"T minus Ten Seconds and Counting; Nine, Eight, Main Engine Start; Seven, Six, Five, Four, Three, Two, One, Solid Rocket Ignition, We Have Lift-Off . . ."

CORPORATE SPACE

To Pat Grigg with Best Wishes For Many Happy Landings

A NOVEL BY

Robert Luther

ROBERT LUTHER

CENTURION PUBLISHERS, HAZEL GREEN, ALABAMA

Published by Centurion Publishers, P.O. Box 248, Hazel Green, Al 35750

Luther, Robert N. Manufactured in the United States of America

Publisher's Cataloging-in-publication Data
Luther, Robert
Corporate Space: Fiction / Robert Luther

417 p. 24 cm.
ISBN 0-9673979-9-5 (alk. Paper)
1. Aerospace Fiction 2. Space 3. Corporate Engineering
I. Title.

PS3562.U874 C66 2005

Library of Congress Control Number: 2005902088

Typeface: Garmond

Printed and bound in the United States of America
By Thomson-Shore, Inc.

First Printing

The paper in this book meets the guidelines for permanence and
durability of the Committee on Production Guidelines for Book
Longevity of the Council on Literary Resources.

Book Cover Design By O'Neal graphics
Edited by Benny Sims

This book is dedicated to all the noble astronauts and dedicated engineers who have made our space program possible. These people have truly reached for the stars and have made a significant difference in all our lives. We can never repay them their just rewards but we must always remember their sacrifices.

First Printing 2005

Manufactured in the United States of America

Published by:
Centurion Publishers,
P.O. Box 248
Hazel Green, Alabama 35750

For information regarding bulk purchases of this book, please contact the Publisher at the above address

CHAPTER ONE

Events were going well for the crew scheduled to launch space shuttle SL-25, the Adventurer. All systems were being checked and double checked on the launch pad at the cape launch site. Roll-out and mating of Adventurer to the launch pad systems that would start it on its voyage into the heavens had been completed. Allen "Ace" Lewis was an old pro, with over ten thousand hours of flight time and two Shuttle missions. When Ace barked the crew responded immediately. Each person knew it was a team effort requiring the best of everyone.

They had completed all training exercises and were within one day of launch. Ace was the first one up and proceeded to knock on doors with "Rise and shine, folks, we got briefings today."

He heard a muffled groan from the room of his co-pilot, Harry Mansfield. "Oh, man, let me have just five more minutes."

"Hey, buddy, we're about to go on a voyage. Rise and shine. Hit the deck."

"Okay, okay, I'm up," came the disgruntled reply.

Ace chuckled as he went to the next door and thought, "What a sack hound." He tapped more lightly on the door to the girls' rooms. "Okay girls. Let's go."

Sandra surprised him by pulling open her door, fully dressed and ready to go in her blue flight suit adorned with all the Space Agency emblems. "Okay, chief, I'm ready and able. Lead me to the chow hall."

At breakfast Ace surveyed his crew: Harry Mansfield, co-pilot and ex-fighter pilot, Sandra Morris, mission specialist and Margo Stroud, mission specialist, who would conduct complex and specialized medical experiments in space; Chuck Hume, navigator and astronomer, who would make observations of solar flares with special equipment he had in the cargo bay; Ted Anderson, who would deploy a satellite and propel it to the correct orbit, and Stan Johnson, who would perform a series of Earth observations for geological resources as they orbited the Earth from over two hundred miles high.

He was proud of these people who had honed their skills to an

1

extremely high level of competence. He thought, *"These guys are truly unique"*, as he sat observing them talking among themselves, excited about their launch tomorrow. Finally, he asked, "Everybody okay for launch tomorrow?"

Sandra, a very beautiful, petite medical doctor, with beautiful flaming red hair which normally would hang to her shoulders, but was now put up in a bun to keep out of the way, grinned at Ace and replied, "Okay father, we're ready, that is if you don't worry yourself to death about us ahead of time."

Ace grinned, as he was prone to do when he was being kidded, and replied, "Well, little one, just checkin'. I want everybody to be ready and able."

Margo interrupted, "Buddy, just you get that thing up there and then land it and every thing will be okay. Think you can find that runway out in the desert?"

Harry commented amid a chuckle, "Margo, you should'a seen us trying to find another runway a few years back."

Now Ted's interest was up. "What's this? You two got lost?"

"Well, Ted," Ace giggled, "not really lost, just a little misplaced."

"Well, I want to know who I'm ridin with on this thing, guys," Chuck interjected. "Did you find the runway?"

"Well, to be honest," Harry continued, "we'd rented a Cessna 210 and were down in El Paso for a party in Wazoo and had to fly back to Albuquerque bright 'n early. We were sort'a spent and it took both of us to get that damned thing off the ground the next mornin. We finally got the gear up after we found the gear handle again, and somehow navigated by followin the highway back to Albuquerque. We left our damned maps and everything in El Paso so we didn't know one frequency from another and couldn't call anybody except emergency and didn't want to do that. We didn't know where the field was and by that time we were a little low on fuel. We landed at a small field I saw out the right side and just acted like it was the most natural thing in the world. We fueled up, bought a map and went on and nobody ever knew the difference."

"Well, friend," Ted replied with a laugh, "we'll know the difference so be sure to take your maps."

The day was busy for the crew. Ace and Harry were once again running through all the procedures that they had been through hundreds of times. Margo and Sandra rehearsed their experiment deployment and timelines again to be sure they had no questions before they left. The preparations were detailed and thorough because the next morning was their big moment. Ace, Ted and Chuck had made previous flights but for the others it was a new experience. Excitement was high.

At five the next morning, Ace made his routine door knock and this time found everybody up, awake and ready to go, even sack hound Harry. All met in the crew chow hall at six and were fed a hearty breakfast. Ace and Harry had their usual eggs and sausage, Ted ate three eggs and four sausages to fill his rugged, six-foot-four frame while the others ate hot cakes, bacon, and grits. No one had coffee because of the tendency of coffee to "run through" quickly. If there were a pad delay, it would be difficult to get up and go to the bathroom.

Sandy was as excited as a child with a house full of new toys. She kept saying over and over to herself, *"I'm really gonna do it! I'm really going into space! I'm really going."*

Margo was quieter than usual. Ace asked, "Hey, you okay?"

"Oh, yeah, Ace, I'm just sort'a stunned to believe it's really going to happen. I've wanted to do this all my life, and it's really gonna happen. It's almost like a dream. Seems like it just can't be happening to me."

"Hey babe, just wait till them big solid rockets ignite and it kicks you in the rear. Then you'll believe. That's a thrill like you can't imagine. I mean, the first time I felt it, I was dumbfounded. That damned thing moves, and I mean it moves!"

At eight thirty after the final briefing by Frank Starnes, Director of Astronaut Training, everyone walked from the crew quarters at the Vehicle Assembly Building to the van for transport to the pad. Frank was quiet that morning, quieter than usual. Margo kept watching him and finally asked, "You okay Frank?"

Frank looked up with a big grin. "Yeah, Margo, I'm okay. Just my usual set of worries, I guess. You know me."

Sandy patted Frank on the arm, "Yeah, father, you always were a worrier. Hey, It's okay. We're gonna do good today."

Shortly the van arrived at the launch pad and the crew exited

3

to the elevator to take them to the dressing level where the suits were stored. Ace had become quiet now, as he contemplated the flight about to take place. He watched each member of the crew don the flight gear and prepare the oxygen system. He watched Sandy wriggle into the suit, a shapely, petite frame with all the curves in the right place. He wondered what had inspired her, a bright, upcoming medical doctor, to want to delay her practice and participate in such a program as this. Then he thought about himself and the inner peace he found in flying space shuttles, or 210 Cessnas, or J-3 Cubs. It became clear to him why she would do this. This was the ultimate flight. All others would become secondary. Shortly, everyone walked to the door and a ground crewman escorted them through, onto the walkway to the Adventurer cockpit. "Okay, kids, this is it. Back out now or you're signed on!"

Harry laughed as he replied, "Hell, man, you couldn't blow me off this thing now." He looked down the sleek hull of Adventurer and over at the two gigantic rockets paralleling the external tank. "Look at that, man, look at that."

Sandy had stopped with Margo and was looking at the ship. "Damn, that's impressive just lookin at it from here. Just wait 'till we're on the way!"

Margo's heart was racing with excitement at the prospect of actually flying. She stopped after another step and held onto the safety rail at the catwalk peering at the structure. She felt a pride she had never felt before, like she really had arrived, like she counted for something in the world because she was actually going to fly into space. She whispered half out loud and half to herself, "Dear Lord, thank you! Thank you! I feel so humble."

Ace had come up last behind Sandy and Margo and began gently, "Girls, it's time. Let's go do it. I know how you feel."

Sandy looked at Ace with tears in her eyes. "Ace, it's beautiful just to look at."

Ace put his arm around her small shoulders, "Yep, baby, it's beautiful to look at but much more beautiful to fly. Let's go get her movin."

Each crew member entered the cockpit and stepped carefully along the walk way area to their respective seat and "sat" down, which consisted of laying down as one would in a chair that had been turned over on its back. The ground crew assisted in getting everyone strapped into the seats and made sure all individual systems were on and working. Intercom systems, oxygen systems, quick-release systems in case of a pad emergency to allow them to get out of the orbiter and onto the slide wire that would take them safely out of harms way were checked and all final preparations were made for each crew member lined up in seats behind Ace and Harry on the flight deck. As the ground crew left, Ace looked around at each person and in a business-like manner, asked each one individually if their preparations were completed. They all were and he keyed the microphone, "Launch control, all preliminary preps completed. Ready to release the hold and proceed with count down."

"Roger, Adventurer. Implement checklist for all switch control settings."

"Roger, launch control." Then shortly, "Uh, launch control, verified."

"Roger, Adventurer. Proceed with control settings checklist."

Ace was slow and methodical. He and Harry progressed through all the checklists and verified all functions and positions. They checked controls that they would use to fly the craft back as an airplane from deep space. They checked communications, range safety, navigation, flight instruments computer systems, and payload information from the cargo bay. Ace was feeling good, having lost the quiet, reverent feeling in the face of all the excitement. He finally keyed the mike, "Launch control, Adventurer is 'go' for launch."

Sandy had been watching every move Ace and Harry made with great interest, hoping to learn to fly herself one day. Margo was concentrating on instructions for her experiments and hoping it wouldn't take long to get to orbit so she could go to work. She looked up with a grin and said to Sandy through the intercom, "Can you believe this? We're about to go into space. Damn!!"

"I know. It all seems too perfect somehow. All the work we went through seems worth while now, doesn't it." Sandy replied, peering from inside her space suit with a huge grin.

Ace heard the count clock over the intercom while he was busy checking and rechecking communications and guidance systems, "T minus 20 minutes and counting. Adventurer is 'go' for launch."

Chuck had been quiet for a few moments, contemplating the impending mission. He looked around at Margo and winked, "Lady, it's close. We're really gonna do it." He had a gleam in his eyes that she had not noticed during training.

"T-minus 10 minutes and counting" came the launch controller.

"Ace, I been thinkin . . ."

Ace looked around at Sandy inquiringly, "Yeah, babe?"

"I never been around the world before. Now I'm about to go around a bunch of times and so damned fast I can't make any stops anywhere . . ."

Ted interrupted, "You mean, like shopping trips?"

"Yeah, yeah, that's what I mean."

Ace smiled as he replied, "Well, tell you what. Pick out a spot and when you get back, just go there and shop till your little heart's content."

Margo couldn't resist the temptation to intersperse her comments, "Yeah, Sandy, I'll go with you."

"Great," Ace replied jovially as he heard the count, T-minus three minutes and counting. "Send us a post card." He then turned his full attention to the control panel with its seeming jungle of instruments and lights. He looked inquiringly at Harry, "Ready, buddy?"

"Hell yes, man, Let's get her on. This ain't no damned 210 Cessna. This baby will *GO!*"

Excitement and exhilaration was running high. The crewmembers were all like children on a great Adventurer. Harry was sweating profusely in the excitement and Ace was straining at all the instruments, making all last minute checks. No red lights.

At T-minus twenty Seconds. Ace felt his heart rate increase as he looked outside at the Launch Support Structure. "Ain't gonna be long now!" he thought.

"T-minus ten Seconds. . . -nine . . . -eight . . . Main Engine Start!"

Ace and the others felt the dull vibrations as the three big Rocketdyne Engines roared to life at the aft end of their ship. Ace watched the thrust measurement instruments as the thrust came up to sixty five percent maximum. "Looks good," he thought. "Feels smooth."

"-Four . . . -three . . . -two . . . Solid Rocket Ignition . . . *LIFT*

OFF!!"

Vibration increased and the rumble now was a heart-rendering roar as the big solid rockets began pumping an additional seven million pounds of sheer brute force into the aft end of Adventurer. Ace looked outside and watched the launch support structure move away as the big machine began to move ever so slowly at first and then started to accelerate rapidly. "Damned computers are right on" he thought as Adventurer cleared the structure and began the roll program to turn the launch down range to the east.

Sandy yelled from her rear seat, "*Yippeeeee*!! Feel that power. God! What a feeling!!"

Ace was too busy to respond but thought to himself, "I know, baby, I know." He had chills running up and down his back at the feeling, like nothing else he had ever experienced. He heard launch control, "Roll program complete." He keyed the mike, "Roger, launch control, roll program complete. Velocity coming up on Mach zero point eight."

"We Roger that Adventurer. Altitude fifteen thousand feet."

Ace felt the vehicle fly, as all experienced pilots do. He had long ago developed the "Seat of the pants" feel for an airplane, and this one was no exception. He muttered to himself, "This damned thing feels a little unstable, like it's wandering on the trajectory some." He checked the instruments and found that the trajectory was close but not exact. "Well, must be a little software problem. I'll sure squawk that when we get back on the ground."

Suddenly launch control burst into life and startled Ace, who was engrossed in the flight instruments, "Adventurer, Max-Q"

Suddenly, Ace responded to all the training and experience he had had, "Roger, launch control, Max-Q coming." He reached over and placed his hand on the throttle. He knew that after he passed Max-Q, the point of maximum aerodynamic pressure and vibration at Mach one-plus he would be requested to increase power to one hundred and ten percent on the main engines. He looked at his gloved hand and saw it tremble with excitement and felt the beads of sweat running down among the hairs of his wrist.

"Adventurer, you are go for throttle-up!"

"Roger launch control, go for throttle-up." Ace pushed the throttles in to the maximum forward position and watched the gages indicate the increase in power and velocity.

Chuck was enraptured as he watched the earth falling away outside the windows. Sandy was speechless, fixated at watching the horizon come into view. Margo laid her hand on Sandy's arm and said, "Look! Just look at that!!"

At T plus fifty seconds, there was a slight shudder in Adventurer. Ace instantly came to attention, "What the hell was that?" He didn't like to feel sudden and strange things in his craft. He had no horizon here, as he did on earth, to judge whether or not he was moving off course. He looked intently at the gages and then at Harry, who had felt the same thing.

Harry asked quietly, trying not to be concerned, "Feel that?"

Ace nodded his head, "Yeah. What was it?"

"Don't know."

As the craft seemed to veer off course again and the computers worked in vain to bring it back onto the programmed trajectory, a strong vibration began occur, seeming to get worse by the second. Ace felt alarm and grabbed the control yoke tighter in preparation for overriding the automatic pilot. Neither he nor Harry said a word, each alarmed and looking from each other to the instrument panel.

Suddenly, the ship veered erratically as the right side booster swung out away from the structure and impacted the forward dome on the external tank. There was a huge spray of fuel erupting from the tank, spraying out in huge quantities over the entire craft. Then there was a powerful jolt as the booster slammed back into the side of the structure. Ace felt panic, helplessness, and sheer horror at the realization he was breaking up in flight. He didn't know what to do. Thoughts were flooding his mind those split seconds between T plus seventy two seconds and T plus seventy three seconds. He keyed the mike to mission control, to ask for advice. He had no idea what to do with this. He had not trained for this contingency. All that he got out was, "Uh--hoo. We . . . "

As the fireball erupted with a thunderous explosioin, all he could see was flame and debris. The ship had disintegrated. He thought about Sandy, Margo, Ted, all the others . . . Were they okay? Was this a dream? . . . *"What's happening to us?? This is wrong . . ."*

He tried to speak to the others but nothing came out. Suddenly he was having trouble breathing. "Emergency oxygen" he yelled and he felt Chuck pushing the emergency oxygen toward him.

He looked around quickly and saw that the cabin area was relatively intact. As he quickly turned on the oxygen, he thought, *How could this be? We blew up! Didn't we? We Should Be Dead!*

He looked back at the others and saw Margo and Sandy with emergency oxygen. Ted was trying to push an emergency supply to Stan but to no avail. Stan was out cold, slumped over in his seat, restrained by his seat belt and harness.

Ace looked out the window of the cabin section as it tumbled over and over out of the debris and flames. He thought, "*Feels like a whole series of snap rolls. But, I'm not doin that. There's the ocean. I can see ships.*"

The craft stabilized itself in a nose-down attitude. Ace was pulling up on the controls as hard as he could, in a vain attempt to pull out of the dive. He had the yoke back in his lap with his right hand, straining, knuckles white and muscles rippling with the control column all the way back. Harry was watching with a calm that was typical in dangerous situations. The cabin began to swing back and forth like a pendulum restrained at the rear, one side of the nose facing the sea and then the other.

The earth was rushing up at them with lightening speed. Ace thought, *Well, this must be the way it is for sky divers.* Then suddenly the full realization dawned on him: *We ain't got no parachute to pull.* He watched for a few more seconds as the ocean got bigger and bigger. "*Why don't we have a parachute? We Could! Couldn't We?*"

He saw a swell in the ocean and the white cap on a small wave. A calm came over him like he had never before experienced.

The cabin section hit the water at two hundred seventy miles an hour.

Then there was silence, except for the waves lapping over each other.

9

CHAPTER TWO

Engineer? Pilot? What the hell, anyhow! Arthur Cannon thought as he loosened the hold down bolts on the exhaust stack of his old Aero Commander, ratty looking, in bad need of paint, oil stains on the top and bottom of the wings, and needing a thousand things he could not afford to give it. Maybe ex-engineer if some damned breaks don't come around soon . . . if the country don't get off its ass and continue with Wernher von Braun's dream of going to the stars.

Cannon looked across the wing at the one good engine and then silently cursed the one that had blown a cylinder on charter the night he and his co-pilot, Ed Stryker, had been forced to make a single engine approach in a howling thunderstorm. He had had to shut the engine down due to extreme vibration from a blown piston that was threatening to come through the side of the cylinder.

What a trip Art thought as a small shiver went through him just remembering that night. Socket wrench idle in his hand, he stood on the ladder by the crippled engine for what seemed a long time thinking of the brush with death and of his good friend, Ed. "Hell of a way to make a livin when you've just come down off a space program. Rather be with some good company on a sweet project like this space shuttle that's gonna get us ready for the stars," he muttered to himself. Patting the wing, he lifted the exhaust stack gently away from the engine. "Well, ole' heap, we made it in. You're hurt but you held our collective asses together. Guess we can't ask much more'n that," he said softly, as if he were talking to a child. He stepped off the ladder and laid the stack carefully on the floor by the other parts. With a greasy hand, he brushed the graying hair from his forehead. Still musing about the flight to Tulsa, Art chuckled silently, remembering how the line boy had paled at the sight of the corpse they'd unloaded from the damaged ship.

He looked out the open doors of the dilapidated, unpainted, almost condemned and worst hanger on the field where he had operated his "flying service" for two years after being laid off during the collapse of the aerospace industry. He thought, "One day, maybe, I'll get back in the business. Sure as hell need to be explorin space instead a haulin cadavers and freight. This ain't exactly my idea of a living. But, hell, Annie and I are still eatin'."

He kicked a hammer laying on floor against his big tool box sitting in front of the plane's nose, the loud clang of the head against the metal punctuating his resolve to return to space exploration. He climbed the ladder to start pulling the alternator off the engine. *"Might as well get the son-of-a-bitch off and then worry about how in hell I'm gonna fix it"*, he thought. He sprawled his 190-pound, 45-year-old frame out across the top of the wing to get a wrench on the bolts. As he applied pressure to the stubborn lower bolt the wrench slipped, raking his knuckles across the sharp edges. "Damn! Damn!" he shouted and rubbed the bleeding, numbed, greasy knuckles on his even more greasy old jump suit doubling as coveralls. As he sat rubbing the skinned knuckles and observing the missing slivers of flesh oozing blood, he became aware of being watched. He jerked his head around to see a slight, neatly-dressed man, graying hair with an open shirt collar watching him intently.

"Hurts like hell, don't it?" the stranger asked with a laugh that seemed to have a rather cocky air about it.

He gauged the stranger carefully for a few seconds and then wondered what he was doing in his hanger, anyway. He decided not to be annoyed at the intrusion and grinned since most of the hurt had gone and the blood was receding. He replied, "Sure as hell does. Looks like I'd learn to quit bustin' knuckles someday."

"Are you Arthur Cannon?"

"Yep. Guess I am," he replied.

"I'm Jack Becker." Art squinted as he studied the intruder carefully from his perch on the wing and waited for him to proceed. "The guys over at the line shack told me where to find you."

"Well, guess you did that. What can I do you for?"

"I'm a student pilot. Well, guess I'm a little better'n that now. I got my private license last week."

"That's nice," he replied forcing patience, as he turned back his attention back to the alternator bolts, resolving this time to be more careful.

"They told me about your approach in the storm last night with a blown engine hauling that dead body. Man, that must have been somethin', especially since they were divertin' airlines."

"Didn't have much choice. Damned thing blew about thitry miles out and there wasn't a better place to go."

"I run the logistics department for Space Corp ..." Art jerked to attention and turned toward Becker with a much different attitude. "I was told that you're a damned good engineer and looking for a job. Is that right?"

Art was excited. He slid off the wing to the ladder and down to the floor. "I sure as hell..." *That ain't the way to approach it,* he thought. "I certainly am," he said, half stammering while stretching out a greasy hand to Becker who looked at it and then took it for a warm and hearty handshake.

"Well, from what the guys over at the FBO said, you might fit into my organization. Can you come in and discuss it." Becker was peering curiously at the engine still mounted on the wing. "I sure can," Art grinned. His heart was pounding at the thought of being able to get into the space shuttle program. He quickly, and perhaps foolishly, threw caution to the wind and continued, "This old bucket of bolts is about due to croak." He glared scornfully at the blown engine and said, "One engine already blew a piston and most likely ruined the cylinder and I don't know how'n hell I'm gonna replace that. When can I come?"

"How about tomorrow?" Becker replied triumphantly. "I'm on the fourth floor. I'm free at three o'clock. Just come to the front desk at our building and ask for me."

Art leaned against the fuselage watching Becker leave the old hanger and felt his dream might be about to come true. He thought about the old programs, the Saturn and the Apollo, mission control, lunar landings, all the satellites he had worked on for so many years. He could not know this was the beginning of an adventure into corporate politics far beyond his wildest dream; that he would be involved in one of the great tragedies of space exploration and that he could have prevented it had the corporate politicians only listened.

When he entered the Space Corp building at five minutes to three, now neatly dressed in a suit and tie, with the grease meticulously scrubbed from beneath his fingernails, Art encountered a receptionist he judged to be in her early twenties with long black hair framing a beautiful face and two beautiful blue eyes and large, well-shaped red lips. "Hello. I'm here to see Mr. Becker."

She smiled and replied easily while pushing a ruled pad over to him, "Please sign in, sir. I believe he's Logistics, isn't he?"

He confirmed that he was, signed the register and began to worry about time. Maybe he should have been a couple of minutes earlier. Won't look good to be late for an interview, especially the first one in months. His thoughts were interrupted by, "This way sir. Are you here for an interview?"

"Yeah, guess I am. Do you work here, too?" Then he thought that was a dumb question since she was obviously there.

A little laugh emerged from his shapely escort as she got up to lead him to his destination. "Only a week now. We're just getting' going and they're looking for some good people to help build the space shuttle, or something like that," she giggled as they stepped on the elevator.

"Do you know Mr. Becker? What's he like?"

"Oh, I only know him slightly. Sometimes he stops and visits with me a little. He seems very nice though. You nervous?"

Art grimaced at her frankness and was saved from further comment by the opening of the elevator door. "This way, sir."

Damn, he thought. Must be gettin old when the secretaries start to call you sir, or else they think you're important, or something. He was ushered into an outer office. "Mr. Cannon to see Mr. Becker." The young escort continued: "I'm very pleased to meet you, Mr. Cannon. They'll call me when you're through. My name is Connie and I'll come back for you. Good luck."

The secretary behind the desk was an ample woman, to say the least, late forties, one hundred seventy pounds if an ounce with short bobbed graying hair. She peered at him with little beady eyes focusing through thick rimless glasses with a look that one would expect from an old Drill Sergeant at the Marine Corps training tenter. She laid her magazine down, scowled at the interruption and replied curtly, "Mr. Becker's expecting you. Through that door!" nodding with the back of her head. Then she yelled, "Jack! Cannon's here!"

There was a rustling in the inner office and Becker, sleeves rolled and tie loose, appeared at the door with a big smile and an outstretched hand. "Come in and sit down. I'll fix you a cup of coffee."

Before Art could say anything, Becker was pouring two cups. "How do you take it, straight or thinned with all the junk."

"With cream, thank you," he replied.

Becker put in a spoon of powdered cream and handed him the cup. "That landing must have been one hell of an experience."

"It did have its moments," Art responded courteously, hoping this wasn't just another aircraft discussion.

"Well, it shows determination and skill. Identifies a man's character. Just like it's gonna take skill and dedication and honest integrity to make this system work. I mean damned hard team work that we ain't never put into a program before."

Art blinked at his intensity. "Well, Saturn/Apollo was a good program. We had lots of people who were part of a real team," he replied.

Jack leaned back in his chair. "I know," he replied wistfully. "I missed that. Wish I could have been a part of it."

Art shifted to a more comfortable position, becoming more at ease as he held the warm, friendly coffee cup, steam wisping upward. He gazed out the window at the huge, rusting test stand in the distance as he replied, "It was exciting. I'll never forget the first full power firing of that big Saturn Five booster. That was really something. Right out there . . ." As he pointed, Art could still feel the excitement and nostalgia for what had been so much a part of his past life and his enthusiasm for what might lay in the future.

Becker pounded the desk. "Cannon, I like you. What do you know about logistics?" Then almost without hesitation before Art could answer, he continued, "What do you know about Space Corp.? Would you like to work for me?"

Art was surprised by the series of questions so fast and direct to the point. He hadn't expected such a machine-gun line of questioning, and stammered, "Here's my resume. I know something about logistics but not too much, and yes I would like to work for you!"

Becker grinned, leaned forward and laid the resume on the table. "You don't need to be a logistics expert. I need a good engineer to run a logistics engineering branch, somebody that knows computers and engineering. Can you do that?"

He still hadn't opened the resume. Art was puzzled by this approach, having expected an in-depth discussion of his education, background, and experience. He decided to respond in kind. "Hell yes! When do you want me to start?" He thought that this was about

14

the shortest and strangest interview he had ever had.

Becker got up, leaned across the desk, and extended his hand. "How about tomorrow, being this is late Monday afternoon. I've got a hell of a problem finding qualified people. I need to get you on board to help me staff up."

Art grinned, extended his hand and felt very good about having a job at last and about this little dynamo of a man. "I can make it!" He answered positively.

"What do you know about our mission here?"

"Not much, but if you had some information I could read tonight . . . "

"Come on," Becker interrupted as he bounded out from behind his desk like a rabbit coming out of its hutch. "I'll introduce you around. Then we'll go to personnel and do the damn paper work."

Art got up to follow Becker out of the office, giving the large lady a wide berth as though she might strike at any moment. As they walked, he listened to Becker quickly describe his organization, its mission and his other groups: supply, transportation, and materials management, and wondered silently what logistics engineering was. "How many people in the department, Mr. Becker?" he asked.

"Call me Jack, Arthur, call me Jack."

"You got a deal. Folks call me Art. Don't quite sound so country."

"Hell, it don't matter where you come from. It's what you can do and how you care about this program that matters. I got six people now but I plan at least 60 when the program gets rollin'."

At an office marked "Supply", Becker steered him inside. "Sonny Leech, meet the newest addition, Art Cannon. Sonny here is going to run our supply operation. He's a retired master sergeant from the air force with lots of experience."

A large, ungainly individual arose from behind a too-small desk surrounded by cabinets and empty shelves, some still in shipping containers. Packing material and cartons, some full and some empty, were scattered in the corners in disarray, begging for organization and cleanup. The stranger stuck out a pudgy hand. Art noted the large stomach hanging over a belt that seemed to be rebelling at the overload and the old plaid shirt that seemed to want to part seams around the shoulders and armpits. "Welcome! Haven't I seen you somewhere before?"

Art experienced the same feeling but an inner voice warned him to be careful. He felt a slight chill go though him. "You sure look familiar," he replied cautiously, trying to remember where he had seen Sonny before.

They stood for a few moments in deep thought before Sonny grinned and raised his hand: "Over at Computer Industries, back in '72 or '73, I think."

Art grinned as he replied, "Yeah. You worked for Gordy Richards, didn't you?"

Jack, obviously pleased to renew old acquaintances, escorted him down the hall a few more doors and announced, "This is where I'm setting up my transportation operation. I've got another old master sergeant running this one, too, name of Zeke Wright."

They entered to find a slight man behind a more suitably-sized desk. "Zeke, meet Art Cannon, our new logistics engineering manager."

"Pleased to meet you." Zeke replied. Art felt neutral about Zeke. Then Zeke asked: "Is he gonna develop that new Optimum Repair Level Analysis computer model for us? You know we need to be getting started on that."

Jack gleefully nodded his head as he replied, "Yep, but don't scare him off yet. He don't start work 'til tomorrow. Got any material he can read tonight?"

At personnel Jack introduced Art to the director of personnel, Dean Aikins, a scrawny looking man he surmised to be 35 years old with big horn-rimmed glasses and large ears sticking out of a mop of curly light brown hair. Dean proudly informed Art that he was one of the people who came from Arizona with the original team, just like four of the others, including Loren Sharp, the executive vice president. "I even hired in ol' Jack here, last month. Got him out of Texas, of all places." Art was uncomfortable with the cocky, obnoxious air Dean showed.

Jack, displaying a definite dislike for Dean, scowled: "Cut the shit, Deanie. Just get the paperwork done. He starts work tomorrow."

Dean glared at Jack with an incredulous look. "Now, you know he can't do that!" Dean said in a high-pitched, whining voice.

16

"Just why in the hell not, Mr. Personnel Man? I got a need. I'm telling you to do it!" Jack thundered as he leaned over in Dean's face and frowned.

Dean suddenly had a pained look on his face; he jerked back, wrinkled his brow, narrowed his eyes and looked as though he would rather do anything than comply. "But Jack, you know I've got to write a letter and schedule interviews with other department managers. Then I've got to do a psychological profile. Then I've got to make him an offer in writing and he's got to accept in writing. Tomorrow is completely out."

Jack was furious as he yelled, "Damn you, Personnel. I got him here and he ain't crazy and you don't need to do no damned profiles. Write him an offer letter now, and I mean *NOW* and let him sign it *NOW*! I want him at work tomorrow or your ass is grass and I'm gonna be the lawn mower!"

Dean tried to continue as Becker moved toward him. He retreated and grudgingly typed an offer letter and shoved over the counter to Art. "Sign it!" he grunted, glaring at Jack out of the corner of his eye as he cautiously gauged the distance between them.

Art was concerned about the sudden change in attitudes and actually felt sorry for Dean, even though he seemed intent on delaying his hiring. He wanted the job and quickly decided to gamble anyway, as he replied, "Thanks, Dean, I'm pleased to be aboard," he said.

Without any further acknowledgment, Dean glanced at Jack who was still red in the face and remarked with a sneer, "Thank you Mr. Becker. Do you have any other requests for Personnel today?"

"Come on, let's get out where the air's better," Becker said. Neither one said anything for a few moments and then Jack, half thinking and half cursing, turned to Art: "That dumb little son-of-a-bitch! Just because he came here from Arizona don't mean he's king shit. He gloats on being a damn bottleneck. Next time I ask him to do something I'll start by kicking him in the teeth. Let me show you where your office is, down on the second floor."

Shortly Jack was in a better mood and as they went down the stairway he pointed, "Loren Sharp's office. He's our executive vice president. Nice guy but nobody can figure him out," Jack mused. "Still can't understand what he's doing here, though. He's a biologist."

"Biologist?"

"Yep. Can't figure what the hell a biologist has got to do with a damned rocket."

At the far end of the hall, Jack opened the door to Art's office, a large room with one wall of windows looking outside at ground level filled with a number of government gray desks, chairs and tables amid a scattering of gray file cabinets. There was one person sitting, feet propped up on a desk, reading as they entered. "Chuck Miller, meet Art Cannon, the new logistics engineering manager. He reports tomorrow if that bastard over in personnel don't screw it all up."

Chuck unfolded from his chair, laid his book down with a big grin and extended his hand. Art felt good vibrations, like here could be a friend. "Pleased to meet you, Art. Are you a logistician?"

"Engineer. But recently I've been running an air charter service and flying school to get by."

"I understand. I've been selling real estate. Now that's a hell of a way for a bonafide logistician to make a living."

"Hey guys, it's almost quittin time," Jack said with a big grin. "I don't want to get whistle bit, so let me walk you back to the front desk. Tomorrow you can get a temporary security badge and go and come as you please. That'll work 'till they get your security clearance reinstated."

Jack escorted Art to the front desk and told Connie. "This is our new Logistics Engineering Manager. He'll be in tomorrow so be sure to take good care of him."

"We've already met, Mr. Becker."

"Oh?"

"Yes, I escorted him in. Remember?"

"Oh yeah. Well, take good care of him. He's another pilot." Jack turned abruptly and walked over to the elevator. "See you tomorrow."

Connie smiled at Art, obviously liking him immediately. "Jack's such a nice guy," she said pleasantly.

"Well, I hope so," he replied, still having some doubt about the personnel incident. "He seems nice but he sure got on Dean Aikins. Is there bad blood?"

"Sure is. As I heard it, Dean wanted to hire a friend of his from Arizona instead of Jack. I heard he tried to cut Jack's salary by two thousand dollars hoping he'd refuse the position and then he could hire his friend. But Jack wouldn't stand for it and made an issue of it . . . embarrassed him real bad."

"Well, that explains a lot."

"Yeah, and besides that, Dean's a pest and a worry wart. He thinks he's God's gift to women. Already tried to get me to go out with him and I know he's married with five kids. How about that?"

"Sounds like a fast mover to me," Art replied with a chuckle.

Connie's eyes flashed with determination. "Well, not as fast as he thinks. I'm sure not going out with him."

"I hope not," Art replied, studying her face intently. "There's too many good, unmarried men out there."

"You're right about that, but the pickins sure seem slim sometimes," Connie replied looking wistfully past Art and out the door.

He laughed as he replied, "Be patient, the right one will come along."

"Look at you," she laughed. "Almost my confidant and advisor already and you haven't even started work yet."

CHAPTER THREE

After clearing Space Center Visitor Control with a temporary badge, Art drove up the hill in the shadow of the towering Saturn V test stands that had been so familiar for so many years. The big test stands stood like a mute monument to the thunderous test firings of the giant rockets, to the shaking of the earth, to the clouds of steam from the cooling pumps with their tons of water, and the sheet of flame from the deflectors. He watched the pigeons flying in and out of the towers and the hold-downs that had locked the giant vehicles in place for test firing, the accumulation of bird droppings and rust streaming down the sides leaving long stains reaching almost to the ground. He was almost overwhelmed with a great sadness of days gone by and the feeling of hopelessness for the future of space exploration that had haunted him for so long. He looked at the front of the building and let his gaze drift over to the row of windows outlining his office. He stared intently for a few moments and somehow felt a renewal, a purpose in life again for the opportunity to once more participate in development of vehicles that would pave the way to conquering the cosmos. He said quietly, almost reverently, to himself, "Welcome home, baby. It's good to be back in business again."

At 7:40, Connie slowly shuffled to her receptionist desk as though she couldn't face the day, hair half combed, make-up unevenly applied and looking as though she had been through a war. Art stood at the door watching her make her way to her desk and carefully sit down. She smiled weakly. "Hi. Thought you'd be here today."

"Are you all right?" he asked gently.

"I'm okay. Just too big a night last night," she replied as she adjusted her position. "Sonny had a party over at his house. Guess I drank too much. I'm not used to that."

"You mean Sonny Leech?"

"Yeah, yeah. That's the one," nodding her head as though she were afraid it might break.

"Well, you better watch those kind of parties. Does he do this often?"

"I don't know. That was my first. Maybe it's the last."

At that moment Jack Becker walked briskly in the front door with his usual race-horse gait. "See you found a sick one. You all right, Connie?" he asked with great concern.

She looked up weakly, closed her eyes and seemed to be about to choke while stifling a belch the best she could. "I don't feel so good, Mr. Becker. Maybe I should go back home."

Jack studied her carefully, noting her pale face and shaky hands. He replied gently, almost fatherly, "You go home and go to bed. Looks like maybe you're catchin somethin. I'll send somebody else down here today." They watched Connie make her way to her car before he turned to Art with a big smile, "Mornin. Let's go to security and get your permanent badges and then you can have free run of the joint. Boy, that kid looks terrible."

At the office security chief Lora Winston searched for Art's file. Lora was nonplused as she finally replied, "I'm sorry, Mr. Becker, I don't have anything from personnel yet."

Jack's face flushed as he reached for the phone with a fury. "Aikins!" he yelled, "If you're not at security in five minutes with Cannon's personnel records I'm comin to get 'em and you don't want me to do that!" Art was sure that Connie must be right about bad blood. "You'd damn well better be!" Jack snorted at the phone and hung up with a bang before starting to laugh sarcastically. "Just got to calibrate the little son-of-a-bitch. I figure he went to Sonny's orgy last night. Probably hung over like hell."

Art was perplexed. "Oh? What do you mean--orgy?"

"Near as I can tell, just a big drunk party. I'd suggest you don't go to one of 'em."

"Don't worry. That's not my thing." Art replied as he adjusted his angle of leaning on the front counter.

"You'd bust every approach for a month," Jack continued with chuckle. "I've heard some bad tales about a couple he's thrown just since he got here."

"Does he do that often?"

"Don't know much about him yet. But I hear he's got a big Indonesian wife who can't speak much English and she's afraid to cross him. He threatens to send her back so, she just puts up with it."

Just under the deadline of five minutes Dean Aikins, pale and obviously hung over, seemingly struggled in and with great effort handed Lora a sheaf of papers. Jack took one step backwards from the office counter and glared at what he considered the "remnants" of the personnel office. Dean pleaded, weakly, "Please don't say it. I don't feel so good."

"I knew it. I knew it! Hung over! Like a damned sot! Boy, you had thirty seconds to spare. Now, get your sorry little ass back up there and don't show your face 'til you can come out smiling."

Dean apparently had no taste for further conflict. He beat a hasty retreat mumbling, "I'll get even with you yet. You don't run personnel."

Lora watched in amazement. Finally she said, "Now I can process your badge, Mr. Cannon.

Art was beginning to worry a bit about Jack's attitude toward Dean and as they left personnel, he casually commented, "Hope you never get mad at me like that, Jack."

Jack laughed out loud. "Don't worry. That little pip-squeak tried to cut my starting salary by two thousand dollars by arguing that he made a typo on my offer letter. Of course, he didn't. . ."

"Seriously?" Art sounded surprised, not wanting to violate Connie's confidence.

"I already negotiated my deal with Loren but he didn't have the guts to make him correct the 'error'. There wasn't no paperwork to show anything different because of the loose way they run this outfit."

"No paperwork," he exclaimed in surprise.

"Nothin' except the back of an envelope where Loren wrote my offer at a bar one night. Deanie almost got away with it . . . but not quite. I still had the envelope."

"That's dishonest, Jack."

"The little bastard don't know nothin about honesty! You can imagine how it pissed me when he whined, 'But Loren, you got to support me, we came here from Arizona together'. Shit, son, I don't care where they came from. Right is right. All I ask is for a straight shake."

When Art returned to his new office, Chuck was sitting in the corner drinking coffee and reading. He looked up with a surprised look, put down his cup and document and studied Art quizzically before commenting. "Boy, that was fast."

"What was fast?"

"The hire, man. The hire. How'd you pull that off so quick?

Art laughed while relating the sequence of events with Chuck absorbing every detail, punctuating the story with genuine cackles and guffaws. "Sure would love to have seen that little sucker. I'll bet ol' Jack burnt him a new one. I guess his wife and five kids get on his nerves."

"How long you been here, Chuck?"

"One month, one day and two and one-half hours. Still ain't figured out this damned program yet. Jack said in addition to runnin' engineering you were going to develop a computer model to figure out where we can expect to repair hardware."

Art had been in his new position only eight weeks and was making good progress in laying out the computer model. Jack, coffee cup in hand and a long, serious look, entered the office and sat on a corner of Art's desk for a few moments without a word. Art looked at Jack quizzically for a moment, feeling all was not well. "How's the model?" Jack finally asked.

"Defined, structured, and about ready to write the code."

"Good, because I hate to tell you, but you got to hire somebody to do that damn thing." Art studied Jack's face but didn't interrupt. "We're going to have to add some people to your group and I know you don't have time to run the organization and do all that too. Does that cause you any problem?"

Art slid back in the government gray chair and put his feet on his government gray desk and took a long drink from his own coffee cup that had an old Ryan STA airplane painted in silver with red trim on it that Ed had given him. He watched Jack intently for a few seconds and replied, "You told me when I first came here we were a team. We still are. Let's get the job done."

Jack beamed and continued with a look of relief, "Damn! I knew I could count on you. You need to hire a good model man, preferably an operations researcher, and two more logisticians. Then we can get a jump on meeting schedules when they start to get jammed up later on. okay?"

After Jack left, Art pondered the worried look. When Jack was out of earshot, he walked to Chuck's desk and sat on the edge. Chuck had been watching the entire proceeding with his seeming indifference but actually with acute attention, as he was very capable of doing. "Why do you reckon he looked worried?" Art asked.

Chuck lowered his glasses and shuffled his small belly a bit to adjust the tight fit of his pants around his crotch to his new position before replying. "Where you been, boy? Ain't you seen the moves going on lately?"

"No. What moves?"

Chuck flinched a little. "The moves Sonny's been puttin on, cozyin with Loren every chance. He makes up excuses to go see him; typical nose job. Sonny's found a soft one and you better watch him, because he's up to no good. Worse than that, he knows how to operate."

Art felt a wave of apprehension because of his first premonition of not trusting Sonny. "What's he up to?"

"Well, in my opinion, he's trying to roll Jack and take over the department. That scares the hell out of me."

Art stood up abruptly. "Does Jack know about that?"

"Yes and no. He suspects, but there ain't much he can do about it. I know for a fact though that an expanded role right now was not in the company plan. Sonny's been talking to Loren about it. Probably while he's been helpin' him paint his house. Looks bad to me."

Art had heard enough and abruptly excused himself. He entered Jack's outer office, skirted the large lady who didn't want to be disturbed reading her novel and burst into Jack's office. "Chief, we started out by being honest with each other and I respect that but I got something I want to talk about," he started with a serious look.

Jack leaned back and replied disgustedly, "I can guess what it is. You've just figured out the knifing he's settin' me up for, right?"

"Damned right, and I'm pissed." he replied curtly as he sat down, observing the pain on Jack's face.

Jack looked at Art with an air of concern mixed with revulsion. "We got a problem with backbone in the front office. If we had an experienced front line manager there'd be a whole different situation here."

"I'll agree that Loren seems gullible. But hell, he's not dumb," Art replied emphatically as he sat down in a chair by Jack's desk.

"He's academically smart but not street smart," Jack replied cautiously. "I don't know anything we can do except do our job and hope for the best. So, don't sweat it. Just keep your gear and flaps down on approach and everything will roll out okay."

Art didn't feel much better. He was quickly trying to develop a strategy to deal with the situation. He thought about other good managers and engineers that he had seen suffer similar fates with merciless consequences. "Jack," he began again, "don't they recognize Sonny for what he is? I haven't seen him do a good day's work yet."

Jack leaned back in his chair with a helpless look, his face taught, unsmiling. "Neither have I, and I'd fire him if I thought I could. But I don't think I could make it stick."

"Well, that ain't worth a damn."

"I know, but let's ride for a while and maybe the right opportunity will come, okay?" Jack replied, trying to be philosophical.

Art walked thoughtfully toward his office while trying to make some sense out of the situation. As he passed accounting he heard the door open and heard, "Well, hello there, Mr. Cannon." He turned to see his young friend, Connie, who had seemingly adopted him as her second father.

"Hello yourself," he answered with a grin, glad to see her.

"Boy, you sure were absorbed. I haven't seen you for several days. You're not mad at me, are you?"

"No chance," Art replied casually, still caught up in the discussion with Jack.

"Well, I hope not. You know how I'm always telling you my troubles and asking you for advice?"

"Yeah. But that's what friends are for."

"Well, I was coming down to tell you something I decided myself." She leaned up against the wall and wiggled her hips in great anticipation of what she was about to say. "I didn't need advice. Aren't you proud of me?" She now had a pixie look on her face and Art couldn't help thinking how cute she was, watching her red lips working in unison and her eyes shining with glee. "Hey, this sounds like a big deal," Art answered with a grin, giving her all his attention.

Connie shifted positions against the wall, head tilted to one side and a big smile as she continued. "You know the boy we talked about so much a few weeks ago, Sammy, my old high school sweetheart?"

"Yeah. You were having a problem deciding 'which one', if I remember right, and I couldn't make that decision for you."

"Wellllll, Sammy and I are getting' married! I'm so happy I don't know what to do. I was coming down to your office to tell you in a few minutes."

"Hey, that's great," he replied with a big grin. He patted Connie on the shoulder while looking into her eyes and noting the look of satisfaction.

"I knew you'd be happy for me," she continued with glee.

"I sure am," Art replied.

"I guess maybe you taught me a lot when we discussed responsibility all those times."

"Yeah, but you're gonna do okay. I'm really proud for you."

"I know. I think you're about the best friend I ever had, besides Sammy of course." Connie giggled a little and turned toward the accounting department door. "I heard there might be a better job open up in accounting. If I could get it I could earn a little more money to help buy the house we want."

"Boy, you're gonna do it big time, aren't you? How'd it go with the interview?"

"Good, I think. You know we just got a new accounting manager and I wanted to get ahead of anybody else. Besides, he's charming and cute."

"Yeah, but you're about to tie a knot and then you won't be eligible anymore."

Connie blushed and giggled as she shifted to her other foot and looked at the floor. "Yeah, but I didn't mean it that way."

Suddenly the door opened and a tall lanky figure filled the outline as he rushed out, almost running over Art in the process. The figure glared at Art and snorted, "Better watch where you stand, fellah. You'll get run over."

Art stared as though he wasn't certain of what he was seeing.. . a cold countenance, tall and thin with coal black wavy hair, small, penetrating, beady eyes covered by heavy black eyebrows, sharp, thin face tapering to a point at the chin with a small black moustache and goatee, as though he were trying to imitate Satan. With that the figure disappeared down the hall without another word. "That's him. Don't you think he's cute?"

Art was slow to reply, "Looks a bit like the Devil himself, if

26

you ask me."

Art excused himself and walked back toward his office. As he passed Sonny's door he heard a hearty greeting from Sonny propped back in his chair with his feet on his desk drinking a Coke. "Howdy there, buddy. How you doin?"

Without slowing his pace or giving into his first inclination to yell "Go to hell!", he grunted, "Okay, I guess."

Art leaned back in his chair contemplating the events of the day when he noticed the clock indicating past quitting time and remembered Annie would be home from school in a couple of hours for the weekend. He thought maybe if she isn't too tired, she might like to go down to Andy's, her favorite place, for seafood.

His thoughts drifted over to Connie's impending marriage and he started to worry about her immaturity. He thought, "Well, she's old enough to make her decision. And, besides, I'm not her daddy anyhow, even if she acts like I am sometimes." Just as he was about to leave his office, Sonny appeared with a big grin. "Workin overtime, huh? That's the way I like to see my people do. When there's work, finish the job before you quit. I'll take care of you for that."

Art gave Sonny a puzzled look, trying not to let the rage and disappointment show because he knew all too well what Sonny was referring to. "What you mean Sonny?" he asked bluntly, squinting his eyes to emphasize the question.

Sonny was obviously uncomfortable as he sidled over to an empty desk in the office and leaned against it. "Well, I can't say any more just yet, but I'd sure like to count on your support. I know I can, can't I?"

A feeling of impending doom swept over Art as he envisioned corporate politics at its worst. He asked sternly, not trying to disguise his hostility, "What's going on?"

Sonny got up quickly and started for the door. "I'll let you know when the time's right but you damn well better support me."

Art dialed Jack's number at home and listened to the phone ring five, then six times. On the seventh he decided he must be out somewhere. Damn, Jack, where are you when I want you, he thought. As he left his office and started down the hall he decided to check Jack's office on the chance that he might still be there. As he topped the stairs he saw, to his amazement, Sonny coming out of Jack's office and ducked into an open door before Sonny saw him. He now had undisputable evidence that Sonny was up to no good.

Art started home quietly contemplating the events he had just witnessed. He felt deep anger and despair at seeing things unravel and resolved to try to do something if he could. As he turned into his driveway he saw Annie rolling to a stop. His heart sped up a bit to see her beautiful legs unfolding out of the little Triumph convertible that she loved so much. "Hi, Beautiful, welcome home. Thought you'd be in about now."

"Were you expecting me?" she teased, as they embraced in the yard. "I'm starving. Didn't eat lunch to get away early to come see you. How about we go somewhere instead of cooking, huh?"

At supper, Annie detected something bothering Art and gently encouraged him, in her own very soft way, to get it out and discuss it. Art finally related his fears about Sonny trying to take over the department, his worries about Jack and about the management of Space Corp. She slid over closer to him and squeezed his hand. "We've worked through some tough ones before and we'll work through this one, too."

"Yeah, sweetheart, I know but I feel so bad for Jack. He's such a decent guy."

"Well, I sure hope you don't get caught up in the politics."

"Well, if Sonny takes over, I can't avoid it. Maybe I can get transferred to another department."

Annie wrinkled her brow. She knew how important the space shuttle was to Art. "Baby, it'll all work out okay. Just wait and see."

"I sure hope so. By the way, I need to find a good, and I mean a really good, operations research analyst. Got any suggestions?"

Annie pondered the question between oysters and shrimp. "How about that fellow you shared an office with when you were working on the Hubble Telescope? Wasn't he good?"

Art sat up with a start. "You mean Eddie Rogers? Hell, he's one of the best."

CHAPTER FOUR

"Damn you, alarm clock," Art muttered as he cracked one eye to face the new Monday. He thought amid a stretch, "Why do we have to get up out of a warm comfortable bed so quick?"

He showered, shaved, ate a quick homemade breakfast and entered his office to find Chuck sitting dejectedly, coffee cup in hand and feet on desk, staring out across the road at a huge Saturn vibration test stand. "Hi, Chief, have a good weekend?" Chuck grunted.

"Sure did. Annie and I flew down to Andy's in Steel City Friday night. Great seafood. Andy has really got the touch." When Chuck didn't answer, Art asked quizzically, "What's troubling you, buddy?"

Chuck slid further down into the gray chair with an expression of disgust. "You know about the new deputy program manager comin' in today?"

Art suddenly became intensely alert. "No! Who?"

"The way I heard it late Friday, this guy's one of the old crew from Arizona that was proposed as Loren's operations man. Supposed to be a good guy but I got my damned doubts considerin some of the rest of 'em." Chuck returned his gaze to the outside with a passive scowl.

While Art considered the significance of this and before he could answer, Connie appeared in Art's office and playfully nudged him on the back of the head. "Wedding's next weekend. Think you can come?"

He had forgotten about the date of the wedding and remembered that he was to help Mack, his aircraft mechanic friend, reinstall the engine in his old Aero Commander. "Gee, baby, I'm not sure," hedging all he dared and genuinely embarrassed that he had forgotten such an important event.

Connie looked disappointed. "We'll miss you. Some of the people are giving us a little reception out at the lake after the wedding."

"That sounds nice. Where is it?"

"I'm not exactly sure. Old fishing lodge out on Exeter Point.

Sonny gave me the directions. He said there's gonna be a lot of Space Corp. people there."

Art looked quizzically at her. "Who?"

"Oh, now, father. Don't worry about me," Connie chided as she came closer and leaned on Art's arm. "I'm a big girl now. By the way, I start in accounting next week. I'm really tickled but I got a lot to learn."

He looked squarely at her and started to lecture about his distrust of the Satanic-looking accounting manager while at the same time worrying about her going to one of Sonny's parties. He held back for fear of alienating her since her mind seemed to be made up and gently tried a different tack. "Connie, be careful. I hear all sorts of bad rumors about Sonny's parties and about that accounting operation, too."

Connie, reflecting her immaturity and youth, sat on the edge of his desk and replied, "Now, I can take care of myself. I heard rumors too, but I don't believe it. Nobody would just force themselves on you that way."

Art leaned back in his chair and took a long drink from his half full coffee cup. He gently, almost instinctively, replied, "Baby, plenty of people in the world would make sex a part of your job description. Be careful up there. Where there's smoke, there's a little fire."

She shifted her long legs, almost brushing Art's. Then she reached over and placed her hand on his on the arm of his chair. She leaned over close, so close that he thought she was going to kiss him. "I know you care," she started. "I guess I really love you for that. But please don't worry! I'll be okay," she chided gently.

He looked straight into her big blue eyes, not six inches from his own as she leaned even further toward him. He placed his finger gently on her nose as he continued to look into her eyes. "Baby, just because he has a satanic look doesn't mean he can't be Satan. You got too many good years ahead to get all messed up."

She took his hand in hers and pushed it aside, removing the finger on her nose but still holding it tight as she leaned further over, kissing him lightly on the forehead. "That's for being my friend and for worrying about me."

"Well, I still reserve the right to worry about you."

Connie moved back to her position on the desk, releasing his hand, and pushed her long legs over against his, teasing him: "Okay, I promise if I need help I'll call."

"Okay. But I still can worry!"

"I'd be hurt if you didn't," she giggled as she slid down off the desk and started toward the door.

When Connie left, Chuck raised up from his seeming concentration on work, drew a long breath and said, "Damn, I couldn't take much of that. I'd at least petted her legs and kissed the hell out of her when she leaned over that way. That is some more woman."

"She's just a kid, Chuck. She's really a good kid but I'm afraid she leaps before she looks. I'm really worried about that. I heard Satan left his last job over some girls he was trying to put the make on."

"I heard the same thing. But I got it straight that son-of-a-bitch gives those girls hell up there unless they go to bed with him. It's easy to tell the ones who have because of the easy jobs they get."

"Well, I sure don't want Connie messed up in anything like that. I'm afraid she's gonna live hard."

Art started to read the memo Connie had left. "Guess I'm supposed to go with Jack at 1:30 to meet the new booster program manager. Looks like he's setting up a program management office. By the way, I need to call Eddie Rogers if he's in town."

Eddie recognized his old friend at the other end of the phone and replied disgustedly, "Just quit this damned job. We had one hell of a disagreement over ethics and honesty." Eddie was vehement, leaving no doubt about his fury.

Art chuckled, knowing very well how Eddie felt, having done the same thing himself once for the same reasons. He was obviously mad at somebody and not too interested in trying to patch it up. "Easy, old friend, easy" Art replied sympathetically.

"Easy, hell! That SOB I worked for until a few minutes ago don't know how to even spell honesty. He thinks I'll beg for my job back. But that day ain't comin."

"What happened, buddy?" Art asked.

"That asshole wants me to charge my time to a program I ain't never worked on so he can keep his funny books. They put people in jail for that, you know." Eddie was getting madder by the moment.

Art capitalized on Eddie's agitation. He could imagine the wavy black hair in disarray, as always when Eddie got upset. "When can you get your butt over here and go to work?" he asked.

There was a sudden silence. "What did you say?"

Art started to laugh and, replied: "I said when can you get your ass over here and go to work. Your desk and first task are ready now unless you plan to retire."

Another pause. "I don't know what to say. I hadn't expected that." came the subdued voice on the other end. "What you gonna pay me?" Eddie was flabbergasted, almost totally without words, which was very unusual for this very bright mathematician.

Art, laughing, replied, "Pay you? Hell, I thought you were a philanthropist. But if you insist, add ten percent to whatever you were making, and I emphasize 'were' making, and get yourself over here. I need you."

Eddie found himself still at a loss for words. After a few seconds, he blurted, "See you this afternoon, and thanks. Thanks a million."

At one fifteen, Art presented himself at Jack's office and described Eddie's qualifications and related past experiences with him. "Man, oh man, Art. This guy sounds great," he replied. "After we get through meeting Loren's new man, go down to personnel and grease the skids. If little Aikins gives you any trouble, let me know. I need to eat his ass out some more anyhow."

"Do you think he's forgotten the last time already?"

"Hell. That little pipsqueak needs it every day. Now, you know that . . ." Jack replied with glee.

Just then Jack's very ample secretary yelled through the door as was her custom, "Mr. Becker, time for your meeting in the conference room with Mr. Sharp."

Jack slipped on his coat and pulled his tie tight as he said, "Let's go see what they've done this time. Maybe we'll both have to leave before it's over." Art gave the secretary a wide berth as they left. Jack started to giggle. Out of earshot he asked, "What's the matter? You afraid of her?"

When they reached Loren's conference room, Art noted the various levels of management people seated around the long conference table. He noted the inordinate number of "managers", and thought of the old axiom about corporate and government structures: The more personnel a manager has, the more power he has and the larger salary he can command. He spotted Sonny Leech, impeccably dressed in coat and tie instead of the usual old pants and plaid shirt, seated at the table across from where Loren and the new man, Jerry Strong, were to sit. He nudged Jack who nodded knowingly as he whispered, "Starting to try to make a move to capture the new man. He shouldn't even be here."

Above the dull buzz of conversations, Art observed Loren Sharp entering the room with a tall, well-dressed man with a definite air of authority slightly behind. As they made their way to the front, the conversation subsided. "Looks like a good man," he commented quietly.

"Sure does. I hope he's good as he looks," Jack replied.

Loren walked to the head of the table as all conversation hushed. "I want you to meet Jerry Strong. Jerry will be the booster program manager and will direct day-to-day operations. He's from Phoenix and has a very distinguished record of developing and manufacturing solid rockets from some of our other operations. We're fortunate to have him join us here in Hawkinsville. Part of his charter is to establish a program management office. With that, I'll give the floor to Jerry."

The large frame covered with thinning blonde hair cut short around the sides, unfolded from the chair. Art studied his face intently as he thought, I'll bet he's a pusher. That's what we need. Somebody to separate the wheat from the chaff.

"Gentlemen," Strong began, "I'm pleased to have the opportunity to work with you. I know Loren has assembled a good staff for the task ahead and I'm looking forward to meeting all of you and getting to know you well . . ."As Jerry droned on, both Jack and Art began to feel a sense of relief. Here, at first impression, was a man that would not put up with mediocrity. Jack nudged Art and nodded his head toward Sonny, who was sitting almost at attention, drinking in every word as though it may be his last. He wondered if any one else had noticed.

Jerry continued for fifteen minutes more, espousing his beliefs and philosophies and closed by saying, "Thank you for your coming."

There was a polite round of applause. Sharp stood up, turned on the slide projector and placed an organization chart on it so that the picture was reflected clearly on the screen. "This is the organization. I don't believe in publishing these things because they're subject to change, so from time to time I'll just show you the chart. Besides, you all know who you work for and who works for you." Both Art and Jack were pleased to see that the logistics department was still shown with Jack as manager. Finally, Loren asked, "Any questions or comments?"

Sonny, obviously anxious, rose, unfolding the layers about his midsection. "Loren, I want to be the first to congratulate you on Jerry. I want to pledge my full cooperation and support to you, Jerry, because I know Loren is going to be making some changes in the organization that I feel will make it stronger."

Loren was uncomfortable with Sonny. He stood and interrupted, "Thank you Sonny. We appreciate your remarks but Jerry and I have another meeting to go to."

Loren quickly exited the room with Jerry in tow. The din in the room rose again as people began to leave and resume their conversations. Jack leaned over to Art in the hall and quietly asked, "What did you make of that?"

Art pondered the question a moment before answering, "In the air force, if I were a private trying to impress my first sergeant I might try to pull a stunt like that. But then, if I were the first sergeant, I'd know better. I think Sonny may have shot himself in the foot. I was watching Jerry and he looked surprised, too."

Jack considered this for a moment. "I think the big son-of-a-bitch was trying to make a move with that little speech."

"I think you're right, but I also believe, at least for now, that Jerry saw through the whole thing."

As Art entered the front lobby area on the way back to his office, his attention was immediately captured by a new receptionist. He saw a girl in her mid-twenties with long flowing light golden brown hair down over her shoulders framing a beautiful face. She had bright, green eyes that seemed to twinkle from any position and soft, red, beautifully formed lips. The long hair extended down over the tops of a pair of beautifully shaped, full breasts and a body that Art was sure would make Venus herself jealous. She was dressed in a tastefully-selected, close-fitting dress, but not too close fitting. As she sat at her desk, from his vantage point, he could see it almost cover her knees, revealing a pair of legs that looked like they came out of a magazine. "Man, oh man! Where'd they ever find one like her? She's almost too good to be true," he thought to himself.

She turned and looked full at Art, who was embarrassed because he was afraid she would think he was staring. She smiled slightly just as Eddie spotted him. "Art!" Eddie greeted enthusiastically.

The new girl looked at them both with a pleasant but business-like look. "Are you Mr. Cannon?"

"Yeah, guess I am. Who are you?" Art thought that was a dumb question because he obviously could see she was the new receptionist.

"I'm Heidi Collins. I just started this morning. I've been trying to call you. Mr. Rogers has been here for twenty minutes."

"Oh, yeah. You replaced Connie?"

"That's correct. Mr. Rogers is signed in and ready to go with you. Was that what you wanted?"

"Oh, sure." Art stumbled. "How you doin', Eddie? Come on, let's go up to my office." He was still almost at a loss for words, which actually surprised him since he usually had no problem relating to people. He puzzled over the effect this young lady had had on him and quickly dismissed it until he could consider it further.

When they turned down the hall, Eddie asked, "What the hell you doin' here? Last time we talked you were flying for a living."

"I got tired of starving. They pay better here than at the airport, so I took it when they offered."

"Great. I'm glad to see you get situated. Let's discuss this 'proposition' of yours. What the hell you need me for?"

Art laughed at Eddie's enthusiasm as they rounded the corner into his office, where he observed Chuck looking disgusted. "You just missed Sonny," he commented wryly.

"Good. Meet the best operations research man in the business, Eddie Rogers."

After he poured two cups of coffee and handed Eddie one, he sat down at his desk facing Eddie and said. "Buddy, I need you. I got more than I can handle. I got authorization to hire you and I got a job for you." Eddie stared at Art intently as he continued, "I need you to finish an optimum repair level analysis model like we did on

Hubble."

"Yeah, that was a good project, wasn't it? Sure hope that one works out. I've always wondered what we'll really see out there."

"Yeah, me too", Art replied with a grin. "But back to business. I started to develop the model but I can't finish it because of an expanded work load in running logistics engineering."

Eddie looked puzzled. "What the hell is logistics engineering?"

Both Art and Chuck laughed as Chuck leaned forward and peered at Eddie: "Friend, you're lookin at it. If Art says he needs you, sign on."

Eddie looked at the both of them quizzically. "You damned guys are serious, aren't you?"

"Yep. Sure as hell am. I wouldn't have asked you if I wasn't. And I know you wouldn't be here if you weren't, so lets fill out an application and report you to work Monday."

Eddie looked surprised. "That's only two work days. You can't move that fast, can you?"

"We got a system here like you never seen before. Come on and watch."

"Aikins," Art bellowed as he entered the personnel office, "Gimme a damned application form."

A startled Dean Aikins emerged from the files and started to groan. "Oh no. Not another one," in obvious reference to Jack Becker. "I know he's put you up to this."

"Deanie, I got an authorization down here to hire this man and I need it done now. I need him at work Monday morning." Art picked up an application form and handed it to Eddie. "Be back in a few minutes, so you can process it."

Aikins was furious. "I told you people it takes at least two weeks to process in somebody! I mean it! Two damned weeks!" He yelled as he pounded the counter with his fist.

Art leaned over the counter as close to Dean as he could get. "Buster, you got five minutes to get your offer letter written. If not, I'll let you discuss it with Becker. Now get hot!"

Dean shrank back, paled, and turned toward his office to write an offer letter, muttering under his breath, "I'll get even with you, just wait and see. I'll get even."

Eddie completed the application form and Art laid it on the desk where Dean was furiously working to get the offer letter done in total abject fear of facing Jack Becker again. Finally he took the letter out of the typewriter and shoved it across to Eddie. "That okay?" he grunted with a sneer.

Art took the letter before Eddie could pick it up, scanned it, and shoved it back across to Dean. "Hell No! You never learn. Now do it over and put another twenty five-huundred dollars on it. Now!"

Dean began to moan a low mournful pout. "I don't have time right now. I got other things to do."

Art reached for the phone on the counter. Dean turned a bright red, and almost screamed, "No! No! I'll do it now!"

"You damn bet'cha because I happen to know that's a memory typewriter and I know you got it stored."

Dean, very grudgingly, corrected the numbers, reprinted the letter and handed it to Art. "That's better," he growled. "Don't try to pull your bullshit on me."

He handed the letter to Eddie who read it and then whispered to Art, "Let's step out in the hall a minute."

"Oh, got a problem?" Art replied. He watched the strained look on Dean's face as he tried to overhear the conversation.

"Art, that's five hundred dollars too much money."

He chuckled at Eddie's worried look. "That's his penalty for trying to short your offer. He's good at that. Now sign the damned thing and let's go."

As they started down the hall toward the office, Art suddenly turned toward the stairs. "Let's go meet Jack Becker."

"Sounds good. I hope you don't talk to him like you do Dean."

"Hah! He's the one who taught me." Art replied with a laugh.

"Sit down." Jack said to them as they entered the office after giving the secretary wide berth. Becker stretched his hand out to Eddie and said to Art, "Boy, that was fast. How did you do it?"

Art snickered as he answered, noting Eddie's grin, "I just had a damned good teacher."

Jack turned to Eddie, still grinning, "Well, Eddie, welcome to our happy home. We hope your stay will be long and prosperous."

Eddie couldn't restrain himself any longer. "What have you

done to this guy? I never saw him get on anybody like he got on that personnel man."

Jack was beaming with delight. "Tell me about it."

Art ushered Eddie back to the front desk where Heidi was dutifully watching the front lobby. He gazed at her again and thought to himself, Yep, that lady's really got class.

As they approached the desk she looked up with a smile, "Hello Mr. Cannon, I didn't expect you back this soon."

"Well, we work fast when we need to. Wasn't no question of hiring, just a question of when I could get him to go to work."

"Oh, then it wasn't an interview after all?" she replied with a hint of teasing in her voice.

"Hey, when you been around together as long as we have, there ain't never any question."

"Must be nice," she replied. "It took me two weeks to get hired."

"See? That's what you get for not coming to the right place. Next time, come see me. okay?"

Eddie was observing the exchange and decided she was attracted to Art. She was grinning as she leaned over to sign Eddie out on the visitors log. "Well, I'll sure keep that in mind. Thank you, Mr. Rogers." Then she turned to Art. "When will we see him again?"

"Monday morning. Call me right away and treat him good 'cause he's one of the 'good guys'."

Eddie was embarrassed at the teasing. "Don't believe half what this joker tells you. I've known him long enough to separate fact from fiction."

Heidi was smiling, eyes twinkling, and obviously enjoying the exchange. "Is he really a joker?" she asked. "I thought he looked kind of serious."

"Me?" Art said with a chuckle.

Eddie stuck out his hand and said gently, "Thanks, buddy. I'll see you bright and early Monday morning."

"Hey, it's really great to have you on the team," Art said as they shook hands.

Art and Heidi walked to the front door and watched him as he left the lobby and turned down the walk to the parking lot. "Thanks for being so pleasant to Eddie. He needs some understanding right now." He turned so as to view the beautiful figure standing there, all five-foot-nine of her. Each part of the beautiful body seemed to be in complete harmony with each other part, the large breasts accenting the small waist and beautifully formed hips and legs. She seemed to truly be from a fairy tale, the rare beauty was almost too much to believe one woman could possess.

Heidi blushed, sensing she was being observed, and sat down in her chair, half exposing part of a full and beautifully shaped right breast with her low cut blouse. "Perhaps he should come to the party next weekend over at the lake. He might get cheered up there," she said.

Art, was curious. "What party? Where?"

"Oh, weren't you invited? I was invited last week by Dean, you know, down in personnel when I checked in." She had become much more casual and friendly, dropping any hint of business formality.

Art felt a wave of anxiety at her mention of Dean. He had only met this beautiful young woman and already he was worried about her. He stopped to consider this a moment and thought to himself, "Hell, I don't even know her. Why should I be concerned?" Then a feeling of concern, or of caring, or of something he didn't yet comprehend, swept over him as he turned to her. "I don't think I'm going and I'd advise you to be careful out there. What kind of party is it?"

"Sonny Leech and some others are renting an old house that's been turned into a lodge over at the lake, Dean said. I won't stay long, but according to him they sure know how to give parties."

"More like orgies, I hear. But then, I never been to one."

"Oh, no, not that nice Mr. Leech. A bunch of us are going. I only met Mr. Leech this morning but Mr. Aikins seems to like him."

"Yeah, he would." Art felt anger he still didn't fully understand. Then his thoughts turned to Connie and her comment about going to a reception at the lake in an old house after her wedding. With that thought in mind, his concern reached high anxiety as he abruptly excused himself, turned and went to Connie's new office. Under the glare of "Satan", he demanded, "Connie, I need to talk to you."

Connie got up from her chair and a low roar came from the back of the room, "Where you going?"

Connie turned to see her satanic-looking boss glaring curiously. "Oh, Mr. Creude, I'm sorry. Have you met Art Cannon, the manager of logistics engineering?"

"I've seen him. What the hell you tryin to do?" Creude growled, "Waste the time of my employees? If you ain't got business here, leave! We got work to do."

Art's surprise turned to disgust and he made little effort to hide it. "I need to see Connie a minute," he replied sarcastically.

"Personal or business?"

"Personal." Art was frustrated. His first impulse was to punch out this obviously arrogant, egotistical bastard but he knew that would cause nothing but trouble.

Connie was embarrassed at the acid-like exchange and asked, "What is it, Art?"

"Come by my office when you get off . . . if you can." Art glared at Creude, turned and without another word, walked quickly out the door.

At four thirty-five Connie walked into Art's office, sat down by his desk and just looked at him for a moment. Art slid back in his chair with a big smile. "Hope I didn't cause you any trouble up there."

Connie, still curious, brushed off the comment. "I was worried there for a minute. I never saw Al act that way before."

Art grinned as he looked at her. "Boy, some guy is getting a lot of woman."

"Quit teasing me and be serious."

"Okay. It's his office, I suppose, and I'm an outsider when it comes to accounting. I didn't have much of an argument anymore than he would have down here if I chose to throw him out."

"You're too nice to do that. What did you want?" she asked as she stared quizzically at Art.

Art looked at Connie seriously. "Connie, you and I are friends and I'm concerned so I'll be blunt. Are you going to Sonny's party next weekend?"

"No, silly. Remember I told you I was getting married that weekend!"

"Yeah, I know and I wish we could come. But I got to help Mack finish installing the engine in the airplane."

"That's the one that failed when you made that night landing in the storm?"

"Yeah. We're going to make the first flight Saturday. But how did you know about that?"

"I heard. I also heard you were lucky to be alive."

"Yeah, well, you had said something about a reception at the lake in an old house and I just heard Sonny was pitching a wild party next weekend. I remember the first one you went to and how sorry I felt for you. I even covered for you."

"Yes, and my dearest friend, I'm still grateful." Connie was grinning as she affectionately patted Art on the arm. "Don't worry. I won't be going. I'll be having too good a time elsewhere, if you know what I mean."

"Well, the new girl, Heidi, told me about it. I wish she weren't going. I feel uneasy about her."

Connie chided, "You've just found another waif to worry about. I'm about to graduate from your advisory class and you just have to have somebody to worry about, don't you?"

"Do you really think so?"

"No, silly. I'm just teasing you. But she is an awfully pretty girl. You're just too soft hearted is all."

"Well, Connie, people are important and I don't like to see anybody mistreated."

"I know. Annie told me how you are and she's exactly right."

"Yeah, well, I was just worried about you."

Just as Connie was getting up to leave, the new program manager, Jerry Strong, entered, seemingly towering over the room. Connie vivaciously excused herself from the room as Art greeted his new guest, "Hi, Jerry. I'm Art Cannon. Sorry I didn't get to visit with you the other day. Sit down."

Jerry sat down in a chair beside Art's desk, smiling, and replied, "I'm sorry, too, but I wanted to visit with you and all the other managers. How long you been with the company?"

Art showed Jerry his badge, Number 93. "Four months. Got a super boss."

"Yeah, I like Jack, too. He knows his business. I heard a lot of good things about you and just wanted to meet you. Also heard that you were a flyer of the highest order."

Art blushed as he replied, "I'm afraid you been hearing some rumors, then. But I do love to fly. How about you?"

"Never had the time but sure got the interest. Maybe we can go bend a wing some day?"

"I go flying at the drop of a hat. Any time you got time, just let me know."

Jerry eased back in the chair, becoming more comfortable and feeling a rapport developing between them. "What do you perceive as problems in this organization? I'm getting bad vibes since I came here. What do you think we need to do?"

Art became serious and frowned at the thought of what he was about to say, and not too sure he should say, because he didn't really know this seemingly-good man in front of him. His intuition was racing ahead and he heard an inner voice saying, *Hey, this guy's okay*. Tell him. Art started slowly and deliberately. "Jerry, I think we need a good systems engineering organization to begin to integrate this vehicle and all the little pieces and parts together into a common whole like we did the Saturn. We need to establish a design and configuration baseline I don't see right now."

Jerry was leaning back looking at the ceiling, forehead wrinkled and mouth set firmly while he considered what he had just heard. He slowly began, as if measuring each word carefully. "I agree that we need a systems engineering group. Would you consider heading up that organization? I've already looked at your resume and you're qualified for that position."

Art took a long drink from his almost cold coffee cup and sat for a moment just looking at the big man and thinking, damn, what a guy. Sure doesn't mind getting down in the trenches and getting level with the troops. "Jerry," he started slowly, "I would be pleased to work for you in that job . . ."

"Go on."

He hesitated to consider his next words carefully. "However, Jack Becker's been so decent to me I feel a strong loyalty to support him. I'd have to consider Jack before I'd just up and leave him cold."

"I understand, and I appreciate that. I like him too. He's got his head on straight and knows where his organization needs to go. I'm just thinking about options."

"Yeah, we always have to do that and I want to contribute the best way I can. This program's very important to me."

Jerry was looking at Art, deep concern showing on his face.

Jerry continued, "I'm concerned about Jack because I don't get a sense of well-being. I probably shouldn't say that just yet so please don't repeat me."

"Jerry," Art began slowly, "if anything ever happened to Jack Becker, the company would be the loser. The man cares, he really cares about the program and he wants to see it through."

"Yeah, that's my sense of him too," Jerry replied while he wrinkled his brow.

"He feels for people," he continued. "That's important. If you can't feel for people and want to treat 'em right, and I don't mean to entertain incompetence just to keep 'em on, but if you don't care about the people, you shouldn't be there. Jack cares."

"I believe he does and that's the way I feel, too."

"My intuition says you do. Otherwise I wouldn't have been so open," Art answered with a feeling of relief at the exchange.

Just as Jerry was preparing to leave Art saw a shadow change from an overhanging light in the hallway. To Jerry's surprise he got up quickly and walked to the door in time to see Sonny disappear around the corner from his eavesdropping position. "Guess we been bugged," Art growled with obvious disgust.

Jerry turned a bright shade of red and said in a high voice, "Is that one of the damned games played around here? Who the hell was it?"

Art deposited himself in his chair and related to Jerry his past experiences with Sonny and admonished him to be careful, concluding with, "I don't understand everything that's going on yet, but I'm worried."

"I can see why. I'll try to do something about it. See you tomorrow, it's getting late."

After a quick breakfast Art drove to his office an hour early to complete his progress report. He was proud of himself for finishing early. "Damn, I'm through and it's fifteen minutes before time to even start work," he mused. As he passed through the lobby to deliver the report he spotted Heidi coming in the front door to resume her position at the front desk for the day. "Hi early bird," he called out as he passed her on the way to the elevator.

"Hi yourself. Looks like you beat me . . . What's up."

"Oh, nothing special, just wanted to get my report in a little early." Then, on an impulse, he asked, "How about lunch today?"

Heidi smiled a huge smile and replied, "Oh, gee. I'd really love to but I'm meeting my mother for lunch. I wish I had known earlier. How about a rain check?"

"You bet," Art replied. "We'll plan it for one day next week." Just then the elevator interrupted the conversation. As the door closed, he pushed the button for the third floor and wondered to himself what kind of a day it was going to be.

Art turned the corner and noticed Loren Sharp's inner office light shining through a crack under the door. He thought, "Guess I'm not the only early bird today". Then he heard Jerry's loud, agitated voice through the door, "Loren, that's the most stupid thing you could ever do. That son-of-a-bitch doesn't know his ass from first base. I will not, and I repeat, *NOT*, have him working for me."

Art froze, fear gripping him as he stood motionless listening. "Now, Jerry," came Loren's smooth reply, "I've been planning this and whatever you think, I'm still boss here. I think the man is brilliant. Besides, I've made a deal to transfer Jack to Arizona and even get him a raise on some of our other projects."

Jerry's voice was growing louder and becoming more excited. "I refuse to have anything to do with that bastard. He's scheming. He's conniving. He's incompetent and he'll not work for me and you can tell your boss Bennie that, too!"

Art turned ashen. He knew too well what was happening. He stood rooted, listening. "Okay, if that's the way you feel about it, he'll report to me. You won't have anything to do with him."

"NO!" came the thunderous retort from Jerry, "It's wrong and it's dumb."

Loren's voice was now louder and more emphatic. "Jerry, my mind's made up. The change is effective next week. You can either work with it or you can pack up and resign. You choose. We've worked together too many years to have a fight like this. Now lets all be friends and get the job done."

Art heard Jerry sigh heavily in despair. "Loren, you'll be sorry. It's a big mistake."

"I don't think so. I've got to go over to the contracts office and inform them of the change."

Art was so weak he could hardly move, but knew he must. He

picked up his lead feet and plodded slowly to Jack's office and deposited his report in the in-basket just as Emma, the ample secretary, entered the office. "What you doin' here this early?" she asked curtly.

Art looked at her without really seeing her. "I wonder." he grunted as he quickly exited.

He took the back stairs to his office to avoid going through the lobby where he knew Heidi, who had quickly become his close friend, would want to exchange pleasantries. When he turned into his office, glad to have done so unobserved, or so he thought, he saw his coffee cup full and steaming. The silence was broken by Chuck. "Hi Chief, what's wrong? You feel okay?"

Art was relieved to see that it was Chuck because he didn't feel like much conversation. Art picked up the cup of coffee. "Thanks, buddy." Then he related the fight he had heard between Loren and Jerry. "I can't believe it. It just doesn't make sense."

"*Shit* Art. Shit is all I got to say. This damned place'll go to hell in a hand basket."

"Yeah, and I just hired Eddie. I guess I got to level with him, too. If he wants to change his mind, he can."

"Yeah," Chuck grunted. "He may not want to stay."

Art slid back in his chair and looked across the road outside their window at a ground hog coming out of its burrow in the far bank and for a moment wished he could change places. Just then Chuck, who had been uncharacteristically silent, stomped the floor and walked to the window. "Dammit to hell, anyhow, I think I'll quit. I ain't going to put up with that fat ass and his shit. You know we got to work for him, don't you?" Chuck's face was red and appeared on the verge of an anxiety attack.

Art commented wryly, "Let's just play the copperhead game for a few days and see what happens. Maybe Jerry can win the battle, okay? So, don't go do anything dumb yet."

Chuck stared at him. "What the hell you talking about?"

"Well, when I was growing up North Carolina I learned some mountain medicine. We can learn a little from the snakes I think."

"From the what . . .?" Chuck asked carefully.

"If you ever watched those little guys you could see an old rattler get all excited and go to pieces with nerves and start to shake his tail. Then you can find him and beat hell out of him before he can

45

strike. But the copperhead . . . now he's different. He lays and waits real quiet and don't get excited and when the time is right, he strikes. Maybe we got to sit back quiet for a while, too."

Chuck grunted, not really seeing him. "Yeah. You damned hillbillies are all alike. Guess maybe I'll hang on for a while--but shit, I don't have to like it."

Art sat quietly gazing outside at the grass and trees without really seeing anything. He was in deep thought as he saw Jack drive up. Chuck motioned and said, "We got to warn him. Maybe he can do something."

Art intercepted Jack as he entered the end hallway door and placing his finger over his lips, motioned him into the office. Jack looked puzzled but complied as Art shut the door before anyone spoke. Jack looked at them both and asked, "What the hell's going on?"

"Jack, we been shit on," Chuck blurted.

Art motioned Chuck to sit down. "Chief, we got a hell of a problem and we got to do something about it if we can . . ." Art related the events he had overheard.

Jack began to turn red and perspire. He stalked to the window like a mountain lion about to spring. "So!" he thundered, "That's the reason for this damned hush-ass trip to Arizona. Those sons-of-bitches don't have the guts to do their own dirty work. They got to have somebody do it for 'em. I thought it was strange when Loren called me at home night before last and asked me to take some damned emergency assignment at the home office. Now I know what kind of a shittin' outfit I'm working for, or at least what kind of a damned boss I'm working for."

Art, fearing Jack's temper might cause him to do something foolish, tried to settle him down. "Now Jack, get hold of yourself. I'm madder'n hell, too, but we need to pull in and do a little thinking. Maybe you should talk to Jerry before you go, do you think?"

"Art, I'm so pissed, I can't even think straight right now. I'll call you later." Jack left the office and he, too, took the back steps to avoid meeting people. Chuck sat at his desk with his head propped on his hands looking like his last friend had just died. They both sat silently looking out the window watching the ground hog making its way along the bank to the fields around the big test stands that stood as mute evidence of a grand era of the past.

Chuck crossed the room to the coffee pot and asked, "Want some more?" Art grunted, which Chuck took as affirmative and slowly poured him a refill.

Just as Chuck finished pouring, the door opened and Connie appeared with her usual big smile. She stopped short of a chair beside Art's desk. "What's wrong with you guys? You look like somebody died."

Art gazed at her and slowly replied, "No, baby, not yet at least. We were just planning our next moves, if there are any. Pour yourself a cup and sit down."

Connie looked serious while pouring her coffee and Art sensed something more than a social visit. "What's the trouble, baby, you look like something's on your mind."

"Art, I'm scared. You know tomorrow's the day for me to get married and I'm worried about my job and about being married, and being tied down, and all that. Is it natural?"

Art laughed, trying to ease her mind, "Baby, when Annie and I got married we were both scared, but we loved each other enough that it didn't matter. We did it and believe me, I'd do it again."

Connie leaned back in the chair and wistfully commented, "Yeah, but you and Annie knew what you wanted." Connie was emphasizing the "knew" very strongly and still had a very worried look on her face.

Art perceived doubts about her new life. Suddenly Chuck exclaimed as he walked rapidly toward the door, "Got to go to the Friday configuration meeting. See you guys later."

"Connie," Art began, waving at Chuck as he left the room, "if you're not sure about what you want, it might be better to postpone it. I would sure hate for you to make a mistake."

Connie seemed uneasy and unsure about what she should say in reply. Art continued, "Is it just the tying down and no more of the romantic chases that you're worried about or do you have some reservations about Jeff? Now, don't answer that if you don't want to, but think about it."

"Well, Art," she began slowly, "I was sure until I went upstairs. Al has treated me so good . . ."

Art's chair slipped and he almost fell. He caught himself on his desk, choking on his coffee at the same time. He recovered and sat a moment in disbelief. He mustered all the composure he could find before he said anything. Finally, "Is it because you got doubts or are you unsure because of Al's advances or what?"

"Oh, he's made no advances. It's just that I think he's so cute and he's so nice to me. I really enjoy working up there."

Art felt rage building because he feared Al's seduction tactics might just be working. "Connie, did you know that man's married and has four kids? What the hell is he trying to do to you?" Art thundered. "Baby, he's trouble. Trouble for you and for all the other girls up there, too."

Connie, sensing that she had upset Art, replied quietly, "He's hasn't done anything to me. Honest. He hasn't made any advances or nothing. I just have this feeling, that's all. I love Jeff and want to marry him but I want to be sure."

"Well, you need to be sure . . ."

"I worry when I have feelings like this. Maybe it's guilt. I don't know. How can I be sure? How is it with you and Annie?"

Art relaxed a bit, believing Al had not made the progress he first feared. "Annie and I have had our share of problems, just like everybody else, but the important thing is we love each other enough to work out things. You got to learn to give and take and learn to negotiate. But most of all you have to respect the other guy. Jeff should be your best friend as well as your husband and lover. Does that make sense?"

"Yeah. I see. I guess I feel better," Connie admitted. "I think it'll work out okay. I know I'm immature and make decisions without thinking much, and I guess I just got worried." She patted Art on the shoulder affectionately for listening.

"Hang in there, Connie. Sometimes people do get nervous before weddings."

"I know. I got to get back to the office. See you later for some more encouragement." Connie dashed out the door, having forgotten how long she had been there.

Suddenly before Art's desk appeared the satanic looking Al, who had stealthily entered. "Saw one of my girls leavin'. What'd she want?"

Art answered as calmly and unconcerned as he could, considering his intense dislike for Al. "Oh, you mean Connie? She just wanted a cup of coffee and to talk a minute."

"About what?" Al scowled, sitting down in a chair by Art's desk.

Art, thinking that Al was now in his territory, gave him a hard look and thought, *Now, you son-of-a-bitch, let's see who can push who around.* Then he remembered that Connie had to work up there and he didn't want to create a problem for her by being nasty. Choking back his desire for confrontation, he answered quietly. "She's nervous about getting married and needed a little encouragement. That's all."

"Oh," Al mused. "I just need to know what goes on with my people. Can't trust 'em, you know. One of the worst mistakes a manager can make is trusting people. You know they all want something, especially those young ones. I give some of 'em a little something sometimes, mostly just to keep 'em happy and make 'em work better. You'll learn that as you go along."

Art leaned back in his chair and stared at the Al in total amazement. He picked up his coffee cup to take a drink and found it had gotten cold. He glared at the cup and sat it back down before saying anything, searching for something to say that wouldn't reveal the ugly thoughts flooding his mind. He could only manage, "That right? Never tried it that way."

Al countered immediately, "That's obvious. That's why you'll never be a great manager, always stay somewhere like this. You know, never progress to the top of the ladder."

Art turned red in the face with anger as he replied curtly, "Al, I'm sorry, but I got to go to a meeting. You'll have to give me your philosophies some other time." With that Art picked up his notebook and left the room.

Jack had been sitting in his office most of the morning quietly contemplating the events and his next move. Because of his fear of a lack of support in Hawkinsville, he decided the best plan was to go on to Arizona and try to solve the problem from there, if he could. He sat watching the old test stands seemingly waving in the breeze and watched the pigeons coming and going. He pondered the trip to the home office in Arizona and wondered what it would lead to. He didn't want to leave Hawkinsville and the friends he had made, and especially he didn't want to leave Art and Annie, and all the flyers at the airport he had come to enjoy so much. His ample secretary,

Emma, waddled into his office with airline tickets and travel authorization in her hand. "Here are your tickets, Mr. Becker. Will you be gone long?"

Jack smiled faintly as he replied, "Don't know, Emma, might or might not. Thanks for getting these."

Jack turned, again facing the window and heard Emma moving across the room toward him, "Is there anything wrong, Mr. Becker?" she asked, changing her tone from the usual gruffness.

Jack turned slowly again and looked affectionately at her, afraid this may be his last opportunity. "No Emma, everything's fine. I don't feel so good today, though, but everything's going to be fine. Don't worry." With that Jack turned again toward the big test stands, feeling defeated and very alone.

The sun disappeared behind some clouds and the wind picked up with an obvious change in direction. Art peered out the window as the afternoon bore on and commented to Chuck, "Looks like we might get a little rain later. Wind's shifted. Guess the cold front came through. By the way, you seen Jack? It's about time for him to leave."

"No, but I wouldn't be surprised if he hasn't left already."

CHAPTER FIVE

While Art dressed for work on Monday morning, his thoughts drifted to Heidi. He found himself worrying and wondering if she made it through the party without a problem. He wondered if his worry was of distrust and intense dislike for Sonny. He decided to put it aside for the moment and then thought of Jack. *Sure hope the guy makes out okay out there. Don't know what we'll do without him. I bet it's gonna' be hell to work here now, what with Sonny and his band of renegades he'll bring in.* Apprehension was building as Art's mind began to consider the day's problems, or at least potential problems. Suddenly he remembered Eddie was checking in this morning and decided he needed to be at the office early to meet him.

Art entered the building at 7:15 and mentally started to lay out work for Eddie while worrying again about whether or not he had done the right thing in offering him a job with the specter of Sonny. He thought, *Eddie won't be in until at least 7:30 and maybe later since he's one of the world's great sack hounds.* Art chuckled to himself. He surveyed the parking lot and saw several people arriving early, including Sonny Leech getting out of his big Lincoln near the front door. He was dressed in a dark blue, pin stripe three-piece suit, large pot belly hanging over the belt and protruding down below the vest. Sonny appeared dressed more for a funeral than for the office. Art laughed to himself at the sight and then thought that it may not be so funny.

Sonny saw Art and waved. "Mornin. Glad to see you early." He raised his fist in the air as a salute to Art's dedication to his supposed agenda. "That's good."

Art, taken aback by the remark, waved back but couldn't muster any response. He walked down the empty hall wondering what all that meant but resolved that he'd find out soon enough. His suspicion was high because Sonny usually didn't dress formally and didn't park in the senior management area.

Art was busying himself by putting on the coffee pot when Chuck arrived. "Hi, Chief," Chuck started slowly as he made his way to the pot to check its progress, "You seen Heidi?"

"No. Anything wrong?" He looked curiously at Chuck who seemed genuinely worried.

Apprehensively, Chuck continued, "I saw her in the parking lot. She looked like hell and didn't walk too stable, like she was hung over or something."

"Well, that's strange. If she's sick she shouldn't be here," Art replied, deciding to go find out about her as soon as he could.

"She didn't have much to say either," Chuck continued. "Wonder what happened to her?"

"Don't know," he replied, "Maybe she went to Sonny's party, but that was Saturday," Art replied with some concern.

"What party?"

"Sonny and some of his cronies had a big bash over on the river. I think she went. Probably had too much to drink."

Chuck frowned and furrowed his brow. "If she went, I bet that's what's wrong."

"By the way," Art queried, "did you hear how Connie's wedding went?"

"No. But I worry about that kid. I'm not sure she's in touch with reality sometimes." Both Art and Chuck emitted a big laugh just as the phone rang.

"Art," came the quiet, weak voice on the other end, "Mr. Rogers is here."

"Heidi, is that you?"

"Yes," came the faint reply.

"You okay?" Art was now more concerned than ever.

"Well, I guess so. Why?" came another weak reply.

"I'll be down in a minute." He hung up the phone and turned to Chuck with a worried look. " Boy, she sounds like she went on the rocks. Eddie's here."

He walked quickly to the lobby where he found Eddie relaxing in one of the guest chairs. "Mornin' Tiger!" he greeted.

Eddie jumped up and saluted with the wrong hand, "Private Rogers reporting Sir. Take my body and do what you will with it."

He grinned at the sight of his good friend and replied, eyeing Heidi out of the corner of his eye, "I've got all sorts of torture planned. Jack's not here today but I got everything ready."

Then he approached Heidi and asked gently, "You okay? You sounded sort of not with it."

She smiled weakly and looked up with a puffy, unmade face and swollen eyes that scarcely had any color at all. Through an obviously forced grin she murmured weakly, "Yeah, I'm okay. Bad weekend. That's all," she replied as she looked down at the desk.

"Well, if I can help, let me know," he responded gently as he and Eddie turned to walk toward the personnel office.

"Boy," Eddie commented, "she looks like a truck ran over her."

"Yeah, or Sonny Leech and some of his crowd."

"Who's that?" Eddie asked cautiously.

"Maybe a problem, but we'll deal with it the best we can."

Eddie looked soberly at Art. "Politics?"

"Yeah. Looks to me like he's trying to take over the department by throwing Jack out. But we'll have to see. Here's personnel."

They spent the next hour getting all the personnel, financial and security forms and other duties taken care of. Finally, Dean Aikins appeared in the office door and saw Art standing by the front counter with Eddie. He stopped abruptly and started to leave as quickly as possible when Art spotted him. He was a disheveled mess, clothes half on, shirt unbuttoned, tie loose and rumpled, eyes red and an obvious red hue to his cheeks. "Don't say a word," he muttered.

"Oh," Art chortled. "I see you been to a party again. Bet it was Sonny's beach party. What did your wife think of that?"

Dean, feeling a terrible upset coming on, tried to yell but could only manage a half croak. "How did you know that, and besides it's none of your damn business." He turned into his office and slammed the door so hard the pictures on the wall shuddered.

Lora, the personnel clerk who had been assisting Eddie, glanced quickly at Art. "Take it easy on the little jerk. You can see he's sick, but I'll bet it's his own fault."

"If he went to Sonny's party, I can understand. There's some more around here the same way," Art commented quietly. "Watch him, he might collapse."

Eddie was staring in amazement while taking in the whole scene. "What kind of a party was it?" he asked, half not wanting to know and half burning with curiosity.

"Don't know, but I'll bet it was wild."

Lora finished the form for Eddie to take to security for transfer of his clearance and said, "I wonder about some of those people. They don't understand what living's about yet. Maybe they never will."

"You're right," Art quipped as they left personnel. "Keep an eye on your delinquent in there."

As they left security, Eddie commented. "Feels good to be a part of a bonafide company again. Looks like this one might be interesting in more ways than one. You know, buddy, this is our third company together."

"Yeah," Art chuckled. "We been gettin around over the years haven't we? Guess you'll have to share an office with Chuck and me for a while. I hope to get us some better office space when Jack gets back." As they turned the corner into the office they would share, Art spotted Chuck sitting with his feet up, looking out the window in a cold, faceless stare.

Art pointed to a desk in the other corner of the room, next to a window. "Eddie, that's your area. We'll go to supply in a few minutes and get Ralph to outfit you." They both were looking at Chuck, who had been sitting poker faced without a word. Art had a premonition, "Okay, Chuck, what's goin' on?" he asked gently. "You look like you've just seen death itself."

Chuck slowly turned around and quietly, matter-of-factly replied, "Chief, I have. I have. Read this." He handed Art a memo that had just come into the office from Loren Sharp, addressed to all personnel.

"As of this date, Mr. Jack Becker has been transferred to our Northern California rocket test range on permanent assignment. Mr. Sonny Leech has been selected to replace him. He will assume responsibility for the logistics department and will report directly to me. I will appreciate your full cooperation with Mr. Leech in the execution of his duties.--Loren Sharp, Executive Vice President."

Art handed the memo to Eddie to read and sank down in his chair with a long sigh, "Well, what next?"

Eddie read the memo and tried to inject a bit of reassurance into the dismal atmosphere, "Hey, maybe it's not so bad. He's got to know something about what he's doing. After all, this guy's a PhD and did make executive vice president."

Chuck frowned at Eddie as he replied gruffly, "One would hope. One would hope."

Eddie looked at both of them quizzically. "Art, I've known you a long time and I know you don't upset easy. Let's give it a chance. He may work out. This job may be what he wanted and now that he's got it he may be okay."

"Remember Neville Chamberlain and Hitler and Poland," Art commented bitterly.

Chuck dropped his feet hard on the floor and growled, "C'mon Eddie. I'll give you a tour of the joint. Maybe it'll work out and if it don't I was looking for a job when I signed on." With that they both walked out the door and down the hall.

Art sat quietly for the next few minutes drinking a cup of hot coffee and pondering his next move. I've got to talk to Jack, he thought. Damn, I hope he's okay. That son-of-a-bitch finally did it. Guess I'd be foolish to walk just yet. Besides it hasn't missed any paydays yet.

Art heard a shuffling noise and glanced up to see Heidi pausing at the door, looking as though she didn't know whether to come in or not. Art gazed for a split second, trying not to be intrusive. Her clothes were still disarranged and completely uncoordinated, hair half combed, no stockings and completely out of character. Her head was down and she had a look of total despair on her face. She appeared to be in anguish, as though she were ill and had lost all will to possess her great natural beauty. "Come in, Heidi. Have a cup of coffee," Art invited with a surge of concern.

She walked slowly and painfully in and sat down by Art's desk. Before a word was spoken, he poured a fresh cup and handed it to her. "Thanks," she said uneasily. "I thought you and Chuck might have some on."

He studied her with a worried look. "What's wrong? Are you sick?"

Heidi didn't respond for a moment and finally said, "Oh, I just had a bad weekend, I guess."

Art took her hand, stroked the long fingers gently, and said, "Baby, do you want to talk about it? You know you can talk to me and it won't go any further."

Her red eyes welled up with tears as she began slowly and haltingly, "Yeah, I know."

"Want to tell me about it?" he asked again gently.

"I don't know too much, but I need to talk to somebody real bad I guess."

"Well, that's what friends are for."

"I know. You're my friend but I'm not so sure about anybody else around here anymore."

She began to cry and Art put his arm around her shoulder to comfort her. "Hey, you sound serious. Let me shut the door for a while."

"Yeah, yeah. That'd be best," she said in a subdued, painful voice. "I just don't know what to do."

Art was feeling deep compassion as he sat down studying her carefully. She continued to cry softly as he handed her a tissue. She wiped her eyes and looked straight ahead. "I don't know if I should trouble you with my problems."

"Hey, we can talk it out. Besides, it's just between us."

"Well, I didn't listen to you and I paid the price. I went to Sonny's damned party, me and my girl friend, Alice Fagan," she began with resolve, as though she had to push to get it started.

"Oh no," Art exclaimed softly, fearing the worst.

"There's a big old house over on the lake that's been converted into a lodge . . ."

He shook his head, "I know the place. I've flown over it; looks remote back there on the river."

"Anyhow, we started out Saturday night, about thirty or fourty of us, mostly people I didn't know. There was a lot of drinking and loud talking and real loud music. About midnight I got a little drunk, like most everybody else I guess," she said haltingly. "Alice had passed out on the couch in the living room and when I tried to get her up Sonny came over and said not to worry, she'd be all right. He asked me if I was okay. I said 'Yeah, I guess I am.' He gave me a couple of red pills and said to take 'em and I'd feel better."

"Did you take them? What were they?" Art asked quietly with a sinking feeling.

"I don't know. I took 'em and then in a little while I began to feel strange, like I was going to fall or something, but I was sitting down. My head was just going round and round. Then I started to pass out . . . I was there but I wasn't there . . ."

"Like you were high on something besides drinks, maybe." Concern was beginning to show in deep lines on Art's face as he genuinely feared what she was going to tell him.

"Yeah, or something. I had the sensation of being pulled up out of the chair and somebody leading me up some stairs. Somebody said 'Come on and you'll feel better.' I remember stumbling on a step and being caught before I fell down."

"Who was it?"

"I don't know, but somebody gave me something else in a glass and told me it would make me feel better. I remember that clearly." A long pause . . . "Well, not so clearly maybe, but I sort of remember . . . Things were just sort of going and coming like I was dreaming."

Art, now very concerned and worried for her, replied, "Go on."

"I remember somebody took my clothes off and pushed me onto a bed. I tried to resist but I just didn't have any will or strength. I didn't know what was happening but I remember thinking they shouldn't take my clothes off. The next thing I remember was somebody forcing my knees apart. I thought it must be a bad dream, that they got no business going in me that way. I tried to move and get away but I couldn't. Then I seemed to sort of float around like I was there and not really there either."

Furiously, he demanded, "Do you know who it was, Heidi?"

"I don't know. I vaguely remember a number of people at different times and I couldn't run or do anything about it. I don't know how many. They were grunting and pawing over me and gnawing on me. I kept wondering 'Why are they doing this to me.' My breasts are so sore and bruised. There were so many, so many times, but then," she hesitated between sobs, "it seemed like a dream too, a long, bad dream."

"Like you were drugged?" Art asked, his body shaking with rage and feeling helpless to do anything to fix it, much less to help her.

"Yeah, but it's so vague. I didn't really feel much except for one. It felt like he was going to tear me apart. I remember the pain at first and then it sort of faded away for a while."

Art's face had turned from red to white with fury. He

watched her intently, gritting his teeth and hate welling up for the people who did this, especially Sonny. He stroked her hand as it trembled and realized how difficult this was for her, the lovely and beautiful Heidi who had been so full of life on Friday and was now reduced to a heap of human rubble.

She continued, not allowing interruption, as though she had to get it out or it wouldn't come. "I guess I must have passed out again, or something but I woke up enough at times to know he was still there. He was so heavy and squeezing and gnawing and slobbering. I tried to get him off but I couldn't. It seemed so long. It seemed like there were others in between and then he came back because I remember hurting bad again . . . and then his smell . . . he stayed so long. . ."

Art was beside himself, still shaking with rage. His first impulse was to kill Sonny. He put his arm gently around Heidi's shoulders and cushioned her head against his neck as he felt her begin to sob almost uncontrollably. He held her tightly and said, "Easy baby. You don't have to go any further if you don't want to."

She pushed her head down closer and sobbed, "I want to tell somebody". She leaned back in her chair, staring straight ahead as she continued, "I finally woke up Sunday morning in a bed on the second floor with the door closed. I had no clothes on, I mean none at all. I didn't know where I was. I was scared and so weak. My head hurt and my body hurt and I felt sick and slimy and dirty all over. I didn't know what to do so I just sat up and started to cry. I tried to throw up but nothing would come up. Then a strange man came in and I tried to get the sheet off the bed to put around me . . ."

"What did he do?"

"Nothing right then. He just stared and said he wanted to see if I was all right. I asked where my clothes were and how I got there and how long I'd been there . . ."

"What did he say to that?" Art asked with a sickness and rage flowing through him like he had never known.

"He said I had been there since about midnight and that Sonny sure knew how to provide entertainment. He said I was the best one he had. Then he said, 'Don't you remember? Several of the guys thought you were the best'. Then he said, 'You were a little drunk but you sure enjoyed it. You enjoyed me more the third time than you did the first time. I just couldn't get enough of you.' I started to cry again and then he asked me if I'd like one more before he brought my clothes."

She started to cry harder and Art, trying his best to comfort her, stroked her arm and handed her another tissue from Chuck's box before he said, "Looks like a case for the sheriff, baby. That's gang rape of the worst kind. Those sons-of-bitches don't deserve to live."

She glanced at him through the tears and patted her eye with the tissue, "He brought my clothes and threw 'em in the floor and said, 'Sure you don't want a little more to get you home on?' I looked at him between heaves of my stomach and yelled at him to get out."

"Did he?"

"No. He grabbed me and punched me in the stomach. I nearly choked to death from his knocking the wind out of me. He jerked his pants off, pushed me over and jerked me straight on the bed, and jumped on me again. I tried to close my knees but he forced my legs apart. I was so sick I couldn't fight back. It hurt so bad. All I could do was lay there and cry and hope he'd hurry. I thought he'd never quit. When I tried to struggle he'd punch me in the side with his fist and threaten to hit me in the face. It was such a long time before he quit. He stunk and slobbered while he chewed on me. When he finally finished, Sonny came in and told him to leave, that he'd take care of me."

"What did Sonny do?" Art asked, shaking with rage.

"He pitched my clothes to me and told me to put 'em on and he'd drive me back to my apartment. He told me not to make any trouble because the papers would love a story like this and it would ruin me. He said I had ten or twelve different men that night, some of them three or four times and all of 'em enjoyed it."

"Damn him!" Art growled.

"He looked at me with a smirk and said he didn't see why I didn't enjoy it, too. I screamed at him to go to hell. I struggled to put my clothes sort of on. I couldn't walk too well but I got out to my car and found my purse and keys and somehow got home. What can I do? What can I do?" She buried her head in her arms on Art's desk and began to sob in despair.

Art put his arm around the heaving shoulders and asked gently, "Was Sonny one of them?"

"I don't know," she replied haltingly. "I don't know who any of them were. All I know is I feel ugly and dirty. I've scrubbed myself until I'm raw."

He looked squarely at her, "Do you know any of the other women?"

"No, I don't know who the others were besides Alice and I haven't talked to her." Heidi looked down at the floor and began to sob again as Art put his hand on her arm and squeezed. She looked up through bloodshot eyes and said, "I'm ashamed to even call her because I invited her to go. I don't know what happened to her. How can I face her?" she sobbed.

"Heidi," Art began gently as he reached for the phone, "you've got to report this to the sheriff. They all can be sent up for a long time, beginning with Sonny. How about if I make the call?"

She paled and pleaded, "No, no! Don't do that! I can't stand the mess and the publicity. I just want to forget it."

He looked at her with compassion because he understood how she felt, the total unfairness of her situation and the unfairness of the media and system for dealing with these kinds of things. "Well, baby, think about it," he said softly, not wanting to push her too hard. He continued, "I'll go with you or help any way I can." Art put both arms around her and as she laid her head on his shoulder he petted her gently, stroking the long brown uncombed hair. "Baby, you didn't do anything wrong. I want to help you and if all I can do is be your friend, then I'll do that."

She shifted her head on his shoulder and cried bitterly for a while. Then she snuggled her head over as close as she could get to his neck, nestling her now-sweaty forehead against the bend between his neck and shoulder much as a little girl who had been hurt playing would do with her father. He could feel the perspiration on her forehead and the wetness in her hair. After a while she began to relax. "I'm glad I don't have any makeup on," she sobbed lightly. "I'd ruin your shirt." She looked up at Art with red eyes and tears streaming down her cheeks, "I'm glad you're here. I needed a friend."

"Yeah, me too, baby. I want to help but you got to decide how to handle it. They all need to be in the penitentiary." Heidi leaned over again and cried for a while longer. He continued to stroke her hair and rub the back of her neck until finally he could feel her begin to relax a little more.

In a few minutes she began to get control of herself and said between sobs, "I feel better. I'll be okay. Don't worry. I've learned a hard lesson and I won't make the same mistake again."

Art replied gently. "If you want to talk more I'll be here any time. I'm your friend and don't forget it."

"I know. I believe you."

"I'll do the best I can for you."

"You don't think I'm dirty do you?"

"No, baby, you're not dirty. You haven't done anything wrong. You have to remember that."

"Okay. I'll try to work on that a while." Heidi's eyes were becoming more swollen from crying and her cheeks were redder as though she were wind-blown. "I think I'll go to the rest room and try to fix up a little," she said slowly.

"Maybe I should drive you home. You don't look like you should drive."

"I don't know. Let me go to the rest room and then I'll let you know. okay?"

"Okay!" He patted her on the shoulder and rubbed the back of her neck some more. "Go fix your face a little and don't worry. I'm here if you need me." He kissed her lightly on the forehead and squeezed her sick body against him.

As she started to leave the phone rang. Art recognized Emma on the other end. "Art, staff meeting in Mr. Leech's office in fifteen minutes." The voice became quiet while Art regained his composure, "You know he's moved into Jack's office. I packed all of Jack's stuff. He wants you to bring the new man, what's his name, Eddie, or something." For the first time Emma was being nice instead of indifferent.

"When did that son-of-a-bitch move into Jack's office?" Art yelled at the phone.

Emma answered in a shocked voice, surprised to hear Art's rage. "He moved in this morning because he's replaced Jack. What happened to Jack, Art?"

"Don't know," he growled as he slammed the phone down while he turned a bright red in the face again. He could feel his blood pressure surging once more and his head beginning to throb. A damned staff meeting on top of what Sonny had done to Heidi was too much. As he was stalking to the door to leave, Chuck and Eddie walked in. He related his conversation with Emma through growls and epithets he rarely used. He thought better of mentioning Heidi and resolved to keep that quiet, for now.

Eddie, knowing Art as well as anyone else except perhaps Annie, studied him. He asked, "You okay? What the hell has he done this time?"

Chuck plopped down and pounded the desk with his fist until the top reverberated like a drum. "That son-of-a-bitch," Chuck muttered under his breath over and over.

Art replied caustically, "You don't even want to know. That son-of-a-bitch has really done it this time."

"You guys really don't like him do you?" Eddie asked curiously.

Chuck quickly retorted, "Hell no. Not no, *but hell no*! He's no damned good."

Art motioned to Eddie, "Chuck, that ain't the half of it. Far as I'm concerned that son-of-a-bitch will burn in hell."

When they walked into Jack's old office, Art looked at his watch and saw he was one minute and thirty seven seconds late. There were others gathered who Art recognized as retired sergeants from the group of buddies that Sonny had quickly surrounded himself with. "Mr. Cannon, I believe," Sonny growled sarcastically. "Now we can get on with the meeting. You're late. From now on when I call a meeting I will not tolerate tardiness. Next time you *will* be on time!"

Art glared at Sonny, trying to contain the deep hatred he felt for what he had done to Heidi. "Sorry," he grunted curtly.

Sonny began his meeting by leaning back in his chair and lighting up a cigar. Art had never seen him smoke before now but decided it was to celebrate his victory, just which victory he couldn't know. "As you all know I have been picked to run this department. There were a lot of things going on here that didn't set well with Loren. He didn't like the lax, inefficient way the department was being run. Now, I'm gonna change that. We're gonna have a reorganization and we're gonna do things my way."

Sonny was beginning to become as fervent as a backwoods Pentecostal preacher in a tent meeting, although totally devoid of any of the religious conviction. He continued, "I will always have an open door policy. If you have any problem or anything to discuss, feel free to come in and tell me about it. I'm strict but I run a good shop as long as you do it my way. If you can't do it my way, I'll help you find another job, outside the company. Any questions so far?"

Art glanced at Eddie, who was squirming uncomfortably in his chair. Sonny had observed Eddie's discomfort and looked directly at him. "Don't worry, Eddie, I've read your resume and I know you're a good man. I'm splittin' off your project into a separate task so you can work on it by yourself. You'll report to me and nobody else." He turned slightly and glared at Art as he continued, "Now, I've previously asked some of you to support me in this department and in one case, I didn't get any response. I'm going to be watchin to see if that improves."

Art's mind flashed back quickly to the time that Sonny made the play behind Jack's back to try to subvert his loyalty in his take-over bid. He thought, "That'll be a cold day in hell." And then total hatred welled up in him for Heidi's rape and he muttered to himself, "Maybe lightning will strike the son-of-a-bitch dead before noon."

Sonny stared at Art. "Did you say somethin'?"

"No."

"Well, soldier, if you got any damned thing to say, don't mumble. Get it out. I just said I got an open door policy." Sonny was enjoying being boss, especially, as Art perceived it, over Art. "Now, if we don't get any more interruptions, here's how we're going to do it, folks, and you can pass the word on down to your troops. We'll report to work at 7:30 sharp, go to lunch at 11:30 sharp and report back in here at 12:30 sharp. No bull sessions during the day, no wasted time. We *will* have the most efficient group in the company. We'll get an award one day because I'm gonna suggest to Loren that we institute my work program throughout the company. If you go visit another office, it had better be on business. If someone comes to visit you, it had better be on business."

Art held his tongue and thought, *'Be cool. Now's not the time to explode. Let's see what this animal is up to."* He sat impatiently listening to Sonny drone on and on. He watched him and began to hate him even more. He wanted in the worst way to see him go to jail. Art turned his attention to the others with clandestine glances out the corners of his eyes. All except Eddie looked euphoric, as though they were hearing from their guru, as though their archangel had arrived and was blessing them before leading them to victory in a great battle.

Finally Sonny announced, "Well, we had a good first meetin'. Here's the new organizational assignments. Rogers, you'll begin to develop the optimum repair level analysis model and report to me directly.

Art, you and Chuck begin to define the support requirements analysis data for the systems on the vehicle and support these other guys in the provisioning and repair. Al Willis is gonna work special projects for me, sort of my trouble shooter like he used to be in the Air Force. Any questions?" Sonny looked around the room and then said, "Let's get to it. We got the best damned group in the company. Let's show 'em."

Art and Eddie left the room quietly, glancing at Emma in the outer office who still appeared to be in shock. As they left, Art heard Sonny call sternly, "Emma, come in here." They walked quietly back toward the office, going down the back hallway because neither of them felt like conversation.

Suddenly Al appeared from the accounting office as they passed the usually closed door. Art greeted casually, "Hello Al, how you doin'?"

Al scowled at Art and grunted, "Don't bother me" as he proceeded at a fast pace down the hall.

Eddie stood with a fixed stare in the direction that Al disappeared. "Did I see what I thought I saw? That one looks bad."

Art explained about Al and his reputation for forcing girls in his office in bed with him or suffer the consequences. "I'd sure love to get him in an airplane for a while. I could really readjust his personality. A good outside square loop would do wonders for him. There's some others around here I'd like to take up and dump out."

Eddie started to laugh going into the office and had to sit down to regain his composure. "I'd wet all over you if you did that to me!"

Chuck was sitting patiently and finally said bruskly, "You damned guys can talk about flying some other time! What the hell happened in the meeting up there with his majesty?"

Art concentrated on pouring himself a fresh cup of coffee with the correct mix of cream while he regained some of his composure after facing Heidi's tormenter and feeling hate like he never felt before. Eddie, still not knowing about Heidi, sat quietly and wondered what Art was going to say while Chuck fidgeted. Art sat down quietly, spinning around to face Eddie and Chuck. "Well," he began, "looks like stormy weather. But Eddie and I have weathered several storms before."

"Hell, I know that," Chuck grunted with a scowl. "But what's his majesty up to? What's he gonna do?"

Art looked through slitted eyes at the both of them as he adjusted his position. "Well, Eddie reports to Sonny. You and I are supposed to continue to development support requirements analyses for the boosters. That's about all I know right now."

Chuck dropped his feet off his desk with a thump. "Shit! is all I got to say."

"Easy Chuck," Eddie chided. "There's more."

"More hell! I'm fed up!"

Art continued. "He's making changes in the department but we don't know what yet. The only thing I know for sure is that I don't like it. I see trouble for anybody he thinks is a threat."

Eddie interjected, "Don't forget about his bunch of goons he had up there. Wouldn't surprise me if he put one of 'em in charge just to make us miserable. That's the first time I really met this turkey and now I understand how you guys feel. Damn!"

Chuck sat up straight, scowling through the window at some imaginary monster. He slapped his knee and stood up. "Hell, I'm gettin out. I ain't gonna put up with this bull shit."

Eddie was afraid his new friend was about to make a hasty decision with as yet little or no valid information. He walked over to Chuck's desk and sat on the corner. "Now Chuck, just play it cool. Don't go off half-cocked. Let's play it close for a while and see what happens."

"Yeah," Chuck replied glumly. "I know you're right. I'll guess I'll ride for a little while."

"Hey, you guys," Art said with a half chuckle, "don't forget the old philosopher's trick of smiling all the time because it makes 'em all wonder what you're up to. I think that's what we got to do right now."

Things were ominously quiet as they each went about their assigned duties in the days to come. Eddie was hard at work on his computer model development and Art and Chuck were busily deriving the logistics support requirements for each major part of the new solid rocket booster. Heidi had settled down but was still nervous and skeptical of everyone but Art. She had become all business with little or nothing to say outside the line of duty. Chuck commented, "Hey, what's with the new girl, Heidi? She won't give me the time of day any more."

Art replied matter-of-factly, "Well, guess she's got a lot on her mind, Chuck."

"Yeah, I think I know what she's got on her mind."

"Oh, What's that?"

"You. You're the only one I see her talking to, at least in the male world. And come to think of it, not very many damned women either."

"Well, guess she doesn't consider me a threat. She knows about Annie and that I'm not gonna try to get her pants off."

Chuck looked perplexed. "Well, I ain't made any moves that way either."

Eddie perceived that Art was having trouble answering Chuck's questions. He didn't know any of the story of the gang rape that she had endured but decided Art needed help and sat down by Art's desk. "Tell me about this integrated electronics assembly. I don't have any data and don't know how to model it."

Relieved at the interruption, he started patiently to describe the box to Eddie and all the electronic interfaces it had with the other booster systems, the external tank and the orbiter. "This box," he began, "is the electronic brains of each of the boosters. There's one outside at the aft end attached to the external tank attach ring and there's one mounted inside the forward skirt. All the booster control and separation functions are processed and managed by these boxes."

"Excuse me a minute," Art apologized as the phone rang for the third time. "Cannon," he answered.

The voice on the other end was a stranger. "This is Mrs. Swann in Mr. Leech's office. Mr. Leech would like to see you soon as you can get up here please."

Eddie had been watching Art's expression of surprise. "What's that all about?" he asked.

"I'm being paged upstairs by a Mr. Leech. Guess I better go up and see what he wants. Who the hell is Mrs. Swann, anyhow?"

Chuck, listening to the conversation, wryly commented, "Shit, it's been too quiet. Maybe something's about to hit the fan."

Art, good naturedly teased, "Now Chuck, you got to admit he's left us alone for over two weeks."

Art arrived at Sonny's office and was surprised at the new secretary in Emma's place. She was tall, well dressed and perfectly made up. Her face was particularly striking with small, penetrating eyes and a small, straight mouth and thin lips surrounded by a short page-boy hair style. "Hi, I'm Art. Where's Emma today?" he asked.

"Emma's been transferred to the typing pool. I'm taking over the office for Mr. Leech. Please sit down until he gets off the phone," she replied coldly and quietly.

Art was surprised at the reception, almost as if she didn't want to bother with him. He started to ask her name but then thought better of it and sat uncomfortably for ten minutes staring out into the hall and at anything else he could find to pass the time. Finally she turned and said very matter-of-factly, "Mr. Leech will see you now."

Art thanked her cautiously and entered Sonny's inner office. Without looking up, Sonny barked, "Shut the door."

Art complied, sat down, and demanded in equally harsh terms, "What do you want?"

Sonny glared at Art and finally said fiercely, "I know what mother-fuckin game you're playin with me, mister. You damned people down there think because I ain't never been to college that you can look down on me, don't you? Let me tell you something, mister smart guy, I'll bury you. You ain't never going to take my department away from me."

Art looked squarely at Sonny and, feeling all the rage and hate welling up in him for what he had done to Heidi, answered in like tones, "Sonny, I got no interest in taking your damned department, and as far as any 'game', I don't know what the hell you're talking about."

"Don't play dumb with me, mister," Sonny roared. "I been hearing about you. I been hearing a lot I didn't know before but I'm on to you."

Art had heard all he wanted to hear of this and glared harshly at Sonny as he answered with great resolve, "Sonny, cut the bullshit. I haven't done anything to you and you know it."

Sonny turned red in the face. "Now you're threatening me. I been hearing about you and those damned airplanes. I heard about your flyin upside down in them shittin' airshows and I been hearin about that wife of yours gettin that damned PhD. Well, mister smart guy, I'm just as smart and don't you forget I got this department now and I'm gonna keep it. Ain't nothin you can do to take it away from me."

Art vainly tried to interrupt Sonny who was becoming more and more agitated with each passing second. He finally got an opportunity when Sonny stopped for breath, "Sonny, I don't want your damned department. I don't want anything you got. Can you understand that?"

Sonny wasn't in any frame of mind to hear anything Art said. His insecurities were running rampant with the belief that Art was trying to unseat him the way he unseated Jack. Art gave up in disgust and started to the door. "Call me when you can talk rationally. I don't have time for this kind of bullshit conversation." With that he opened the door as Sonny choked on his cigar, quickly stepped through and slammed it shut to emphasize his point. The new secretary looked shocked as he glared at her for good measure and quickly left. He walked hurriedly to the elevator. When he reached the first floor, he started through the lobby at a fast pace to his office, temporarily forgetting about Heidi at the front desk.

Heidi, concerned about him, said lightly, "Hey, preoccupied, you look like you need some counseling, too."

He looked up to see her grinning and replied, "Hi, beautiful. Maybe I do. Maybe I do."

"Well, if I can help, you know you can count on me."

"Thanks, baby." He walked over to her and rubbed her on the back of the head, feeling the soft texture of her hair again, and continued to his office, still wondering what triggered Sonny and how to deal with it.

Eddie noticed the worried look on Art's face. "What happened? Get fired or something?"

"Worse than that." He gave Eddie a description of the scene just played out in Sonny's office before asking, "We've worked our way through a few before, old buddy. What do you make of it?"

"Obvious." came Eddie's measured response. "Extreme paranoia brought on by a terrible inferiority complex. I don't see a good solution yet but he's afraid of you for some reason."

Art leaned back and pondered Eddie's conclusion for a moment. "Yeah, I believe you're right, but I don't know why unless it's because I wouldn't prostitute myself when he was unseating Jack."

Eddie propped his feet on his desk and assumed a counselor's role, which he enjoyed. "Now he's afraid of getting the knife from you just like he put it in Jack. Looks like an unworkable situation at best. Why don't you just play it cool and see what happens?"

"Yeah, you're right, but I'm not going to stand for anybody attacking Annie for anything. Nobody's givin' her a damned thing!!"

"Now settle down," Eddie ordered. "Remember, if he gets you mad he's got you hooked into his game. You can't play if you're playing by his rules."

CHAPTER SIX

Things remained quiet for the next few days after Sonny canceled his staff meeting on Monday morning. The three of them wondered why until late Wednesday afternoon. Art commented, "Perhaps no news is good news." Wondering ceased when Albert Willis swaggered in and sat down in front of Art's desk. "I been appointed supervisor and you damned guys work for me now," he bragged with an air of authority only present in a buck sergeant looking for promotion.

Chuck choked on a drink of coffee at his desk in the corner and Art looked at Albert in disbelief. "When did that happen?" he demanded.

"This morning. Sonny thought you guys needed some leadership and delegated me to manage you. I want you guys to look alive and shape up down here. Cut the bull and keep working and we'll get along okay. I'll take care of staff meetings and then I'll tell you what to do."

"Wellll," Art said slowly, "I guess since this is Sonny's department . . ."

"You got it, baby. That's the way it is." Albert got up to walk out the door.

Just then Eddie entered the office and Albert turned to Art. "Your first assignment is to brief this clown," obviously referring to Eddie.

Chuck slammed the door before venting his rage. "Dammit to hell! Dammit to hell! Do you know what that SOB was? Nothing but a damned 20-year supply buck sergeant and now we got to work for him. He don't know shit about nothin! If he's anything he's a third-grade drop-out. I'm gonna . . ."

Art interrupted as Eddie sat down heavily in his chair, "Now settle down, Chuck, and listen a minute." Chuck turned and almost fell into his chair with a scowl. "It's just like Eddie told me earlier, don't let 'em get you mad because then you're hooked into their game. We want to play by our rules, not theirs."

Chuck heaved a big sigh. "Yeah, yeah, I know."

"That's better. Now see if you can continue and grin just like a mule eatin' briars when you see one of 'em. Then maybe we can sort this thing out a little."

"Shit! It ain't resolvable!"

"Yes it is. The one thing he's got going is he's Sonny's buddy and that makes him somebody we got to deal with. Don't say anything you could regret."

"Okay! I'm not dumb, you know. I know when to keep my big fat mouth shut."

Eddie, watching the exchange, posed a tactical question. "This is a new company. You been here about six months, Art, Chuck a little longer and me about four weeks now. I once heard from a great philosopher that if you don't like the way a large company is going, just wait, it'll change. Maybe we either transfer to other divisions or wait for something to change. What do you guys think of that?"

Chuck looked worried as he turned to Eddie and asked, "But what if it changes for worse instead of better? What then?"

Eddie was obviously amused. "How can it get worse?"

Chuck looked at the wall clock and grunted, "Damn, I've got to go to a meeting I almost forgot about. I'd better hurry or I'll be late." In his rush to get out the door he almost ran over Connie coming in. "Excuse me, Connie. Congratulations."

Art greeted Connie with a big smile. "Welcome, old married lady. How does it feel to be a bonafide housewife?"

Connie laughed out loud and clucked, "Nut, what makes you think I'm a housewife. I've got a new husband in training for that." She held out her hand showing off her new wedding ring. "See my new ring?"

"Wow, that's pretty. Looks like you're pretty special to somebody. When do we get to meet this new superman?"

"What do you mean 'superman'?"

"Hell, he must be. He was good enough to get the prettiest girl in the company to marry him. If he's anything less, I'd be disappointed."

Connie had sensed the presence of Eddie sitting at his desk quietly observing. She looked at him inquiringly and, before she could say anything, Art, embarrassed at having failed to introduce them, said, "Connie, this is Eddie Rogers. He's new in the company. Eddie this is our newest bride, Connie Minor, just back from her extended honeymoon."

71

"Very pleased to meet you, Eddie," Connie said. "Are you a friend of Art's?"

"Art and I been bumping around together for a lot of years. Where do you work?"

"In accounting upstairs. I just came to visit today. Monday I go back to work. I got married and begged for time off to go to the Bahamas." Connie beamed as she held up her new ring for Eddie to admire.

"Well," Connie replied with a smile as she got up, "got to go. Can't keep my new husband waiting too long. He'll be home soon. By the way, we're looking at new houses just across the state line. I think we found one we may buy."

Eddie watched her disappear into the hallway and remarked, "Wow, what a looker. Where'd you run into her?"

"She was on the front desk when I came in. She's a good girl but sometimes she leaps before she looks. I worry about her."

"Oh? I'm sorry to hear that," Eddie replied.

"Yeah. I'm afraid Al's gonna make a play for her. You know the rumors up there?"

"Yeah, I've heard. I hope they aren't true but if they are, I hope she's got more sense than that. She's a grown woman now; got to make her own decisions."

"You're right. It's after quitting time. I'm going down to see Jerry. He's been scarce lately for some reason."

Art found Jerry Strong busily working on a report for the home office in Arizona. He pushed a chair up to the table in front of Jerry's desk and sat down. Jerry grinned, pushed back his chair and said, "I've been meaning to come down but I've been so covered up trying to straighten things out here that I haven't had a chance. How's things going?"

Art sucked in his breath for a moment and narrated the events that had been unfolding with Sonny and Albert. Jerry's face turned red as he commented quietly, "That son-of-a-bitch. I was afraid of something like this. We've got to figure out a strategy to show Loren how wrong he is."

"Well, we'll agree to that."

"It's not that simple, I'm afraid. He's stubborn as hell when he makes up his mind, especially in these situations. I've seen it before."

"You mean he won't listen?"

"When he gets sold a bill of goods he won't admit it. He won't change anything because he doesn't want to admit he's wrong."

"Jerry, how about the systems engineering group we were talking about? Is there any possibility to initiate that?"

"I'm afraid there isn't right now. The Space Agency has to give us a contract change and they want to retain that responsibility for the time being. So, I guess the answer is no for now, and maybe no for a while."

Art looked disappointed and Jerry asked, "What do you want to do?"

"Well, Eddie, Chuck and I want to get away from that situation and there just doesn't seem to be much hope, does there?"

Jerry leaned back in his chair and scratched his chin. "Well, you know I've initiated a program management office and staffed it as far as the contract allows right now. Again Loren has edicted an old buddy on me, a fellow named Billy Ghote, and don't laugh at the name. Maybe we can do something there. Eddie's a good man. I've checked his credentials and he has an excellent reputation."

"Yeah, but what about Chuck?"

"Chuck's a problem. He's always been a loggie with a degree in business. That's not bad but he's in a technical area and needs a scientific degree. Let me see what I can do and we'll get together next week. okay?"

Monday morning the alarm clock went off with a deafening roar and Art rolled over pulling his pillow over his head. Suddenly he felt the pillow being moved up ever so gently and felt the long dark blond hair he knew so well being pulled over his face.

"Hey, sleepyhead, it's time to rise and shine," came the voice from beside him, sounding ever so sleepy too. Without opening his eyes, he reached over and pulled the smooth, shapely body close, engulfing her in his arms and, feeling the warmth and soft tenderness, he gently stroked her. "Hi, beautiful, I'm sure glad to wake up and find you."

"Me too, but we better get going," Annie commented as she wriggled in a little closer. "We've both got a busy day ahead, you and your politics and me and my drive back to school."

When Art drove into the parking lot he saw Connie pulling into a space near him. As she opened the door she spotted him and waved, "Hi there. I made it back."

He walked over and teased, "Why shouldn't you. How's it feel to make your first day as a married woman?"

Connie eased her long legs out of the car and looked up with a big grin. "We decided to buy the house. It's so cute," she bubbled with excitement. "You and Annie have got to see it when we get moved in. Please," she begged.

Laughing at her excitement, he replied, "Sure we will. I'll be talking to Annie tonight and I'll tell her. I'm glad you're planning to get it."

"I love all the little shrubs and flowers. And it's got one big old oak tree in the back yard. Perfect to lay in the shade."

While Connie and Art discussed the house, Al Creude walked by as Connie locked the door of her car. "You two riding together, now?" he growled. Art glanced up to see a terrible scowl. Al squinted at them as he grunted, "You got about five minutes to be at your work station, lady," He turned and walked briskly toward the building.

She looked perplexed while Art smiled at her. "Connie, I believe he may actually be a little jealous. Come on, you better not be late."

She giggled and poked Art playfully on the shoulder. "Let him be jealous if he wants to. I don't care."

Art sat down at his desk to the smell of fresh hot coffee Chuck had put on and wondered where he had gone to so early. Then he realized Eddie had not made an appearance. *Bet he ain't turned over the first time yet*, Art thought as he chuckled to himself. But he also knew Eddie would give good measure of work, much more than was required. While he was sitting pondering Eddie and secretly laughing about his sack hound tendencies, Chuck entered the door, "Mornin Chief, how was your weekend?"

Before he could reply, Albert appeared in the door with the look of a First Sergeant eyeing over a group of recruits. "Just checkin. It's five past. Where's Rogers at?"

They both stared at Albert in disbelief. Art demanded, "What do you mean, 'where's he at'. He obviously ain't here."

"You heard Mr. Leech give orders you'd be here on time and

that your lunch period would be exactly one hour. No more. No less. I mean to enforce that."

Art fired, "How about the professional aspects of this organization? Doesn't that mean anything? If you're going to enforce strict hours, mister, you had better know we quit at exactly quitting time and to hell with whatever we're doing. We're not a damned platoon in the Air Force."

Albert turned red, obviously not used to confrontations with lower echelons of his platoon and started to sound like a drill instructor in the Marine Corps. "We're a unit. We will work as a unit. We will take orders from Mr. Leech. If he says we be here at a certain time we be here at a certain time. I'm writin' up Rogers for being late. See it don't happen again!"

Chuck was sitting up straight in his chair and staring in disbelief. "Okay. okay. We'll tell him, but he may quit and then what the hell you gonna do for that ORLA Model?" Art growled.

"Don't you sweat it, big daddy. We'll roll another one in from where that'n come from."

Art jumped to his feet and started menacingly toward Al. "Shit, son! Don't you understand? You can't get a man like that every day. He's almost one of a kind. Back off or you'll lose him."

Albert, thinking retreat better than confrontation, backed away from Art toward the door, defiantly pointing a pudgy little finger at them both. Art wondered if the finger got that way because of staying in the Air Force kitchen too long as he watched it wag up and down. "You damn guys better be here and I mean it!" Albert thundered and quickly exited.

In less than a minute Eddie walked in with his usual big morning smile. "Hi guys." He perceived all was not well. "What's Albert doin here this time of day?"

Art was red with rage and Chuck was sitting dejectedly at his desk staring at Eddie. "Shit," Chuck barked. "We just saved your ass, man. We just saved your ass."

Art regained his composure and said, "Settle down, Chuck." Then he related the confrontation to Eddie.

"Did he make any threats?" Eddie asked.

"None directly. He'll leave that to Sonny."

Eddie was evaluating this as the room grew quiet. After a few moments he looked up with a serious expression. "Seems to me the only thing to do is all of us transfer away from the 'sergeant corps.'"

Chuck had regained his composure and was ready to fight. He replied, "Yeah, that's okay but our task has got to be done by people that understand it. If we left what the hell would he put in here?"

Art leaned back in his chair and agreed. "Yeah, you're right but we can't worry about that. Eddie could do his work in another department, like maybe Systems Engineering . . ."

Art was interrupted by the phone. Eddie answered "Logistics, Rogers." He scowled at the phone before answering, "Of course I'm here." A pause and "Just a minute." He put the phone on hold and looked at Art with a sympathetic look, "Sonny. Sounds mad."

Art groaned as he reached for the phone, "I thought we weren't supposed to talk to Sonny except through Albert."

"Search me, but you better talk to him, I guess."

"Yeah, I guess," as he pushed the blinking button on the phone. "Cannon," he answered sharply, expecting the worst.

Sonny's mode quickly changed. Charm seemed to pour out of the phone, making Art even more suspicious. "How about coming up a few minutes?"

"Okay," he answered cautiously, puzzled at the switch in attitudes.

"What's he want?"

"Don't know. No damned tellin'."

Eddie was looking serious. "If he's appointed Al our supervisor, he'll be there because the Air Force recognizes the chain of command. Be careful and don't let 'em get you mad."

"Yeah. I'll try to follow my own advice," he replied half heartedly.

When Art arrived at Sonny's office he saw the new secretary displaying a name plate, *MRS. LISSIE SWANN*, and the next line, Departmental Secretary. She looked up and asked coldly, "Can I help you?"

He looked beyond her to see Sonny's office gray with smoke, which he surmised must be from more than one cigar. "Sonny In?" he asked curtly.

"One moment please," as she went to the office door, "Mr. Leech, you have a visitor."

"Is it Cannon?"

She turned to Art. "Your name please?"

"Art Cannon."

Lissie turned to face the smoke filled room, "Yes sir, it's Cannon."

"Send him in."

She turned with a straight-lipped smile, "You may go in now."

Art sat down at a conference table Sonny had pulled endways to his desk as a status symbol to convey to visitors that he first, held meetings of importance, and secondly, was too busy to use a conference room. Art looked through the dense haze and saw Albert and two other people he didn't recognize, all puffing cigars that reminded him of the old five-cent ones he had seen hobos smoke when he was a child back in the mountains. "Cannon," Sonny started, "We need to clear the air of some problems."

Art leaned back apprehensively, expecting the worst. "Okay?" he replied cautiously, trying to appear casual but very aware of the pitfalls of this situation.

"You know I reorganized the department and you guys work for Al down there now, don't you?"

Art looked at Al grinning like a horse eating briars. "That's what Al said."

"Good! You accept that?"

"Sonny, it's your department and you can run it any way you want. You don't answer to me at all."

Sonny choked on his cigar, abruptly changed his attitude and growled, "Just what do you mean by that, soldier?"

Art knew he probably should have chosen his words a bit more carefully and took a different approach. "What I meant, is that you are the person designated to run this department and I don't have any right to tell you how since I don't share that responsibility."

Sonny leaned back in his chair, obviously more comfortable. "Glad you figured that out, soldier. I was afraid for a minute we still didn't understand each other. Now, I want to tell you how the organization is gonna run."

Sonny puffed on his cigar as he looked out the window. Then he began, "This organization is going to be the best logistics group in the entire center. We have the experience and the know-how to make it that way. I want you to be a sort of straw boss down there and see that Rogers and Miller do their work. I've appointed Al here as your

77

manager but he's got other things to do, too. I know you need help and we're gonna build that area up to be a big one. I been lucky enough hire two real experts in the field. Meet Don Wicks and Cig Luciano. They both gonna be discharged next month and move into the office with you."

Art looked at the two new faces and wondered if these two came from organized crime or were actually coming from the Air Force. He was certain they would be loyal only to Sonny without question. "Pleased to meet you," Art answered, measuring his reply and trying to smile the best he could.

Sonny looked pleased, thinking Art was coming around to his way of thinking. He turned to the two strangers and said proudly, "You guys gonna enjoy working with old Art here. He's a damned good engineer but we got to train him a little yet. He's short on our kind of experience but he'll come on okay. If he gives you any trouble let me know. I believe we're beginning to understand each other."

Art felt panic and said to himself, *I got to get out of there.* Then he answered carefully, "Pleased to meet you fellahs."

Sonny turned to Al, Don and Cig with a big grin. "That's all. I need to talk with Art a little before he goes." With that the three of them filed out in step, and disappeared through the outer office.

Sonny turned to Art with a steely glare. "I want you to know that I know you were in Jerry Strong's office last Friday for thirty three minutes. I hope you ain't plotting nothin with him. Are you?"

Art looked at Sonny in disbelief. Rage suddenly engulfed him as he faced Heidi's and his own tormenter. He wanted to punch Sonny but an inner voice said, "Not yet, not yet." He leaned back in the chair and stared at Sonny. "Of course not. You just said we were all a family and Jerry's interested in flying. I was just outlining a course for him. I hope that's okay."

Sonny had a very suspicious look on his face, as though he didn't believe any part of Art's explanation. "I hope so fellah, I hope so. I'd sure hate to have to fire you for going around me. You be careful now, you hear?"

Art had enough and retorted, "Do you want me to transfer to another department?"

"Hell no! I don't want you to transfer. First you're too good an engineer and I know that and secondly, I want you where I can watch you. Got that!" he boomed. Sonny was leaning low over his desk and breathing hard. Art knew from past experience that he was beginning to get excited.

"Sonny, if you don't want me to transfer all you have to do is tell me. I hope we can work things out."

Sonny seemed to be relieved. "Yeah, me too. Unless you got something else, you can be dismissed."

Art walked into the front office in time to see a pretty, rather tall, willowy blonde girl in her early twenties that he had not seen before. As he went out the door he heard, "But mother, I want to start work here week after next, not next week because I want to go to the beach with the crowd."

Art surmised this was Lissie's daughter. He stopped outside the door to listen. "Your daddy told you he wanted you to let those people alone and he wanted you to help pay for that new car you promised him you'd pay for. Besides, Mr. Leech has it arranged for you."

Just then he saw Dean Aikins come around the corner and feigned a moment of forgetfulness. He stood with his hand on his chin and Dean, in his usual childish manner, quipped, "What's the matter, Cannon? Lost?"

"Oh, hi. Do you know where they moved the new program management office? I thought it was up here somewhere."

Dean looked at him with a funny look. "Are you losin' it since your buddy Jack got fired? You know that group's over in the lower wing of the building. What the hell's wrong with you?"

"Gee, thanks." As he walked quickly down the hall in the direction indicated, he turned to see Dean walk into Sonny's office.

Back in his own office Art poured a cup of coffee, sat down and looked out at the test stands across the road. Suddenly he saw the little ground hog that lived in the bank on the other side of the road come out to forage along the top near some big bushes, but never getting too far from its hole. When a truck appeared the ground hog panicked and ran waddling until it dove into its hole as the driver passed threateningly near. He watched its tail quickly disappear down the burrow. "Gee, little guy, I know how you feel," he said to himself.

He sat contemplating the ground hog's dash to safety as Eddie quietly entered. "Glad you're back. What was it all about?"

He looked at Eddie with an untypical feeling of helplessness and despair. "Guess we'll have two more new sergeants in here soon. That's all in the hell we need."

Eddie poured himself a fresh cup of coffee and sat down. "I been expecting something like this. Let's look at it logically. The Cat Fish has an ego big as all outdoors but he's very insecure. He knows he's in over his head, or at least he perceives, he is. He has to control you, and us, because he thinks we're some kind of threat . . ."

Art interrupted Eddie's very logical analysis. "Yeah, you can say that for sure. For some reason he's afraid of me. I think he still believes I'm trying to take the department away from him."

"Yeah, he thinks you'll try the same game he did on Jack. The way he's chosen to combat that is to demote you and try to minimize your stature in the organization and then to bring in his own people to keep surveillance on you. We've got to make a move soon."

Art nodded agreement as he responded, "Yeah, but what?"

"Well, we sure as hell got to figure out one."

"Shit," Art mumbled. "Think I'll take a walk."

"Go ahead, I'll mind the phone."

When Art walked through the lobby he saw Heidi looking wistfully out across the front lawn. When she saw him, her face changed expression from melancholy to a big smile. "Hi friend, how's it goin'?" she responded cheerfully.

He smiled at her, quietly replying, "Wish I knew, baby, wish I knew. How about you?"

"Okay, I guess. You look to me like you need a little cheering up. A few weeks ago it was me. Can I do anything?" She took Art's hand and squeezed it affectionately. "You know I really owe you one."

He smiled with great appreciation for a friend he had grown to like and trust. "You don't owe me anything. I'm just not sure where we're going right now but we'll figure it out."

"I know Sonny's giving you trouble because I overheard those two new goons talking as they left. One said that he knew Sonny would get you in line. Then there's that awful woman he hired up there for his secretary, and now he's hiring her daughter. What's he doing?"

"Who knows? Just keep the faith and it'll all work out somewhere."

"Yeah, I know and I believe that, but doesn't our management know better than to put somebody like him in charge of a whole department? I've already seen him leave with that woman. She's so fictitious and cold and formal that she gives me the creeps."

"Heidi, just be sure you don't get involved in any of the stuff flying around. I don't want to see you get hurt anymore." Art patted her on the back of the head and ruffled her long hair.

"Not me. Say, did you see the way that Dean Aikins took off after the daughter? You know how he delays everything and has to do all the official things he likes."

"Yeah," Art replied.

"Well, Maggie told me that when he got his tongue back in his head he processed her in fifteen minutes. Then he padded her salary a thousand dollars over her offer. How do you like that? And that little squirt with five kids, too."

Art laughed, reflecting on the gross stupidity of the whole thing and walked off shaking his head. Heidi called gently, "If you need to talk, I'm available."

"Thanks hon, I'll remember," he replied as he continued to the back of the building. He went down the stairs leading to a big grove of tall pine trees with interspersed benches that had sheltered the building from rocket engine test firing noise from the big Saturn V test stand about a mile away in the test area.

As he reached the lower floor, opening out on ground level at the rear of the building, he saw Jerry Strong coming down the hallway. Jerry threw up his hand in a friendly greeting. "Hello there, I was just thinking about you."

"Well, I hope your thoughts were good," Art replied as he approached.

Jerry laughed and said, "How about coming down to the Program Office and let me introduce you around. I told Billy I wanted you to help out and he wants to meet you."

Art's heart leaped at the prospect. "Great," he said but then thought he had better fill Jerry in on his status.

As Art talked, Jerry's face turned red as blood flooded the small veins and capillaries. "That son-of-a-bitch! I'll have his head if it's the last thing I do."

They arrived at the program management office and Jerry ushered Art in. It was a long office made up of a central secretarial bay with offices going off the sides. He entered one and said, "Billy, meet Art Cannon."

Billy was a small, gray- headed, wiry individual with a seasoned face such as one might expect on a sailor who had many years before the mast. Art sensed immediately that Billy didn't trust anybody. "Pleased to meet 'cha. . .", he half grunted in a high-pitched voice that had a definite California twang to it.

"This is the engineer I want to help Elmer Russell on the electrical systems. I'll make arrangements for him to work over here on loan 'til we can bring him over permanent."

"Okay, if you say so, Jerry. I don't know what Loren will think."

Jerry, very calmly, replied, "Billy, you worked for Loren for a long time but don't forget that you work for me now. okay?"

"Yeah. okay." Billy was studying Art carefully over the top of his glasses. "When can you start?"

Art studied Billy, and answered slowly, "How about tomorrow?"

"Fine, come down and I'll introduce you to Russell."

As they left, Art was contemplating the new position. He was pleased but he was very distrustful of Billy and wondered if he should go through with it. Then he thought, It can't be any worse than where I am, so I guess I better go for it. He stopped, turned to Jerry, who looked at him questioningly, and commented, "Gee, Jerry, I didn't expect that."

"What?"

"I started to go out under the trees to sit on a bench and lick my wounds. Here I got another job. Damn!"

"Well, that's what you wanted, wasn't it?"

"Hell yes. I just didn't expect it to happen that way or that quick."

"Hey," Jerry answered with a chuckle, "don't look a gift horse in the mouth. Now we've got to try to make it permanent."

As they approached the stairs to the ground floor, Jerry sensed Art's doubts and said, "Art, he's okay. Just a bit eccentric and insecure. He was a Seattle beat cop while he went to engineering school. I'm not sure but what he's still just a beat cop, but he is a good engineer. He has a lot of years with the corporation. He'll play the game."

Art replied, "Jerry, I'm grateful. I hope we can do something for Eddie and Chuck."

Jerry looked pensive for a moment. "You know we're moving to a new building off the center."

"No, I don't guess I heard that," Art exclaimed.

"Well, it's not been formally announced but I'll be setting up a computer department to support both the Hawkinsville and the Cape operations in the new facility."

"I don't know what to say."

"Well, we need more space now that the company's over five hundred people. I've got my eye on a guy by the name of Carr to run it, if I can get him. Maybe we can move Eddie in there."

"Great. I'm sure Eddie would appreciate that. What can we do for Chuck?"

"Don't know yet but let me work on it." At the top of the stairs, Art thanked Jerry again and started back to his office.

Connie was coming at a brisk walk down an adjoining hallway with her long hair flowing. As she rounded the corner she ran straight into Art. Her papers went flying in all directions. "Connie, I'm so sorry," Art said apologetically as he tried to catch the papers and her at the same time. "Gee, I hope I didn't hurt you," he said as he stooped to help her pick up the scattered papers. Connie was laughing as she and Art finished recovering the stack of papers. "I was just coming to see you, and all of a sudden, splat, right here."

Art invited her into his office for an afternoon cup of coffee. "Well, how is it up there? I'm sorry I haven't been up but your boss is a little stingy. I don't think he likes me much."

"I know," Connie laughed, "I do and that's all that counts."

"Well, what can I do for you?" Art asked when Connie had settled down in a chair beside his desk.

"Nothing. I just wanted to check in and say hi. I didn't want to be replaced by the new girl up front, if you know what I mean."

"No chance of that," Art answered firmly.

"I don't know. She sure seems to have taken a liking to you."

Art smiled as he replied, "Does it show? She's a really good soul."

"I know. I like her a lot, too. Just don't replace me! Okay?"

After Connie left Eddie walked slowly through the door and glanced at Art. Without a word, he went over to the pot and drained the last part of the afternoon coffee. Art knew something was wrong and he knew Eddie would tell him when he was ready. He sat down and banged the desk with his fist, almost turning his cup over. "Damn, damn, damn. Those idiots up there don't even begin to understand this model. They just don't know. They don't have enough background to appreciate what we're trying to do. I think that damned Cat Fish has got shit for brains."

He gazed at Eddie sympathetically. "Why do you call him Cat Fish?"

"Because he's all mouth and no brains and you can make book on that, buddy! That's straight! None of those damned people he's surrounded himself with, and especially Albert, ain't got any brains."

"What else is new?" Art replied with a chuckle.

"I think they're all third grade dropouts. They don't know an algorithm from a biorhythm. If they think this is a simple job, they're wrong."

"Hey, buddy, they ain't got any background in either mathematics or modeling. Period. They'll never understand," Art said, trying to comfort Eddie.

"I don't care what kind of models they say they had in the Air Force, this isn't that kind of model. This is very complex and can't be worked out on a hand calculator."

"Settle down, buddy. Maybe I got some good news."

He related his conversation with Jerry and watched Eddie's mood change. "Well, guess I'll tolerate 'em 'til I can transfer. Are you coming, too?"

"No. I'll work in the program management office as a loaner and then I'll try to transfer in there permanently."

"Art, that could be dangerous. That damned Cat Fish won't like that and he'll try to block you."

After a long evening to contemplate the possibility of a new position, Art walked into his office ten minutes early the next morning to be sure he didn't offend Albert, and saw Eddie and Chuck coming across the parking lot. Suddenly the phone rang and Albert growled from the other end, "You got desk and office space down there for Don and Cig?"

"Yeah, Albert, and we're all here—early."

"Don't get smart with me, mister!" the voice almost screamed into the phone. "You're talking to your boss, you know!"

"Yeah, Al. We know," Art slowly replied, chuckling quietly.

"Well, I just wanted to be sure you birds was there," Al blurted, forgetting about the first excuse he gave for making the call. Then, just as suddenly as he had called, he hung up without another word.

When Eddie and Chuck entered the office Art related the scene and Chuck started to laugh. Eddie looked somber before commenting, "Bed check, huh? Well, I sort of expected that."

"I don't believe Sonny has the guts to try to fire any of us. He needs us and he knows it. Let's just sit back and watch the action," Art replied.

"However," Eddie, raised one finger to signify an important point, "when the Cat Fish finds out you're supporting the Program Office part time, I think we'll see fireworks."

Art checked his work schedule and saw that he was caught up, since Sonny had made his organizational changes, and decided to go to the Program Office. As he passed an alcove near the head of the stairs he saw Al and Connie standing in front of the soft drink machines with Connie giggling at something Al had said. Art thought, *"Well, she's trying to get along up there, anyhow."* He turned rapidly down the stairs to the Program Office.

"Hello, Billy!"

Billy Ghote, the new program manager, looked up over his horn rimmed glasses and replied gruffly, "Hi. Sit down."

Art slid into a chair beside Billy's desk and waited for him to finish what he was doing. "So you want to work in program management?" Billy grunted without ever looking up.

"Yeah, Billy. I think I can help you guys."

"Do you really think you can help us?" Billy queried, still not looking up.

Art was getting a bit uncomfortable with this line of questioning. "I think I can. Not only that, I want to transfer in permanently first chance."

Billy dropped his pencil and leaned back, studying Art. "Don't know about that. I'll have to see what you can do for me first. I need help and Jerry wants you to help. That's the way it is for now."

Art was carefully observing Billy to try to develop an approach that would be non-threatening and comfortable. He decided Billy was a special individual to be handled with care if you wanted to get any positive results, one who didn't trust anyone and probably had no close friends. He could see insecurities boiling inside and wondered why he was picked for an assignment like this. He decided too, that, with care, Billy might do just what he wanted and get him away from Sonny. "Come on, I'll introduce you to Russell. He's the one you'll be working with," Billy said.

After a quick introduction, Billy turned and walked back into his own office, shutting the door.

"Elmer, I'm glad to meet you," Art said as he extended his hand to the well-dressed and perfectly manicured individual.

"Sit down," Elmer replied in a friendly tone, motioning to a chair beside the desk. Art wondered about the tall, good looking individual before him who looked more like a college professor than he did a program manager on a space program. He wondered how he would be to work with and what sort of background he had. "Tell me about yourself," Elmer continued.

Art looked at him with a straight but friendly look, not wishing to give the impression he was shy. "Well, not much to tell, about seventeen years' experience in engineering, both in management and design, professional engineer's license, pilot, married to a school girl, and run part of the logistics department. I want to get into program management. Here's a resume." Art handed Elmer a copy of his latest resume.

"What do you mean you're married to a school girl?"

"Got a wife in her PhD program up at Alfoxton University."

"Oh." Elmer looked up with a big smile. "I know about those things. I went through two PhD programs myself. Hard road. Hard road. What's her field?"

Art was feeling more comfortable and impressed to be

working with a person with a PhD, much less two PhD's. "English Literature."

"Well, I'm impressed because those people are the keepers of the language. Without them we'd still be living in caves."

"Correct," Art replied. "But what can I do to help you? What are your responsibilities?"

"From talking with Jerry, there's a great deal. I have sole responsibility to get designed and built all of the electronics, instrumentation, and cables on the solid rocket boosters. I need someone to work instrumentation for me and get all that stuff built and help me with the electronics. Your resume shows a strong design background in electronics. Are you interested?"

Art was leaning forward, intensely interested and trying not to appear too eager. "From what I see so far, the major portions of the instrumentation measures pressures, temperature, vibration, heat, stress and strain, and velocity."

Elmer grinned and leaned back in his chair. "Hell, you already know as much as I do. What do you know about the integrated electroncis assembly?"

"Well, not too much yet. I'm familiar with its specifications. I know that it processes data from all areas of the Boosters and controls functions of the vehicle. Art went into a rather lengthy explanation of the systems and their operations, including the protocols for the computers to interface to the integrated electroncis assembly.

Elmer slid back in his chair and looked at Art with an inquiring, studied look. "Damn, how long you been on the program?"

"I been here about six months."

Elmer extended his hand with a gracious gesture and smile. "Welcome aboard, Mr. Program Manager Assistant. Maybe we can get you transferred over here permanently. You just stick with me and I'll take care of you."

CHAPTER SEVEN

Eddie was staring out the office window deep in thought, slouched down in his chair with his feet on an unruly desk, as Art entered with a big smile. "Damn, fellow," Eddie exclaimed, "you look like you just ate the canary. What happened?"

Art plopped down in his chair, propped his feet on his desk and leaned way back like a new proud father. He looked as though he didn't know where to start and wanted to tell it all at once. Eddie was studiously observing, wondering what the good news was. Finally after a few moment's reflection he began, "Well, I got the job, part time so far. How about that?"

Eddie's face became one big grin. "Damn, I'm glad. I was afraid Sonny'd screw it up."

"Oh, he'd try if he knew. I wonder how long it'll take him to figure it out."

"Probably not long, I'll bet. Better watch for more screaming phone calls."

"Well, Jerry's supposed to tell him. I guess I'd rather he did that."

Eddie started to comment when Jerry entered with a grin. "Good show," he croaked in obvious glee, "I knew you'd set their eyes on fire down there. Russell was so tickled he couldn't see straight."

Eddie said jovially, "Well, I could'a told you that."

Jerry turned to Eddie, now looking serious and said, "Don't give up on me. I need you and I'm working your problem, too."

"I know, and I appreciate it. I won't go away as long as I believe there's hope."

"Good. Guess I better drop the news on Sonny about Art. He won't like it, but if he gives you any trouble let me know."

Art gave Jerry his all-approving look as he replied, "Don't worry, we took the first step. I'll handle Sonny. I'm looking forward to working with somebody with a PhD."

Jerry stopped short of getting up and looked strangely. "What do you mean, PhD?"

"That's what he said, or at least that's what he inferred to me.

He asked me all about Annie's program."

"Let me set the record straight at the start, Art. He didn't complete any PhD that I know of."

Art was taken aback, "Well, that's interesting."

Eddie chimed in with, "It'll be an improvement over a third-grade drop-out."

They all laughed at Eddie's confidence as the momentary tension drained. "Yeah, you're right about that," Jerry commented jokingly as he left to go visit the Cat Fish.

Just before quitting time Heidi burst into Art's office with a pale, excited look on her face. "Art! Art! I got to talk to you."

"What's wrong, baby? Sit down," he said as he pulled a chair over close, fearing the worst. She plopped down looking as though she were grasping for a place to start. Then suddenly she exclaimed, "I heard an awful argument about you between Mr. Strong and Sonny. Mr. Strong threatened to fire him and he kept saying that he was going to fire you. Something about you thinking you were too good to work in logistics and he wasn't going to stand for you to share your time. Is that true?"

He grinned at Heidi, who had become a totally loyal friend and self-appointed caretaker as he patted her thigh. "It's okay, baby," he replied gently, taking her shaking hand in his. "It's okay."

"Are you sure? I don't want anything bad to happen to you."

"I'm sure. I'm going to spend some time in the Program Office and Sonny's not going to fire anybody. Now don't worry." he said as he squeezed her hand and watched the stress drain from her .

"Then you already knew?"

"No, but I thought it might come to that. Where were they arguing?"

"In Mr. Strong's office. It sounded awful. Sonny doesn't have any respect for him at all."

"Was Loren involved?" Art asked, now studying her carefully.

"No, he's not in this afternoon."

"Well, pretty lady, don't worry. Jerry knows him for what he is and he won't get away with anything."-

"Well, it scared me. It scared the hell out of me."

"Thanks for caring, baby," Art said softly, staring at her while continuing to squeeze her hand and thinking about the horrors she had endured and was now worrying about him.

"You know I care a lot. I don't want anything bad to happen to you."

"Well, you're very special to me, too. You know what I told you once, 'We either hang together or we'll surely hang separately.'"

"I know and I believe that. I'm glad we're here."

"I'm glad, too, hon. Come on and I'll walk you to your car."

Early the next morning while Art was busy making the morning coffee he saw Eddie and Chuck crossing the parking lot. He laughed to himself thinking, *That sack hound finally learned to get up and to quit on time. Let's see how long this is gonna last.* In the middle of his thoughts he heard the office door open and saw Albert standing in the middle of it. "Hi, Al. I'll have some fresh coffee soon as it runs through. Grab a cup."

Albert was in no mood for conversation and glared at Art with a very disdainful stare. "What's this I hear about your going to work in the Program Office?" he growled in his best drill sergeant mode.

Art returned the stare as he responded, "Yeah. Guess you heard right Al, but they need help. You're bringing in two new guys Monday and Chuck is still here full time. There isn't enough work to keep two people busy full time, much less four so I'm going to help out in the Program Office part time."

Al turned red, so red that Art thought he could almost see his ears begin to glow. "Mister you didn't clear that with me first. You don't shit here unless you clear it with me first. That's disapproved, NOW!" Al yelled.

"Al, I'm sorry if you got your feelings hurt . . ." Art began.

Al interrupted, "Feelings hurt? Hell this has got nothing to do with feelings. You've violated the chain of command. You can't do that."

Al was on the verge of hysterics when Eddie and Chuck stopped at the door in wide-eyed amazement. Al stormed out of the office looking at his watch to be sure that Eddie and Chuck were in before starting time. Eddie called out as he rushed down the hall, "We got five more minutes, Al."

Eddie and Chuck entered gingerly, as though trespassing on a battleground. "Fresh coffee, guys?" Art offered with a grin.

Eddie picked up his cup fearing the worst. "What's going on with little Al? He looked like he was about to have a seizure."

Chuck, never wanting to miss anything or not be in on the action, moved to where he could see and hear. "Has Sonny called yet?" he asked cautiously.

"Slow down guys. Sonny hasn't called but he will. You can bet Al's in Sonny's office right now."

Eddie started to pour a cup of the fresh hot brew when he started to laugh uncontrollably, as he was known to do at times. Finally, he managed to croak, "I can imagine that conversation."

Just then the phone rang. Art looked at his watch, "Seven thirty-five. Wonder why they waited so long."

The phone rang again. Chuck replied nervously, "I bet it's Sonny."

Eddie retorted, "Hell, let it ring again. Don't be so damned available."

He picked up the phone after three rings. "Logistics, Cannon."

Both Chuck and Eddie could hear Sonny yelling, "Cannon, report to my office NOW!"

"Sure, Sonny. What's up."

"Don't play none of your damned games with me! Get your ass up here NOW!"

They all heard the phone slam down and imagined the rage at the other end. "Well, fellows, if I don't survive, it's been nice knowing you," Art laughed as he walked out the door.

He entered Sonny's office cautiously and saw Lissie carrying a fresh cup of coffee through the inner door to Sonny. He observed the smoke coming from the room and surmised there must be more than one person in the room because that amount of cigar smoke would be far too much for one person to generate. Lissie emerged and with a cold stare, glared at Art, "You're Cannon, aren't you?"

Art nodded his head without replying and wondered if this was just her way of being cold or she really had not been able to learn who he was yet. After all the trips up into Sonny's office lately and the arguments he had survived she surely did know who he was. He mentally noted, *You can go to hell, too.* Lissie motioned toward the door with her head, "He's waiting, I believe," she grunted sarcastically.

He saw Sonny seated with his back to him while he fumbled around in his credenza behind his desk for another cigar and then through the haze he saw Albert seated in a chair behind and to the left

91

of Sonny's desk. Albert frowned and announced: "He's here!"

Sonny growled, "He damned well better be." He turned around in the chair and adjusted the mass of body as though he expected an onslaught. "What's this bullshit I hear, Cannon? Ain't we good enough for you? What the hell you think you're doin' anyhow? Al's your supervisor, and buddy, you blew it. You don't do nothin' without consulting your supervisor. Don't you know that?"

Art had prepared himself mentally the best he could for this and sat for a moment wondering if he had been able to prepare well enough. Then his mind flashed back to the times he had worked as an expert witness investigating industrial accidents. He thought of some of the lawyers he had faced on depositions and on cross examination and this gave him assurance. Hell, he thought to himself, they were professionals at intimidation. This here's not even a good amateur. He quickly decided the best approach would be a frontal attack. He faced Sonny squarely without flinching and asked directly and calmly, "Why was Albert appointed my supervisor, Sonny? What qualifications does he have?"

Al jumped to the floor in panic and yelled, "I'll tell you why I'm your supervisor, mister! Because your boss said I was!"

"Sit down Albert." Art barked. "I'm talkin to your supervisor!"

Sonny had turned even redder and stormed, "I picked him because he's a good man. I got confidence in him! I can trust him! That's why!" Sonny was waving his hand up and down at Art and almost screaming; he didn't see the large, glowing cigar ash drop on his pants.

Momentarily Art saw smoke curling up as Sonny's pants began to smolder. He chuckled and found himself anticipating the result with glee. Finally Sonny saw the smoke, jumped up from the chair furiously brushing his pants and screaming, "Shit! Shit! I'm on fire! Damn! I've ruined this suit!"

Al quickly handed Sonny a glass of water which Sonny started to dump on the smoldering hole. At the last moment he caught himself. He turned his fury on Al, who was looking like a rat cornered by a big cat, and screamed, "Idiot, what are you trying to do, drown me!" He slammed the glass down on the desk, spilling water over a large stack of papers.

Al jumped up to rescue the papers and tripped over the waste can that Lissie had put at the end of Sonny's desk and sent it flying, spreading trash, cigar butts and ashes over the carpet in that end of the room.

Sonny focused his rage at Art, screaming and red in the face. "Cannon, this is all your motherfuckin' fault. You caused it and by God, you'll pay for this."

Sonny had put the smoldering fire out by beating it with his hand while yelling at Lissie, "Get a damned paper towel and clean up this mess."

Lissie promptly appeared with a stack of paper towels and dried up the water the best she could without a word. She took the papers that Al was holding up to drip and dried them off before hurriedly exiting as though she thought she might be next.

Sonny, still red in the face, regained some of his composure and glared at Art. "See what you've caused? You're a disaster! I think I'll fire your ass right now!"

Art chuckled as he answered Sonny very matter-of-factly. "Sonny, that wouldn't be a good idea."

Sonny roared, "How in hell did you get involved with that damned Program Office? Those people don't know from nothin about this program. I'm ordering you right now to quit. I ain't authorized you to do that and by damn, you're not gonna' do anything that I don't authorize you to do and that includes even go shit. Do you hear me, Cannon? Do you hear me?" Sonny was sitting straight up in his chair pounding on his desk with his fist. Al looked in shock and fear of what might be coming next.

Art knew that he had Sonny on the defensive from watching his body language and listening to the inflections in his voice. He knew Sonny was thoroughly mad and had lost his ability to reason. "Sonny," he began, "we could have been good friends but you didn't want to. Those people need help and I'm gonna help 'em."

Sonny squirmed in his chair, carefully watching Art out of the corner of his eye as he relit his cigar. He started to interrupt but thought better of it. Art continued, "After all, you hired two new people and told me how good they were, so when the chance came, I took it."

Sonny had settled down some and Art sensed a new direction in his attack. "Well," Sonny started more calmly, "Jerry thinks you're some kind of gift to 'em down there. I talked to Loren about it last night and he said to let it go for now and he'd try to deal with it later."

"Loren doesn't have anything to do with it, Sonny."

"Like shit he don't. So, mister smart guy, you may be fired after all. If you screw up I'll fire you. I don't give a damn about your airplanes or your flying or your wife, or even your damned cat. So, mister, watch it!"

Art smiled calmly at Sonny, as he had learned to do in court, while he replied coolly, "Fellah, I watch you all the time. I learned that the hard way."

Al, who had been silent, saw an opening to show Sonny that he was still on the job. He leaned forward in his chair, his eyes flashing the fire of a thousand demons. "Don't you forget who your supervisor is, mister, because if you do I'll bust you down to recruit!"

Art, ignoring Al, asked with a little smile. "Are we through, Sonny?"

Sonny sensed that he hadn't succeeded in intimidating Art the way he wanted and yelled, "Get out of here!"

Al, beaming approval and still trying to impress Sonny, yelled, carefully after Sonny was through, "Yeah, get out of here. I'll call you when we want you again."

Art was thankful for the opportunity and walked out into the outer office where Lissie glared at him as though he had done something to her as well.

"See you, Lissie."

"From the way you're goin' you may not!"

Art felt he had won an important battle. He now knew that he could hold his own with Sonny and Al but he was even more aware of the need to get out of Sonny's department and into the Program Office permanently. As he walked toward the stairs he noticed the accounting office door standing open, which was unusual. As he passed, he saw Connie sitting at her desk with Al standing beside her, arm around her, leaning over as though he were showing her something on a report. His stomach tightened in disgust because it was obvious he was gradually penetrating Connie's outer space and he was sure he would soon be working hard on the inner space. He stopped, put his head in the door and asked curtly, "You got your door open, Al?"

Connie looked up with a start as Al jerked his arm away. Al growled in an obvious attempt to vindicate himself. "Any idiot can see the air conditioner ain't working."

Connie blushed, knowing that Art would disapprove. "Hi, Art, I didn't expect you up here."

He returned to an empty office, glad for the quiet, and thought about the two goons, Don and Cig, to contend with, coupled to problems he anticipated with Sonny. He wondered if it was all worth it and decided to pour himself a fresh cup of coffee to replace the cold one. He soon engrossed himself in instrumentation systems, wiring systems, and interconnect philosophy for the new booster designs when Jerry appeared. "Goin to lunch, Art?"

He looked up with a start. "Yeah, sure, Jerry, I just sort of lost track of time."

Jerry responded good naturedly, "I see you're deep into the systems. Hell, you'll be the resident expert in no time at all. Let's go get a sandwich and talk a little."

They walked to the parking lot in time to see Sonny's big Lincoln driving off with Lissie sitting close. Jerry shook his head and said, "I don't understand, but I can't convince Loren. So I guess we'll just have to live with it."

After a good lunch and Jerry's pep talk, Art felt there was a good future at Space Corp. He had new resolve to do a good job in the Program Office and decided the smartest thing to do was to minimize contact with Sonny and Al. Jerry said, "Art, I, and we, the company, need people on this program that have integrity and capability. We desperately need you and Eddie. Loren is a smart man, but he's hard headed. I'm trying to work things out for you guys but it's not easy. Fighting some of these corporate bureaucratic systems can be deadly." Art was pleased with Jerry's honesty and sincerity and was convinced if he had any hope, it probably would be with Jerry.

After returning to his office he checked his logistics work responsibilities to be sure that there wasn't anything left undone. Finally he opened his center desk drawer and was stunned to find it had been rifled with no attempt at concealment. He found his address book containing old business contacts had been moved from one side of the drawer to the other and other items had been shuffled around and left in disorder. Now why would anybody do that unless they were looking for something to try to make a case out of for some reason? He decided to remove everything personal from the desk. He checked the other drawers and found they had been searched as well. As he walked to the Program Office he thought, "Maybe two can play this game."

He passed through the lobby where Heidi greeted him with a big smile. "Hi there. Haven't seen you today."

He smiled, glad to see her, and stopped. "I've been hiding," he teased. Then he asked, "Did you see anybody go into my office during lunch?"

"No, but I took a bathroom break. Why?" she asked with alarm.

"I was just wondering." He started down the hall and then stopped and turned. "I'd appreciate your keeping a watch down that way for me."

"You know I will. Who you looking for?"

"Don't know but I'll explain it later. Okay?"

"Sure. I'll let you know," she replied as he turned toward the Program Office stairs.

"Hi Elmer. I'm ready to go to work," Art announced with a grin as he entered the office.

Elmer Russell, his new part-time boss turned from his worktable piled high with a mass of paper with a big smile. "Great. I want you to take the instrumentation initially and when you figure that out I'll give you most or all the electronics. I've got a hell of a rats nest on my hands to build these damned cables."

Art was pleased to finally be getting an important task assignment. "I can handle that easy," he said as he sat down beside Elmer's table.

"We're responsible for all design and procurement including installation and check-out through flight. I'll help you understand the systems the best I can but I don't know much about 'em myself yet. How are you at negotiating contracts?"

"Okay, I guess, but we'll use procurement for that, won't we?"

"Yeah, but you'll have to guide 'em and show 'em what you want and then you'll have to prepare purchase requests." Art gave him a questioning look. "Yeah," Elmer replied, "this is where the buck stops. We have responsibility for the entire vehicle."

"That's a big responsibility, Elmer."

96

"You're right. The entire company was designed to support this office. We have any group or department, theoretically, at our disposal."

He was impressed and leaned forward a bit. Elmer continued, "When we get engineering staffed and assume design responsibility from the Space Agency, we'll have a handfull. Now that's the good part. The bad part is that we're responsible for design, production, technical correctness, schedules, budgets, contracts, and things that we ain't even thought of yet."

"That's the first time I've heard that. Looks like a hell of a job."

"That's why Jerry is setting us up like the Space Agency. I don't know how he'll make out, given all the politics, but we got to support him."

"I see why you need help," Art said thoughtfully. "Sounds like it could be fun, though."

"That's why I signed on. I want to be a part of this and get experience in big programs. Hope you still want to help."

Art faced Elmer with a big grin. "You damned bet I do. Looks like my kind of animal."

"Great. Tomorrow I'll divide up the hardware and give you the files so you can start developing specifications and writing statements of work for your contracts and getting phased into the operations. I hope you'll have a lot of time."

"Yeah, me too. I'll really enjoy this."

As Art shaved for work the next morning he wondered how Sonny was going to react today. Then he thought of Albert. What a pair, he thought. They'll really be after my ass. He dressed appropriately for the program management position with a suit and tie instead of the usual open shirt and casual pants he was accustomed to. In his driveway he surveyed the tires on his old Buick that had served him so well for so long and thought, "Well, old gal, not long till new shoes for you." He got in and soon pulled into traffic on the street leading to the main gate entrance on the east side of the space center. Out of the corner of his eye he saw a big red Lincoln Town Car on an intersecting street. *H'mmm, just like Sonny's.* When the car approached the intersection he saw the driver *was* Sonny as the Lincoln turned onto the street going into the space center main gate.

The light turned yellow on the other side and he saw a yellow Chevrolet bearing down on the light with a vengeance, with Lissie at the wheel.

Art was puzzled because he knew Sonny lived on the west side of town and entered the west gate instead of the east gate. And what was Lissie doing following him? Art was suspicious, and knowing Sonny's tricks, especially with women, was sure they both were up to no good. Then he thought, "Hell, she's a married woman with a family. I shouldn't do that to her."

When he drove into the parking lot at his building he saw Connie getting out of her car a few spaces down from him. "Hi there. You look bright and shiny today."

Connie didn't look particularly happy when she turned and replied, "Hi."

He studied her carefully with a worried look. "Anything wrong, Connie?"

"No, nothing's wrong. We had our first big fight last night and I lost," she complained as she approached Art's car with a downcast look

"Well, gee, can I help. . .?" he offered.

"My new husband has a jealous streak I didn't know he had."

They walked across the lot toward the building as he tried to sooth her hurt feelings. "Well, Connie, we all have our insecurities but that's part of what marriage is about, to help each other deal with problems and to reassure each other. Know what I mean?"

"Yes, but he doesn't understand anything . . ." She began to talk faster and to open up a little. "He doesn't understand that we were able to buy that house because of my getting a better job so we could qualify for the loan and that I'm grateful to Al for that."

"Is that the only problem?"

"Well, no, it isn't," she conceded. "I promised Al I'd have lunch with him one day and I don't see anything wrong with that, do you?"

"No, so long as the lunch is an innocent one between two friends who are not trying to make time or get commitments from the other. You know it's not everybody you can have lunch with and get away with it. Do you see what I'm saying?"

She stopped under a small pine tree and he saw tears coming into her big blue eyes. "You mean sort of like us, just like buddies?"

"Yeah. We're good friends but that's all there is to it. We respect each other's territory. I respect your husband and you respect my wife and we have established lines in the friendship that we won't cross."

She looked long at the trees on the other side of the parking lot in deep reflection. "I see what you're saying, I guess, but it's so hard to know . . ." Her voice trailed off.

"Baby, you have a little voice inside. You know whether it's right or not. Just stop and listen."

"When did you first know you loved Annie, Art?"

"The first time I ever saw her I loved her, I think," he replied thoughtfully. "But it took a while to overcome dumb and really admit it. Sometimes we don't show great sense and have to get hit in the head once or twice."

She was pensive. "I hope I did the right thing. Now I'm not sure I did because he's so possessive and jealous."

"I think 'immature' would be a better word. You both have to grow up some more. You haven't been out in the world much yet and neither has he, so just give it a chance and it'll work out okay."

Art opened the door as they entered the end hallway. "Gee, I don't know what I'd do without you when I get in trouble. Sometimes I think you're almost my father," she was now smiling for the first time.

He grinned and patted her on the shoulder. "That's what friends are for, but promise you won't do anything dumb."

"Okay, buddy, you got it," she replied jubilantly. "If I do, you'll be the first to know."

Art entered his office feeling relieved, knowing that Al's pattern was to force women rather than to charm them into submission. *Ain't no charisma in that snake*, he thought. The smell of hot coffee attracted his attention as Chuck sat consuming a cup. "Mornin Chief," he greeted.

"Mornin, early bird, you sure got out early today. How'd that happen?"

"Couldn't sleep. Buddy, we got to do something. We got two goons that just hang around in Sonny's office and shoot the shit about old times. They don't know nothing about logistics."

"Yeah, I know," Art replied quietly. "I think the best thing is to quietly explore the outer compartments of the company to see if there's another position."

"I been doin' that. But you know you can't transfer in this damned company without your supervisor's approval. He's not about to let either one of us go."

Art poured himself a cup of coffee, sat down at his desk and watched Eddie cross the parking lot. "Look at that. Early again."

Chuck looked out the window and laughed. "Well, one thing about it, they got Eddie calibrated."

"Yeah," Art chuckled. "But back to the transfer business. I think as long as Jerry is here we don't have to worry too much about them firing us. So I believe if we make the Cat Fish as miserable as we can, he'll be glad to let us transfer."

"I hope you're right about . . .," Chuck started as Albert appeared in the doorway.

"Mornin Al," Art said, and Chuck added, "Mornin' glory, you sure bloomed early today."

Albert scowled at both of them. "Where's Rogers?"

Art, without blinking an eye, looked at him and calmly admonished, "He's trying to get in the door that you're standing there blocking. Besides, *sir*, he has two minutes yet."

Albert wheeled around and looked at Eddie. "Where you been, mister, you're supposed to be at your place of business."

Eddie was elated at the opportunity to drive another nail into Albert's thin skin. "I been standing here waiting on you to move. You're obstructing the entrance and wastin Government money standing there like that. Besides, you're a fire hazard."

Albert looked as though he could eat Eddie in one bite and replied sharply, "Just checkin on you damned guys. I can't trust you one inch. Now look busy."

Chuck hopped quickly to his feet, clicked his heels and saluted as Albert turned to leave mumbling, "Smart ass."

"By the way, Al, where's Cig and Don this morning? It's after starting time and I don't see much of 'em down here working," Art said.

Al turned, eyes flashing, "Don't you worry about them, mister! They're professionals and if you really want to know, I left them in Sonny's office in a meeting."

"Just checkin' Al. Just checkin'." Art laughed as Albert stormed out the door. He propped his feet on the desk to enjoy his first cup of coffee of the day.

Eddie entered laughing so hard he could hardly walk. "He's paranoid about us now, you know," he got out between heaves.

Art looked at Eddie with a big grin as he said, "But watch the little beggar. He might slip up and really do something if he can find the right opportunity."

Chuck, who was not laughing, interrupted, "That's for damned straight. You guys got a chance to get out. I still ain't found me a tube to float on."

Eddie, feeling compassion for Chuck, replied, "Hang in there. You will. Besides, I'm not out yet and neither is Art."

"Eddie's right, Chuck, but we got to work the problem. Just keep the faith a while."

In the program management office Art found Elmer and Billy Ghote sitting around Elmer's work table. He noted a big frown on Billy's face. "Here's your new guy," Billy said and started to get up from the table.

"Hi, Billy. Don't leave on my account."

"Hi," Billy grunted as he slowly rose and started to the door.

Art stood a moment watching Billy disappear into his office and shut the door. He wondered if there were a problem, but thought better about inquiring yet. "Come in, come in," Elmer greeted. "I got this stuff laid out and Billy agrees on the distribution," pointing to a large stack of documents and specifications. "You can start reading specifications for your hardware."

Art wrinkled his brow, looking at the volume of material, and said, "Wow!"

Elmer grinned as he continued, "Also, here's a list of the people in Engineering to support us. You need to get acquainted with them."

"Looks like a lot of hardware Elmer. Sure looks like a lot of reading."

"Yeah, but you'll absorb it with your background. Lots of repetitious boiler-plate. Now, let's go over the list of items that you'll be working and I'll help you get started."

Art was eager and for the next two hours he and Elmer discussed various systems and how the Program Office must respond to requirements imposed by the Space Agency. He was saturated, or so it seemed, when Elmer picked up the last file. "This is all I got on this thing right now. We have a requirement to develop a force sensor using an aft strut clevis end."

"What's a clevis?"

"The clevis is one end of the aft attach strut that connects the solid rocket booster to the external tank at the rear during launch. The clevis has a big set of ears where a large pin connects it to a fitting made onto the SRB aft attach ring. It's a critical piece."

"You mean it actually forms one end of the strut?"

"Yep. It's made of 718 Inconel steel. The mechanical design was done by the Space Agency and qualified for flight. I believe they've issued a certificate of qualification for it."

"You got a copy yet?"

"We don't need it for a government-furnished piece. What you have to do is design and install instrumentation to measure the tension and compression loads during propellant loading before launch and then measure the loads and shocks during launch. The Space Agency designed the data collection system so you won't have to bother with that either."

"Elmer, there's a lot we need to know about that system first. Can we get the design data?"

"I've talked to their instrumentation specialist and he doesn't know much about it yet. I don't know who designed the system but it's frozen. You'll just have to work with it."

"I don't know if I like that or not."

Elmer grinned as he said, "I see the design engineer comin out. I'm sure it's okay. They wouldn't give it to us if it weren't."

"Well, I don't mean to be picky but these are important details."

"I know. But you'll just have to work with their guy to get a suitable sensor design and qualify it to prove it works and survives in a space environment. We got no assigned responsibility in the data acquisition system."

The file contained a large stack of drawings that Art recognized as an aft strut assembly, a five-foot or so tubular affair with a set of big ears on each end to accommodate the attachment pins. He examined the drawing for the tubular connector, or "frangible nut," as it was designated, that each half of the strut screwed into to complete the assembly. Next he examined the drawings showing the hollow inside areas of each end where the shaped charge pyrotechnics would go that would blow up and split the nut, causing separation of the boosters from the orbiter after they had burned out. He wrinkled his brow and commented, "Looks like they want to put the instruments inside the barrel behind the separation pyrotechnics."

"Yeah, in the half on the booster side but that may be tricky because of interference with the pyrotechnics inside that splits the center nut between halves of the strut on detonation at separation."

"That's at about 250,000 feet?" Art asked, pondering optional locations.

"Yeah, about there on a nominal mission."

Art scanned the drawing carefully before commenting, "I hope everybody's aware we're going to blow the instrumentation to hell at booster separation."

"Yeah, but then we're through measuring loads anyhow, aren't we?"

"True. Guess we don't need it anymore," Art replied.

"Exactly. Then when the ends of these struts are recovered with the SRB from the ocean you'll have to install all new instrumentation and recalibrate before another flight."

"Elmer, this looks like an interesting system. Let me be sure, before I read the requirements documents. I've got to measure the force on these struts during vehicle roll-out to the launch pad, during propellant loading, and during launch through separation."

"Right. I think there's a small company here that does strain gage work. It'd be best to keep it local if possible so you can work with your contractor."

"Okay. I'll investigate 'em and some others, too."

Two days later Art visited engineering. He decided to follow protocol and start with the director even though Jerry had called him a "wimp." Art entered Sam Hardiman's outer office and faced a stern looking secretary. "May I see Sam?" he asked with cautious courtesy.

Shortly he saw a very prim, properly dressed young man, youthful-looking to be director of engineering and silently marveled at the quality and detail of his clothes. He thought this guy looked like some of the magazine ads. "Hello, Sam, I'm Art Cannon," he greeted warmly.

Sam stood up behind his massive desk and put out his hand.

"Pleased to meet you. Sit down."

Art explained his mission with Elmer and Billy while Sam sat listening. Finally he answered, "I've been told we were supposed to support you guys, but I don't think I have the support you need yet. I'm trying to hire engineers anywhere I can find 'em." Sam looked wistfully as he asked, "You're probably from the old Saturn team, aren't you?"

Art nodded. "There's still a few of us around."

"It's a shame the team was allowed to break up and dissipate the way it did. I think this program would be a lot further ahead if we had all you old guys back."

He flinched a little at the word "old" because he was now approaching forty-five and beginning to be more sympathetic with the "over fourty" people. "However," Sam continued, "you need to meet Danny Belcher. He's an old Saturn man and my supervisor of electrical engineering. He'll steer you straight to the right people."

Art thought, as he walked down the hall to the designated door, *Sam can't be over 35. Awful young to occupy a position like that. Must be a whiz kid or something.* Shortly Art saw the name, Danny Belcher, and turned into the office where he saw a large, flushed, red-faced man with unkempt, bushy red hair in bad need of cutting, at the desk, feet propped up on a pile of papers, documents and other assorted litter, talking to someone on the phone. He was obviously not pleased at being interrupted. He glared and replied gruffly, "Can't you see I'm talking on the phone? Wait out in the hall."

"Oh, excuse me." Art beat a hasty retreat to the hall, not wishing to offend this unwelcome looking character.

He waited fourteen minutes and twenty seconds when he heard the phone hang up and a blunt, gruff , "Come on in, if you're still out there."

Art entered the office and extended his hand to Danny, who returned the handshake with what he liked to call the 'dead fish'. "Art Cannon, Danny." He wondered how he was going to deal with this big, blustery individual. He studied the red, ruddy face and large bulging eyes framed under a very receding hairline and opted to reserve judgment for now. He explained his position with the Program Office and his conversation with Sam Hardiman.

Danny interrupted curtly, "He didn't tell you I was being

reassigned to the Cape did he?"

"No. He didn't."

"Yeah, I'm going down there and take over engineering. I hired a guy I can trust to run electrical here for me 'til I get back and take over all the engineering here at the home office. Then who knows where from there."

Art was uneasy at the bragging and gloating. He wondered what engineering school produced this one or if he just bluffed his way through. Danny continued, "You guys don't need to worry about that engineering shit. We'll take care of that from the Cape. We know how to build rockets down there better'n anybody else."

Art knew immediately, reflecting back on the fierce inter-center rivalries that had been so rampant over the years between Hawkinsville and the Cape, that this must be what was referred to in Hawkinsville as a "Capie". He responded cautiously, "Well, 'til you get it under control at the Cape, I guess we'll have to work on it some up here. Seems like that's what the company wants to do."

Danny stared, not quite knowing what to make of him. "Yeah, yeah, but when I get to the Cape, mister, some things are gonna change. Guess you need to see Elton Jones, three doors down the hall."

"Thanks. Guess I'll go see him." He left quickly into what seemed to be a fresh breath of air. As he walked to Elton Jones' office he saw Connie in a lower hallway. "Hi, Babe, haven't seen you in several days. How's things?""

Connie returned the greeting, stopping under a large clock mounted in the hallway. "Great! I went out to lunch with Al a couple of times and my new hubby seems to be taking it okay. I told him what you said and he settled down."

Art felt his stomach tighten just knowing that she had gone to lunch with Al even once. He stared at her, contemplating his next statement: "Connie, be careful. Al's not in your league."

She started to giggle as she continued in her own naive way, "He's precious. You've got him all wrong, Art. He's really nice to me. We've gone to some neat places for lunch."

"Do you know he's married with four kids?"

"Sure, but so what? I'm married, too, and I can take care of myself."

"Gee, baby, I sure hope so." Art studied her with a worried

look, fearing for her and her tendency to jump before she looked.

"Now Art," Connie chided, "don't worry. I know what I'm doing. I'm a big girl. He's really sweet and I like that little beard and goatee. He's really nice when you get to know him."

Art furrowed his brow and drew a deep breath. "Okay, baby, see you later. I got to go see some people." He spotted Elton Jones' office and opened the door to see a large room with a number of desks piled high with papers and drawings.

"Elton Jones? ' he asked quietly.

A young man looked up and pointed toward the far corner. "That's him over there."

Art thanked him and walked to the far corner of the room. "Elton Jones?"

"Yep. What can I do for you?" came the slow reply from the small, gray-haired individual at the desk filled with drawings and documents.

Art relayed his last two conversations with Sam and Danny, being very careful what part of Danny's conversation he mentioned. Elton smiled broadly through tobacco-stained teeth, leaned back in his chair to adjust his small build and lit a cigarette. Art thought that the teeth needed a wire brush instead of a tooth brush. He peered through thick, brown-rimmed glasses that made his eyes look strange as though they were squinting through marsh gas in a swamp. "You're in the right place. We got the mission to support you but right now I don't have the people," Elton replied.

"How many engineers you got?"

He looked embarrassed. "So far I'm the only engineer, and I graduated in 1947, so you can see what I'm up against."

Art, in disbelief, surveyed the room. "What are these people?"

Elton squirmed, searching for an answer. "The philosophy is to do this job as cheap as possible. Danny decided we can only hire non-degreed people. Later on we can hire some engineers . . . I'm told. I suppose I'll just wait and see about that."

Art had a sinking feeling while he looked squarely at Elton and asked, "How do you propose to assume design responsibility for these systems?"

Elton was uncomfortable with the direct questioning. He responded slowly, "I don't know, but if I do I've got to hire the kind of engineers I need. Right now Danny is driving the train but I hope

I can do something about that later."

Art stroked his chin and began to feel sorry for Elton's position. "Danny tells me he's going to the Cape to take over engineering down there. Is that true?"

"Where'd you hear that?"

"From him."

"Well, okay. I guess I can comment since he told you. Yeah, he plans to move most of engineering down there. He wants me to come too, but I'm not sure I want to. You know, he's from there."

Art leaned back in the chair, feeling he was gaining some of Elton's confidence. "I gathered that from what he said. But I'm afraid that won't work. The design of the vehicle is here in Hawkinsville. We need these functions here if we're going to support the program. I know I need my support here. I got no intention of going to the Cape."

"That makes sense but I'm not drivin' the train. I guess Danny's planning to go down there in about a month. He says he's leaving me in charge here."

"Well, Elton, I'll work with you any way I can to keep the programs going, but you're going to have to hire some good engineers soon or you'll drown."

"I know", he replied pensively. "Get me some budget and I'll try."

"Well, I'll be back and we can discuss it some more." Art left and quickly walked to the Program Office where he narrated the events to Elmer, who leaned back in his chair and furrowed his brow.

"That's what I've been afraid of all along. Some of these people don't seem to understand the problem. They've got a bunch of technicians trying to design cables to Space Agency standards and they just can't get it right."

"Elmer, we got a problem."

"Yeah, we do and I don't know enough about these things yet to be much help either."

Art peered out Elmer's door across the inner court yard, at the arrangement of offices. He saw signs reading *Range Safety, Structures, Pyrotechnics, Thrust Vector Control,* and others beside the doors. He took a deep breath because for the first time he realized there may be a real problem. "Looks like engineering is concentrated here, but we can't do it all. It simply can't be done."

107

"I know. We should be engineers, managers, accountants, negotiators, and a hundred other things, but we *do not* have time for the detail engineering."

Art propped his feet up on the worktable amid many files and other piles of paper and leaned back in the chair as he replied, "Well, we'll just do the best we can. But these little economies may cost a fortune later. It's better to do the job right the first time than do it over."

Elmer nodded and continued, "One word of advice. Watch out for Danny, he's ruthless and overbearing. He's got Elton in there because he can control him. But, if I'm right, when Danny goes to the Cape, Elton will turn on him and then there'll be another battle. I've known Danny for a long time and I know what kind of snake he is."

Art looked puzzled and asked expectantly, "What university did Danny graduate from?"

"He didn't. He's a third rate technician with a high school education and a big mouth. He has taken Loren in totally."

Art dropped his feet off the desk with a thump and a look of astonishment. "You mean here's another one that's taken Loren to the cleaners? Hell, what's wrong with that fellow?"

"He's just an incredibly bad judge of character, I guess. He's too nice a guy," Elmer replied quietly.

Art became very concerned about the design of the aft strut clevis end force measuring system. "Elmer, who in that engineering department can design the instrumentation that has to go into that clevis?" he asked pensively.

Elmer glanced out the door to watch some people go by as if he was trying to measure his answer carefully. "Nobody. It's gonna' be tough because there's no good way to place the strain gages to measure the load directly. Why don't you go over to the Space Agency lab and talk to Cal Thurgood. He's supposed to be their engineer that knows all this stuff."

Art felt relief and grinned as he replied, "First thing in the morning."

Art walked up the back stairs from the ground floor to his own floor, thinking, *What a day. What a day.* When he arrived he saw Eddie and Chuck intently staring out the window. "What you guys got treed out there?"

"Watch," Chuck croaked with glee. "We just saw Sonny kiss that new secretary and then get in her car. Damn, don't they care what they do?"

Art peered out the window and saw Sonny in the midst of a big bear hug on Lissie and then kiss her again. Just then he heard someone enter the room and turned around to see both Cig and Don. "What you damned guys lookin at?" Cig demanded.

Eddie, being quick with his wit, moved forty-five degrees to the right, and motioned, "C'mere, Cig, and watch. See that hole over there? There's the cutest family of ground hogs livin in there. A strange ground hog just went in and the old mama came out on top of him clawin like nothin you ever saw. The stranger took off and we're waiting on her to come back."

Just then, as if pre-ordained, the ground hog reappeared and started to enter its hole. Eddie nudged Cig on the arm and pointed, "Look, there she is. See her?"

Cig looked out the window and motioned for Don. "Whatt'a 'ya make of that?" he asked excitedly.

"Hell, I never seen one of them damned things before. You sure that's a ground hog?" he asked, looking at Chuck.

Chuck laughed as he replied, "Hell, man, what 'ya expect. They ain't got none of them damned things in Brooklyn. Sure, that's a ground hog."

Art stood up and locked his desk drawer, keeping one eye on the parking lot as he saw Sonny and Lissie drive off in their respective cars. "Well, guys, see you tomorrow."

Art and Eddie walked to the parking lot chuckling about the ground hog incident. "Quick thinkin there, old buddy."

Eddie started to laugh so hard that his sides were heaving. "How'd you like the way I fixed that groundhog's arrival? Now that's what I call real plannin."

"You're about the luckiest rascal I ever saw, is what I think. I don't know anybody else in the world that would happen for."

"Well," Eddie commented between laughs, "when you live in a small Peyton Place you got to be prepared. By the way, what do you suppose Sonny's doing with Lissie?"

Art propped his foot on the rear bumper of the old Buick. "Sonny's up to his usual tricks. He's imported this one for his own use, apparently, or else he's got lucky. I'm not sure how he latched onto her. He didn't like the one Jack had because she was loyal to Jack."

"Yeah, and Sonny can't deal with anybody that's not totally loyal and continually demonstrates it."

Eddie turned and surveyed the old Saturn test stands standing on the east side of the building across the road, well spaced out to prevent interference with one another. His mind drifted back to the old days as he said quietly "Sure wish I could have been here during the good old days."

"Hey," Art interrupted, "these days may be the good old days, too. We just got to wait and see."

The morning arrived with a gentle rain coming from a layer of low clouds. As he drove into the main gate through the rain he again saw Sonny's Lincoln and Lissie's Chevrolet two car lengths behind. "Guess they're starting early today," Art thought as he grinned to himself, trying to be unobvious.

Art entered the office that he now shared with four other people. "Sure hope I can get myself a transfer out of Logistics and into the Program Office. I can't work in this confusion all the time," he thought. Then he saw Chuck coming in with a large pot of water to put into the coffee pot and checked the time. It was now fifteen minutes before starting time, which Sonny had set strictly at 7:30 a.m. "Mornin' Chuck," he replied easily.

Chuck was all smiles and quickly responded, "Did 'ya see which gate Sonny came in this morning?"

"Yep, sure did."

"Well, did you see where he left from?"

Art's curiosity was aroused, "No. Where?"

Chuck grinned from ear to ear as he continued, "From the Plantation Motel. I got a buddy there that's in maintenance and he told me he and Lissie checked in last night and stayed a while. Then they came back this morning, stayed a while and left. Now what's that tell you?"

Art watched him pour water into the coffee pot and mused, "Well, Chuck, about all I can see is it's not worth much unless you plan to blackmail him and I don't think I would do that just yet."

Chuck's grin was replaced with a serious look. "Yeah, I see

110

the point." Then he started to grin again, "But it sure is interesting."

Art pointed to Eddie crossing the parking lot. "Yeah," Chuck replied, "Sonny's got him calibrated to the clock. He's got four minutes."

"By the way," Art queried, "have you seen Don and Cig yet?"

"No. They're probably upstairs with Sonny. Have you noticed they don't drink much coffee from our pot?"

Art eased into his chair and opened his desk. His face turned red as he saw his center drawer has been thoroughly searched again. "Shit! They struck again."

Eddie entered the office and looked curiously at Art. "Who struck again?"

"Hell, I don't know," Art roared. "But look! This time they went through it good. What the hell are they looking for?"

Eddie surveyed the crudely-attempted reordering of the contents. "Obvious. They're lookin for anything they can find to use against you. Maybe we can set a trap."

"What do you mean?"

With a big grin Eddie motioned to Art, "Let's go for a walk. The room and maybe the phone might be bugged."

"Okay. But let's put things out on our desks so when Albert comes down he'll know we're here. Chuck can tell him we went to get some data or something."

Chuck stared seriously at them both for a moment. "Buddy, that ain't all I'd like to tell him."

Eddie ushered Art out to the back of the building into the rear parking lot. Then he began to unfold his plan. "Let's put some notes in your center drawer like maybe you were thinking about a contract to get Sonny knocked off. We can word 'em in such a way that there could be several meanings. Then we can see who gets nervous or if there's a change."

Art finally agreed to the plan. As they walked back to the building, he announced his intention of going to the Program Office to discuss the clevis force sensor problem with Elmer. Eddie laughed out loud as they parted and chided, "Watch out for Albert."

Art found Elmer engrossed in a large pile of documents and drawings. "Hi. Got a few minutes to talk?" he asked.

Elmer smiled and said, "I'll bet that clevis is buggin you."

"How'd you guess?"

"Because it's buggin me, too. Have you been down to see Cal yet?"

"No. I was planning to this morning. Got any words of wisdom?"

"No. But I'd suggest you develop a statement of work and get something working soon. Maybe Cal has some ideas since he has Space Agency responsibility. He might even have a specification you can use."

Art returned to his office to find Albert coming out. "I brought you a present," Albert quipped, as he speedily departed the area.

Art saw Eddie and Chuck leaning back studying a small black board hanging from a nail on the wall by the door. "What's that?" he asked.

Chuck glanced at Art with a pained look. "Sign out board. You got to sign out to even go to the bathroom. Notice whose names are on it, too."

Eddie chided, "Better still, notice whose names aren't on it." With a scowl he surveyed the board as though it were a festering boil. Art took the piece of chalk and wrote "Meeting" beside his name. "That's the way you deal with that."

"How about the blank for the phone number? You can be sure they'll check." Eddie grunted.

"Simple. Just leave it blank until they start to bitch and then we'll figure something else."

Chuck walked over and scrawled "quit" beside his name. Eddie frowned with slitted eyes, "I hope you aren't serious. Don't let those clowns get to you."

He looked pensive for a moment and studied the new sign-out board. "Yeah, you're right. Guess I ought to change that to 'lookin'."

Art drove to the Space Agency Research and Development Lab, a large cavernous building made up of many wings that housed many different electronics laboratories for development of space flight hardware. He entered one and among the work benches and rows of test equipment he found an old man sitting with his back to the door engrossed in reading the morning paper.

"Cal Thurgood?"

The man, clad in an old rumpled suit, no tie and unlaced wing-tip shoes, smoking a pipe, turned slowly. He looked for the best of him to be retired already. "Yeah. I'm Thurgood," came the gruff reply.

"I'm Art Cannon from Space Corp. Are you responsible for strain gages over here?"

He looked at Art with an icy glare. "It's about time some of you folks started to show an interest in this damned thing."

Art was surprised at this attitude and replied cautiously, "Well, I'm sorry if somebody dropped the ball."

"Sure as hell did," Thurgood snapped.

"Well, I just got the problem and now I'm here. I want to get started on whatever we need to do."

Cal appeared to relax as he rummaged around in a desk drawer, finally producing a document. "I'm getting' ready to retire and I want to get this thing goin' 'fore I do. I was beginnin to worry about you people."

"I'm ready to run with it," Art replied, trying to smooth over the obvious discontent.

"I hope so, son, I hope so." He pointed to a small sheaf of papers on the corner of the desk. " That there is the specification you'll have to live to. Read it and if you got any complaints, let me know." Cal leaned back, staring at Art as though he wondered if he was really ready.

The specification looked very much like others, typical jargon, lots of standard and detail information. Art leafed through to the drawings section and saw the tiny leaf-like strain gages arranged in a neat pattern to measure the stress and strain in the aft strut clevis. He could see Thurgood out of the corner of his eye studying him. He decided to try to convert him to a friend and cautiously commented, "Looks like you put in a lot of work on this."

Art noted the grin of satisfaction from the old man. "You think they'll work at the bottom of the barrel inside there like I got 'em?"

Art studied the sheet carefully before replying, "Don't know. Have you had the stress people analyze it to see if that's the best place?"

113

"Hey, you've done your homework," Cal chuckled, now becoming much more friendly. "Stress agrees that's the only place we can put 'em, in a circle like that," pointing to the drawing with his finger.

Art studied the drawings intently for a few moments and then asked, "How about putting gages outside on the ears? Looks like that would be best."

Cal leaned back in his chair and contemplated the question a moment. "Well, I considered that but with them damned orange pickers assembling the vehicle at the Cape they'd be destroyed by handling." Cal leaned back in his chair and took a deep breath before continuing, "By the way, have you talked to a little company named StressCo here about installin' them things and doin' the testin'?"

Art acknowledged that he had not and Cal pulled out a local Hawkinsville phone book. "Write down this number and address. I've talked to 'em a lot and I think they're the ones you need, so go see 'em."

"How about today?"

Cal smiled at Art, obviously pleased. "Sonny, I believe you're gonna' move out. You come back over here any time."

Art drove to his building and entered the Program Office where Elmer was shuffling through huge stacks of paper trying to get his cable work started. "Hey, struck oil," Art cheerfully announced.

Elmer looked up momentarily and grinned as Art sat down across the littered table behind Elmer's desk. "Glad somebody did. I'm just gettin in deeper," Elmer replied, casting a hard look at the many drawings and specifications strewn across the table and piled in the floor. He asked, "What did you learn?"

"Got a spec. I think I'll go down to StressCo like Cal recommended after lunch and talk to them. Right now I'm going to run a copy for Engineering and get their inputs."

"Thought there was nobody in electrical that could support us," Elmer replied, looking quizzically at Art.

"There isn't, but I'll give 'em a copy to make 'em feel like they're part of the team anyhow," he replied with a furrowed brow.

"Good idea. We can make our own decisions, but who knows, they might have a good idea or two." Elmer turned back to his drawings and documents with a vengeance, as though he were about to tackle a real elephant in his back yard.

Art returned to his office to find Heidi coming out. "Oh, hi," she said with a big smile, looping her arm through his. "Chuck said you were out of the building."

"Yeah. I was. Come on in." He stroked her arm as she held tight and asked, "What can I do for you?"

"Not what can you do for me, dear boy. What I can do for you!" She giggled as she threw her long hair back and wiggled her hips at him.

Amused at her antics, he replied coyly, "What'd you have in mind?"

Heidi stepped closer, tightened her grip on his arm and tugged at him to follow. "I'm on break. Let's walk around the little park out back and get the kinks out."

She seemed insistent and Art, now sensing her feeling of urgency, agreed. As they approach the tall pines bordering a small grass area she said, "Chuck tells me you think your office is bugged."

"Well, Eddie thinks it might be. He used to be with the CIA and I respect his judgment."

"You're kidding!" she replied,

"No, but don't say anything. Sonny doesn't know and it would complicate our life more. Besides, it might upset our data sources."

"Well, you know you can trust me," she replied.

"I'm sure of that," Art said, still holding on to her arm.

"You bet you can, to the bitter end."

"Well, my beautiful friend, what's going on? You invited me out here to this park bench." he teased.

Heidi playfully pushed on his chest to signify to him to sit down on a bench under a large pine tree. When he had done so, she followed suit, sitting close as she could without actually pushing up against him. "I overheard Cig and Don discussing some things they found in your desk and I promised I'd let you know if I found or heard anything."

He looked off in space for a few moments and then at Heidi, who was studying his face intently. "I wasn't sure just who but I figured as much."

She watched him half admiringly and half in worry. Then she

grasped his hand and rubbed it, uncertain whether or not she should continue. "There's another rumor, too, that you ought to know."

"Oh, what's that?" he responded as he returned the caress on his hand and watched her smile.

"Sonny and Lissie have something going and it's pretty strong from what I hear."

Art put his hand on her shoulder. "I know. I also know you hate the son-of-a-bitch and with every right, too, but just forget that one. I don't want you involved because I don't want you hurt again. okay?"

He saw a tear well up in her eyes with all the old hurt trying to come to the surface. He wanted to take it away somehow, but there didn't seem to be a good way to do that. She responded quietly, remembering the night she had spent at the mercy of Sonny and his drunken cronies. "Thanks. I just don't want you hurt. I know they're out to get you."

"I know, but I want you to stay clear. Promise me you will."

"Okay. But I sure as hell don't want to see you hurt either."

He looked admiringly at the very beautiful girl sitting beside him and continued, "Baby, when it's all worked out maybe I'll tell you all about it. But I've just got some stuff to work through or quit a program I love. You know I really want to be a part of this. It's my world."

"I know and you should be a part of it." She hesitated, checked her watch and said grudgingly, "Well it's almost time for my break to be over, but you know you can count on me."

"Yeah, I sure do," he replied with an air of confidence. "It's good to have you for a friend, baby."

Art knew he should never visit a company to talk business, even technical business, without informing the procurement department. He thought this was reasonable and asked a clerk in Procurement who was handling the StressCo contracts. The lady looked at him strangely. "The who contract?" she asked impatiently.

"The StressCo contract," he repeated.

"Let me check the log." She pulled out a large book and thumbed through the pages. "We don't have that company."

"Oh. I didn't know. Who should I see?"

The secretary gave Art a sarcastic look. "What do you mean?

You want to contract with 'em?"

"No, not yet. Which buyer would handle the account if we did?"

"I'm sorry but I don't make those decisions. You'll have to see Mr. Van Monroe about that."

"Okay. Where do I find him?" he asked in an exasperated tone.

She pointed to an office three doors down a hall. "There. Whom shall I tell him is coming?"

Art had gotten tired of the game and when he looked sternly at her he saw she wouldn't return the gaze. He thought, *Ha! Chicken livered. Just a bluff.* "Just tell him that Mr. Cannon is here to see him."

Art was announced and explained his mission while Monroe leaned back in his chair skeptically. "I can't believe this. You're the first one of those people to come see us before goin' out to a vendor's plant. I've had a hell of a time about that."

"Really?" Art replied.

Van smiled big and continued, "You bet we'll support you." He pulled out a list of procurement people and asked, "How about a super sharp guy we just got in from the ship yards? Excellent man and he's not loaded up yet."

Art flinched and asked, "Does he understand our business, I mean, being from the shipyards and all?"

"Oh, hell yes," Van replied. "He's worked on large missile programs for the Air Force and for some of the large aircraft companies. He's held responsible positions. I think he used to be an old Air Force fighter pilot, too."

Art mulled this over before he said, "Sounds like my kind of guy."

Shortly he was ushered into the office of Charles M. "Tex" James by the large secretary, whose attitude had improved. Tex was sitting with his back to them on the phone when Art heard him say, "You bet I will. See you later."

Tex turned to face Art. Before he could say anything the secretary injected, almost like a rifle shot, "Tex, this is Art Cannon. Van asked me to bring him down."

"Yeah, I was just talking to him. Sit down," came the warm greeting from the tall, well-built man whose graying hair was beginning to get a little thin, but who had an experienced face with a big grin. Art noted the open collar and the easy, informal attitude and thought this one would do very well.

When Art was in a position to see a picture of a North American P-51D Mustang fighter in full battle dress on the wall he stepped back in admiration. "Damn, that's a beauty. If I ever can, I'm sure as hell going to own one of those."

Tex was grinning really big. "That one was mine during the war. We got shot down over France and I lost her. Had to bail out. I loved that ship. She was a really good one. I had some others after that but never one I liked as much as that one."

Art stared lovingly at the picture and finaly commented, "Those are dream planes now. Something every pilot that's worth a damn dreams of during his saner moments."

"Yeah, she was a beauty. Hated like hell when some damned Jerry shot holes in her tryin' to kill her."

"Well, I know you're busy. . .," Art started.

Tex jumped up out of his chair like he had been shot. "I know where I heard that name now!"

Art peered at Tex with a startled gaze. "What name?"

Excitedly Tex said, "You're the one somebody out at the airport told me about makin a single engine ILS in the middle of a hellish rainstorm a few months ago. Haulin' a dead body, too, wasn't it?"

"Yeah. Guess I'm guilty of that," Art replied with a grin. "But, hell, we've all been caught. I bet you could tell some better'n that, gettin shot down and all."

"Yeah. Reckon I could. Most fighter pilots could if they wanted to. But, hell, it's gonna' be good to work with a professional pilot."

"Well, I guess I gotta tell you I'm green with envy every time I get around one of you old P-51 drivers."

He blushed a little and propped his feet up on the desk, obviously comfortable. "Well, Van told me a little bit about what you want to do and I'm ready to help any way I can."

"Great!" Art replied.

"I think the first thing we need to do is to pay 'em a visit and look 'em over. If the Space Agency people know 'em they're probably okay," Tex continued enthusiastically.

Art grinned.

Tex dialed the number at StressCo and soon had an appointment with the president, Sam Kelley.

CHAPTER EIGHT

Tex and Art were greeted at StressCo in a makeshift lobby of an old building in a rather seedy part of town. The receptionist's youthful looks, long brown hair, blue eyes and innocent face gave the lobby a fresher look. As they entered the lobby she asked pleasantly, "May I help you?"

Tex, without cracking a smile, leaned down to the visitor's sign-in book required by security and answered, "Well, what did you have in mind?"

The girl, very self-assured, as though she had heard it before, answered, "Well, that depends on how much money you have."

As Art signed the register, a trim, stately, gray-headed gentleman neatly dressed with an open collar, appeared at the front lobby. "This is Mr. Kelly. This is Mr. Cannon and Mr. James from Space Corp," she said.

The old gentleman extended his hand. "Pleased to meet you. Come in."

He ushered them into his office that Art quickly surveyed. Not too plush nor was it totally sparse, about what he would expect for a growing, aggressive young company. It reflected taste with a certain amount of austerity, he thought.

"Well, Gentlemen, what can I do for you?" Kelly asked.

Tex began, "I believe you've been talking to the Space Agency about instrumentation and testing on the aft strut clevis units. Is that correct?"

He leaned back and considered his answer before he responded. "Yes, we had some meetings on how those things should be instrumented and tested. We think we're correct in our approach. This type of thing, as you may or may not know, is our main line of business."

Art peered studiously at Kelley as he asked, "Well, to be honest, nobody has ever done anything quite like this before, so we may plow some new ground. How about showing us around your plant."

"Sure. Be glad to. Call me Sam. We're an informal little company and titles don't mean much."

Tex grinned at Art as he responded, "I'm sure glad to hear that. Call me Tex and this is Art."

As they approached the lab where the testing would be done, Sam led them into a small adjacent office. "I want you to meet our chief designer, Edgar Randolph.

All shook hands and Edgar asked, "What kinds of load limits are you planning to test your units to?"

Tex looked at Art for an answer. "We'll need 400,000 pounds in both tension and compression. During the tests we'll take data and then analyze it at specific points to see how the gages are performing. Then we'll draw a calibration curve so we can measure loads during launch and flight." Edgar was listening intently, watching every hand motion and gesture that Art made in describing the operation of these force sensors. "This measurement is to determine the loading of the flight structure between the booster and external tank during launch through separation," Art added.

"That way you compare calculated values to actual measured loads. Sounds good," Edgar commented thoughtfully.

"Well, you see the importance of doin' this job right," Tex interjected.

Edgar nodded in agreement but looked perplexed. "Sure do. If we screw up, we could blow one of those things up, couldn't we?"

Well," Art replied, "let's hope the worst thing that would happen would be some lost measurements."

Sam quickly interrupted Edgar. "I'm sure we can work out the processes because we'll work with you every way we can."

Tex peered steely-eyed at Edgar and then at Sam. "If we should enter into a contract we expect to almost live with you."

Sam was beginning to squirm because he really wanted the business. "Tex," he started, "you tell me what you want and when you want it and it'll be done that way to that schedule. We'll worry about how we have to do it. I've been in this business a long time and I know what it takes to meet a schedule."

Art had begun to develop a warm feeling about Tex. Here's a real professional, he thought to himself. Sam and Edgar seem sincere, too. The plant looks good so far. Not great, but good. However, Sam said they are going to move into new quarters soon and that should remedy that problem. Art suggested, "Let's see your equipment."

"Sure. This way," Sam motioned as they left Edgar's office and entered the Force Lab. In the laboratory they saw a large, formidable looking Tinnius-Olson Press. "This unit will go up to 520,000 pounds force in both tension and compression and includes a standard load cell measurement system," Sam continued, pointing to a foot long cylindrical object six inches across, with large fittings on each end, "calibrated to National Bureau of Standards. We use that to make an independent measurement of input force loading."

"How do you take the data?" Art asked, looking around for a computer or some other data acquisition system.

Sam blinked a little, as if slightly embarrassed. "If we have a weak link, that's it. We take all our data by hand by reading a meter."

Edgar added, "Of course there are other considerations to this project, but I'm sure you know that."

Tex was shaking his head "no".

Art grinned slightly as he replied, "I know. A problem I have is placement of the gages and calibration with this odd shape."

Sam suggested they go back to the conference room and discuss the possibility of performing the job to Art's requirements.

For the next two hours they engaged in a technical discussion that included testing, theory of strain gages, system errors, system linearity, and other subjects. Finally Edgar asked, "What kind of a data acquisition system does the vehicle have?"

Art gave him a blank look. "I honestly don't know. The Space Agency people told us not to worry about that. They're still designing and say it'll work. Our job is to meet this specification."

Sam sounded like a Pentecostal preacher at a revival. "Cooperation is what you got when you deal with a small company like us because we ain't got all that damned bureaucratic bullshit. We can respond instantly."

Art looked at him quizzically as he asked with a grin, "Instantly? Do you really mean instantly?"

"Well, you know what I mean. We can be fast," Sam replied with a slight blush on his ruddy complexion.

On the way back to Space Corp. Art asked, "What do you think?"

"Well, they sure want the job. I got some references I want to check. Then if you still want 'em, I'll help you because I'm impressed with their can-do attitude."

"Yeah, I believe we'll get a fair shake from 'em," Art replied with a grin.

"I'll get the low dollar, too. I don't want them to know they're sole source yet because I'll issue a request for proposal and see what they come in with."

Art was disturbed, not knowing Tex any better than he did. "I don't want you to kill 'em on negotiations. I want 'em to have a fair price and a fair profit."

"Hey," Tex asserted, "I'm in total agreement. I'll be sure they get a fair profit and a fair price. But I'm not going to let 'em have an excessive profit and I'm not going to let 'em hide costs on me. I don't know these people yet but I will."

"Well, I got to be sure they do a good job and if they're short on funds they'll try to cut corners on us."

"I'll treat 'em fair or I won't be your buyer," Tex replied almost vehemently.

When Art arrived at his office he saw Eddie staring out the window with a frustrated look. "Hey, anything wrong?" he asked.

Eddie turned slowly. "I just had a big battle with Sonny. He just doesn't understand what the hell this logistics repair model is all about. He accused me of empire building and trying to circumvent his authority and of just a bunch of bull that even he doesn't know what he's talking about. I'm tired of it."

All Art's ebullience he had felt before was gone. He sat down at his desk after pouring what would be his last cup of coffee for the day. "What the hell does he want to do?"

"He wants to understand everything I do, every data source I consult, to approve everything I do ahead of time. Worst of all, he barely understands grammar school arithmetic. He knows nothing about calculus or tensors or any higher mathematics beyond grammar school arithmetic. He just doesn't understand."

Art leaned back, taking a long drink of coffee and swatted at a fly buzzing around his cup. Then he commented carefully, "I suppose all you can do is to try to play his game 'til you can get into the new group. Have you talked to Jerry yet?"

"No, but I will first thing tomorrow. I suppose they'll start searching my desk now, too."

"Yeah, you're probably right. Guess you need to plant something in there like we did in mine."

"Trouble is if you show him something he doesn't understand, he thinks you're trying to talk down to him and he gets defensive and hard to deal with. I've never seen such an ego. I can't do this model any other way that would make sense. If we put this thing on the computer using third grade arithmetic there's not a damned computer on the Space Center that could run the program, if you ever got the damned program written."

"I agree, buddy. Besides I don't know any languages that he would understand. Certainly not clear English."

"Yeah. By the way, he's after you, too, so be warned. I don't know what for but I can guess."

Just then Cig came in the door and scowled at Art. "Boy, are you in deep shit."

Art smirked cynically as he replied. "What else is new?"

"What's new? What's new? I'll tell you what's new! Sonny's pissed about you being AWOL. That's what's new."

Art shrugged his shoulders, closed his desk and walked out without another word. As he approached his car he thought to himself, *What a hell of a way to end a day that started off pretty good.*

Art entered the office building the next morning hating to leave the brilliant sunshine and the inviting sky. He looked up and thought, "Boy, I'd love to be up there pursuing the Old Master's "Lines and Symmetry." Art was thinking of one of his all-time heroes, Dwayne Cole, one of the great masters of aerobatics that he had watched in awe so many times, rolling, looping and tumbling with perfect precision through the sky. He wished again, as he had often done, that he had Cole's touch with an airplane. But then, almost no one else does. He grinned as his thoughts returned to reality. When he entered his office and saw Don and Cig making their usual trek to Sonny's office for their morning coffee and wondered what skullduggery would be hatched today. He knew all too well that they'd be down in about an hour or so and that Albert would be in just before 7:30 to check on himself, Chuck and Eddie. Before he could sit down the phone rang. He looked at his watch and saw it was only 7:20. *Can't be Sonny yet. Or can it?* He picked up the receiver: "Logistics. Cannon here."

"Cannon, I want you in my office at 8:30," Sonny roared.

"Okay. What you need?"

"I want you, mister," he yelled. Then *click*.

Art looked at the phone with disdain as Eddie walked in. "Don't tell me. Sonny called."

Art grinned slightly. "I didn't know it showed. Wonder why he put it off till 8:30?"

"Obvious," Eddie chided. "So he and the goons can have their morning meeting with coffee and cookies. You could be a part of that if you'd knuckle under and throw away your principles."

Art winked at him and chuckled. "Of course. Then where would I be?"

Eddie leaned back in his chair with his cup of coffee. "Buddy, we got to do something. We got to get clear of this mess. These people ain't got the foggiest notion of what they're doin'."

Art was about to reply when Jerry Strong entered the room. "Hi guys," Jerry greeted with a smile as went straight to the coffee pot. "How's it goin'?"

Art studied Jerry for a moment, as if measuring his reply carefully. "Jerry, you don't want to know. If you did you'd just get mad."

Jerry's mood became serious as he looked from Art to Eddie and back to Art. Finally he said, "Well, I can imagine. But I got some good news for Eddie. We've got the go-head for the computer center and I'm making an offer to Ben Carr, the one I told you about. I told Loren I was going to transfer you to a lead position because you have credentials that Ben needs."

Eddie's face suddenly became a big grin that Art hadn't seen for a while. He stood up and extended a hand gratefully. "Thanks, Jerry. I can't wait. I'll go now."

Jerry laughed at Eddie's enthusiasm. "Don't get impatient. It's gonna' take a little time to get it started. I just sent the offer out. He's got to accept, give notice and report in. Then I can transfer you in a week or so after that."

Eddie sat down and stared at the floor. "So we're talking about three weeks to a month?"

"Yeah," Jerry replied quietly, detecting the disappointment in his tone. "But hang in. We'll get there."

Eddie turned to Art and asked dejectedly, "Can we last a

month?"

"Sure we can. This looks like it might be good."

He stared at the floor again and then at Art. "Okay. If you can tolerate that damned Cat Fish for another month, so can I."

"What's going on? Do you guys have a problem?" Jerry asked.

They related the events of the last twenty-four hours about to Eddie's experience with Sonny's lack of understanding and Art's assumed battle coming at 8:30. Jerry's face turned red as he replied, "Shit. Loren's got to listen to reason. Maybe I made a mistake refusing him because then I could have tried to fire him. I'd recommend you don't go up there, Art, or maybe let me go with you."

"No. I can handle it. We've squared off before and I've learned how to get to him. Besides, it'll only cause you more problems with Loren if you interfere."

At the appointed time of 8:30 Art entered Sonny's office and greeted Lissie, who was sipping on her usual morning soda pop. "You're Cannon. Right?"

"Yep. I'm Cannon," he declared with gusto. Art was silently chuckling at her obvious effort of disassociation.

Suddenly, before Lissie could direct him into the office or announce him, Dean Aikins appeared in the door. "Have you seen Candy?"

Lissie looked at Dean as though she thought he had lost his senses. "Well, nut. No. I haven't seen her. Isn't she in her office where she's supposed to be?"

Dean saw Art, turned abruptly and walked out without another word. "Cannon is here." Lissie curtly announced, obviously annoyed.

"Send him in," came the rather civil-sounding reply from inside the room.

This quiet command was unexpected, especially considering others that had been issued recently with such vehemence. He entered the room, surprised to see Sonny alone and wondered, *Now what's he up to.* Art cautiously took a seat at the conference table. "You're a damned good engineer," Sonny started.

Apprehensively, Art squirmed in the seat because he had seen this approach before. "Well, thank you Sonny. I appreciate that," he replied cautiously.

"I've decided to make you a part of my inner circle and quit fighting. Would you like that?"

He was more suspicious than ever but decided to play out his hand and see where it led. "Well, it would be good if we could get along better," he replied cautiously.

Sonny leaned back and grinned. Suddenly his stomach heaved as he coughed from smoking too much. Art watched the large belt line to see if anything split but nothing did. Finally, after getting his coughing settled, he replied, "I knew you'd see it my way. We got a good thing going here and I need you to help me with it."

Art shifted positions and looked at him curiously. "Just what you got in mind?" he asked cautiously.

"I'm settin' up a new branch and I want you to head it up. I'm gonna' call it the Logistics Engineering Branch and we're going to do a lot of engineering design. You'll have Cig and Don as deputies." Sonny shifted his cigar a little, picked up his coffee cup and pointed it toward Art. "I know those guys can't run a branch the way you can, but they'll be a lot of help. What do you say?"

Art was uncomfortable wondering where the real catch was. He knew Sonny wouldn't throw out bait like this unless he was desperate for something. "Well Sonny, that sounds almost too good to be true . . ." he replied cautiously.

Sonny interrupted, "Hey, buddy, that's just the beginning of what I can do for you. The sky's the limit. Okay?"

"Suppose we did do that, what do I have to do to earn it?"

Sonny pulled a long draw on the cigar and leaned back in his chair. His eyes shifted from Art to the outside where the breeze was waving the pines back and forth. Then as suddenly as he had looked out, he turned back. "Do? You don't have to *do* anything. Of course, I'll need a little help along with problems but you can do that for me, can't you?"

Art felt a big knot trying to form in his stomach. He knew Sonny was trying to use him for something. He responded carefully, "Of course I'd help if I were on the inside, but I'm not aware of any problems."

"Yeah," Sonny beamed. "I got me one hell of a problem down there in your area with Rogers." Art grimaced as Sonny continued, "Rogers comes up with all that damned high falutin math shit that I don't understand and I know ain't worth nothin'. Anybody talks like that's up to no damned good. I think he's got a plot up with Jerry to try to take over this department and then you'd have to work for him. Hell, man, you hired him. It'd be an insult to have to work for him, too. I'm not sure he's all there anyhow." Sonny thumped the desk with a very big but very fat fist. Art almost choked to keep from bursting out laughing. He watched Sonny's very ample belly as it undulated under the strain of trying to solve a perceived problem the best way he knew how--fix a deal with another deal. Sonny droned on, "Then, too, you'll have to get out of that damned Program Office. Ghote don't give a shit about you and Elmer's just using you. I know that SOB and he ain't no good for nothin'. Thinks he's some kind of a damned doctor or something. Hell, he don't know one end of a fuckin pill from the other. What the shit does he know about bein' a doctor?"

Listening in disbelief at Sonny's rambling summation, he asked, "How long have I got to think about it?"

"Think about it?" he stormed. "Hell, I want an answer now. I ain't used to waitin'." Sonny impatiently shoved the phone across the desk. "Here," he roared. "Here's the phone. Call em' and tell 'em you changed your mind."

Art faked a sorrowful look. He was afraid to answer for a moment because of sarcasm he knew he couldn't hide. He drew a deep breath and finally replied, "Sonny, I'm not willing to give up the Program Office and I'm not worried about Ghote. I got no illusions about him."

Sonny choked on his cigar, stomped the floor, got out of his chair and started around the table. He suddenly thought better and retreated to his safety zone behind the desk as Art uncrossed his legs. He sat down in the chair hard, almost falling into it. Art watched the frame bend as though it were about to rupture. Then he yelled, "All I can say for you, is you're crazy! You don't give me no choice but to fire you!"

He felt this was the point that he and Sonny would eventually arrive at. "On what grounds?" he demanded, mustering up his best glare.

"Grounds? Hell." Sonny stormed, "I don't need no god damned grounds. I can't trust you or that damned Rogers, neither."

Sonny stood up again, his voice getting louder and more shrill with each word. "I call you in here and make you an offer that only a damned fool would refuse and you ain't grateful enough to take it? What kind of idiot are you?" He was breathing hard, holding his cigar between two fat fingers and waving both arms like a semaphore operator.

Art, raging inside, remained outwardly calm, frustrating Sonny even more. He knew Sonny couldn't deal with calm. "Sonny," he began, "you wanted me to give up something that's important. Those people need me. Then there's the other issue, you want me to spy on one of the best friends I've got. I'm sorry."

Sonny was beginning to hyperventilate while he paced back and forth carefully remaining in the sanctuary behind his desk. "Cannon, you're fired, go clean out your desk. Get out of here. You got fifteen minutes to clear the building."

Rage was taking over Art. He stood up and pointed his finger, growling, "You don't have grounds to fire me and more than that, you ain't got the guts to fire me. I defy you to fire me! You'll look silly as hell in court trying to defend yourself because you know I'll take care of you." Art, red in the face, glared at him and continued, "Further more, mister, I don't want your damned goons searching my desk or anything else I got. There's nothin there that's any of your damned business. I mean it. *STAY OUT.*"

Sonny was sputtering as though he didn't know what to say next. He stammered, like a kid caught with his hand in the cookie jar. "What you talkin' 'bout, boy? I ain't never been in your desk."

Art moved around the side of the desk closer to Sonny's sanctuary and spotted a copy of his telephone list sticking out from under some papers on Sonny's desk. He grabbed it and shoved it at Sonny as he replied sternly, "Don't you lie to me. Your goons stole this and hell only knows what else. But, fellah, I'll tell you one thing, every damned number on this list is official business. Now, get off my ass."

Sonny paled and sat down. He finally mumbled, "You won this one, buster, but watch me 'cause you might not win the next'n. Now get out."

Art scowled and stormed, "With pleasure." As he exited he saw Lissie coming in and decided to exercise her a bit, too, especially since he was in the mood. He pointed his finger at her, glared and roared, "Don't you forget my name's Cannon the next time you see me."

She was shocked and quickly moved out of the way. As he rounded the corner in the hallway he saw Lissie's daughter, Candy, and Dean Aikins in a close conversation at almost a whisper. Dean was looking at her like he wanted to get much closer. Art, still mad, glared at them and grunted, "Get the hell back to your hole and stay there." Dean looked like a wounded pig and grimaced as Art walked rapidly to the elevator.

He had momentarily forgotten about Heidi when he left the elevator. She looked up, smiled and asked gently, "Hey, you just bite a nail in two?"

"Does it show?" he asked, slowly regaining his composure.

"Must have been a big one. Want to talk about it?"

"I been up to Sonny's office and you know what that means," he replied as he approached her chair. He felt a flood of relief coming over him at just seeing her smiling and cheerful face.

Heidi laughed as she responded, "I can imagine, but remember what you told me once, 'Keep smiling no matter what because it makes them wonder what you're up to.' That's good advice."

Art ran his fingers through her long, soft hair and stroked the back of her head as she leaned forward for more. "Baby, you're a jewel. Thanks for being my friend. I wish we had more like you here."

Heidi blushed a little, adjusted her position in the chair so she would be a little closer as he stood by her, and looked up, eyes dancing with a broad smile on her face. "That goes two ways but I don't know about more. I don't want the competition."

He laughed and leaned down to look her straight in the eye with a big grin. She squirmed in her chair, as if to ward off the expected teasing. Art said affectionately, "Baby, you don't have any competition."

"Now that's what I wanted to hear."

"Heidi, I don't know what to do with you. For that matter I wouldn't know what to do without you either. You're a wonderful mess."

She giggled, "I know, I know." Then she became serious. "I sometimes wish it could be different, though, Art. Know what I mean?"

"Yeah but don't worry. It'll work out."

"I'm afraid not the way I want it to, though."

A tear appeared in her eye and as she quickly changed the subject. "Oh, by the way, you'll be interested in this . . ."

"In what?"

"I've seen Sonny and Candy going out at lunch a couple of times the last few days after he sent Lissie somewhere else. What do you suppose is going on up there?"

"You mean he's going out with the both of them?" Art stared at her in amazement.

"Appears so. I'll bet Lissie doesn't know it either."

"Wellllll," Art mused. "Ain't that something. Wonder if he's got 'em both in bed yet?"

Heidi laughed with her eyes twinkling. "You can bet he and Lissie aren't playing gin rummy in that motel over there. I hear Candy's got an apartment somewhere, so if they're going there that's cheaper on him"

"Don't kid yourself. This could get very expensive before it's over. I hear he's got a wife and two or three kids."

She frowned, feeling sorry for the wife. Art smiled at her, put his finger on the end of her nose and grinned, "Keep the faith, sweetheart, and keep your eyes open."

As Art entered his office Chuck jumped up from his chair and came around the desk. "What the hell did you do to Sonny?" he asked, almost panicked.

Having calmed down, mostly due to Heidi, Art started to laugh. "What do you mean?"

"Hell, Sonny just called down here and said to tell you he didn't really mean to fire you. I was scared shitless. What the hell went on up there?"

Art was about to relate the story when Eddie came in the office door. "Guess what I just saw?" he exclaimed excitedly.

"What?" Chuck asked eagerly.

Enthusiastically Eddie exclaimed, "I just saw the Cat Fish and Candy drive off."

Chuck was wide eyed and Art was laughing half in disbelief and half in cynicism. "You're kiddin?"

"I ain't kiddin. I saw it. She was sittin mighty close, too."

Art looked out the window and down the road as he asked, "Which way did they go?"

"They went toward the main gate." Eddie was excited as he continued, "We knew about Lissie, but, hell, what kind of operator can get both mother and daughter? He must be a dealer sure enough."

Art dialed Heidi and asked, "Hey, baby, did you see Sonny and Candy leave?"

"No," came the surprised answer. "But you know they could have gone out the back door. Did you see them?"

"No, but Eddie did. How about calling up there for Sonny and see what story you get. Then call me back."

"Call you right back."

Art hung up the phone and Chuck renewed the original question he asked before Eddie came in.

Art explained the proceedings of the last half hour or so to Chuck and Eddie while Eddie rocked back and forth in his chair laughing so hard he could hardly control himself. Chuck stared at Eddie with a scowl as he grunted, "I don't see what's so damned funny."

Eddie finally got control of himself and when he could again breathe comfortably, answered, "Hell, Chuck, Art faced him down. He knows he can't fire any of us for that matter. He'd have to deal with Jerry and he's too big a coward. I think it's funny."

Just then the phone rang. "Hey," came Heidi's familiar voice, "Mr. Catfish Leech has gone to a meeting at the headquarters building and won't return until after lunch. He left orders not to disturb him there. Then I called Candy to see if she was in and she had a dental appointment. She'll be back this afternoon, too. Looks like Eddie scored."

"Thanks beautiful. You do good work."

He turned and repeated what Heidi had just related as Eddie took out a notebook and started to make notes. Art watched curiously and asked, "What you writing down?"

"I want a record of this. I'm starting a notebook so I can keep it all straight."

Art quietly, matter-of-factly commented, "Yeah, ol' buddy, and you'll share it with Cig and Don, and Sonny, and all the rest." His face froze as his pen stopped. "Damn, I forgot about that. They haven't searched my desk yet but that don't mean they won't."

"That's right. The best way to keep a secret is to file it in your

132

head. Then there's no trail." Art stood up and started toward the door. "See you guys later. Got to see Elmer."

After a review of the statement of work for the aft strut clevis instrumentation project with Elmer, Art asked, "Well, Chief, are we ready to go for a contract?"

"Yep. Now we got to wait on the procurement process. Let's write a purchase order request and get it typed. How long do you think that will take?"

Art bounded up from his chair. "I'll have that done today. Then we can get on with it. I'll go see Tex and alert him that it's coming. Who does our typing?"

Elmer leaned back in his chair, obviously amused at the enthusiasm. "Well, whoever you can get. Do you have anybody in Logistics that types for you.?"

He thought for a moment. "No. Anything I do there I have to take to the typing pool. I'd rather not ask Lissie."

"I understand. We got a couple of people in this department but they're usually so snowed under they can't do anything quick."

Heidi flashed across his mind. "I know how if we don't get caught. She's supposed to type for the front office but she'll help me."

"Who you talkin about?"

"You know Heidi, on the front desk."

"No, but I sure wish to hell I did. She's one beautiful gal."

"Yeah, she sure is. I think she'll help me."

"Well, try your bootleg route first and then if that doesn't work, we'll try to push it through here."

Shortly Art was at Heidi's desk. "Hi, beautiful . . .," he started.

She smiled big as she teased, "Keep it up, I love it. However, I know you want something."

"Well, yes, I do . . ."

She interrupted with a laugh, "Name it. You got it."

"Gee, that was easy. I didn't expect you to give in that quick."

She grinned and moved her chair closer to her desk as though she were symbolically protecting herself. "For some people, I'm difficult. For others, I'm damned impossible. For you, name it."

"Well," he began, "since you're so cooperative, if I were nice would you do some typing for me?"

Still teasing, she looked up with her best pouty look. "Is that all you wanted. I'm disappointed." She watched Art's little blush and started to laugh. "Hey, I'm only teasing. You know I'll type anything for you. You're priority one."

He felt the blush fade and looked down at her smiling at the prospect. "Heidi, you're really impossible, did you know that?"

She officiously took the papers from his hand. "Only for almost everyone else in the world. Is this all you need?"

"Yeah, for now."

She motioned to the chair next to her desk. "Sit down. I'll only take a minute."

When she had finished, he put his arm around her shoulders and gave her a big squeeze, as she wriggled in closer. "Thanks a bunch," he said affectionately.

Art returned to his office to find Cig searching his file cabinet. "Can I help you?" he asked.

Cig jumped at being caught unexpectedly, "Uh, uh, no, I was just looking for the electrical requirements document. You got it?" He approached him with a straight, stony stare, "No, Cig, it's laying on your desk. There's nothing there that you or Sonny would be interested in."

Cig quickly looked at his desk. Feigning surprise and embarrassed at being caught, he exclaimed, "Well, well, there the damned thing is after all. How could I have missed it?"

Art glared at him without another word and thought, *I got to get reassigned soon.* Cig fumbled over to his desk and then walked out of the room without a word. He was sure Cig was on the way to Sonny's office to report. He gathered the documents to go with his purchase order request and assembled an orderly package with the neatly typed request on top. He noted it was quitting time and resolved to get the request into the procurement system tomorrow first thing.

As he approached his car he saw Heidi waiting by the driver's door. He was puzzled by her waiting after hours for him that long and then out by his car, too. "Hi beautiful. Waitin on me?" he greeted with some apprehension.

"Do you see that goon standing in the door talking to Loren Sharp?"

"Yeah. Danny you mean?"

"Did you know that he's going to the Cape to take over engineering?"

"That's what Loren said."

"Did he also tell you that goon hasn't the intelligence to find the toilet door if he had diarrhea? What's wrong with him? I heard them talking about it in Loren's office and all his big plans and everything. I got sick." She moved up against the car door and held her stomach as if to throw up.

"I know, Baby," he replied with a grin. He placed his hand on her arm and squeezed it gently. "That's their problem, isn't it? Let's not worry about it. Okay?"

"Cannon, I know you too well to know better than that. I care about this program and as little as even I know, I know a real loser when I see one."

He leaned closer, put his arm around her and ran his fingers up through the long brown hair scratching the back of her head gently. He felt her relax as she leaned up against him, the large breasts pressing against his shirt, presenting a firm pillow for his chest. He gave her a big, reassuring squeeze, for the moment feeling her soft body compliant with his. Then he looked at her as he fought to suppress the desire to invite her further. "Go on home, baby. We've worried enough for one day."

She poked him in the ribs with a playful jab, "Yeah, you're right. See you tomorrow." He watched her walk to her car as she seemingly floated across the parking lot, a pair of beautiful legs and a gorgeous body effortlessly working in perfect harmony.

After a good night's sleep, Art arrived at the office early and thought he'd start the office coffee before Chuck, who usually got there first. After everyone had poured their first fresh cup for the day, Eddie sat at his desk, feet propped up and leaned back in the government-gray swivel chair and announced, "Well, Jerry's guy accepted the job. I'm burning up to meet him. Sure hope he's everything Jerry thinks he is."

Chuck looked both disappointed and happy at the same time and commented quietly, "Sure hope that works out."

Art was lost in thought, wondering how he was going to escape into the Program Office, or somewhere where he could work uninhibited.. Eddie, looking contemplative, thumped the floor with his foot as a big grin came over his face. "Hell, maybe you should try to transfer into engineering and work a deal there, as bad as they need engineers."

Art considered this a few moments and finally responded, "Okay, you talked me into it. It just might work."

"Hell, it's worth a try," Eddie replied confidently. "The very worst is they can refuse you and if you don't try, then you'll never make it anyhow."

Art looked at Eddie a few moments and replied, "I agree, buddy. I'll give it my best shot. See you guys later," he said as he started out the door with his procurement package.

"You goin now?" Chuck asked, almost in despair, thinking of his own meager possibilities.

"Right now I'm going to procurement to start this contract."

As he entered the hallway he saw Connie coming in the end door a few minutes after the designated office hours starting time..

"Hello, there. I haven't seen you in several weeks, where you been?"

"Hi," came the pleasant reply. "I've been busy. Al's given me a lot of new responsibility and I'm trying to learn a new job. He's teaching me accounting."

Art felt a large jolt of concern. "What do you mean he's teaching you accounting? I always thought you went to school to learn that."

"Oh, I don't mean I'll be a CPA or anything like that. I'll just be a good accountant and then I can move up into a better job in the office later."

"Connie, just when are you learning this accounting?" Art asked suspiciously.

Connie looked uncomfortable and turned her head slightly, "Well, we've been working in the office, mostly. But he's just trying to help me. He really is and I think you've treated him unfairly. He's not at all like you described him. Not at all." The pitch in her voice was higher, which concerned Art even more.

He knew it wouldn't help to get mad or lecture, so he spoke gently. "Connie," he started slowly, "please be careful. I don't want to see you get messed up. Okay?"

"Okay. I promise." she relied evasively as she quickly turned to go up the stairs.

As he started to enter the lobby he saw Al Creude rushing in the front door in a hurry, also late and wondered if it were only coincidence that they were both late on the same day and about the same time.

"Mornin Al."

"What the hell's good about it?" he grunted as he rushed past Heidi and the front desk to the elevator.

"Didn't say it was good. Just said 'mornin'."

As Al disappeared up the stairs Art heard him mutter "Smart ass." After greeting Heidi with her usual exchange of pleasantries, he proceeded to procurement. He saw Tex entering his office with a disgusted look and sit down hard at his desk with his back to the door glaring at the speaker phone. "Mornin, Tex."

Tex turned around slowly and grumbled, "Shit! I'm glad you didn't say that with a 'Good' on it. Sit down."

"Anything wrong?"

Tex, in his usual methodical fashion leaned back in his chair with a scowl. "Wrong? Wrong? Here? Anything wrong? Hell no, nothin's wrong except that I got to work for a bunch of fuckin' idiots that don't understand the first thing about contracting and won't listen. I got two layers of management above me that couldn't go out and buy nails for their own damned coffin. Other'n that, everything's fine." Art noted a small sweat coming up on Tex's forehead as he stared bitterly at the wall.

Art was unsure about what to say next. He felt he had to say something instead of just looking dumb. Finally he asked, "Can I do anything?"

"No, I don't reckon," Tex replied disheartedly. "I'll just have to figure a way around those dumb bastards to get the job done and not go to jail. All I'm going to say, and you better never repeat it, is that when I get a competitive bid there's no way in hell that I'm going to fix it. Those sob's want me to take care of one of their buddies and I'm not in the business of takin' care of anybody. I'm in the business of doin' business exactly by the regulation. I ain't deviatin." Turning redder in the face, Tex pounded the desk with his fist as though he were taking out all his rage on it alone.

Art was concerned because he knew he had a tendency to high blood pressure. He asked quietly, trying to hold the disgust in his voice to a minimum to avoid upsetting Tex any further, "What did you do?"

"Hell, I pitched the damned file on Monroe's desk and told him I wouldn't touch it. I told the sob to get himself another buyer."

Art started to laugh and was relieved to see some of the tension draining off. "Bet that pissed him off."

"Let's say he weren't too happy about it," Tex laughed. "But, hell man, in this damned business, all we got is our integrity. We make mistakes the very best we can do but it's stupid to ask for trouble."

"I'm sure of that. Will he get somebody else to fix it?"

"Hell," Tex began as he got up and shut the door, "it goes on all the time with some of these guys. Some of 'em make more on the side than they do for salary. But they got trouble sleeping at night. I don't."

"I'm glad to hear you say that, Tex. It's gonna be a pleasure working with you."

Tex had by now returned to his normal, jovial self. He continued with a big grin, "I think we get on real good and we can do some good things here if we try. What you got?" pointing to the folder Art was holding.

"StressCo package and sole-source justification written up like you said. If it's okay with you, I'm ready to submit it."

Tex studied the file intently, checked the list of specifications and read the Statement of Work. "I just want to be sure that I don't ask somebody to do something that they don't have the capability or the information to do," Tex muttered as he studied the documentation. Finally he replied, "Looks great. Let's submit this for approval and I'll start to write the contract so when it gets back I'll be ready.

"Great. Come on and I'll buy you a cup of coffee."

Tex gave a hearty laugh and peered at Art over the top of his glasses. "You're on. By the way, when we goin flyin' in that Commander you got?"

When Art left Tex he had a feeling of accomplishment at getting his first procurement package out. He saw the movers packing various offices now for the move off the Space Center into new quarters and thought, "Guess I better get my stuff together." Then he remembered his resolve to see Elton Jones about a transfer to engineering as a means of circumventing Sonny until he could get in to the Program Office full time.

Shortly he saw Elton bending over a large set of drawings on a worktable, obviously intent on some portion of the electrical systems in the booster. "Hi, Elton. Can we talk a little?"

"Sure. Here or your place?"

"Here, if that's okay?"

"Sure. Sit down."

Elton pulled up an ash tray running over with ashes and old butts and inserted a cigarette between tobacco stained teeth. "What's on your mind?" he asked as he lit up.

"Well," Art began, "you know I'm formally attached to Logistics. I want to transfer into Engineering until I can get a permanent slot in the Program Office. Can you help me?"

Elton leaned back, took a deep draw on the cigarette and laughed as he responded, "Can't you get along with Sonny, either?"

Art felt he should not talk about his boss to a relative stranger. He considered the response and replied, "Well, you know he's difficult at best."

Elton leaned forward in the chair and emitted a hearty laugh that was somewhere between a shriek and a cackle, so virulent that it completely caught Art off guard. He hadn't expected Elton, a small, heavily bearded, slightly shriveled man, sixty plus years old and balding with nicotine stains all over his hands and teeth from chain smoking, to be capable of such a laugh. "Do I? That sob is impossible," he roared as he pounded the desk and rocked back in the chair. "I'll sign the transfer but you got to get Sonny to sign it, too."

Art was elated. "Great. But you understand it's temporary until I can get a slot in the Program Office. I don't want to mislead you."

"Oh, don't worry about that. You aren't misleading me. There's a lot we can do to support the Program Office and I'll work with you. But you'll be free to work with the Program Office, too."

Art smiled and shook Elton's hand. "I'll get the ball started now."

At personnel Maggie appeared to be alone. No sign of Dean, for which Art was just as glad. "Howdy, lady. I need your help," he said as he entered.

Maggie put her finger to her lips indicating to Art to be quiet. He looked at her curiously and then overheard Dean through his closed office door interviewing a candidate. "What do you like to do in your spare time, you know when you're not working?"

Then he heard the feminine voice reply very calmly, "Well, sir, in answer to that question and to the other question that you interrupted me in answering, whatever I do in my spare time is my business and I sure won't spend it with a personnel rep."

Art cackled out loud and Maggie almost choked trying to keep from bursting out laughing. "What's goin on in there?" he whispered.

She explained that the woman was already hired by directions from the home office and all Dean had to do was to process her in. "There's no way he can't hire her and she knows it," Maggie explained. "But you know that little pipsqueak. He'd mount a fireplug."

Art almost burst out laughing. "You mean he's trying to get next to her already. Hell, she hasn't even checked in yet."

"True. She's not checked in yet but from what I've been hearing she's damned well checked out. Dean hasn't got a chance." Maggie walked to the front counter and asked quietly, "What can I do for you?"

"Oh," Art chuckled, "I almost forgot. I need a transfer form."

Maggie gulped in surprise. "You're kidding. You really going to transfer from Sonny's group?"

"I'm gonna try."

"He'll kill you. That's the ultimate insult to that ego maniac. Have you got it arranged already? Because if you haven't he'll kill it."

"I think so. I'll get Jerry Strong to help me."

"Here's two forms, but be careful. I've seen some of the other people try and nobody's made it yet." Maggie was looking worried. She leaned over the counter close to Art and said quietly, "Let me know if I can help. If you figure it out, most of the others'll follow, too."

Art reached up and pushed gently on the end of Maggie's nose. "Okay," he laughed. "If I find the secret I'll tell you and you can sell it."

After carefully closing the office door Art and Eddie filled out one of the transfer forms and with a ceremonious stroke of the pen, signed it. "Done," Eddie cried in defiance. "If you get this through we all got a chance."

Art looked quizzically, "What do you mean?"

"Simple. Of all the people down here he thinks you're the biggest challenge and therefore he likes you least. But, I'm close."

Eddie jumped up with his coffee cup and held it high, almost spilling hot coffee, and began to chant, "A toast to the Cat Fish! A toast to the Cat Fish!"

Art leaned back in his chair laughing and between heaves, gasped, "Fellah, you're too much. Now I know why I've put up with you these last ten years. You're a damned nut."

Eddie walked over as though he were going to christen Art with the coffee. "Yeah, Yeah," he sang. "But I was sane before I met you and damned sane before I met Sonny." Then he chanted again, "A toast to the Cat Fish! A toast to the . . ." Just then Jerry opened the door with an astonished look.

"Anything wrong, Eddie?"

Eddie looked sheepish at getting caught in his antics but quickly responded in a high pitch, "Art's finally going to jump ship."

Jerry turned quickly. "What!" he exclaimed. "You're not quittin?"

He liked seeing the look of concern because it made him feel somehow still an important part of the group. "No. Better than that, I'm transferring," he said, shaking his head for emphasis.

Jerry sat down at the table beside Art's desk with a look of relief. "Hell, don't scare me like that. Where to?"

"Well," Art began, "Elton agreed to allow me to transfer to Engineering and continue working with the Program Office without interference. That means I can put my full time in there and won't have to worry with Sonny."

"That sounds good," Jerry replied. "But how well do you know Elton?"

"Not very well, but he seems okay."

"Neither do I, but I don't get good vibes. I know he's running electrical engineering, or at least he's supposed to be, although I still have a problem with Frank and Danny over that."

Eddie had settled down from his antics and asked quietly, "Danny still thinks he's running engineering and working for Frank, doesn't he?"

"Yeah, that's the problem. The other thing I came down to tell you guys is that I'm being replaced and transferred back to Arizona. My replacement will be in next week and I'll be here two more weeks after that."

Both Art and Eddie stared at Jerry in shocked silence. Fear gripped them, fear that everything they had accomplished so far would come to an abrupt end with Jerry's departure. Both knew that Art's path out of Logistics depended on Jerry's support and Eddie's departure depended on the new man coming in to run the Computer Department. Art got up, went to the window and looked out across the road at the ground hog hole. All three were silent for a few moments before Art commented, "Sometimes I think that old mama groundhog over there is a hell of a lot smarter than we are."

"Yeah, could be," Jerry responded quietly. "I don't want to leave yet." Jerry's face had taken on a serious, solemn look that Art had never seen before. He looked disappointed at leaving a job partly done and at leaving his good friends.

Art turned to lean against the window-sill and gazed at Jerry as though he still didn't quite believe what he had heard. When he continued, he said quietly, "You can't leave here. There's too much to be done."

"Well, I don't want this to go any further but I wasn't sent here permanently. It was always planned that I would go back to Arizona one day. However, Frank has hired my replacement about a year before I expected it."

Art responded with an acid tone, "I'm certain it's because you opposed him on issues like Sonny and Danny. I think he can't deal with somebody he thinks knows more than he does."

Jerry laughed lightly, almost sadistically, "Well, I wouldn't say that I know more than he does, but I think your analysis is pretty accurate. Anyhow, the new guy will be in next week. I just found out last night myself."

Eddie studied Jerry seriously for a moment, no more antics or joking. "Jerry," he started with a sad, serious tone, "this program is going to suffer and I mean it's going to suffer big. Doesn't he care about that?"

Jerry shifted uncomfortably in his chair and frowned. "He has one primary concern that's edicted on every corporate manager and that's his bottom line, his profit and sales. As long as that looks okay he'll survive."

Art shared Eddie's concern about the program. But even more, he was opposed to losing another good friend and especially one he considered an outstanding manager. "What's the new guy like?" he asked quietly.

"Don't know. All I know is that he's a retired Navy Rear Admiral. I don't know much about him except that he's supposed to have a lot of experience in Navy rockets. Hey guys, give him a chance. Okay? He doesn't know and he's comin in cold." Jerry was trying his best to play the corporate role ingrained in him for so many years and put a good face on the change even though he was opposed to it.

Art grinned as he said, "You know we'll give him every chance if he's okay. I just hate to see you leave."

"Yeah, guys, I'll miss you, too," Jerry continued. "However, Eddie, I'll get your transfer set up so you don't have a problem. Ben Carr will be in a couple of days and Art, if you have any problems with yours I'll try to help you, too. I got nothing to lose now."

After getting Elton's signature on his transfer paper Art decided to confront Sonny. He entered Sonny's outer office and noted Lissie's absence. He wondered where she might be this time of day and then heard a slight giggle from Sonny's office. She heard Art enter and suddenly appeared in the door. "What do you want, Cannon?"

"How about that? You remembered who I was. You're doing better," he commented sarcastically.

Lissie was not pleased. "Well, what you want?"

"I want to see Sonny."

She turned at an angle facing Sonny's desk, "Are you in?"

Art heard him growl, "Send him in. Go get us a cup of coffee. He won't be long, I guarantee." With that she swept past Art with her unseeing glare as she stalked into the hall.

"What the hell you want up here? I didn't call you."

He sat down at the conference table pulled endways to the desk and gave Sonny the best authoritative glare he could muster, expecting the worst. "I'm solving a problem for you." He handed him the transfer and pointed to the signature line. "Just sign there and your problems with me will be over."

Sonny picked up the piece of paper and glared at it. "That's a damned transfer!" He threw the paper on the table as though it were a serpent. "Hell no, I won't sign it. I'm gonna' keep you where I can watch you, smart ass. Tear that damned thing up, *NOW!*" he roared.

Art felt sick at the thought of not getting the transfer but resolved to fight to the end with whatever it took. "Look, Sonny," he tried to reason, "you know we don't get along and I'm trying to help us both by getting out. If you'll agree to the transfer I won't be a problem any more."

Sonny got up from his chair and walked around the desk to stand beside Art. He pointed a very fat, stubby forefinger with a very dirty nail at Art's nose and started to wag it up and down. "Mister, you'll always be a problem to me. I hate your guts, you and that damned Eddie Rogers. You think you're both so fuckin' smart. Cig told me about you calling me Cat Fish. Well, mister, I'll tell you right now, I run this damned show and you'll do what I shittin' tell you and I'm tellin' you that you'll tear that thing up *NOW.*"

He was beginning to get red in the face and Art sensed the conversation was going to get nasty before it got any better. He decided the best defense at this point might be a strong counterattack. "Sonny, I came up here to try to be nice," he began, "but you apparently don't know what that means. I want you to sign that transfer and I want you to sign it now!" he boomed.

Sonny got down in Art's face, breathing hard and exhaling a foul odor of heavy cigar smoke. "How the hell do you plan to make me do it, mister smart ass?"

Art's mind was racing and he decided the only thing left was to play dirty, too. "Sonny, you're goin to force the issue but if that's the way you want it, okay. I'll release all the pictures I took and then corporate won't have any recourse but to fire you."

Sonny was raging. He walked over and slammed the door and stormed back, "What you mean, boy, what you mean, pictures?" He was excited and Art felt the tide of battle was about to turn.

"You know damned well what I'm talkin' about, over at the Cross Inn, room 224 with Lissie and then at the Duck Inn, room 118 with Candy. I'll bet even Lissie don't know about that."

Sonny was beginning to breathe hard, his enormous stomach heaving in and out and threatening the puny-looking belt that was all there was between his trousers' survival and demise to the floor.

"How'd you know about that? How the hell did you know about that? You been followin me?" Sonny's volume and pitch were both increasing rapidly.

Art looked at him as steely-eyed and sternly as he could. "Your big ass really shines in the room. Lissie doesn't look too bad, either, but that Candy, now that's really something to see. She's sure got a cute ass." Art was bluffing for all he was worth, and starting to worry that Sonny would call the bluff. Then he thought, since he didn't really have any pictures, he could do no less than carry it to the end. "Want me to describe Candy's nipples to you, Sonny? Want to hear a recording of her when she comes?"

Sonny was pacing the room now like a wild man.

"Damn you, Cannon. Damn you. Damn you and that som'bitch Rogers too! Damn you both."

Art drove the bluff for all he could. He was feeling desperate to win and scared that he wouldn't. His thoughts of consequences if he lost were running like wildfire while he maintained an outer calm and cool that amazed even him. When Sonny walked around to his desk and sat down hard with a pale look, he knew he had captured him mentally but he had to get the signature. He instinctively decided to drive another stake into him while he was worrying about his job and Lissie. "Your wife and kids might care about this, too, Sonny. Now, I mean for you to sign this damned transfer and get me out of here or I'll make your fucking life so miserable you'll never survive. *Sign it!*" Art stormed, using his best courtroom tactics.

"You would, too, wouldn't you. " he snarled.

"You're fuckin' right I would Mister. Just try me."

Sonny's hands were shaking when he picked up a pen on his desk and signed the transfer paper. He slammed the pen down on the desk and screamed, "Get out of here. I don't never want to see you again. Get out."

With a great feeling of relief Art knew he had won. He reached for the transfer paper and shoved it into his pocket and then thought of the extra copy Maggie had given him. Then, with a feeling of renewed strength, he looked at Sonny as sternly as he could and said, "Thanks Cat Fish, but we ain't through yet."

Sonny jumped up. "What else you want?" he whined painfully.

Art jerked out the extra form and shoved it at Sonny. "Sign

this one, too."

"Ain't nobody's name on this'n" he feinted, trying to dodge the necessity of signing another one. Art grabbed the form and pulled out his pen. He wrote "Eddie Rogers" in the blank and then shoved it back at Sonny. "Sign! *NOW!*"

Sonny picked up his pen and with shaking fingers signed the form. Art grabbed the form from the desk and shoved it into his pocket with the other one. "See you, buddy," he gloated.

"You know this is blackmail, don't you? I could send you to prison for this," Sonny whined.

"I don't think you want to get too close to the law, mister." Art turned and walked swiftly toward the door.

Sonny was in a panic. "What about them damned pictures?" he yelled. "Where the hell are they?"

Art stopped at the door. "Don't worry. I won't show 'em to anybody."

Sonny looked up with a very pale face and smiled weakly. "You won't?"

Art grinned, savoring the sweet moments of triumph. "I promise I won't as long as you leave me alone. Thanks for the forms." Before Sonny could say anything else Art quickly exited the office and went directly to Personnel.

At personnel he saw Maggie at her desk in the rear of the office laughing so hard she had tears in her eyes. "What's so funny, Maggie?" he asked.

"Dean . . ." she gasped between breaths of laughter.

"Dean?"

"He had Candy in his office trying to put the make on her, right in the office."

Art looked at her in disbelief. "You got to be kiddin! Did he make it?"

Still laughing, Maggie replied between heaves of her chest, "Even she's got more sense than that. But she did agree to meet after work."

"Well, I'll be damned." He wanted to tell her about Candy's trysts with Sonny but thought better of it for now. "Be sure to see if he comes in the morning with a smile on his face and let me know, will you?"

"You bet I will. What can I do for you?"

With a quick flick of the wrist he handed her the transfer form.

"Process this for me, will you?"

She picked up the form and exclaimed in disbelief. "How the hell did you get this?"

"That's Sonny's signature, right there," Art replied, pointing to the proper line.

"Yeah, yeah, I know. How'd you do it? I want to know." She asked excitedly.

"Well, let's say that Sonny and I understand each other now. Not only that, but he signed one for Eddie, too."

Her mouth opened as though she wanted to say something but couldn't. She realized she was standing with her mouth open and quickly closed it. Then she began to quiz Art in earnest. "What happened?? I thought you'd have to kill him over this. How . . . tell me how . . ." she exclaimed excitedly.

"Well, let's just say we came to terms he can understand. Okay?"

"But, but, Art . . . I don't understand. How?"

"Better you don't know, baby. Just process it, and don't forget to let me know about Dean."

Eddie was at his desk going over a set of mathematical equations and curves he had plotted for his computer model. He glanced up as Art entered the room, "You just missed Jerry. He wanted to know what all the shouting was in Sonny's office. He said he could hear it down the hall. Did you have another run-in?" He was now looking seriously at Art and expecting the worst.   Art sat down on Eddie's desktop and leaned over quietly. "I got my damned transfer."

Eddie bounded up from his chair in surprise. "You did what? How the hell . . . ?"

"That's what the noise was about. Not only that, I got you one, too."

CHAPTER NINE

Space Corp's move to new quarters was conducted with the usual chaos. The Electrical Engineering department was temporarily housed in separate leased quarters in an empty area of another company nearby because of a lack of space in the new building. Elton assigned Art to the remote site with an office out in the middle of a big "bull pen" area along with everyone else in electrical engineering. The "small" cubicle contained some thirty people, which reinforced Art's philosophy that creative thought was impossible in a bull-pen environment.

Elton had placed Art's desk across the aisle from his office, the only private office in the area. For the moment that did not bother Art because he was spending most of his time in the Program Office working on Elmer's table. The most unsatisfactory part of separation from the rest of the company was from Eddie, Chuck, Heidi, and the program management office.

He had not seen Tex for the first week of the transition but decided he should go check progress on issuing his contract with StressCo. As he entered Tex's office on the first floor inside hallway of the new building, he was greeted with, "Where the hell you been? I been searchin this company over for you," Tex exclaimed. "We got to negotiate a contract tomorrow at "oh nine hundred". Can you go?"

Art, surprised, finally stammered, "Already?" as he sat down by Tex's desk.

Tex grinned and asked, "Did you think I wouldn't get it done?"

"I thought you'd do it but I didn't expect it this fast. It's only been three weeks since we started this thing."

"Hey man, don't ever let it be said that old Tex can't get the job done. Here's a cost breakdown."

Art took the sheaf of papers and began to study hours estimated and costs. He made a number of calculations and finally commented, "Looks like a fair composite rate, Tex."

"Yeah. Looks like they're gonna treat us good. I'll negotiate that some but I think it's fair. I won't try to get much out, if anything."

Art was pleased and decided to share the good news with Elmer. When he entered Elmer's new fourth floor office, still cluttered with boxes and books from the move, he saw Billy Ghote propped up in a chair beside the very cluttered table. "Come in," Elmer invited. Art slipped into the room and seated himself in a vacant chair at the opposite end of the table. "Billy was telling me he doesn't see any chance for the next little while to transfer you into this office permanently but he's working on it."

"Yeah," Billy grunted in his usual non-committal fashion, "I'll keep trying to get a slot. Since Jerry left and Harry Engle came in I don't know where I stand."

He stared thoughtfully at Billy for a moment before replying, "Don't worry about it. I got away from Sonny and so long as I can continue this way we'll be okay. But I do need a desk over here somewhere."

"How about if I put one in one of those empty cubicles out there?" Billy replied, pointing to an area of the floor that was as yet unoccupied and intended for bull pen type of offices with the classical junior walls. Art didn't like junior walls because of the noise that flowed over them and the lack of privacy but for an interim solution, he was willing to accept it, especially if it could cement his relationship further with the project office.

"Great. Then I could move all the files back over here and keep it all closer together."

"Okay. But let me tell you something. Keep an eye on Jones. He's been around Danny too long."

Elmer crossed his legs and leaned back, as was his manner when he was about to say something he thought was profound. "Billy, you don't trust anybody. He only worked for Danny for about six months."

"Don't you think that's six months too long? And you're right, I don't trust nobody. I learned that on the San Francisco police force, so watch it." Billy chuckled and bounded out the door to answer his phone.

Art relayed the news of the impending negotiation while Elmer smiled at his enthusiasm for the project. When he finished, Elmer replied: "Okay, go negotiate it and then run it. We need some good hardware out of those people."

Art felt good to see this display of confidence. Then out of courtesy, he asked, "Do you want to go?"

"Why? You can handle it."

"Well, sure. But I thought you might like to sit in."

"Hell, I got more to do than I know what to do with now. I don't want to hear anything unless you got something you can't fix."

He felt his blood rush a little with excitement. "All right buddy. It's in good hands," he replied with a grin.

"But don't forget to put it on the master schedule board for the monthly reviews with the Space Agency." We're going to start giving monthly presentations on program status and you'll have to present all your projects and defend 'em before the Space Agency management."

Art was somewhat taken aback at this new development. "I thought you'd do that."

"Nope. I don't plan to know all the details of your programs like you will."

This was good news. Art felt now that he was really a member of the team. "What kind of charts do they want?"

"Oh, you know, the typical schedule chart that shows status and deliveries of your hardware, where you are in meeting that schedule and an outline of problems."

"What kind of problems do they want?"

"All, I guess," Elmer countered. "Technical, schedule, cost overruns or underruns, and your concerns. Their program management office needs to know how we're progressing so they can manage the program from their side. We'll have to work together as a team."

Art sat for a moment looking studious before asking, "By the way, which cubicle do you think I should move into?"

He thought for a moment and then stood up. "Lets go pick one before anybody else gets to that space." They examined the empty area and selected one. "Too bad we don't have a desk to put in there now," Elmer said.

Art's mind was racing about how to protect his 'squatters' rights. Peering into the vacant area, he spotted a large cardboard box that had been left by the movers. "Look there, a desk," he said as he pointed. "Help me carry that thing over here and we'll create an office."

Elmer was thoroughly puzzled. "How the hell you gonna do that?"

"Just watch," Art replied gleefully. He carried the box into the cubicle and laid it on it's side, carefully positioning it as one would a desk and stood back to survey it. "Looks okay. Now let's get one of Billy's extra chairs to sit by it and then put a bunch of papers on top." Shortly he emerged with a chair with Billy laughing at the scheme. He placed it beside the box and continued, "See? Now lets get some of those old folders and put on it and I'll put my name on the post here on a piece of masking tape and then we'll be in business."

Elmer grinned and said, "We're in business. Looks like the Dynamic Duo struck again. Next we got to steal an extra desk and desk chair."

"Don't worry, I'll take care of that. Ralph, down in the store room owes me a favor or two."

As Art prepared to leave the building he stopped at the new supply room and greeted Ralph Garner, who was busy unpacking boxes and putting materials on his new store room shelves. Ralph looked up and greeted him with a smile, "I'm up to my fanny in boxes. How you doing?"

"Fine, but I need some help if you can do it."

Ralph flashed a big grin. "Just name it, you got it."

"I need a desk and a chair put in a cubicle upstairs there where I'm settin up shop. Can you help me?"

Ralph nodded at a series of new desks still in the cartons. "I'm supposed to have authorizations for all that furniture to be moved." Art looked a little disappointed and started to excuse him from the request but Ralph raised his hand: "But they's somethin' they don't know."

"What's that?"

"The folks in accounting screwed up. Those people don't seem to know what the hell's goin on anymore. They's a bunch of them desks and chairs that's not on the property books but they're company property. How many do you want?"

He felt a surge of adrenalin. "Oh, just one, and a chair."

Ralph grinned as he replied, "Want a wooden one and an overstuffed chair?"

"Hell no," Art gulped. "I want a used, Government gray desk with a used government gray chair and a file cabinet. I don't want to attract that kind of attention."

"How about one of the new brown metal ones that belong to the company? I'm gonna replace all those program people's desks with those in a couple of days anyhow."

"Great. If you're going to give those to everybody up there. I don't want to look conspicuous."

"Well, that's what I thought I'd do with 'em. You might's well have one too."

"Gee, I really appreciate it."

"Not nearly as much as my kids appreciated that airplane ride. They're still talkin 'bout that."

The next morning Art failed to check in with engineering because of the impending negotiation he and Tex had with StressCo and instead he went directly to the program management office. He found Elmer standing in the door in amazement. "What's up, Elmer?"

"Have you seen your damned cubicle?"

"No, not yet."

Elmer shook his head as he motioned Art to follow him. As they approached the cubicle in front of them, with all the shine brand new furniture could have, was a gleaming new desk, chair, and file cabinet. Elmer looked at Art for a moment and then finally managed to say, "Look at that. If I didn't know better, I'd say you were mafia or one hell of a dealer. We can't even get this stuff."

Art couldn't resist the temptation to tease his friend a little. "Well, would you all like some of that?"

"Seriously?"

Art couldn't keep it in any longer. "You guys are gonna get this, too. I don't want to be conspicuous, but If you want anything, let me know and I'll try. I won't guarantee, but I'll try."

Elmer peered across his glasses with a very studied look. "You know, I'm beginning to believe you, the way you got away from Sonny and pulled that slicker into engineering. I heard that you got Rogers out, too. Is that true?"

"Yeah. I had a hand in it," Art replied jovially with a quick sweeping hand gesture. "He wanted out as bad as I did."

Elmer sat down, picked up his coffee cup and gleefully declared, "Well, I got to toast the biggest comshaw artist in the company. By the way, when do we get ours?"

"Oh, I think probably in a couple of days. I still got to get a phone and speakin of phone, guess I better call over to the other building and report in."

Elmer, still shaking his head, watched Art as he dialed the number. "Welcome aboard. Billy's gonna shit when he sees this."

Clara, the tall, willowy, very beautiful black girl who ran the secretarial desk in Engineering, heard the phone ring at Art's other desk. As she leaned over to answer it, Elton Jones appeared in front of her. "Where's Art this morning? You seen him?"

Clara held up her finger for a moment's pause. "Engineering, Clara."

Art announced his location over at the Program Office and informed Clara that he was going to go out and negotiate a contract in a few minutes. She acknowledged his statement and then said, "Hold on a sec, Art."

She turned to Elton, "It's Art. He's going to negotiate a contract."

"Let me speak to him." Elton grunted gruffly as he took the phone from her hand. "Art, I would appreciate it if you'd check in here first," he began sarcastically.

Art was surprised to hear this tone and replied cautiously, "Gee, Elton, I didn't know I was supposed to. We didn't discuss that."

"Yeah, I know. That was down in the fine print. Since you work for me I need to know where you are and what you're doing all the time."

"Well, okay. I don't have any problem with that but sometimes I might not be able to check in there and then drive over here."

"Well, when you can't come over on regular time, you can come in early and sign out or you can call me and tell me and I'll sign you out. I'll be here."

Art had a sinking feeling and was afraid that he had another situation similar to the one he was in before. He thanked Elton and sat down in Elmer's chair beside his work-table with a troubled look.

Elmer peered at Art over his glasses and asked, "What did you know about him before you transferred?"

Art shot a quick glance at Elmer and without a word, got up and went over to the coffee pot in the hallway outside the office. When he returned he sat down and said quietly, "I really didn't know anything about him, except that he seemed to be a nice guy and acted like he wanted to help me get away from Sonny. Maybe Billy is right."

Elmer leaned back and slowly answered, "He often is but there's a couple of things you need to know about Jones. First, that he has a degree in Electrical Engineering but it's an old degree from the late thirties. He hasn't kept up at all so I don't consider him much of an engineer. He went back to school and got himself another pair of degrees in Philosophy. Billy and I are convinced he was trying to figure himself out moreso than anybody else."

"You're kiddin?"

"No. Danny brought him in because he thought he could control him. He wasn't really interested in helping you as much as he was in getting a shot at Sonny. They quarrel frequently and dislike each other intensely."

"That's interesting. I never knew they quarreled."

"Well, the next thing is that you're the only bonafide engineer he's got, or at least the only one that knows anything about rockets and he's not going to turn you loose if he can help it. I was afraid he'd want you down there solving his problems."

"Hell," Art exclaimed defiantly. "I thought we had that problem worked. I'll have to deal with him differently than Sonny. I could blast Sonny and manipulate him. I'll have to study this one a little, but now I got to meet Tex and get out to StressCo."

"Hey, good luck out there. Elton's goin' to have a fit when he sees your office over here so be thinkin' about it."

"I'll see you when I get back. We've got to figure out somethin, 'cause this one's a lot smarter than Sonny."

As they drove to StressCo in Art's old Buick, Art turned to Tex, who was beaming brightly at the prospect of getting this contract in place. "Do you know Elton Jones?"

"Yeah, slightly. What about him?"

"Well," he said quietly, "I work for him now."

Tex turned his head quickly with a surprised look. "I didn't

154

know that. When did that happen."

He was quiet for a moment. "Last week. Now I'm worried."

"Don't tell me, let me guess. He's started to put the screws on you. Right?"

"Yep, I'm afraid he's trying to do that."

"Well" Tex said quietly, "let me tell you how I got him figured. He's a hell of a nice guy until you work for him. The truth is he's scared shitless of his shadow. He's making a move to take that department over since Danny's left. He don't trust anybody and he'll do anything he can to control you. But, mind you, it'll be subtle and quiet."

"Yeah, that's the impression I'm getting, too, and it worries me. I don't want to work in his department and we agreed it would be just a parking place for me until Billy could get me a place in his group."

As they entered the driveway at StressCo Tex looked up with the true skepticism of a contract negotiator as he commented, "You believed him without a written contract. I got to teach you how to negotiate, boy, providing he don't do you in."

At the front entrance, Art laughed and pointed his finger. "You ought to know better'n that, Tex. I'll just have to find a way to work around him."

In the lobby of StressCo they met Sam and his accountant, Randall Eversley. "Well, gentlemen," Sam said jovially, "I see you made it okay. Come on in. We got a fresh pot of coffee in the conference room."

After all were seated in the conference room, Tex outfumbled Sam for the end seat at the conference table, which Art had learned was a strategic advantage. Sam called, "Tina, come pour some coffee and bring in the doughnuts." Then he looked at Tex for approval.

Tex had a noncommittal look on his face. Sam took note and asked cautiously, "That's okay isn't it. You don't consider this a gratuity or anything do you?"

"If you could buy me for that, I don't need to be here," Tex commented dryly, using all the psychology he had learned over the years as a contract negotiator. He opened his copy of the proposal and laid it on the table and began with, "This price is ridiculous. I sure as hell ain't goin to buy that."

Sam choked and Randall squirmed. "You mean you don't like

the price?" Sam hedged, trying to recover from the initial shock.

"Hell no. I ain't about to buy no bottom line price until I know exactly what goes into it and what I'm getting for my money."

After two hours of intense discussion and examination of every part of the proposal, including the technical approach and management, Tex studied Sam intently for a moment, considering the position he had arrived at.. He noted the worried look on Sam's face with the sweat inching down his forehead. Tex began an intense set of calculations with tape spewing from his calculator like spaghetti. Suddenly, he paused and looked at Sam with a big grin. He extended his hand. "Done on that part." Then he turned to Art and asked, "You got any further questions?"

Art replied, "Oh, yeah. I've got a big one."

Tex pointed to the table. "Let's get it out right here."

Sam looked nervous again and began to fidget. "What is it? Is there another problem?"

"Not yet, Sam, but there will be." Art pulled out a sheaf of papers and began, "Go to your sheet where you proposed quality inspection hours."

He fumbled nervously through the papers. Randall finally pulled out the sheet and laid it in front of Sam, who appeared to study it intently for a moment. Then he peered at Art over the top of his glasses and asked cautiously, "What's wrong?"

Art grinned at Sam and began, "Sam, do you think you can really build this hardware with those inspection hours?"

Sam squinted and shifted his position as though the chair had suddenly become uncomfortable. Art was carefully watching the body language and knew that Tex had already analyzed it. "Well, they may be a little shy but we're willing to give you that free if we needed more."

Tex thumped the table with his fist, startling Randall and Sam. "Rule one fellas. Don't forget it. I pay for everything I get. I pay a fair price and I damned well get what I pay for. I don't want any more than I pay for and I sure as hell ain't ever gonna take less. You people are here to make a fair profit. You can't do it that way and you know it."

Tex asked Art, "What do they need to do that job right?"

Art smiled, glad for the support. "Well, it's my opinion that using a half-man effort on this job when the assembly people are installing instruments and testing isn't enough. I think they need a full man monitoring, working data and writing test procedures."

Tex had calmed down and took his estimate form, studied it a moment and said, "Okay, we'll double those hours."

Sam stared in disbelief. "Tex, in all the years I been negotiating contracts I ain't never had a customer put more hours in. Usually they want to take it out."

Tex smiled and pointed his finger at Sam. "Then you ain't never had one more serious about doin' a good job. I can't stress that enough. This is important work, man. I ain't gonna accept anything but right." Tex thumped the table with his forefinger for emphasis.

Sam looked pleased as he said, "Tex, I feel good about the hours now. I'll admit I had some worries before."

"Good. And I'm sure you don't expect me to pay you fifteen percent profit either."

Sam grinned like a Cheshire cat. "We'd like it."

Art chuckled as Tex continued, "Yeah, but you know I ain't gonna do that. I'll make you one offer and if we can agree on that we'll be done."

"What's that?" Sam was eager now.

"Eight and one-half percent profit and that's a half percent over what I usually allow big companies, but I know you're small and growing."

Sam looked serious for a moment, pulled an envelope from his pocket and scribbled on it. Art silently laughed because he knew Sam was going to counteroffer at ten percent, which was where Tex had wanted to get to in the beginning. Finally Sam smiled and said, "How about ten?"

Tex countered, "I'll split it with you, but hell, I hate to go that much."

Sam grinned and said with a gusty thump on the table, "Done. I'll take nine and one-quarter percent profit. Do we have a contract?"

Tex stood up and extended his hand to Sam. "Sir, we have a contract."

As they drove back to the office Art was mulling over the events he had just witnessed. He noticed Tex intently watching some cows out the window with a satisfied expression on his face. "Tex, I think we got a good contract and I think we got a good contractor."

Tex grinned and gently slapped him on the shoulder. "You nearly blew him out by adding hours onto the contract. He ain't used to that."

Art laughed so hard he almost ran off the road. "I know. He didn't quite know what to make of it. But I want him to have the manpower to do a good job."

"Yeah. If a company isn't happy with the contract they won't do a good job and they'll try to dollar you to death. You'll have to watch it technically and I'll watch the contract side."

Art replied with a big grin, "Soon as you get the contract out there I'll start transfer of new strut clevises and we can get rolling."

Tex pulled out some notes and studied them for a moment. "If you want, I'll give him an advance authorization to proceed and he can get started ordering his parts and material."

"Great. I wasn't aware you could do that."

Tex looked at Art with a kiddish grin, "Hell fellah, your contracting officer can do anything. So far as your contract is concerned he's almost God himself."

When he arrived at the Program Office Ralph's moving crew was placing new furniture into Billy and Elmer's offices. Elmer grinned and commented, "Boy, you did it this time. This is great. They gave me a whole new compliment of furniture, even a credenza. We should 'a had you up here a long time ago."

Art laughed as Billy approached. "How the hell did you do that, Cannon?" he asked abruptly.

Art grinned at Billy, not wanting to say too much but feeling he had to say something fast. "Billy, I always take care of my friends. Don't ask, just enjoy."

"Well, I'm glad to see Elmer picked help that can make deals. If I'd 'a done it, I wouldn't tell you how neither."

"I know," Art replied with a grin.

Art invited Elmer into his newly furnished cubicle and sat down on the new furniture. Elmer sat quietly for a moment surveying the newness of everything before commenting, "I still say Elton will shit when he sees this." Then he asked, "How'd the negotiation go at StressCo?"

Art laid a magazine on the desk before propping his feet up so as to not scratch the new finish, "Well, that's what I came to tell you about."

He gave Elmer a detailed account of the negotiations and studied him intently to see if he was satisfied. Elmer slid back in the new chair and watched Art for a moment before replying, "Sounds good. I'm glad you made 'em put the inspection hours back in, too."

"Well, I just believe in a good quality program on flight hardware," Art replied.

Elmer raised up in the chair and surveyed the office area. He stopped at the location of the coffee pot and thought for a moment. "The only drawback now is the proximity of the coffee pot. We got to do something about that and we'll have it made. By the way, you had a call from somebody named Bob Strothers, or something like that. Know him?"

"Yeah, he's the lawyer from Toponacah, Georgia that I told you about, the one that I've got to appear in court as an expert witness for."

"Oh yeah. I remember him. Is the case set?"

"Must be. Guess I better call him tonight and see."

"You'll have to go to court on that, won't you?"

"Yeah, federal court."

Elmer flinched and frowned, "Hell I ain't never been to court. I don't know how I'd do with that."

Art chuckled at Elmer's curiosity. "They're just people, too, out there trying to do the best job they can for their clients."

"Well," Elmer said, as he got up, "let me know when you need to go and I'll cover for you. Better let Elton know, too."

That night Art called Bob Strothers and made arrangements to appear in court under subpoena. He always liked to have the attorneys subpoena him when he appeared as a witness to preclude any question of his court appearance. The next morning Art dutifully checked into Engineering where he saw Elton sitting in his office and decided this was a good time to inform him of the impending trip. "Mornin', Chief. How's it goin'?" he greeted pleasantly.

"Good morning," Elton said bruskly, while taking a drink from his cup of hot coffee he had just poured and laying down his cigarette in the overflowing ashtray. "Glad to see you checking in."

"Oh, that's no problem, but I thought I better let you know that I have been subpoenaed as a witness in a trial on the 28th and I'll have to be in Atlanta on the 27th."

Elton looked startled. "What kind of a trial?"

"Aircraft accident. I'm the expert witness. I was asked to investigate and arrive at the cause. Then I have to testify about my findings in court. You know the routine."

Elton looked disturbed and faced Art with a disapproving frown. "You know company policy doesn't allow that kind of thing, don't you? You got to get approval to work outside the company."

Art grinned good-naturedly as he answered, "Yeah, I know, but this case was one I had prior to my employment. I discussed it when I was hired and was assured there's no problem. Besides, they're issuing a federal subpoena for me."

Elton, still looking troubled, asked, "What kind of accident? I don't know if I can approve this or not."

Art was rapidly becoming impatient. "Well, Elton, all I can say right now is that it's an aircraft accident that happened on the western coast of Florida and I can't discuss it. After the trial I'll tell you about it."

He was not satisfied. He continued, "Well, you better let me know where you are at all times so I can call if I need you. You know you're working on some pretty important stuff here. Who's going to cover for you?"

He looked steadily at Elton, who was fidgeting in his chair. "I've already made arrangements with Elmer." He reached into his shirt pocket and pulled out a folded sheet of paper. "Here's the hotel and phone numbers and the clerk of the court at the federal court building. Is there anything else that you'd like?"

"You got any more of these things around anywhere?"

Art was trying to not let his frustration show. "No, this is all and I made a full disclosure about this one when I came here."

"Well," Elton began slowly, as if thinking deeply. "I guess you can go but you'll have to take leave without pay."

"No problem." Art excused himself from Elton's office and signed out on the sign-out board.

As he completed the sign-out, Clara, who had been sitting quietly observing the proceedings commented, "Gave you a pretty rough time, huh?"

"Yeah, Clara. But it's okay."

She looked at Art. "I hope I can make it. I'm about fed up,

too. He's changed so much since Danny left. Doesn't trust anybody at all."

Art patted her on the top of the head, where he liked to pat her when he was teasing her. "Baby, we'll be okay. Just hang in there with me. You're important as hell here and don't forget that."

Clara grinned and then started to giggle as she teased, "Brother, for a honkie, you're okay. I'm glad you're here."

"Yeah, me too, baby. You and a few others make this mess worthwhile."

"You know you can't see me blush, but I am," she answered with a big grin.

As Art entered the new building where most of the company was located except for the Engineering group, he saw Heidi sitting at the front desk in the lobby, as she had done in the old facility on the Space Center. "Hi beautiful," he called.

"Hello yourself. You been avoiding me?"

"Hell no. You know better than that," he replied as he walked over to her desk.

"Well, I just been missing seeing you as much as I did over at the old place. How's your new position in Engineering working out?" Art grinned at her inquisitiveness. "Well, it's interesting to say the least. You know I got an office over here, too."

"Yeah. I already been up there but you were gone. It must be nice to be important and have two offices."

Art was afraid he had disappointed her. He leaned over the desk to stroke the long hair and kissed her lightly on the forehead as she leaned forward to get closer. "Baby, you're important, too. Especially to me."

She quietly replied, "I know. It's friends like you and a few others around here that keep me goin'. I've been thinkin' of quittin', though."

Art was shocked. He straightened up and sat down on the edge of the desk, placing his hand on hers. "I'd sure hate to see you do that."

"Yeah, I know," Heidi answered quietly as she rubbed the top of his hand with her free one. "But I can't forget that damned Sonny and what they did to me, and the way that hussy Lissie and that damned daughter of hers treat me. I think they know."

"Baby," Art began, moving to a chair beside her desk, "You got to let it go. Put it away and forget it. You've got too much ahead of you to dwell on that."

"I know what you're saying and I appreciate it and I appreciate you. But every time I see him or one of his damned henchmen or that damned hussy or daughter, it all comes back. I hate those people."

"Heidi," Art pleaded, "you've done well and I don't blame you for hating them. They're the dregs of civilization, but don't let it destroy you."

"If it doesn't, it's all because of you. You know that, don't you?" she replied, squeezing his hand harder.

Art stroked the back of her head and stood up beside her as he replied,. "Baby, you're tough and you can do it, but I understand. All I ask is for you to consider it for a while before you actually do it."

"By the way," she continued with a cynical laugh, "little Dean Aikins has been hanging out with Lissie's daughter, Candy. Did you know that?"

Art laughed as he turned toward the elevator, "I suspected that but they probably deserve each other. Does Dean know she's shacking up with Sonny?"

"No. I'm sure he doesn't. It would be interesting to see him find out, don't you think?" She started to laugh at the thought of such a revelation.

"Now Heidi," Art teased. "If he finds out it won't be from us."

"You're right about that. I ain't gonna get involved nohow for no reason." She grinned, now having recovered from the moments of sadness that still emerged from time to time. "Oh, I meant to tell you the other sad story, too, about Connie."

Art's attention was instantly focused, "What's wrong with Connie? I haven't seen her in a month or so."

"She's been avoiding you. She's seeing Al on the sly now. I see them out sometimes and see them come and go. Of course, from here in the lobby I can see a lot that other people can't see, too."

Art looked down at the floor for a moment and shook his head as though he were in deep thought. "Damn." he exclaimed.

"Hey," she said gently, trying to console him, "Connie's a big girl. She's got to make her own decisions and her own mistakes.

Nobody can make 'em for her."

Art finally replied in a quiet, painful tone, "I know, but she's so young and had so much to offer. I hate to see her get all screwed up now."

"Now listen to old mother hen a minute. Stay out of it. Let her make her own decisions."

"Yeah, I will, but I sure hate to see it."

"I know I'm right. Besides," she giggled, "you got me to worry about now."

"Yeah, but you're a whole different matter. You got your head bolted on straight and I know you're going to do okay."

"Think so?"

"Yep. It's such a shame, her new husband of only six months and her new house. Oh Well."

Art went to the Program Office, placed his files in the new file cabinet and then into Elmer's office where he was busily working on a cable wiring list. "Have you figured out all the cables in that thing yet?" he asked.

Elmer leaned back and blinked his tired eyes. "What do you think?"

"Well, knowing you, I'll bet you're close."

"You know these damned cables are always the last thing to be defined and the first thing they want when assembly builds up a booster stage. There's no way for me to get caught up. I'll always be behind and I know I'll always have last minute design changes. How's the clevis contract?"

Art settled himself down in one of Elmer's new chairs and stretched out his legs under the table. "It's working well," he answered. "They've ordered all the materials and I've had our shipping department transfer all the clevises to 'em, six full flight sets and one set of spares, total of forty-two units. Guess I'll get Tex and go see how they're coming with writing procedures and doing their planning."

"Good idea. Looks like you got everything going okay."

Art stood up and breathed deep. "I sure hope so but it's a hell of a job keeping all the balls in the air at once."

Elmer grinned approvingly as he looked at Art. "Now you see why Jerry thought I needed you. This office could never handle all the electronics, instrumentation, cables, and everything else. I don't know why there wasn't more planning put into organizing this damned job."

He peered at Elmer and laughed as he responded, "Well, buddy, ain't no body ever built one of these things before. Nobody really knows what it'll take."

Elmer lifted his coffee cup in a toast, "I agree with that. Sometimes I wish I had help on these cables. I sure don't get much from Engineering." Elmer leaned back in deep thought and contemplated his next comment: "You know, I just had a brilliant idea."

"What's that?"

"I'm gonna' call Elton's outfit *'F-Troop'*. Yep. I sure as hell am." He slapped his knee, stood up with a hearty laugh and raised his coffee cup, "A toast to F-Troop."

Art was laughing so hard the tears were starting to flow. "I love it," he cackled. "We got a logistics group run by a Cat Fish and an engineering group called *'F-Troop'*."

Suddenly Billy yelled across the open area between the offices. "What the hell's so damned funny with you guys over there?"

Elmer couldn't resist the temptation to carry it further. "Well, we just decided something, Billy."

"What?"

"We got an engineering department named F-Troop and a Logistics Department run by a Cat Fish. How about that?"

"So what else is new? You damned guys just now figured that out?"

Art couldn't resist and joined in the fray. "Well, what we're really doin' is trying to figure out how to use the F-Troop for fish bait to catch us a Cat Fish. Got any ideas?"

"Hell, that whole bunch wouldn't make good fish bait, especially that little shit that runs it. I don't know about you damned guys."

Elmer peered out the door across the room at Billy's open office door. "What don't you know, Billy?"

"You damned electrical weenies. You all walk to a different drummer."

They relaxed at Elmer's work table, satisfied they had stirred Billy enough. Art became serious and continued, "Well, I got to go to

StressCo. You know I'll be leaving tomorrow morning?"

As Art turned the corner to go to Tex's office he saw Van Monroe, the director of procurement, coming out with a serious look on his face. He hoped Tex wasn't in any difficulty. As he turned the corner he saw his friend facing the wall and quietly shaking his head. "What's the matter?" he asked.

Tex turned around with a hard scowl as he replied, "That dumb son of a bitch."

"You mean Van?"

"Yeah, Van. He doesn't understand the first thing about contracting or terms and conditions, or anything else. He just gave your integrated electroncis assembly contract to me."

"Hey, that's great," Art beamed. "That means we can really get things done now."

"Don't bet on it. He ain't got no idea what a warranty clause is or what it does. He thinks I should negotiate the contract and forget the warranty, but baby, that's bullshit."

Art sat down with a frown. "Tex, we got to get a warranty on those things for parts and workmanship through the first flight. Then what happens after they fly is our responsibility."

Tex grinned, some of the stress obviously drained. "See? See what I just said? You're not even a contracts man and you can see that. He can't. We'll get a damned warranty in spite of him. I'm not gonna pay over a million bucks each for damned black boxes without it."

"Hey, I agree. We'll work it out. Let's go out to StressCo to see how they're doin."

"Yeah, good idea," Tex grinned. "I need to settle myself down a little and those are good folks out there."

Sam ushered Art and Tex into his inner office. "Coffee?" They both accepted as Sam continued, "The units look good and the procedures are under way. We got the parts and as soon as you approve our procedures we'll start installing strain gages."

"Great," Art replied with satisfaction. "Let's go look at the hardware and see what we got. By the way, Sam, I've got a real sharp quality engineer assigned to the project by the name of Chip Harrell. He'll work with you on test procedures and monitor work in progress."

"Good. When will he be out to see us?"

"Tomorrow," Art replied, as they entered the laboratory area.

Shortly Tex, with his trained machinist's eye, was inspecting one of the clevis units. He suddenly said, "Art, look at this thing and tell me what you think."

Art walked to the workbench where Tex had one of the large clevises turned up on end, studying it in detail. "Looks like a tough piece of hardware, Tex. I just hope it's tough enough." Then Art's eye was caught by a line on the side of the unit. He bent over to take a closer look. "Look at this," he exclaimed, pointing to an obvious large scratch on the side of the unit.

"Yeah," Tex replied in a high-pitched tone, "that's a tool gouge from manufacturing. I can't believe that."

Art pulled an inspection light closer to the side of the unit for a closer look at the cut. "Have your quality people inspected these, Sam?" he asked.

Avery stepped in front of Sam and took command. "Yes sir, they have. Those marks are covered by waivers from the Space Agency. They say it's no problem. Use as is."

Art furrowed his brow and took a deep breath. "I wonder if they considered the possibility of a stress riser forming along the bounds of that cut?"

He turned the unit over to look at the other side. Tex, having been a master machinist before becoming a contract administrator, quickly recognized the significance of what he saw. "How many others like this, Sam?"

"I don't know for sure but Avery tells me several of 'em have some cuts and dings."

Art looked up and commanded, "Get me the waivers these things came in on. I want to see what they say."

Avery disappeared through the door to his office. Sam was worried and beginning to fidget as he asked, "What's wrong? What caused that?"

He explained, while Tex nodded approval, "When a piece of material has a defect, and particularly a cut or deep scratch, it causes a stress concentration in the region where the defect is and it could cause the part to crack."

Avery soon reappeared with the waivers. "See? *Defect not*

considered excessive. Use as is. It's signed off by the manufacturer's engineering people, accepted by the government inspector and the Space Agency quality person. It must be okay."

Art was still skeptical. He replied slowly, "Well, the paper's clean so we got no choice but to continue, but I sure as hell don't like it. These things should be smooth with a fine grain finish."

Sam looked more worried than ever. "Tex, what do you want us to do with them?" he asked nervously.

Tex grinned while watching him, "Continue unless I tell you something different. You're clean."

Art and Tex left StressCo worried about the defects. He commented to Tex as they walked into the Space Corp main building, "I'm going to get our Quality Control Office to go look at those things, Tex. I'm scared if one broke on launch, we might lose a vehicle and a crew."

When Art returned to program management, Elmer came into the cubicle before he could sit down. "What's wrong, Art? You look like trouble found you," he asked casually.

He explained the defects he had seen in the clevises, the succession of paper work that had approved the units for use as is and the apparent lack of attention the problem had gotten up to this point. He explained, "Al Bryant is gonna get his quality engineering and our stress people and check it out, so be aware that they may come to you before I get back."

Elmer leaned back in his chair and said calmly, "Remember what we named that group? I'll watch it and if there's any development, I'll call you."

"Okay. I don't know yet, but my gut feel says there'd be one hell of a catastrophic failure if one of those things broke."

CHAPTER TEN

On the 27th, Art arrived in Atlanta to meet Bob Strothers for the aircraft accident trial beginning the next day. He had no inkling of the stress that he would undergo during the next week; three days on the witness stand under relentless cross examination by seven different lawyers whose capability ran from expert to very poor, some of which he enjoyed swapping jabs with and matching wits. Finally, at a recess on the third day of testimony when he had a chance to get his breath, Strothers confided, "Hey buddy, I think we got this one won. You've done a hell of a job containing Glenn Downing. That's no small trick."

Art grinned and replied confidently, "I think he's about run out of questions. I don't think he's gotten to me yet on any answer."

After the jury was escorted to the deliberation room, Art, Bob and Jim walked out to the hallway to relax. Art grinned at them and declared, "Well, fellows, not much I can do now. If you don't need me anymore, I'm going to Northboro and visit a beautiful blonde who's getting ready for her PhD comprehensives next week."

Art woke Monday morning with a feeling of accomplishment. His call on Sunday night from Strothers announcing the winning verdict was good news. Also, his week-end with Annie after the trial had given him a new lease on life. Sharing the moments of high drama and frustration with her was not only a pleasure he looked forward to but a catharsis of sorts. Even the drive from Northboro hadn't bothered him as much as usual, hating to drive as much as he did. He bounded out of bed and into the shower, immersing himself in the hot water and soap, absorbing the friendly heat. Shortly his mind turned to his projects he had entrusted to Elmer and decided there must not be any problems since he had received no calls.

He drove toward the new office complex and saw Al and Connie entering the main parking lot together, sitting close. "Well, I'll be damned," he said to himself, "they must be living together now or they wouldn't be coming in that way this early." Art thought about Connie's new husband and the absolute snake she had taken up with.

He purposely let them get further ahead as he experienced a strong feeling of lost trust and friendship.

He parked in front of his building and saw Heidi sitting in her car anxiously waiting for him. He thought it strange that she would be sitting in this parking lot instead of going to her own building. He got out and greeted her, "Hi, beautiful, haven't seen you for a while."

She was panicked as she opened the door and commanded, "Get in, Art"

Puzzled, he slipped into the empty seat expecting the worst. "You don't know what happened yet, do you?" she blurted.

"What do you mean?" His pulse grew faster, fearing the worst for her. "What have they done to you, now?"

"Not me. To you." she started. "I tried to call you last night and even went to your house at eleven but you weren't home. I thought you'd probably gone to Northboro."

"Yeah, I got back about twelve or so. What's going on?"

"Elton Jones doesn't like you, Art, and he's trying to fire you."

He sat bolt upright in disbelief. "What are you talking about? He can't fire me." Art stared hard at her, trying to decipher what he was hearing from this most trusted friend. He continued in a high voice, "I told him where I was, gave him phone numbers and told him when I'd be back. He knew where I was and what I was doing. I don't understand."

"Buddy, with him, you don't have to understand. He's gone off the deep end since he took over that department."

"Yeah, I know," he replied, staring at Heidi and trying to understand what was happening.

"I think that since he thought he couldn't totally control you he'd get rid of you any way he could." She reached took his hand and held it with her own sweaty, worried palm.

"But Heidi, he had no reason. I haven't crossed him. I've done what he's asked and he had no grounds. Besides, I was in federal court on a federal subpoena. He knows that."

"Well, babe," she said excitedly, "let me tell you that he tried. He processed the paper all the way to personnel and little Dean was going to go through with it until he got scared. And that's the only reason he didn't, just because he's too damned chicken hearted to do it."

"I can't believe they'd be that stupid. I can't believe it." he

said, squeezing her hand and staring at her, still in disbelief.
"Well he did. I wanted you to know before you walked in cold."

"That son-of-a-bitch," Art muttered out loud. "He can't get away with this."

"Easy, Art. Remember what you always tell me. Settle down and don't let 'em spook you."

"Yeah, yeah, baby. You're right." He leaned over and gave her a big bear hug, which she returned with all the strength in her. He kissed her lightly on the cheek, and continued, "I really appreciate you, hon. I'm sure glad you're here."

"Yeah, me too," she whispered, as tears welled up in her eyes. She reached for his hand again and squeezed it. "Be careful."

"I will. You took a chance coming over here. I'll take it from here." He reached over and kissed Heidi on the cheek again as he opened the car door. "Now don't be late. I don't want them to get on you." Her eyes welled with tears as she backed out of the parking space.

Art rushed angrily to Elton's office with his eyes flashing, looking for a major confrontation, only to find it empty. Claire appeared behind him as he turned to storm out. She stepped in front and ordered, "Slow down cowboy. The little sob ain't here this morning. He really tried, didn't he?"

"So I hear," Art said. "Where the hell is he? I want him and I want him now."

"Art!" Claire commanded sternly in a loud voice, with her big brown eyes flashing, "Slow it, man, slow it. You got to think this one out. You're mad. Get over that first."

He stopped cold as he started to push past her. He sat down on the top of a desk and reflected for a moment. "Yeah, you're absolutely correct, as usual. I'm madder'n hell and that ain't good."

"Mad? Buster, you're worse than mad. If you go around like that they'll chew you up to nothin. Now cool it."

"Damn, Claire," he said apologetically. "I hadn't realized how mad I was." Then he took her hand, pulled her over and hugged her in a deep bear hug. "Thanks, Baby. You saved my butt again. I was ready to kill him."

Claire hadn't expected that and laughed as she said, "You sure can hug a girl, you know that?"

"Gee, Claire, I hope I didn't embarrass you, but I'm glad you're on my side."

She giggled and struck him lightly on the shoulder with her fingers. "I'm so embarrassed that you can do it again if you want to, but not now. Somebody just came in and I don't want to get no rumors started."

He felt stress diminishing and his whole body beginning to relax from the strain. "Claire, you're a real sweetheart. If I didn't already have a beautiful wife, I'd be over at your house, that is if your daddy wouldn't shoot me."

She blushed as much as she could and wanted to change the subject for fear of being overheard. "He took the day off. He said he had some business to take care but I know it's because he didn't want to face you. That's the way the little bastard works, underhanded and devious."

"Thanks baby," Art replied as he started out the door. "I'm going over to the other place by way of Dean's office in personnel. See you later."

Claire again felt fear as he started out the door. "Art," she called, "Promise me you won't do anything dumb. Please."

"You got it, lady. All I'm gonna do is to quote the law to him about harassment and intimidation of a federal witness."

Art walked into the personnel office with a gait he seldom used, as though he were ready for war. However, thanks to Claire, he had developed a plan of action that he knew would work. "Aikins!" he yelled. "Where the hell are you?"

He perceived movement inside the room as he jerked Dean's door open. Then he saw Dean down behind the desk as though he actually was trying to get under it. Art stopped short, put his hands on his hips and put on the best glare he could muster. Then he yelled, "What's the matter with you? Did you lose something down there? Or maybe you're trying to hide your skinny little ass?"

Dean was pale, having never seen Art in this frame of mind before. "What can I do for you?" he asked in a high voice that almost squeaked.

Art stared at him and took a step closer to the desk. "What the hell do you mean, you little snake? Haven't you already tried to do enough?" He was laughing inside at Dean cowering behind the desk as though his last moment may be near. "You ever been in jail?" he asked.

Dean jumped up straight. "You can't put me in jail. It was Jones' idea to fire you. You should be grateful I stopped it."

"Stopped it, hell, you little pip squeak. You stopped it 'cause you're a damned coward. That's why you stopped it. " He moved closer.

Dean paled even more and expected the worst. "Don't you touch me, Art Cannon. Don't you dare!" he croaked as his voice began to fail him.

Art took another step forward as Dean backed into the corner. "I mean it," came the shriek.

"Hell," Art said. "I wouldn't waste the time. What I am gonna do is report you and your henchman to the federal court judge in Atlanta and let him deal with you. Do you know the penalty for harassment and intimidation of a federal witness?"

Panic set in. "You weren't a federal witness, were you?" Dean asked brokenly.

"Under federal subpoena," Art yelled. His eyes narrowed to slits. "Do you know what that means? Do you realize what the hell you've done?"

"It was all Jones' idea. I swear it was. I had nothin' to do with it." Dean was begging now. "Don't lie to me, Aikins," Art roared again. "I'm gonna let the feds take care of you two. Maybe you'll get a year or two over in the Big House in Atlanta. That's where they usually put those kind." He turned and started out, "You'll hear from 'em."

Dean was shaking as he ran from behind the desk. "Please don't do that, Art," he begged. "It was all Jones' doing. He did it. He wanted to get rid of you."

Art glared at him. "You both lie. Now I've got you two where I want you."

Dean began wringing his hands and reaching out to touch Art, then thinking better of it and continuing to wring his hands. "Think of my family. Think what it'll mean to them if I go to jail. Please, Art, don't do this. *Please!*"

Art turned to him as he stood in the office door. "On one condition," he said.

"Name it. Just name it. I'll do it. I swear I will."

Art, chuckling inside but with his sternest look outside, demanded, "I want a transfer out of his group into the program management office now."

Dean fell back against the wall. "I can't do that. That's up to the department manager."

"Then you better be out there negotiatin, son, 'cause I'm gonna go see the judge."

He grabbed Art by the arm. "Wait, wait," he shrieked. "Give me a couple of days. I'll try. I'll try!"

He pointed his finger at Dean's nose. "Okay squirt, you got two days. Now get your ass in gear."

He left the office chuckling, grateful for Claire's counsel and for Heidi's early warning. Maybe this'll work out fine after all he thought, as he turned into his new cubicle.

Art leaned back in his chair with a cup of hot coffee and began to reflect on the events of the morning. Just as he had allowed the first swallow of the golden brown liquid to go down ever so smoothly Elmer entered the cubicle with a worried look on his face. "Where the hell you been? I been trying to call you all week end."

Art smiled and dropped his feet from the desk. "Well, when I got through in court Friday I went to Northboro to see Annie and stayed up there until late last night. Then I drove back here and here I am."

Elmer sat down in the new side chair with a perplexed look on his face, crossed his legs with a fixed gaze that Art had learned to expect when he was worried. This time the gaze seemed to be more fixed than usual. He took a deep breath and said slowly, "Did you know you been fired?"

Art crossed his legs and took another drink of coffee before he answered. "No way, old friend, I ain't been fired. My good friend Elton Jones tried but Dean chickened out at the last minute and it's a damned good thing he did."

Elmer breathed a long sigh of relief and shook his head. "Well, Friday afternoon I heard it from Billy, who heard it in a meeting. He got all upset and asked me what the hell was goin' on."

Art started to laugh and recited the events of the morning, excepting Heidi. He dwelled on the part where Dean was begging him not to prosecute and concluded with, "That was beautiful. That little bastard really squirmed."

Elmer chuckled with relief and re-crossed his legs to a more comfortable position. "I sure would have liked to have seen that. What'll happen next?"

"Well, I got to get Billy to transfer me. I obviously can't continue to work for Elton."

"I agree that's the logical move and I've already started that ball rolling with Billy. We were afraid we'd have to rehire you."

Harry Engle, who had replaced Jerry Strong in the organization, suddenly turned the corner of the cubicle and in the true form of an admiral who expected to be answered immediately, asked, "What's going on with you damned guys? What the hell was Ghote talking about? I can't make any sense out of him. Cannon, why the hell did you get fired and if you got fired why the hell are you here?"

Elmer was startled and perplexed. He started to stammer, "Well, sir, he didn't get fired . . ."

Art interrupted, "Let me explain. I think I can clear it up."

"Well, I sure as hell hope so. I consider you a key player in this office."

Art's heart leaped and he felt his pulse quicken. He wasn't aware that Harry hardly more than knew who he was since he had given him only a couple of program review presentations. He had an instant like for him.

"Well, let me explain . . ." Art went through the pertinent details and when he got to the discussion with Dean Aikins, he said, "I left it with Dean that he had better talk Elton into approving a transfer into the Program Office for me or else. Guess I threatened him a little, but that's what I wanted to do."

Harry relaxed and started to laugh. "My secretary informed me Friday afternoon that you'd been fired because you appeared in court under a subpoena."

Art grinned and watched Elmer fidget, as he replied, "Well, that's basically what happened, I guess."

"Well, that scared the hell out of me. That's harassment, or something like that and I don't need none of that." Harry shifted to a much more comfortable pose standing in the door of the cubicle. He asked, now relaxed, "You got any hard feelings toward the company or do you plan any legal action?"

"No. I like this company. I like these guys up here and I want to work with 'em. It's just been a hell of a hard time trying to get to do it," Art replied.

Harry shifted from one foot to the other and extended his hand. "Well, you're transferred now. I'll cut a directive to personnel this morning. Billy wants you and I know Elmer needs you so let's make this team work."

Art stood, almost floating, still feeling the warm strong grip of Harry's hand. "Gee, thanks. You don't know how much I appreciate that. I'll do the best job I can."

"I know that and I'm depending on you."

Elmer beamed and added, "Harry, you sure got a way of solving problems."

Harry turned to leave and as an afterthought, "Tell Ghote I solved the problem and he can quit fidgeting."

The both of them, resting comfortably for the first time this morning, leaned back with their feet on Art's desk and reflected on the events. "Sure as hell moves fast, don't it, Chief?" Art chuckled.

Just then Billy Ghote rounded the corner and without waiting for an invitation, interrupted, "Cannon, that's the quickest damned transfer I ever seen. How the hell did you do it?"

Elmer couldn't resist the opportunity to tease Billy. "What's the matter, you want to learn the technique?"

Billy chuckled, which was rare with his usually dry humor and expressionless face, "Yeah, I might want to use it sometime, maybe on you."

They both related the events as Billy laughed heartily and replied, "Well, we got your ass now. I expect a full day's work."

Art grinned and replied easily, "Good deal. That means I can slow down if you only want one days work at a time."

Billy walked out of the cubicle with his gruff humor, "I see I got to watch you damned guys closer. Next thing I'll find is a conspiracy."

"Well, what happened while I was gone? I mean on company business. I think we've beat the other stuff to death now," Art asked, finally feeling comfortable after an eventful morning.

Elmer recalled the key events of the past week in Art's area of responsibility and began to enumerate. "First, StressCo completed installation of strain gages in your first clevis end and expects to start testing this week when you approve their procedures. Next, Procurement placed your order for pressure transducers for the aerodynamic pressure measurements on the aft skirt." Then he paused with a pensive look, "You sure those transducers will do the job that needs to be done back there?"

Art stared at the wall for a moment in deep thought. "No, I'm not certain. That's why I only bought two flight sets worth for initial delivery and optioned the others for a staggered delivery. However, if the Space Agency's aeroballistic model is correct these units should work fine."

"Well," Elmer replied slowly, "I don't know a better approach." He continued with significant events. "You got a delivery problem on thermocouples for measuring temperatures on the engine nozzles. Then looks like you may need to go to Palmdale, California for a design review on the acoustical sensors for measuring sound pressure levels in the aft skirt. Also, you may need to go on up to San Francisco to check on accelerometers for measuring low-frequency vibration."

Art leaned back and took a long drink of coffee. "Looks like a typical week, doesn't it?"

"Oh yeah," Elmer continued. "I almost forgot, you need to check with Configuration Management on some engineering changes that appear to have problems and then you need to check with engineering to schedule a review of the instrumentation junction box design."

Art smiled and replied, "Well, I'll do those things in my spare time. Did I get authorization to proceed on building the new integrated electronic assemblies?"

"No, not yet, but I talked to Mr. Morgan out there and he said they expected to get that budget authorization in sometime this week. You know it had to go to Headquarters because it was over $25 million."

Elmer stood up slowly. "Well, welcome aboard. I got a cable meeting out at the Center in half an hour. I'll see you later."

Art sat for a few moments and pondered where to attack the myriad of problems facing him. He decided to go to StressCo first to review the procedures so testing could begin. He was worried about schedule because of the sheer amount of work to be done and wanted to check on development progress for the computer programs to take test data from the calibrations in both tension and in compression.

He thought for a moment and decided to invite Tex to go along. As he entered Tex's office he saw a new picture of a P-51 Mustang in full battle dress on a dirt strip, obviously a combat strip from World War II, over his desk. "Hi buddy. I sure like the picture."

"Welcome home." Tex replied easily with a big smile. "Yeah, that's my old baby I flew in North Africa. She's got a few kills to her credit. Think we need to visit StressCo? They're about ready to do something on the first test."

"I came down to see if you could go with me."

On the way to StressCo Art related his transfer as Tex laughed almost uncontrollably. "That's the funniest thing I ever heard," he croaked, almost in tears from laughing. "That little sob. Damn I'd 'a loved to seen him under that desk beggin'. You know what they did is a felony, don't you?"

"Yeah, but I made my point and I don't see any need to pursue it. I don't want to cause trouble for the company and it might reflect bad on management."

When they entered the room where the instrumentation installation was being performed, they saw Edgar, the resident engineer on the project. "Hello, Mister Cannon," He greeted with an extended hand. Then he turned to Tex. "Hello, Mister James, glad to see you again."

"Hi Edgar, my name's Tex and his is Art."

Edgar blushed and shifted his weight from one foot to the other. "Yes sir. Tina told me. Anyhow, here's the first unit. We thought you'd like to see it before we started testing."

Art and Tex inspected the inner barrel area of the clevis with the small wiring and the strain gages so skillfully placed in their proper positions and cemented to the surfaces of the metal inside the bottom end of the seven-inch diameter barrel. As they were surveying the workmanship Sam asked, "Now you fellows know I don't understand technical stuff at all, but why the hell are those strain gages at the bottom like that instead of the outside end where we could get to 'em easier?"

Art patiently explained, "Well, Sam, this thing forms one end of an aft strut used to attach the booster to the external tank. Remember I showed you there are three struts, each made up of two clevis ends and a center nut assembly. This two-foot long clevis forms the end of one of those struts; the other end attaches to the external tank attach ring."

Sam nodded as though he now understood. "You mean these things actually attach the SRB to the ET?"

"That's right. Notice the threads out here on the outer surface. That's where the clevis screws into the center body we call the nut. Then the other clevis end screws into the other side of the nut and you have a strut. It's sort of like sticking two long tin cans into a large pipe with a snug fit, except the clevis ends screw into the center pipe."

Sam was intently interested and exclaimed, "Hell, man, that's an important piece. I had no idea it was that important."

Art smiled at Sam's enthusiasm and turned to Tex, who was watching closely. Then his gaze went back to Sam. "Now to answer your question about why the gages aren't at the top of the barrel. Remember what I said about the center part of the strut, that it was shaped like a hollow cylinder with threads on each end to screw each clevis into. That's called the nut, except it doesn't have flats like a regular nut. It's a big, round cylinder."

"Yeah."

"Well, imagine this unit screwed into the nut, or cylinder, and another clevis screwed into the other end to form a long, tubular looking strut nearly five feet long. Now, between the two clevis ends there's some hollow space inside and in that center area there's a shaped pyrotechnic charge and a detonator. On each end of that shaped charge is what, for the lack of a better word, I'll call *'waddin'*, sort of like in a shotgun shell."

Sam looked perplexed. "Why in heaven's name do they put pyrotechnics in that damned thing?"

"At separation of the boosters somewhere around 254,000 feet altitude, the detonation of the shaped charge in the center of each strut splits the barrel nut just like you cut it with a knife. That happens at the same time the ball joint at the forward end of the booster is separated. Then the separation motors are fired and the SRB is pushed away from the external tank and orbiter that's now on the way to orbit using the three main engines on the aft end of the orbiter. It's still on top of the External Tank and drawing fuel from the tank for that part of the flight until the tank runs dry. At that point the Orbiter separates from the tank and finishes orbital insertion using the Ohms Engines at the rear and fuel stored on board the Orbiter. "

Sam was clearly impressed. "Then if the gages were at the top end of the barrel they'd be destroyed when they put in the wadding."

"Correct. End of lesson."

Sam grinned and shook his head. "Just think. Little old StressCo is doin' a major job on the Space shuttle. Damn. I'm proud of us."

Tex laughed at Sam and couldn't resist a bit of kidding. "If you don't do a good job, friend, you ass is grass and I am the lawn mower."

Sam slapped him on the back, "Don't you worry about us, buddy, we'll do it right."

Edgar asked, "What do you think? Look okay?"

Art was inspecting the workmanship with a large, illuminated magnifying glass to be sure before he committed himself. Finally, he stood up and laid his hand on top of the clevis. "Looks damned good to me. I'm amazed at the way those tiny hair wires are cemented in there. Whoever did that was good."

Sam was beaming as he replied, "Was there ever any doubt?"

Art beat Tex to the answer, "If there had been we wouldn't be here."

Sam turned to Edgar and commanded, "Go get Sara. I want these gentlemen to meet the young lady that did that."

Edgar left the room and soon returned with a woman in her early-forties, dressed in old sockless tennis shoes, faded blue-jeans and plaid shirt with her hair on her head in a big bun. She looked as though she just came in off the farm. Art noted her complexion, rough and ruddy, like a long-time farm girl who worked in the fields beside her man day in and day out. He noted that she also was a liberal snuff user from the traces on her lips. Her fingers were long and finely formed but rough. She was shy but there was a friendly twinkle in her eye as she shuffled up to the work bench where the unit was displayed. Tex was standing back looking in amazement and wondering, *Who the hell is Sam kiddin now?*

Sam said proudly, "Gentlemen, meet Sara Taylor. She does all our precision work."

"Howdy," she said shyly. "Pleased to meet you'ns. I been hearin 'bout you and wonderin' if we would get to meet 'cha, too."

Tex was beside himself. "You mean to tell me she did this?"

Sam grinned and put his arm around Sara's shoulders. "She sure did. Sara's the best."

Art was staring in amazement. He finally managed, "Sara, I'm pleased to meet you. How do you feel about working on Space shuttle hardware?"

"Wellll . . . hit don't make me no never-minds, I reckon."

"But this is so important to the Space shuttle flight that if this part here failed it could cause a catastrophic failure and kill the entire crew."

Sara was more at ease. Her self-consciousness had settled into a deep, easy smile characteristic of most farm folk. "Well, sir," she drawled, "If you'ns'll tell me whur to put them gages down and show me whur you want 'em connected, you won't have no problem with my stuff."

Art was beginning to laugh and realize what a total jewel Sam had uncovered. He commented with a big, friendly smile, "Sara, the work in that thing is beautiful. Just keep it up through the rest of 'em and I'm sure everything will be fine."

Sam was beaming as he perceived Sara's acceptance. Tex wasn't totally convinced yet, however, and asked, "Sara, you're a certified solderer, been through the schools, and all, haven't you?"

Sara, without blinking, replied, "Yes sir. Duh' ya want me to go git my certificates?"

Tex backed down quickly. "No, no. I'll take your word for it. Besides, the quality inspector is responsible for that."

Sam patted Sara on the shoulder and excused her. She turned and left with a gait that Art was sure she had to have learned behind a plow and a horse. He reflected on this for a moment and remembered his own early days of plowing with a team of horses. He had taken a definite liking to Sara.

Art asked Edgar, "Has Chip Harrell reviewed your procedures yet?"

"He's in my office right now doin' that. He said you wanted to see 'em and would sign off the engineering block on the front."

As they walked to Edgar's office they passed the instrumentation lab where Sara was working. Art stopped outside the door where he could observe, watching the long fingers working down in the barrel of a clevis with such deliberate precision that he was amazed. Then she picked up a soldering iron to solder a connection down in the bottom of the unit where she must solder wires not much bigger than a human hair. He shook his head and commented, "Amazing isn't she?"

"Sure is. Sam really found a jewel there," Edgar commented.

"Where the hell did he find her?"

"So far back in the woods you wouldn't believe it. A couple of years ago she came in to work and didn't know anything. Sam said, 'Hell, teach 'er something. I told her we'd put her to work.' So we tried to teach her soldering and assembly. She's so good that all the other women are jealous."

"I can believe that," Art replied.

"When we have a problem we have to solve, she does it. She's an amazing woman, highly intelligent."

Slowly Art turned to walk on down the hall and quietly commented, "That was my impression. You got a real sleeper there. Too bad she couldn't have been an educated woman. But then, who knows, those skills may not have developed like they have."

In Edgar's office, quality engineer Chip Harrell was sitting at a table with a large collection of manuals, documents and papers spread out. He looked up and smiled as he greeted warmly, "Hi, chief. Glad you're here."

"How they look so far?"

"Good. I got a couple of small changes to make, mostly procedural. I already checked the software when we made a dummy run on the computer."

"Great. Looks like we're about ready to test."

As they drove back Tex leaned back in the seat and took a long breath as though he were considering his question carefully. Then he asked, "What do you think?"

"Well, we can't ask for more than that, can we?" Art replied.

CHAPTER ELEVEN

Art, Tex and Chip arrived at StressCo early the next morning to begin testing the first clevis. Soon the procedures were checked and Art said with a commanding voice, "OK, guys, let's get started."

After the clevis was mounted securely in the big Tinnius-Olson press, a power-up sequence was initiated to assure that the test system was on and working. Great care had to be taken because a mistake here could cause serious damage to the hardware or even death to members of the test team because of the extreme forces they would be applying.

The computer passed one final simulation test and Edgar started the motor on the big press. The gears whirred and meters began to read out the changes of voltage as the strain gages dutifully responded to the applied compression load. Art watched the computer print-out as it spat out it's incessant stream of data until Edgar brought the load up to 200,000 pounds compression and said "Let's let it sit there for fifteen minutes and stabilize so we can get a better test."

At the end of fifteen minutes Edgar commanded, "Recycle to zero pounds force and then go into the tension mode." He placed the switch in reverse and engaged the clutch. The gears whirred in the reverse direction. All stood quietly and expectantly as the voltmeters showed a smaller and smaller voltage while the load was released on the clevis. As the press approached zero load the meters all read zero.

Art looked at the meters and commented quietly, reflecting his satisfaction so far, "Look at that, would you. I wouldn't have expected them to be so well behaved. They're both on zero, at the same time."

Edgar smiled and said confidently, "Let's see what it does at 200,000 pounds tension." He placed the selector switch into position and the large press began to apply a pulling force to the clevis. The meters reading the two strain gage bridges inside the clevis read out voltages that were almost identical, which said that they were tracking each other and the tension in the metal closely. Edgar slowed to a barely imperceptible movement and stopped on 200,000 pounds. Then he said, "Okay, 15 minutes stabilization."

Art, studying the printout, commented, "Looks like we had excellent data correlation."

Art turned to Tex and asked, "What do you think?"

He looked thoughtfully at the press and the clevis mounted in the tooling before replying, "Looks good to me. I'm ready to go back to the office if you are."

On the way back to the office Tex commented philosophically, "Kind of exciting watching your first piece of hardware?"

Art was thinking about the testing that would be run. "Sure is," he finally replied. "I'm anxious to see how the curves plot out. You know, that specification has never been used."

"Yeah, but all of 'em got to start somewhere, buddy. Besides, the data will tell you real quick if you need to revise the spec."

Art and Tex parked in the rear of the building and went in through the back door. When Art turned into his office area he saw Heidi coming down the other side of the large open space toward him. He waved and noticed a worried look on her face. He laid his sheaf of papers on his desk and sat down as she sat down beside his desk.

"Hi beautiful," he greeted before she could say anything. "What's up?"

She sat there a moment, as if organizing her thoughts and finally said, "Art, I got to talk to you now."

He was more than mildly curious because of the seriousness that seemed to be consuming her. "Sure, baby, you know you can."

She sat quiet a few seconds, her long brown hair draped over her shoulders and big green eyes fixed on the corner of the desk with a serious look covering her face. "I think I still want to quit. You know what a mess this place had been for me."

He studied her with an understanding look. "Yeah, hon, I know. But all that stuff is behind you now."

"Yeah, thanks mostly to you. The problem is that if I do quit I feel like I'm deserting you. I'm afraid you'll think I'm not a friend and don't appreciate you. You know I do, don't you?" She dropped her eyes toward the floor with a worried expression on her face.

He laid his hand on her arm and faced her straight on before he answered, "Heidi, I know you're a true friend and I want what's best for you and if you think quitting is best, then you should. But think about it and don't quit till you have a job you want."

She jumped upright in the chair. "Oh," she exclaimed. "I didn't tell you about the job offer, did I?"

He smiled and said slowly, "Noooo, I don't believe you did."

"Well, I have a friend I've known for a long time and she's started her own real estate agency. She wants me to come in as a partner because I still have my realtor's license. She's got more business than she can handle. I can more than double my pay, too."

Art leaned back in the chair with a feeling of relief that she wasn't in trouble again. He replied slowly, "If you have a good relationship with this woman and can make a good deal, I think it sounds good. But, hon, please be sure you get a good contract."

She laid her hand on his and squeezed gently as she asked, "Then you think it's okay? And you won't be mad at me or think I've deserted you to the wolf pack here? She's offered me a contract and wants me to have an attorney approve it. This lady was a good friend of my mother and I've known her all my life."

"Well," Art replied, "I'd say go for it. I'll be in your corner whatever you do." He was experiencing a lost feeling in the pit of his stomach at the thought of losing her almost daily contact. He had grown more than fond of her and looked forward to seeing her.

She grinned with a feeling of relief and replied, "I still want to be friends. I know you have a beautiful wife and I know you love her but we can still be good friends. Okay?"

He leaned over and rubbed her cheek. "You know I don't want to lose you but baby, you got to do what you think is best for you and not worry about this place."

She sat quietly for a moment before replying, "When I'm gone there's nobody to keep you up on all the gossip here. And then there's the emergency typing you need."

He got up, put his arm around her gently and said, "You got to do what's best. Don't worry about me."

She interrupted excitely, "You'll call me occasionally and we can have lunch sometimes?"

"You bet we can," he replied.

"Art Cannon, I'm really gonna miss you." She looked up at him with tears in her eyes and pressed closer to him as he stood by her chair. Finally she stood up and put her arms around him and squeezed him as tight as she could, he returning the hug and felt her warm body against him.

She released him and as he ushered her out of the office cubicle toward the door of the big room, he said, "We're friends for life. Don't forget that." He saw a small tear come up in her eye again and rubbed it away with his finger. "Hang in there, you're very special to me."

"I know," she replied quietly, "I know and you know that goes double for me, or maybe a thousand times. Who knows? Thanks a bunch."

She turned and walked down the hall toward the stairs while Art watched the rhythm of her body as she walked and thought, *"Gee, she's really beautiful. If I were single she'd be one hell of a catch."* Just as he was about to turn around and go back to his cubicle he saw Elmer coming down the hallway quickly with a worried look on his face.

"What's the problem, Elmer?"

"You know those damned qualification cables we were startin' to test?"

"Yeah."

"Well, we just failed the salt exposure test on the biggest one of the damned bunch."

"Damn! What happened?"

"We got salt water penetration into the connector through those new seals that were supposed to be so great. Hell, I don't know what to do now. We'll have to repair it and start over with another connector, I guess, but that invalidates the whole test."

Art looked at the floor for a moment and thought through the design and the fabrication of the cable and then asked, "Have you done a failure analysis yet?"

"No, not yet. It's in process at the plant. I'm goin over there right now. Want to come?"

"I will if I can help, but I've got the first clevis in test now and we do have that status review to get ready for Monday. I was planning to try to help you on that if I could because I know what a load you got."

Elmer stopped cold. "I completely forgot about that damned review. I'll never get ready and retested before that. They'll kill me."

"Hey, buddy," Art said sternly, "it's not your fault. We don't have design responsibility yet and you're dealing with a vendor that was directed on you by the Space Agency. Settle down. It'll work out."

Elmer stopped at the door of his office and reflected on this for a moment. "Hell yes, you're right. Guess I better get up there, though, and supervise that failure analysis. You know these damned cables are always the last thing designed and the first thing installed and always going through changes."

"Well, that's just the nature of the beast."

"I don't know if I'll ever get on top of this mess or not." As Elmer turned to go into his office, he continued, "I sure would appreciate any help on that presentation."

"Hey, I'll be glad to," Art called as Elmer hurried out the door with his briefcase and an arm load of drawings.

Art sat down with a warm cup of coffee, his last of the day, to welcome the waning of the afternoon.

Just as he started to put his feet up on the desk and lean back Eddie Rogers turned the corner and asked, "Got any more of that anywhere?"

Art hadn't seen him in some time to sit and visit. He jumped up, "Hey, stranger, come in, come in. Here's a cup and over there's a pot," pointing at the corner where the coffeepot was kept. "Help yourself and sit down."

Eddie poured himself a cup, walked back into the office and looked around. "You got it made up here, fellah."

Art laughed at the kidding as he replied. "How you figure that?"

"Hell, look at the new furniture and all that. Next thing I know you'll have a private office."

"Well, we're supposed to move pretty soon into new quarters and I suppose then I'll have one. At least, that's what Elmer tells me. How's things with you? I haven't had a chance to catch up with you lately."

"Goin' my way now. I sure appreciate your help in getting away from Sonny. I'm glad you got separated from Elton, too. I never did trust him."

"Yeah, that was a good move," Art concluded.

"I tell you one thing, though," Eddie continued, "I sure do like my new boss, Ben Carr. He's sharp and the nicest guy in the world to work for but he's a stickler for detail. He wants it right or not at all."

"Well," Art commented after drinking a long drink of coffee from his oversized cup, "I guess I agree with him. If it ain't right, it's not worth much, especially in this business."

"By the way," Eddie started with vigor, "Al has moved in with Connie. Her husband caught her shacking up with him and kicked her out. I understand he's filed for divorce. Then Al's wife actually caught him and Connie in bed together and kicked him out. So they just moved in together."

"I guess that's why she avoids me now," Art mused. "I'm sure sorry. I thought she had so much on the ball."

"Hey, don't forget that's a two-way street. She had to be a party to it, too."

"Yeah, I know. I think she got sold a bill of goods, mostly because she has a beautiful ass, pretty face and not much brains. I'm not gonna push it anymore," he said dejectedly.

"Hell no, you tried to get her started right, just like you've done Heidi," Eddie replied philosophically, shifting his position in the new chair.

"Yeah, but I think Heidi's gonna do okay. She's thinking about quittin and goin back into real estate. I think that might be a good move. Then maybe she'll meet somebody and fall in love. I hope so."

Eddie chuckled and leaned back as he replied, "I think she's already done that, if you ask me."

Art dropped his feet and looked straight at Eddie. "How you know that? She hasn't told me."

"Idiot. Can't you see it? She's crazy about you but she also knows where the bases are. She won't trespass."

"That's the craziest theory you ever came up with. I don't believe that at all. Why, we're nothing but good friends. That's nuts."

"Well, be careful and don't hurt her. By the way," he continued, "I was wondering if you got that clevis part into test yet and how it's working out?"

"Yeah, as a matter of fact, we started the first one this morning. They'll need a couple of days to make all the data runs and then reduce it but it started off good."

"Good. I've been looking at that specification and wondering how it was working out. Since this is a new piece of hardware I was wondering how it might fit into the refurbishment scheme for my model."

"Well," Art said as he shifted positions from his favorite "feet on desk" to leaning back with his legs crossed, "I don't know what you would do to refurbish it. It's just a big chunk of Inconel 718 steel."

"That's what worries me. How do we know if it's cracked or not?"

"Seems to me you could x-ray it for internal cracks. A die-penetrant test would show any external cracks. Guess the best thing to do would be to go see the metallurgical people about that. This Inconel 718 is supposed to be tough stuff."

"Yeah," Eddie replied, "but it's been my experience that some of these exotic materials also have some problems that need to be considered before we give 'em full blessing. Guess I'll go research it when I get time."

Suddenly the phone rang and they both jumped with a start. Eddie looked at his watch and saw it was past quitting time. He started to get up as Art answered, "Program Management, Cannon here."

Eddie watched a big smile cross Art's face and decided to stay and see what the good news was. Then he heard, "Great, Chip, get 'em started early tomorrow. I'm real anxious about this first one. Sounds like everything is working good."

Art leaned back after hanging up and grinned with satisfaction. "Well, the first day of testing went well. No problems."

"Hey, that's great. You got Chip Harrell out there?"

"Yeah. He's good. Really knows how to run tests."

"I hear he's one of the best. I'm glad you got him."

"If all goes well tomorrow, Chip thinks he'll finish and get the data reduced by Friday. Looks like we're about to complete the first one early."

"That's good," Eddie commented as he started out the door. "Come down first chance you get and I'll show you our new quarters. We're right by the computer room."

As Eddie left the door Billy Ghote appeared. "Hi Billy, haven't seen you all day," Art said.

"Yeah. Been busy," he grunted. "Too many damned meetings. Seems like all I do is go to meetings. Do you know what happened to Elmer's cable qualification test?"

"Well, just from the little he told me, it sounded like he had a workmanship problem. I don't know though. He's gone up there to watch the failure analysis."

"Good," Billy grunted.

"By the way, I got a letter go-ahead for you to buy those integrated electronics assemblies and multiplexers/demultiplexers. Looks like about $26 million or so?"

"Yeah, about that. I recommended twelve forward and ten aft units and twenty-four MDM's. Is that what I got authorization for?"

"Uhuh," Billy grunted. "But why do you need two extra MDM's?"

"Spares. We could slip a schedule if we don't lay in some spares."

"Yeah, I guess you're right, but you better be prepared to run your ass off between New York and Denver." Billy stood a moment in deep thought before he continued, "Oh yeah, I almost forgot to ask you if you're ready to go to San Diego Friday."

Art looked puzzled. "San Diego? What the hell for?"

Billy snorted, "Didn't Elmer tell you?"

"I guess not. What's he supposed to tell me?"

"About that damned instrumentation conference out there. I think it starts on Saturday or something. You need to be there to represent the company and more important to find out what the hell other organizations' thinking is."

"Sounds important. Guess I better find the memo and get ready if you think I should go."

"Well, I've already authorized your travel and the travel office was supposed to have everything ready for you. Guess you better check with them in the mornin'. I'd go but I don't know shit about that stuff and I don't think Elmer knows very much. You're the one, buddy."

Art laughed as he replied, "Okay, I'll check it out tomorrow morning. How long is the conference?"

"Hell, I don't know, two or three or four days I guess. I think that's why they decided to start it on the week end. You'll have to miss the monthly review but Elmer an I'll present your stuff."

"Thanks, Billy, my view graphs and handouts are all ready."

Billy hesitated a moment as he started to leave the office and looked questioningly at Art. "Tell me something . . . "

"Sure", Art replied. "What you want to know?"

What the hell is an MDM? Is it part of that damned expensive integrated electronic assembly."

"A very important part," Art replied. "It is the data interface between all elements of the IEA that the various systems communicate through. Without it the electronics assemblies couldn't communicate with each other and no commands could be processed from the computers."

Billy shrugged his shoulders as he turned, "Too damned deep for me. You electronics weenies better know what the hell you're doin'."

Art's trip to San Diego was uneventful except for the many discussions of the methods of making various measurements, the kind of sensors to use and the method of data capture and reduction after the flight.   He voiced severe reservations about the planned methodology of taking data using on-board recorders. He favored a telemetering link back to the ground station where the data could be received and recorded on an electronic data link.

"How about if we lose a booster in descent? How would we know what went wrong?" he asked the conference.

A seeming committee from the Space Agency descended on him with a vengeance. "We represent the preliminary design group for this data system and we don't believe we need this kind of sophistication. Besides, who ever said we were going to lose one?" a short, balding man who appeared to have more mouth than anything else, stood up and demanded to know.

Art smiled at him and replied, "Well, I know the track record for these kinds of flights is impeccable, but my friend, our luck could run out and then we'd like to know, wouldn't we?" The debate ended in a stalemate and he felt he had failed against such formidable opposition.

At the end of the conference while Art drove to the airport to return home, he began to wonder how the testing on the clevis went. Chip hadn't called, so he could only assume that there were no problems. Then he thought maybe he should have called Elmer to see how the qualification problems were going. As the big Boeing

727 lifted off the runway and began a very smart climb through the perpetual overcast with the mountains in the distance he looked forward toward the cockpit and mused, "I'd sure rather be up in the front office than back here in the big tube. Oh well, can't have everything, I guess." Soon he was fast asleep.

When Art arrived at his office building he decided to go in the front entrance to see if Heidi had made any decisions about her future. He entered the lobby and saw her coming in fifteen minutes early, about her usual time. "Hi beautiful," he called. "Are you awake yet?"

She turned with a start and flashed a big smile across her face. "Gee, I'm glad you're back," she gushed. "I want to talk to you and show you my resignation letter."

"Then you decided to do it?"

"Yeah. I hate to leave here in a lot of ways, but I finally made a decision yesterday."

Her eyes were twinkling as she rounded the desk, poked him playfully in the ribs with a good-natured tease, and continued, "And, my fine feathered friend, I made this decision myself. You weren't here for me to run to for help. What do you think about that?"

He chuckled as he replied, "Well, I never had any doubts about your decisions in the first place. You're a very smart lady, if I do say so."

She teased with a big smile, "I'm glad to hear you finally admit that."

He read the resignation, looked at her over his glasses and asked, "Have you already turned this in?"

She looked alarmed. "I'm going to. Is it okay?"

He couldn't resist laughing. "Of course it's okay. It's great. If I had a criticism I'd say you were too gracious. They don't deserve this up there in that personnel office."

She relaxed and asked quietly, "Did I make the right decision?"

He patted her cheek and responded gently, "I think you did. I want to see you happy and I know you haven't been for a long time." She looked up, smiled and said quietly, "I can always count on you for good advice. That's why I like to ask your opinion."

Art turned toward the elevator. "Got to go see what trouble

I'm in since I left. I'll see you later."

She smiled, threw her long hair back across her shoulder and grinned as she answered happily, "You can count on that, buddy."

As he walked into the program management office area he saw the light on in Elmer's office. "Hi, chief," he greeted.

Elmer turned around, obviously tired and exhausted from what Art presumed some long days at his cable manufacturer's plant. "Damn, I'm glad to see you," he replied, blinking as if to keep his eyes open.

"How's the world of cables?"

"Never worse. I think we found the problem, but I wanted to get your opinion. Got a little while?"

"Sure. Just let me put this stuff down and get a cup of coffee."

Elmer handed him his cup. "How about bringing me one, too. I just made a fresh pot when I came in."

Shortly Art returned with two steaming cups of coffee. Elmer took a long drink and relaxed. "Damn, what a week this has been. The people in engineering can't seem to come up with a cause for that salt water leak and I'm as puzzled as they are. I been up there almost continuously since you left. I left here this morning at 1:30 and was back at 6 a.m."

"Now, Elmer, you know better than that. You lose efficiency so bad you can't be even ten percent productive."

"I know, but this thing is bugging the shit out of me. I took a hell of a beating in the monthly review and was told by the Space Agency people to get it resolved this week or else."

Art studied the cable drawings in deep thought as he mentally fit all the parts and pieces together. He recalled the processes required to fabricate the wires into the connector and then to waterproof the cable with the back shells and cable sheathing intended to keep the moisture out. "Is the cable still relatively intact?" he asked.

Elmer nodded that it was and pointed to a large stack of photographs and X-rays. "There's the pictures we made. I wouldn't let 'em tear it down any further til we're ready for the next step."

Art studied the stack of pictures intently for about thirty minutes and compared all the visible parts to the drawings spread out in front of him. Then he asked, "Where is this little O-ring that goes into the back shell against the grommet?"

Elmer jumped up, "What O-ring?"

He pointed to one on the drawing and then to the photo, "I don't see that one there. It's tiny but it's important."

Elmer squinted at the photo and said, "What's that?" pointing to a little black appendage protruding through the rear of the back shell with a curled shape.

He got out his magnifying glass and studied the black object. "I don't believe that's it. I know you're tired but we might should go look at it."

Elmer leaned back in the chair with a look of exhaustion covering his face. "I don't think I can drive up there again. I'm totally beat."

Art grinned and replied, "I know a better way, let me make a call. I think we can get us a chopper to run up there in if it's not being used."

Elmer sat up straight and looked curiously at Art. "What you talkin' about? This company don't have no chopper."

"I know, but I got a friend who has a Bell 47 we can use."

Elmer was alert now. "Hell, let's go if you can fly it."

Once inside the plant, Elmer introduced Art to Seth, the company's project manager.

"We thought this might be important enough to come up as fast as we could. Let's look at that damned connector one more time. I think Art's found something.

In the lab Art carefully removed the screws from the back shell retainer on the connector and slipped the halves of the back shell away from the wire.

He pointed to the spot where the small O-ring should be, "Not there. There's your problem."

Both Elmer and Seth looked in amazement. Finally Seth exclaimed, "Why in the hell didn't we find that?"

Elmer was standing in amazement and shaking his head. "For one thing, neither of us is much of a hardware engineer. I had to get the expert to look at the pictures."

Art blushed a little as he replied, "Really and truly, you guys were too close to the problem, too involved to see the forest for the trees." He continued a detailed inspection of the connector and the wiring going into the grommet that retained the pins in the connector. "Looks nice otherwise, Seth. I think if you'll replace this one where the salt water penetrated, she'll qualify for you." Art turned to Elmer and continued, "I think we better go back and send you home for a nap, old friend. You look worse than beat."

Art checked his watch as he started to walk toward the front lobby and saw it was lunch time. As he entered he saw Heidi checking in three visitors. When she beckoned to him, he walked over to her desk and said, "Hi, lady."

She finished instructing a rather impatient young man on how to fill out his visitor form and then said quietly, "The Admiral had been looking for you, and Tex asked me to page you. Where you been?"

Art grinned and said quietly, "Mississippi. Solved a problem for Elmer."

She looked up in wide-eyed amazement. "How did you do that?"

"Simple", Art chuckled. "In a helicopter."

She looked even more amazed. "You have a helicopter, too?"

"No, but I got a friend who does. I taught him to fly it when everybody else gave up on him. He lets me use it occasionally."

Heidi took his hand and pinched his little finger. "Why didn't you tell me. What else do you do?"

The visitor, who had finally filled out the form, looked curiously first at Heidi and then Art. She grinned at him and said, "Don't mind us. You know how big brothers are, don't you?"

He nodded, "Oh, sure, I got some of those myself. And a big sister, too."

"Good. Then you do understand." Turning to Art, she continued in the same breath, "Better call the Admiral first, then Tex. See you later."

Art patted her on the head, rumpled his fingers through her long, light brown hair and said to the visitor, "Works wonders for keeping sisters in line. Better try it sometime."

As Art entered the door to the Admiral's office, Marty looked up and said, "That was quick. I was just looking for you. Go on in."

The old Admiral, whose head had now become shiny on top

instead of full of hair as it once was, turned from his credenza where he had been thumbing through a file and said, "Art, we got a problem. I been talking to Eddie Rogers and he said I should see you. I'm sorry you weren't here last week. Those damned nincompoops in engineering don't know their ass from first base."

Art chuckled silently and offered, "Well, sir, how can I help?"

"We got the hell beat out of us on that cable qualification in the monthly review earlier this week. We looked bad and Elmer didn't have any right answers. The Space Agency is down on us hard to get that qualification testing completed and Rogers said you are about the only engineer we had. That's not true is it?"

"No Sir. Eddie's very generous. You've got some people that just need time and experience."

"Well, I hope so. Frank seems to think highly of the management he's put in there but I'm reserving my opinions on that for a while, just like I am in another department."

Art was feeling comfortable now. "Well, Sir, the cable problem is solved. The repairs are being made right now and I think the qualification testing will go on okay."

"How do you know that?"

"Well, when I came in this morning Elmer showed me some pictures of the assemblies and the drawings. I got lucky and saw something they hadn't seen before and went out to the plant to check it out."

"To the plant?" the Admiral asked with a shocked tone.

"We found they had left out a little O-ring in the rear of the connector back shell that allowed the moisture to get in. They plan to start testing again, probably tomorrow."

The Admiral was on the edge of his chair. "You say you went out to the plant to check it out? I'm talking about today, this morning. You couldn't possibly have gone out there. It's only 12:30 and I happen to know it's over a hundred miles over there."

"Yes sir," Art replied. "It's exactly 136 air miles over there. We went over by helicopter. I have a friend who loaned me a Bell 47 and we took it over there. It's pretty fast as helicopters go."

The Admiral was looking in disbelief. "You're a helicopter pilot?" he asked.

"Yes sir. I fly a little."

The Admiral sat back in his chair with a grin that almost

covered his entire face. "Well, I'll be damned. I had no idea. Are you sure about the qualification problem and the fix?"

"Yes sir. I feel like we got it solved now. It was just a simple mistake in assembly."

"That's wonderful news," Engle replied with a big grin. "I hope it's gonna work out now."

"I'm sure it will," Art replied as he rose to leave.

"By the way," Engle continued, "there's one more thing I have to mention."

"Yes sir," Art answered as he started to leave.

"Company policy does not allow any private flying in anything. Don't mention that trip."

Art checked his watch and saw it was nearly one o'clock and he had talked right through lunch. He decided to go to Tex's office to see how things were progressing at StressCo. As he turned the corner he heard Tex in an excited voice, exclaim, "I don't know where he is, Chip." Tex saw Art and jumped up excitedly from his chair, "Here he is. Hold on." He quickly shoved the phone to Art and said, "Here, talk to Chip. He's got a problem."

Art asked excitedly, "What kind of a problem?"

"Hell, I don't know. Talk to Chip."

. He took the phone and turned on the speaker so they both could hear. "What's the problem?"

"Don't know but we just had a weird thing happen."

"What do you mean, 'weird'?"

"I mean weird, man, weird. That damned clevis popped like a rifle shot during test."

Art looked at Tex, who shrugged his shoulders as if to say he didn't understand either. "How do you know it was the clevis? Did something break?"

Chip became calm since he found Art and replied with much less panic, "I don't think so. I was standing right by it and it scared the hell out of me. It seemed to come from the clevis just as we went through 290,000 pounds compression load."

"Okay. Stop the test."

Before he could complete the statement Chip blurted out, "Hell, I already did. I been scared of this thing anyhow. Do you realize what would happen if we broke something at one of these high loads?"

"Okay Chip, settle down. Tex and I are on the way out right now."

He looked at Tex, who was looking as blank as he felt at the moment. "What the hell do you suppose could cause that, Tex? Must have broken something in the press or something slipped."

Tex was putting away things on his desk and stuffing his contract into his old brief case. He replied excitedly, still stuffing files and folders into his desk, "Sounds bad to me. If something came off that damned thing at the loads we're running, we might kill somebody."

CHAPTER TWELVE

Art and Tex arrived at StressCo quickly because of their concern about breaking either a clevis or the press at the high force loads that could quickly result in death and destruction from shrapnel-like parts. Sam and Chip were standing out front waiting when they arrived. "Hi, guys," Art said as they got out of the car. "Find anything yet?"

"Not yet. The test setup is still just like it was. We haven't changed anything," Chip answered.

Tex replied, "Good. We need to see it before you change anything."

As they entered the building Art asked, "Has this machine ever done this before?"

Sam, looking worried, responded, "Not to my knowledge, and we've run it a thousand times."

Tex replied gently as they entered the lab, "That may be the problem."

Chip pointed to the clevis still mounted in the press, "That's right the way it was. I backed the pressure off as soon as it happened."

"That was smart. At these loads we can't afford to take any chances." Art replied, peering at the press and the clevis. "First, I want to look at the outside of the tooling and while I'm doing that, Sam, how about getting your mechanical guys to take a close look at the press."

"Sounds good," Sam croaked, less than enthusiastic about disturbing his press and possibly delaying the program.

The five of them worked late into the night examining all aspects of the tooling and looking for cracks. When it was finally evident that fatigue was setting in, Tex suggested, "How about we hang it up until tomorrow?"

Sam, who had been sitting quietly in a chair for some time stood up and asked, "How about my schedule? We got to test this thing."

Tex glared, obviously irritated. "Sam, you may not test anything else on this press. Ever! We're gonna examine every part.

Don't worry about schedule. I'll handle that."

"Sam, you don't want to kill somebody here," Art added sternly.

Sam flinched and answered sheepishly, "I'm sorry, fellahs. I just don't want to be late on your job."

Tex, with a more kindly look, responded, "I appreciate that, but this here's serious. Did you ever have an accident with one of these presses?"

"No. Never did," Sam replied quietly.

"Well," Art grunted, "this damned thing could be a cannon ready to go off if something broke. In fact, I'm considering requiring a blast shield. I'm honestly afraid of it."

The next morning the group reconvened in the StressCo lab at 7:30 where they repeated the tooling and mounting examinations from the previous night. Finally Art asked, "Chip, just where were you when the noise happened?"

Chip was frowning as he relived the experience. "I was standing here," indicating the spot, "and that pop came from up there", pointing to the area where the clevis was secured in the tooling.

Art considered that a moment and asked, "Are you sure?"

"Of course I'm sure."

Edgar volunteered, "Chip's right. I was here, too, and I'd swear we had a thread slip," pointing to the mounting block where the clevis screwed into the test fixture.

"How about you, Brady? You still agree with that?"

"Yep. It come from up there. Sounded just like a rifle shot," pointing to the same spot that Chip had pointed to earlier.

"Well, you know what you guys are saying, don't you? That it was either the tooling or the clevis,"

Chip looked at Art quizzically. "So?"

"So," Art began, "since nothing broke I think the only thing left to do is to run a magnaflux test on all the parts to see if there's any cracks." Art turned to Tex. "Do you agree?"

Tex thought for a moment and replied, "Yeah, but I think we ought to take the gears and drive shafts out of the transmission and do them too. And then, maybe we'd be smart to take the vertical screws out of the mounts and do them. Maybe something in there cracked we ain't found yet."

Sam stared over his glasses first at Tex and then at Art and then at Tex. His expression was one of deep pain as he asked, "You're serious, aren't you?"

Tex squinted as he answered, "You're damned right. I want to know what cracked or broke, or shifted, or what the hell happened."

"Okay," Sam grumbled. "Let's get on with it. It'll take two or three days."

Art glanced at Chip and asked, "Can you stay with this till it's completed?"

"You're damned right. I want to know, too."

"Great. Call me if you find anything. Tex and I have got to get back to the plant."

They were almost silent on the way back, each in deep contemplation about the strange noise. As they arrived at the parking lot, Tex, frowning, commented, "It's got to be either the press, the tooling, or the clevis unit itself." He squirmed in the seat and adjusted his glasses to get a better view of Art as he parked his old Buick in the lot under a pine tree.

"You're right," he answered jokingly, "but as any damned fool can see, it's got to be one or the other."

"Yep, that's what we got to figure out old buddy," Tex replied.

"Well, we got the ball rolling in the right direction. I hope that magnaflux testing shows some cracks in the press parts. I think it will."

"Well, if it doesn't, I don't know what to do next, but I tell you what I think I will do. I think I'll go talk to Wayne Ingram about it. He's an old ICBM man. Maybe he's seen something like this before."

"Sounds good," Tex replied, "Maybe you ought to touch base with Al Bryant over in Quality, too. There's a lot of experience in that old boy."

"Good idea," Art replied, as they entered the front lobby of the building where he saw Heidi sitting with a big smile.

"Hi beautiful, you sure look spiffy today. Is that a new outfit?"

"Sure is," she bubbled. "Like it?"

Art stood back and surveyed the sheer silk, light brown dress clinging tightly to her perfectly-shaped figure filling it out correctly in all the right places. "Stand up. Let me see all of it."

Heidi stood up and walked from behind her receptionist desk. She whirled around on her three-inch heels as the dress rose with the motion to reveal a pair of beautiful legs. "Like it?"

"Absolutely beautiful. I even like the dress, too."

Heidi giggled and poked him in the ribs playfully. "Nut, I meant the dress. I know what you think of the girl."

He wanted to put his arms around her and give her a big bear hug in the lobby but was afraid someone would walk up. He took her hand and squeezed it tightly and smiled at her instead. "They're both beautiful, especially the girl."

She smiled as she got as close as she dared in the lobby. "I really wore this for you today hoping you would notice me when you came in."

"Well, baby, it worked. But you know you don't have to dress for me to notice you." He watched her carefully, thinking what a beautiful thing she really was. He almost hated the rules of society when he thought of the pleasures of a woman like this.

"Yeah, I guess that's one of the frustrating things about you, Art Cannon," she answered.

He gazed into her big green eyes that were crying out for love and affection. "Heidi," he started, "you're one of the most beautiful women I know and I assure you that if I could, I'd be knocking on your door."

She sat down on the edge of her desk, displaying her long legs dangling off the edge, as she leaned forward looking like a school girl in love. "I know that and that's one of the great things about you. You know how I feel and I can't help it but I would never want you to betray a trust."

"I appreciate that."

"Yeah and if I were married to you, I'd like to know I could trust you, too. But then sometimes . . . "

He patted her on the back of the head and then ran his fingers through the long, soft hair as he stood in front of her. "I know, Heidi. Believe me, I know. To me you'd look great in anything." Then he squeezed her shoulders and kissed her lightly on the end of the nose. "I got to get up stairs before I got us both in trouble. See you later."

"You can count on that."

As the elevator opened he turned to her, "I meant to ask you, if you don't have any other plans, I'd like to feed you lunch on your last day."

She beamed as she answered, "I was hoping you would. I'm totally available."

As the elevator door closed, he saw her turning to her typing and thought, *Gee, what a woman.*

Art went straight to Chief Engineer Wayne Ingram's office. "Wayne," he began as he seated himself at the table in front of the desk piled high with technical journals and books of one sort or another, "you been around this business a long time. I need some help or at least some advice."

Wayne laid down his calculator and pencil, realizing that the visit was more than social. "Sure. Any way I can help I'll be glad to."

Art outlined the problem and when he finished, Wayne leaned back with his hands behind his head. After a few moments contemplation, he responded, "Well, I agree with your approach so far. I think you need the magnaflux testing but you need to consider the next alternative."

"What's that?"

"Well, if the magnaflux doesn't show anything, I think you need to bring that clevis here and do an X-ray, just to be sure. I think that if you've got an internal crack it'll show up."

"How much resolution can we get on an internal crack?"

"If you're asking how small a crack we can see, I'd say we could see one less than one thousandths of an inch across. But it's also possible Inconel 718 steel is so dense our X-ray may not be able to see it. You need to talk to the non-destructive testing people."

"Does the Space Agency have that capability out at the Center?"

Wayne was staring out the window thinking. Slowly he responded, "I think so. Have you talked to them about the problem yet?"

"No, but I don't see any need to excite them yet. I'd rather solve it and go ahead if we can."

"I agree," he answered quietly. "But if there does appear to be a problem in the clevis we need to let 'em know in writing through contracts as a formal submittal."

"Okay. I'll keep you posted."

"Fine," Wayne replied. As an afterthought he commented, "You might want to talk to Alf Bennett. You know he's a metallurgist."

Art sat up with a start. "I didn't know that. I sure will and I'll try to get him to coordinate the X-ray if we do it."

"I'm sure he will."

Art went back to his office and sat down with a cup of fresh coffee to work on other pressing problems in the electrical and instrumentation system. He was immersed in review of a proposal for the integrated electronic assembly when Elmer sat down with a big grin. Art looked up and greeted in, "Hi, Elmer, what's up?"

"The cable qualified after we put that o-ring in. Boy, what a relief. The Space Agency inspector just bought 'em off." Elmer was elated.

Art leaned back and smiled. "I'm sure pleased to hear that. That's really good news."

Elmer slapped the table with the palm of his hand. "Man, that's team work. We're building a hell of a team in this office."

Art laughed and waved his hand, "Just wait, friend. You haven't heard it all. I got problems. Maybe you can help solve mine."

Elmer quit celebrating and looked concerned. "What problems you got? You mean with that clevis?"

He shook his head affirmatively and proceeded to brief Elmer. While he narrated his discussion with Wayne Ingram, Elmer leaned back and put his feet up on the desk, seemingly to be able to ponder the problem more efficiently. "Well, looks like you got the bases covered so far," he finally replied.

"Yeah, I think so. In a couple of days we ought to know the results of the magnaflux testing. Then we'll know where to go from there."

The next morning as Art reached his office his phone rang before he could get his usual morning coffee. Must be mighty important to call this early, he thought. "Art, Sam Kelley. We completed the magnaflux last night about midnight and we couldn't find any cracks anywhere in anything, including the clevis."

"I didn't know you were going to work last night. Was Chip there?"

"Yep. He offered to help when I told him I wanted us to get this testing done. I'm still scared of your schedule in spite of what Tex says."

"Sam," he replied sternly, "Tex told you he would cover you contractually."

"I know and I believe him. I just want to maintain it if I can."

"I appreciate that. Tell me about the magnaflux."

"Well," Sam began, "we put each piece in the machine and got no crack indication anywhere, including the clevis."

"Did you do all the parts, gears and all?"

"Yep. Everything," he declared.

Art was quiet for a moment as he considered this and quietly answered, "Well, I don't know what to think right now. I'm puzzled. I'll get back to you after while." He sat down and then smelled hot coffee brewing. He poured himself a cup, even though it wasn't quite through; looked at the color and decided it was strong enough. As he turned to go back to his desk he greeted, "Mornin' Elmer."

"Hey, you're early. You must be thinking about that clevis."

"I sure as hell am. How about we caucus when you set your briefcase down."

"Sure thing." Shortly Elmer sat down, held his cup up and declared, "Now that I got my second cup I can think better. You look puzzled."

Art squinted out the window across the aisle from his cubicle and replied, "I'm damned puzzled. I just talked to Sam and he assured me there's no cracks in any of the parts or in the clevis but I'm afraid to continue testing until we know what caused that damned pop. What if there's a problem somewhere that we ain't found and that thing broke in flight?"

"Hell, man, don't even think about it. It'd be bad."

"Elmer, if we broke a piece of that thing out at 400,000 pounds it could go completely through the plant, building, people and all."

Elmer sat pensively for a moment. Then he responded, "Maybe you should put a blast shield up. Why don't you talk to Safety about it?"

"I think I will. Tex wants to, too, but that doesn't solve the noise problem."

As Art took a long drink from his cup he saw Chip Harrell

coming around the corner at a fast clip. "Hi guys. Did Sam call yet?" Chip asked.

Art nodded affirmatively and replied, "It don't sound good. I was hoping we'd find a cracked part."

Chip seated himself in an extra chair, leaned back and eyed Elmer's coffee. "Where'd you get that?"

Elmer pointed to the pot over by the wall. "Help yourself."

Chip poured himself a cup and returned to the perch he had occupied. "What do you think?" Art asked.

"I still think it's that damned clevis."

Elmer sat up straight, not wanting to hear that answer. He knew Chip wasn't prone to make snap judgments, which fueled his concern even more. "What makes you think that?" he asked.

"Because of the location I was standing in and the type of sound it made. I'll grant you there's other parts that could make a similar sound but we'd find something broken. The big pieces would have made a duller sound. I'm convinced." Chip shrugged his shoulders for emphasis.

Art studied him intently before asking, "But you found no evidence of cracking in the magnaflux. How do you explain that?"

"I don't know, I just believe it was the clevis. Don't ask me how, I just feel it."

"Yeah. In this quality business you just learn to feel things sometimes," Art replied.

"Well," Elmer began, "I know one way you can eliminate the press."

"How's that?" Chip asked.

"You could reassemble it and then proof test it."

"What if it broke?" Art asked.

"Proof test it gradually. Don't load it all the way the first time. Just bring the load up incrementally without any tooling the first time and then if everything checks out on those runs install the tooling and repeat the process."

"Might work," Art replied quietly, contemplating the possibility. "I'm game to try it if you feel comfortable with it, Chip."

"Well, we aren't gettin' anywhere this way," he replied with a grin. "We need to do something to eliminate something."

"Okay. Why don't you go out there and supervise the reassembly of that damned thing and then lets do it. I'll clear it with

205

Tex for contract coverage."

Art briefed Tex, who sat quietly. Finally he responded, "Well, I agree. I'll call Sam. Why don't we go out, too? This son-of-a-bitch is buggin' the shit out of me."

He laughed at Tex and remarked jovially, "Old machinists never die, they just keep right on turning."

Tex turned red and snapped, "It's too early in the morning to be kidded, especially by a damned spark chaser."

Art moved so he could get a clearer view of his face and remarked, "Spiffy this early ain't he?"

"You damned guys better be glad you got a contracts man that understands your problems. One of these other suckers around here wouldn't know which end of this damned thing to start on." He sat down and muttered quietly, "There ain't no damned humor in a piece of machinery I don't understand and so far this shittin' thing don't make no sense."

"Nor any of the rest of us yet," Art consoled. "But you can be sure that we will before it's over."

Tex instructed Sam to begin to reassemble the press without the test tooling. The reassembly, under Edgar's skillful guidance, was completed just before lunch. Art stood for a moment and observed the monolithic machine towering over the room, with it's top protruding up into a recessed area in the ceiling. He asked Chip, "Satisfied with the assembly?"

Edgar nodded his head and responded, "Satisfied. Let's install the dummy clevis simulator and get started."

After completion of the simulated clevis tooling, Art commanded, "Okay, lets's take it up in steps. Fifty thousand pound increments for the first 200,000 pounds. Then 25,000 pound increments for the next 200,000 pounds and the last 50,000 in 10,000 pound increments. We'll stop and examine it at each increment. Any objection to that process, anybody?"

They studied the press for a moment and Tex finally nodded his head in approval. "Sounds good to me," Edgar replied and turned on the power.

As Edgar brought up the load to the first 50,000 pound increment Art held up his hand to signify a stop at that point and commanded, "Let's look at this thing to be sure we don't have anything that appears to be about to fail." They completed inspection of the major components of the press at the first load and Edgar asked, "Ready for the next increment?"

Art looked at Tex and Chip and got a confirming nod from each one. Edgar repeated the process again and again with the detailed inspections taking more and more time as the load was gradually increased to 400,000 pounds. Just at 400,000 pounds the quitting time buzzer went off in the manufacturing assembly areas. Tex and Art jumped as though they had been electrified and drained of all strength. "Damn Sam," Tex finally stammered, "why didn't you tell me about that son-of-a-bitch'n thing. That scared the hell out of me. I thought somethin' broke."

"Hell, fellahs, I'm sorry," Sam replied repentantly. "I just plain forgot. I been so concentrated here on this thing that I ain't been thinkin' about much else."

Art finally laughed good naturedly, although still somewhat shaken. "Well, it sure as hell got our attention," he replied.

The atmosphere seemed to be electrically charged; apprehension and worry was evident. The slightest noise out of the ordinary was cause for alarm. Sam, still sitting in a chair by the door, had broken out into a profuse sweat. Tex had nothing to say as he studied the huge machine straining and groaning. This process continued until the force readout indicated 450,000 pounds; everyone was quiet, listening to the agonized whirring of the gears driving the large screws that applied the loads to the press. The gears now turned slowly, protesting each turn, pulling the structure ever tighter down on the lower platen.

Sam was wiping his brow and saying nothing. Tex moved to the press and began to inspect his areas. Without a word each person followed suit and for the next thirty minutes performed a detailed inspection. Edgar emerged from behind the gear box and asked, "Can we let her down? It ain't broke yet."

Art pointed to the control panel. "Yeah, start down slow and give everything time to settle out. Then let's do it again in tension. I don't see anything wrong in compression."

As the pressure was reduced, Sam relaxed and stopped sweating proportionately.

"Are we gonna take the tooling up to the same loads?" Chip

asked as they completed the inspection.

"Yeah, I think we got to," Art replied as he crawled from behind the big gear box. "We got to have confidence in the whole system, not just part of it."

Tex looked over his glasses. "I agree, but I don't have to like it."

The remaining tests were performed without incident or indication of any problem and the load was reduced to zero from the tension mode. Edgar shut down the system and looked at his watch. "Hell, it's after 11 o'clock," he grunted.

Art and Tex stood looking at the tooling for a few moments. Tex felt of the main screw block where the clevis bolted into the base of the platen and commented, "That damned thing ought to stand about anything."

Chip asked, "Satisfied that the press is okay Art?"

"Yeah, but all that means is we may have a problem in the test tooling."

The next morning, Saturday, while Art poured a cup of fresh coffee Sam had made, the others arrived ready for the days testing, apprehensive of the unknown. No one said much for a while but when all were gathered in the room housing the monolithic monster, as Chip called it sometimes, Art asked, "Tex, ready to go?"

Tex took a large swallow of coffee and grunted, "Yeah. But I'm still worried."

"Me too, but we'll know soon," Art replied quietly.

They watched Edgar and Chip install tooling and the dummy clevis, which was nothing more than a large chunk of solid steel twenty-four inches long and seven inches in diameter with fittings machined onto the ends to simulate the actual flight clevis.

After the tooling installation was completed and every detail checked, Art commanded, "Take her up just like we did last night." At the 250,000 pound load point Sam sat down in the same chair he occupied the previous night and began to sweat through his old plaid shirt. He decided against any comment because he, as well as the others, knew that this could be the most crucial of the tests. "What load did the other one pop at?" Sam asked.

"290,000 pounds compression. We're approaching that now," Tex replied.

Art interjected, "Well, if we had a tooling crack I'd think we'd have an indication by now."

"Yeah," Tex replied cautiously, his years as a machinist beginning to show. "I'm beginning to agree with Chip about a cracked clevis."

The balance of the tests were completed and except for the usual creaking and groaning of the joints in the press, there were no anomalies. When the press was finally recycled to zero load, Art sat down on a table and peered questioningly at the others. "Well, guys, it's opinion time."

They stared at the floor and after a long silence Edgar answered, "It's like I told you before, when Chip and I were standing here. We got a clevis problem."

Tex peered at Edgar pensively. "Yeah, I hear what you're saying, but what about the magnaflux? It didn't show any problem and if that thing had cracked inside it should show up."

Art stood up and shook his head, "Well, I think we've eliminated the press and the tooling. Now I think we need to talk to Alf and Wayne on Monday and see what they think our next move is."

Monday morning as Art pulled into the parking lot his watch read 7:05 am, which was twenty-five minutes ahead of his usual starting time. *Damn*, he thought, *I could have slept a little longer this morning.* When he entered the lobby on his way to the elevator he thought of Heidi and her last week at Space Corp. He turned the corner into the main lobby and saw that she hadn't arrived. *Good girl,* he thought, *I wouldn't be early either, if I were quitting.*

As he got on the elevator he saw Sonny and Lissie coming in together and thought, *Another example of Peyton Place. I wonder how Sonny's wife is taking all this.* Art had seen Sonny's wife one time at a company party and thought, *What a rotten deal that lady must have gotten in life. I wonder what kind of line he fed her over there.*

Just then the elevator door opened and he stepped into the hallway leading to the Program Office. He saw movers scurrying about with little trucks moving furniture and wondered what everything was all about. As Art turned the corner to his cubicle and found it empty, he heard a snicker behind him. He turned to find Elmer about to choke to keep from laughing. "What the hell's goin' on, Elmer?" he asked cautiously.

"Well, I thought I'd surprise you, old buddy. You've surprised us some so I thought I'd just not tell you until it happened."

"What do you mean, not tell me? What?"

"Well," Elmer chuckled, "we're moving down to the third floor. You know that suite of offices over on the south side of the building? Billy finally got 'em and he agreed to give us two offices over there with nice windows."

Art looked at Elmer incredulously. "Well, I'll be damned. I never knew."

"Yeah, you been too busy. Now we'll be near the main conference room so we can have better access for meetings. Besides, there's a lot of moving scheduled to go on around the company this week. I think Configuration Management is supposed to move in here."

"Where's your office?"

"Right next door to yours. By the way, so you don't get surprised, Heidi's down there straightening out for you. She came in yesterday and packed your office."

Art looked at him with surprise, "You're kidding? Heidi did that?"

"Yep. She's a strange girl. Nobody's ever been able to really make friends much with her but you. How the hell did you do that?"

"Oh, I don't really know unless it's because I treated her like a lady and an equal. She appreciates respect, you know."

"I tell you, man, that's one beautiful woman. Most of the men in this company would give anything to have her."

"Maybe that's the problem. They try to put the make on her first."

"Hell, I guess you're right. But you got to admit she could excite a damned man a hundred years old."

Art walked down the steps to the South side of the third floor and saw an office with a large window that already had his name on the door. He took note of the carpet and thought, *Damn, this is nice.* As he entered, he saw Heidi in the office dusting the window sill and straightening the curtains. He walked quietly on the soft carpet until he was behind her, reached out and took her by the waist on each side and pulled her up against him. "Hi, beautiful," he said gently.

She turned quickly, startled, and then fell over on Art's shoulder, the long hair falling down over his white shirt. "You scared the life out of me."

He looked at her as he still held her close and felt the warmth of her body penetrating his. She put her arms around his neck as if to support herself and snuggled in closer. He felt the two large, beautifully shaped, breasts against his chest and felt her heart beating faster as he held her. "Baby, you didn't have to do all this."

"But that's what's nice about it. I did it because I wanted to do something for you."

Art squeezed her in a big bear hug, feeling her firm, warm body molded into his as she pressed closer. "Thanks baby. I appreciate you."

She pulled away a little and stared into his eyes, her eyes searching from one to the other, as if she would find a simple answer. "I'm gonna cry in a minute and then I'll ruin the makeup and buddy, you'll be in trouble."

He released her and laughed as he teased, "Well, I sure don't want to get in trouble with you, lady."

"I mean good trouble . . . the best of trouble."

He proudly surveyed the office and the neat job she had done. "It's a hell of an improvement, isn't it?"

She looked thoughtfully out the window at the pigeons flying to and from their perches. Then she turned around to face him with a serious look. "You deserve the best, Art Cannon. By the way, how'd the tests go this weekend?"

"How'd you know about that?"

"Tina's a friend and she called me late Friday night in a panic. I finally convinced her you knew what you were doing and everything would be okay."

He was dumbfounded, "Tina's a friend of yours?"

"Long time. We went to high school together. By the way, did Annie know what you were doing?"

"No, I thought it'd be best not to tell her."

"That's what I'd expect. You should keep her informed. She has a vested interest, too, just like I do and I mean to see our interests are taken care of."

"Oh?" he replied.

"Yeah. So boy, the next time you stick your neck out, you better tell her and you better tell me."

Art laughed, side-stepped the issue, and replied, "I sure

appreciate all this. You're a real sweetheart."

She walked over close to Art by the windows and he took her in his arms again and held her. He saw a little tear forming in the corner of her eye that he spread with his finger before it could cause any makeup problems and kissed her nose gently.

Heidi laid her head on his shoulder and said quietly, "I don't think I can leave, Art. I won't see you very often." He released her and she turned slowly toward the door, "but we're still on Friday?"

"You bet we are, but I'll see you before then."

"You better, or I'll come huntin' you," she laughed as she walked out the door.

He seated himself at his desk in the new office and turned to look out the window. *Damned nice of Elmer to get this one for me,* he thought. Elmer soon appeared with a concerned look on his face. "How'd the tests go this weekend?"

Art responded quietly, thinking back over the weekend, "That damned system worked fine. I think the next move is to discuss it with Wayne and Alf Bennett. Chip and Tex should be here in a few minutes, if they can find me."

"Yeah, I agree. Why don't you call Wayne and get with him soon as possible."

Soon all the principals were seated around Wayne Ingram's office table and Art made a mental note of attendance. Wayne, Chief Engineer; Alf, metallurgist; himself; Chip, QC Engineer; Tex, Procurement Officer; and Elmer, Program Manager for Electrical and Instrumentation Systems. Wayne turned to Art and said, "Well, the floor's yours."

"Thanks Wayne," he replied as he proceeded to outline the activities and results to date. He summed up with, "I guess we could use some guidance about how to proceed."

Wayne leaned back in his chair, carefully considering all that he had heard. He put his hands behind his head and crossed his legs in deep thought. He finally responded, "Well, it sounds like you've done all the steps correctly so far. I wouldn't change anything you've done."

Alf nodded his agreement and added, "I think, though, that you need to consider a blast screen around that press. Some of those exotic metals will shatter . . ."

Wayne interrupted Alf, "I think the next thing in order is to write this up and submit it through our contracts office to the Space Agency Structures Lab and let them send a copy over to the Materials Lab. I think they need to get involved now since they still have design responsibility."

Alf was looking ponderous and sat for a few moments before saying anything, as though he were trying to measure his response. He finally said, "Inconel 718 is a very tough material. I don't know much about it, but I know it has some excellent tensile stress capability . . ."

Art interrupted, "But Alf, the problem occurred in compression, that is if we even have a problem."

"Yeah, that's what keeps bothering me. I don't know that much about the compressive side of that material. But I think you should do what Wayne suggested and I'm sure the Materials Lab will have some experts in that area."

Over the next two days, Art researched all available data on the popping, and summarized the work that he had done. When he had completed a detailed report and obtained Elmer's and Wayne's concurrence, he commented to Wayne, "I'll feel better when we get those guys involved because of their expertise. I'll run this down to William in contracts and get it out."

William Bagley, the Contracts Manager for Space Corp, studied the letter report and wrinkled his brow. "I don't know if we ought to tell 'em their hardware's bad or not, Art . . . "

Art was irritated and interrupted, "William, I'm countin' on you. This is important. This is the twentynineth of August, and I want an answer by the fifth of September. Understand?"

"I don't think they'll respond that quick to anything?"

He was becoming frustrated. "Well, they'll respond a lot faster if you get that out there today. Art lowered his eyes and looked straight at William as he continued, "And you better not screw up my schedule, either."

William flinched and squirmed in his big over-stuffed chair, "Okay, okay. I'll get it out there today."

When Art arrived back at his office his phone was ringing. "What's the verdict, Art?" Sam Kelly asked apprehensively.

"We sent the report to the Space Agency, Sam. All we can do now is wait on 'em to respond, so just sit still and let's see what they want to do. By the way," Art continued, "I want to plot out the data we have so far."

"Sure. We can use our plotter out here."

When Art arrived at StressCo, Edgar was busily entering data into the computer. Finally he was through and gave the little machine a plot command. "Won't be long, now," he commented as the plotter pen started to draw a curve from the data that had been entered.

Art pulled the sheet off the plotter and held it up for closer scrutiny. Then he quietly commented, "This curve isn't right, Edgar. Look at this damned thing."

Edgar examined the plot with a furrowed brow. "Looks like it's got one hell of a hysteresis curve on the compression side, to me, if the plot's right. But look here at the tension side. It's well behaved."

"Yeah, it's weird. Look here at the compression curve. The load goes up to 400,000 pounds sort of ragged like with an error from the standard of less than one percent. We can live with that. But look, when you start down with the load from 400,000 the curve doesn't come back down the line it made going up. The damned curve almost goes straight down and then bends back to the origin sort of like a gourd shape."

Art continued to study the curve. He finally broke the silence, "I'm gonna ask Eddie to come out here."

He dialed Eddie's number and heard, "Rogers here."

"Eddie, I need your help a few minutes."

"Sure. I'll come right up. I'm not doin' anything especially important right now."

"I'm not in the office. I'm out at StressCo."

"Be right out."

"That guy sounds like a character."

Art grinned at Edgar's perception of Eddie. "He is. That's what makes him so priceless and probably the best operations research man in the city."

Soon they laid their data plots on the table in front of Eddie. "Look at this," Art commanded. "That's the weirdest damned plot I ever saw."

"What's it of?" Eddie asked as he intently studied the curves. As was so typical of Eddie, who was a fun-loving individual until it came to business, then he was all business. His analytical mind began to work like a mainframe computer, spitting forth either solutions or questions like a machine gun.

"It's the response of a clevis to the loads input through the press in both tension and compression compared to response of the very linear standard."

"Is the standard calibrated?"

"To National Bureau of Standards specifications. The load cell has an almost perfectly linear, straight curve everywhere."

"Let me see the calibration curve on the load cell."

Shortly Edgar returned with the calibration curve which Eddie scrutinized carefully. He laid it down on the table and placed a straight edge along the curve. "Looks damned near perfectly linear."

"Let's do a data dump and look at the numbers on several of the runs they made and see how they look," Art suggested.

"Good idea," Eddie concurred, as he sat down in front of the computer and instructed the little machine to dump all the data on six of the calibration runs, three in tension and three in compression.

When the printer quit, they began to study the numbers printed in neat columns and rows. "The load increments look right," Eddie commented. "I don't see anything that would skew the data but look here in the compression side at the intervals of the read-out from the strain gages inside the clevis. You can see that the intervals between the clevis data and the standard diverge and make the curve go down when the load was decreased instead of following the curve back down the same path it made going up."

Art asked, "Edgar, I know you been in the load cell business a long time. Ever seen anything like this before?"

"No. Never in ten years of designing these things."

Eddie was silent for several moments while he pondered the strange curve. He peered at Art over the top of his glasses and suggested, "Lets put some test data in the computer that we know will give us a linear plot on both the compression and the tension side and see how it plots out. If it skews, we know we have a computer problem. If it doesn't, well . . ."

Art thought for a moment and finally said, "Let's simulate the

215

loads from zero to 400,000 in both tension and in compression."

Eddie studied the numbers Art proposed and replied, "That should plot linearly on both sides of the curve." Then he busied himself typing the test data into the computer. Without looking up, he replied, "I think I'll do a graphics plot first." He keyed in the plot commands and watched the plotter needle begin to move. To their dismay the curves plotted out a straight line.

Eddie took the paper off the plotter and laid a straight edge on it and commented slowly, "Buddy, you couldn't got a more linear plot than that. I don't think there's a machine problem. I believe that's the way that damned data came out of your test."

Art sat down by the computer with a long, serious, questioning expression. "Must be something wrong in the strain gages. No piece of steel would display a characteristic like that."

Eddie put his feet up on the computer table and leaned back looking at the screen. "Well, right now I'm inclined to agree. I've never seen anything like that."

Edgar had been listening intently. Finally he broke in. "I supervised the installation of those gages and Sara put 'em on. She's the best there is and I'll bet my reputation they're put in right. They're exactly like the manufacturer's requirements."

They became silent as they both tried to sort out a possible cause. Finally, out of desperation, Art suggested, "Let's run the data on the clevis that popped and see how that plots out."

Eddie, eager to proceed, leaned over the computer. "One hell of a good idea."

He searched the disk files, entered the commands and quickly was plotting data. "I'll make a plot of the stabilization runs because they're lower loads and then I'll plot the full-up load to see where the thing popped and Chip shut down." Shortly the plots were complete for the first stabilization run to 200,000 pounds.

"Look here, Art," Eddie said. "This damned thing was following the same curve shape as the other one." He pointed to the tension side of the curve plot and continued, "It's showing almost no hysteresis in the tension side, one percent or less. But here, on the compression side, it's got that damned gourd-shaped curve."

Art wrinkled his brow with a large frown. "Shit. I'll bet it's going to be in all of 'em. Let's look at the next one."

Eddie changed paper and started the plot program again.

Shortly the second stabilization was plotted. Eddie placed one plot over the other and held them up to the light. "Look here, this one lays over the other one almost perfectly. That says the strain gages are installed and working correctly."

"Yeah. Otherwise it wouldn't be repeatable."

Eddie, displaying frustration, entered the command to the computer to plot the next curve to 290,000 pounds compression where the "rifle shot" sound occurred. All three watched the plot intently as the tension side of the curve was drawn. "Looks good so far," Eddie commented as the pen switched sides of the vertical axis in the plot and began to draw the compression side of the curve.

As the pen reached 290,000 pounds it jumped and made a narrow spike on the paper that appeared as a vertical line downward and then off the paper above the plot line, forming a very compressed "Z" laying on its side. It returned to the plot line, to began it's plot upward again and abruptly stopped. "That's where Chip shut down," Art commented, "at about 292,000 pounds."

Both Art and Eddie studied the curves for several minutes without saying a word. Finally, Art pointed to the spike and quietly said, "Almost looks like the material yielded here, or at least it sure as hell relieved itself."

"Yeah, but what does it mean?"

"Right now I don't know, but I'm getting a definite feeling that this material has some funny characteristics."

Eddie raised an eyebrow and looked at the clevis laying in it's storage box. "Well, we may have a real problem."

CHAPTER THIRTEEN

Art and Eddie drove back to Space Corp after finding the very strange hysteresis curve displayed by the aft strut clevises. This curve, indicating the reaction of the metal to the forces applied, confounded their expectations and limited knowledge of metallurgy. It defied their logic or reason for such systems and raised great fear that there may indeed be serious design problems that each knew were so critical to survivability of any Space shuttle launch. They firmly resolved that the problem, if it was a problem, must be investigated and thoroughly understood, especially since the strange and as-yet undefined rifle shot-like pop had occurred.

As they entered the lobby to the elevator Heidi came through the swinging doors leading into procurement and personnel. "Well, well, if it isn't the dynamic duo," she commented with a big smile. Eddie peered at her over his glasses. "At least she recognizes talent," he teased.

Art smiled at her as she came up closer and greeted her pleasantly, "Hi lady. How's it goin'?"

"Chip's been looking for you and I think he just went out to StressCo. How'd it go out there?"

"Baby, we may have a real problem. There's some things we just don't understand yet," Art replied as he pressed the elevator button. "We're still on for tomorrow?"

Heidi looked pleased and brushed her hair back over her shoulder as she replied, "You bet."

Eddie had been observing the looks that she gave Art. After the elevator door closed he commented observantly, "Better watch it, friend, I think she's got it bad."

Art replied quietly, "Yeah. I got to do something for her without hurting her. She's walked through the gates of hell and back and she's still afloat."

"Yeah. She's a beautiful girl." As they stepped into the hallway from the elevator, Eddie continued, "Well, it's probably a good thing she's leaving. A little distance will help. She'll get over it."

Upon arrival at Art's new office, Eddie stopped at the door, his eyes twinkling as he peered in. "Howdy, howdy. How did you get this, buddy? Even got carpet."

Art smiled as he ushered Eddie in. "Well, to be honest, Elmer did it. I really appreciate it, too."

Just then Elmer appeared in the door. "Did I hear my name?"

"Yeah, you sure did," Art chuckled, "but not in vain."

Elmer laughed as he replied, "Yeah, I know. How'd it go out there this morning?"

Art spread the data plots on the table and pointed to one of the hysteresis curves as he asked, "What do you make of that?"

He studied the curves in silence. Finally he replied, "Looks like the plot of the clevis strain gage output versus the output of the NBS standard, but it sure as hell don't look like I would expect."

Eddie issued a cynical laugh. "Well you could have knocked us over with a feather when we saw it."

Elmer, still examining the curves intently, asked, "That's one hell of a hysteresis, I think, isn't it?"

Art furrowed his brow and replied, "Well, that's what it appears to be but so far we're not sure. I think we need to understand that material a lot better."

"Well," Elmer began, "technically speaking we got no responsibility for the material. Those parts were given to us by the Space Agency and under the strict interpretation of our contract, we have to use those parts. They did the design and qualification."

"That's true, Elmer, but this phenomenon may be a problem that our instrumentation just picked up and even more, it may be a tipoff to worse problems."

"Well, you may be right. At least, we need to understand it," Elmer commented quietly. "But I got to get to a meeting out there in *'Cableland'*. I know those things are gonna drive me nuts yet."

"Well. Good luck. If I can help, let me know," Art replied pensively, pondering the curves.

"I appreciate that, but you got your hands full right now. It's my opinion that whatever you need to do to understand this is what you should do."

"Thanks, Elmer. You know I'm gonna get to the bottom of it if I can."

As Elmer left, Eddie spotted Chip coming around the corner of the hallway. "Sorry I missed you at StressCo," Chip said breathlessly.

Art laid the plots out in front of Chip as he seated himself beside the work table and asked quietly, "What do you make of that?"

He studied the plots, turning them around upside down and then right side up before asking, "What the hell is that?"

Eddie, almost in seeming defeat, replied, "Those are the plots of the clevis data compared to your very linear NBS-traceable load cell standard we took. The last sheet was the one that popped."

Chip was intense, leaning forward studying the curves. He shuffled from one to the other until he finally responded intently, "Hell, man, this is crazy. We don't have nothin like that in the system. Our curves won't even begin to look like that. This tension curve's about what I would expect but damn, this compression curve is ridiculous."

Eddie raised his eyebrows as he said, "That's what we thought too, till we validated the plot program and it works. Believe me, baby, those curves are what the computer saw from the testing."

"What does it mean?" Chip asked in a very flustered tone. Art had noticed that when Chip got flustered the pitch of his voice came up in almost direct proportion. Now it was almost a shriek.

"Don't know yet, but we got to find out. I think we need to research the material and see what characteristics it has."

"Who makes it?" Eddie asked.

"Don't know, but I bet I can find out through our Quality Department sources."

"Well, Chip, maybe that's a piece you could research while we look at other data."

"OK, I'll do it. What other data you going to look at?"

"Well, for one thing," Art began, "I'm going to look at the instrumentation system design and then I think Eddie should start to research the material from the handbooks. Let's get back together in a couple of days and compare notes. I'm still waiting to hear from the Space Agency on my letter."

"Well," Eddie interrupted, "I got to get over for a meeting with Ben and some other people on the installation of our big Univac 1108 computer we got coming."

Art looked thunderstruck. "Our what?"

"Oh, didn't I tell you?" Eddie grinned as he prepared to leave. "Ben's got us one hell of a fine mainframe computer coming in here to handle all this stuff. Loren should have hired him first thing, but we got him now and I'll tell you another thing, that cat's super sharp. He has experience out the gazoo."

Art grinned at the thought of finding another of the rare professionals in Space Corp. "Sounds like our kind of guy, Eddie. I just hope we can keep him."

Chip settled back in a chair. "I hope we can resolve this. I don't know what to do if we don't find the answer to that curve."

"Me either. I suppose I worry more from not knowing than anything else." Art sat back in the chair and looked out the window for a moment and continued, "We need a duty coffee pot now that we got a new office."

Billy Ghote suddenly appeared in the door as if from nowhere. "We got a damned duty coffee pot, right out here in this here alcove. I just made the first pot." They turned to see Billy standing in the door grinning, which was an unusual occurrence.

"Hi, Billy. I didn't hear you come in."

"That's why I picked this office area, fellah. I wanted the carpet so you damned guys couldn't hear me comin'," he kidded.

Art picked up the curves and handed them to Billy, who studied them for a moment. He finally asked, "What the hell's this?"

Art explained the curves as Billy stood studying the strange shapes. Then he responded, "Don't mean nothin'. I'm sure the Space Agency's seen all that shit before. Besides, we got nothin in our contract about doin that kind of analysis. I wouldn't give it another thought."

Chip was furious. "How can you say that, Billy. I, as QC, want to understand it. I'm not gonna sign those things off 'til I do."

Billy smiled with his little straight-line smile and quipped, "Well, mister, I'll tell you one thing about that. If you don't your boss will when I get through with him."

Art had heard enough and interrupted in a stern, lecturing tone he had found to be effective. "Now Billy, there may be a problem. You can't dismiss it like that. We got to know what's going on there."

"I didn't dismiss it", Billy replied defensively. "I gave you my opinion. This here young whippersnapper jumped to a conclusion." Billy suddenly turned, quickly exited and disappeared down the hall.

Chip sat staring disgustedly at Art for a moment. "What in the hell was he trying to do?"

"Billy's okay. He just marches to a different drummer, that's all."

Chip, still unhappy, wryly commented as he got up to leave, "I'm going home. It's after quitting time."

The next day was Friday, Heidi's last day. At noon Art walked to the lobby where she was sitting, dressed in a soft dark blue low cut sheer silk dress clinging as though it had been especially fitted by a fine seamstress. He surveyed her as she sat grinning, and said, "Wow, what a woman. You sure look sharp today."

Heidi stood up, twirled around, pleased at knowing she was dressed in something he liked, and asked, "Like it?"

Art observed the dress and the rare beauty of the form inside and the almost perfect match of the two. "Gorgeous. I've not seen that one before."

"I bought it special for lunch today. I wanted this to be one of the good memories from here. You haven't taken me out to lunch for over a month now."

"Really? Has it been that long?"

She smiled and replied teasingly, "August fifteenth and here it is September fifteenth. That's a month even. You thought I recovered and you'd cut me loose, didn't you?"

"Now you know better than that," he teased.

"Seriously, I've missed it."

He escorted her to his old Buick where she perched herself on the front seat like a catbird on a limb. As he got in the other side she looked at the dash of the old Buick and commented quietly, "You really like this old car, don't you?"

"It's an old friend. And like old friends, they're valuable. I don't let them go easily."

She dropped her eyes for a moment, the dancing gone. "I hope not, Art, I sure hope not."

He patted her softly and slowly on the knee, running his fingers around the smooth hose behind as she pressed her long legs closer. He gently answered, "I won't Heidi. Count on it."

"Promise?"

"Promise."

As he drove out of the parking lot she moved over closer and said gently, "I know Art. I don't want to lose track. You're one of my best friends in the whole world."

He smiled at her and again felt a flash of sorrow that he couldn't reciprocate all his feelings and feelings that he knew were in her. He studied her through the rear view mirror, sitting, smiling and gazed at the beautiful face with the soft, full lips, the gorgeous full breasts showing through the low-cut V-neck dress, long, beautifully formed legs, the long, light brown hair fixed so perfectly, and thought, *Man, what a catch this woman could be. It's no wonder people stop to stare at her.*

He turned into the Hollow Log Lounge and Restaurant and asked, "Okay?"

"Sure. Anywhere would be okay today."

As he parked and opened her door he noticed a small tear in the corner of her eye. "Hey, baby, this isn't the last time we can have lunch," he said gently. He tenderly wiped the tear, kissed her eye and said quietly, "Come on, beautiful, let's go feed your face."

She regained her composure and began to tease, "What you're gonna do is fatten me up so nobody will notice me any more."

He laughed and replied, "You know better than that. What you got I don't think you'll ever lose. Come on."

She slipped out of the car and put her arm through his as they walked across the parking lot. She looked up admiringly and commented, "Gee, this is fun."

The receptionist seated them at a small table covered with a white tablecloth set with real silver in a corner of the building where it was quiet. She looked around the area surrounding their booth and smiled at Art sitting across from her. "This is such a nice place. "I've never been here before. I know it's expensive."

"Yeah, but you're very special and I only bring very special people here."

"Oh, do you bring your other girls here, too?" she teased. After the waitress brought the menu he ordered each of them a glass of white wine, to which she asked, "How'd you know I like white wine? You never bought me any before."

"Ah, but I know you're a lady of great and discriminating taste so I know you like good white wine."

"You know so much about me, and I feel I know so little about you. Somehow it just doesn't seem fair."

He blushed a little and countered, "Not really. Sometimes I

inadvertently get myself into messes because I'm not perceptive enough about people and their motives."

She stared quietly at the corner of the room where there were plants in large copper pots branching out to form a small umbrella, seemingly offering shelter and perhaps isolation from the world. She continued wistfully, "I know how you are. Annie's the luckiest girl in the world. I'd give anything to trade places with her."

"I know. I finally figured it out," he answered quietly.

"I don't want to cause you any problems. Ever. I hope you're not mad at me. You're not, are you?"

"Of course I'm not. I'm honored that somebody like you would care for me. Heidi, that's a great honor because I know you're genuine."

"Yeah. But what good has it done me so far?"

"A lot baby, a lot. For a long time I had no idea how you felt. I thought we were just real close friends. I kept hoping you would find some very lucky guy and fall in love."

Her eyes were wet as she continued, "I knew that. That's the reason I haven't really bothered you. I know you love Annie and I love you for loving her that way. But it just sort of happened. I couldn't help it."

He was feeling deep compassion for this beautiful creature that he knew he could love very dearly if things were different. She took his hand and squeezed it, "Art, I love you deeply but I also respect you. I don't want to come between you and Annie. I couldn't live with that. Please believe me."

"I believe you. I had planned to try to set things in order today but it looks like you're the one setting things in order. You're a wise and precious person, Heidi."

"I hope so. I'm trying my best to be. I knew all along that we couldn't be any more than we are but I don't think it's wrong for me to love you, too, so long as I don't cause Annie or you any problems."

Art was almost at a loss for words. He placed his hand on top of hers and looked her in the eyes, eyes that were still damp with tears and crying for love. "Heidi, I have to tell you the truth. You have got to know how it is and then it won't hurt so much, and the last thing I want to do is hurt you."

"I know, and the last thing I want to do is hurt you, either," she replied gently.

"It hurts me very much because I know I'm hurting you, but if things were different, I could love you intensely. I do love you very much. There's something about you that is extremely attractive to me. You're a magnificently beautiful woman both physically and intellectually. If I were married to you, which I would be very honored to be under different circumstances, I wouldn't cross the line then, either. Do you understand?"

"The hell of it is, I do understand," she replied with a sad smile curling her lips ever so slightly. "And I know I'll meet someone one of these days and I'll love him very much, but I want to say one last thing."

"What's that?"

"Whoever he is or wherever he is, I know I could never love him like I could love you, like I do love you now."

"Heidi," he began, "I'm deeply honored."

"One last comment on love and then I think we need to change the subject before I cry all over you."

"Sure," he replied with a grin. "What was it?"

"Well, you know how I felt dirty for so long after that Leech incident?"

"Yeah, but that wasn't your fault and you know that."

"I know that now, and I assure you no man has touched me since. That's been nearly a year and a half."

"Yeah, baby, that's all history."

"Well, I'm going to tell you how it is with me now. If you want me, any time, Art, I'll be there. I feel like I do have something to offer now. I feel like a real woman again, thanks to you."

"Heidi, . . ."

"Shush, shush. Let me finish or I'll never get the nerve to say it again." She squeezed his hands tightly and shifted her feet uncomfortably under the table, afraid perhaps she had said the wrong thing, but resolved to continue. "I felt so bad for so long, I decided no man would ever touch me again. You changed that by showing me that all men aren't bad, which I knew at some level anyhow. But I really mean it, I'm yours to use, to have, to love on or to cry on any time you want me. I come with clothes, or for you, with no clothes. Just tell me, or better still, just take them off and take me. I'll love you for it either way."

Art sat ponderously for a moment and finally replied quietly,

"I'm honored and I know you mean it. You've got a body that I know in some circles men would pay almost any price for. But the next time you give it, it has to be the one that you plan to spend your life with."

She blinked back more tears and squeezed Art's hands. "I know, but I'm making a commitment because I don't have anything else to give you. I'm serious. Now or any time in the future, anytime you want me, just take me. I'll only love you for it."

Art didn't know what to say. He'd never had such a temptation thrown at him. He stared into her eyes as he replied, "Heidi, you're a precious person and I'm so totally honored and overwhelmed that you feel that way, I just don't know what to say."

"Then don't say anything. Just leave it where it is. We both know how it is and that's the way it will stay." She stroked his hands while holding on with her other and gently, quietly said, "I just want to give you something that I can give you in return if you ever want it."

"You already have, baby, you already have," he replied gently, "You have honored me more than you know just with your love."

"Yeah," she replied gently with a smile as she squirmed around in her seat, stretching her legs out under the table against his, "but it's always there as long as I live. Now let's drop it before I cry. Allright?"

Art looked at her with renewed compassion and affection. He pulled her across the table until he could reach her beautiful soft lips. He kissed her tenderly and said, "Done, baby."

During the rest of the meal Heidi talked about her new venture and it's possibilities while Art, listening intently, was pleased at the enthusiasm she showed for her new career. He thought the real estate business should really do well for her. "Looks to me like you're ready to set fire to that market. I bet you're already looking at sales numbers and lining up prospects?"

"No, not yet. I had to get my head together a little more and," as she closed the car door while Art started the engine to drive out, "I sort of had to come to terms with some things. We did that today."

She got quiet again, leaned over and kissed Art on the cheek as she replied, "Thanks. You saved my butt again, I think. I was about to go off in the doldrums but now I feel good about things."

"Great. That's the way I want you to feel."

She smiled and snuggled closer. "I know that. But I wanted you to know how it was before I left."

After returning to the building and watching Heidi make her way toward Personnel, Art unsuccessfully tried to work on a test plan. He turned and stared out the window at the pigeons going and coming from his window sill. He was feeling lonely and at a loss when his phone rang and Chip entered simultaneously. He waved to Chip as he answered, "Program Management, Cannon."

"Mister. Cannon," the voice on the other end said, "this is Bert Ellis with the Space Agency. I've been assigned the action item created by your letter to us on the clevis."

"Great. Do you have an opinion yet?"

"Well, as a matter of fact, we do. We want to meet you at your contractor's place Monday to run some tests. Is that convenient?"

Art was elated and jubilantly replied, "You bet. Name the time and we'll be there."

"Good," Ellis said. "There'll be myself from Structures Lab, Freddie Engle from Materials Lab and Harry Andrews from Instrumentation."

"Sounds like a good start. Do you need anything special, any facilities that we can provide, or anything else?"

"No," Ellis replied, "I think we have everything we need. We'll see you about 9:30."

"That's great," he agreed, thinking of the program review on Tuesday and how it all will fit together nicely. "We'll look forward to it." After hanging up the phone he jubilantly turned to Chip and said, "Sounds like they're sending some talent to look at that clevis. I bet now we'll get to the bottom of this thing."

Chip grinned as he sat down. "Well, the ball's rollin' again. You want me there?"

Art gave him a serious look as he replied emphatically, "Hell yes. You know I always want Quality involved. Besides, you're the one that found it."

Chip beamed at being considered such an important part of the team. "Well, I researched the material and found out who made it. It was Inter-Steel in Philadelphia."

"Hey, that's a good lick. Did you talk to 'em yet?"

"No, I thought you should do that but I did find out who to talk to. I finally got the name of the chief metallurgist who developed the material, fellow named Dr. Philip Arnette. Here's his phone number at the plant."

He approvingly read the notes Chip had made. "You're a damned wizard, Chip."

Art looked at the clock on the wall. "It's almost six o'clock, too late to call today. Let's call him Monday after we get through with the Space Center people."

"Damn," Chip replied, "I didn't realize it was that late. See you Monday."

After Chip left Art again sat staring out the window thinking of the events of the day as the sun set and a soft darkness began to fall over the complex of buildings which Space Corp had evolved into. He watched the pigeons finding their roosts for the night and marveled at one old bird he had seen around for a long time as he wondered where this quest would lead. Then he started to worry about Heidi and her new career. He again felt a great void at her leaving but knew it was best for her and perhaps him, too. He leaned back and watched a flock of birds go over head and thought, *Gee, it'd be nice to go out flying. Think I'll call Ed and see if he wants to go if he got back from his Miami charter trip.* Then he remembered he was supposed to call his chief aircraft mechanic and inspector friend, Mack Murray, about an electrical problem he had promised to help him with on Saturday.

As he reached around behind for the phone he felt himself engulfed in a set of arms with the back of his head buried in the midst of two firm, large breasts that felt like angelic cushions that could only be Heidi.

He wished for a moment that he didn't have to move but could just stay there. Finally, without a word, she released him, moved to the front beside his desk and looked down, staring into his eyes, with tears forming in the corners of her own, "I had to come and say goodbye. I saved the best for last," she opened with a quiet, sad wistfulness.

She turned to sit on the desk, the blue silk dress halfway up the beautiful thighs. She made no effort this time to pull it down, any shyness now replaced by desire combined with a feeling of loss and fear of the emptiness she was so afraid of. "I thought you were leaving just after noon," Art finally responded.

"No. I insisted on finishing out the day so I wouldn't feel they gave me anything."

"Yeah, I understand how you feel, baby, but don't go out bitter."

"Oh, I'm not bitter at the company, just some individuals in it." She was quiet for a moment. Finally, "I'm sure gonna miss you. I won't let you forget me, either." Heidi looked sad and lonely now.

Art studied her and gently caressed her thighs as she sat close to him on his desk. He began to share her desire, feeling the currents of excitement coursing through him and wondering if he would really see her again and being afraid he might not. "I won't forget you, baby. How could I? We can talk anytime. But you know that . . ."

"I feel better about us now and I don't want you to worry about me. I'm going to be okay," she replied gently. "But I wanted to see you just once more before I left. I don't know who's gonna look after you now."

He smiled at her as she slipped off the desk and stood in front of him, her legs up against his. He stood up and took her in his arms and held her for a moment. "Baby, you know you're irreplaceable."

"I'll call you next week and let you know how things are going. Okay?" she continued quietly.

"Sure," he said gently. "Be sure. You know I care." His blood was rushing faster and faster as he held her, feeling her close and feeling the magic from her as he had never felt it before, feeling that fine wave of communicative energy that passes between two people who are tuned to each others souls.

"I know . . . I just wish it could be different, if for nothing else, just a little while." She pushed in closer, forcing her breasts tight to his chest, feeling her heart pounding hard in the cavity.

Art looked down at her and felt all the temptations he had ever known rushing through his body, his very soul, and squeezed her close. She tried to get as close as she could, pressing her body tightly, flattening herself even more against his chest as the long hair engulfed his shoulder. He wondered for a moment if it would be wrong to just enjoy this lovely thing once. Then he knew if it were once, it might be more than once. It tore at his very fiber. He released her and she slid back a bit, looking up. "Guess I better be going, huh?"

He nodded and replied hoarsely, " Yeah, baby, you better or I might not let you." She started to walk slowly to the door and he felt himself begin to sweat and to shake, if only inwardly. He stopped, pulled her against him with his arms around her, holding her close and again feeling her heart beat through the two firm breasts again pressing against his chest and then the full glow of her body as she pressed close. "Baby, take care." He pushed the door closed as the shadows of evening were beginning to fall long across the office and then turned off the light, welcoming the dim dusk.

She turned her face up, pressing her lips in a long, tender kiss as he unzipped her dress and let it fall. He unhooked her bra and watched it fall to the floor as she quickly slipped her panty hose and pants off and urged him down to the carpet as he removed his clothes in almost a frenzy. They paused for a moment while he was immersed in the beautiful, full breasts smothering his face, while she groaned little whimpers of ecstasy and expectation. Shortly he felt himself penetrate her soft, eager, body to a depth that even surprised him and they became oblivious to all other earthly surroundings, events, and sounds as they plumbed the very depths of each other's soul. Finally, when they both lay limply on the floor she spoke the first word. "Oh, God, Art Cannon, that was wonderful. I always knew it would be."

He looked tenderly at her and kissed her in a deep, wet kiss. He said haltingly, "I didn't really mean to go this far, Heidi."

"I know. I didn't either, but I'm not sorry."

"Me either. I guess it had to happen sometime, didn't it?"

After another half hour of ecstasy, they lay exhausted, enjoying the moment, the afterglow and the closeness. Art looked at her with a loving look and kissed her deep and long, absorbing as much of her as he could while giving himself to her totally. Finally he said, "We probably better get up before someone from security starts to make a night round. They're not due for a while yet, but you never know."

"I guess you're right," she whispered hoarsely. "I'm so happy. I love you so much and wish we could continue all night and forever."

He held her tightly, feeling her bare breasts against his chest and feeling the deep warmth and beauty of her body. He said, "I really love you too, baby. I really do but guess I always did."

"I know," she whispered hoarsely. "I guess I always knew somehow."

"Well, we gave you a hell of a sendoff didn't we?" he said gently as he reluctantly released her.

"The best," she replied quietly as he got up and started to put on his clothes. She slid her panties on and then her panty hose. He took her in his arms before she could put on her bra and said gently, "I love these breasts, baby."

"I love for you to love them. I've wanted this for so long," she replied as she pushed against his bare chest while he stroked her breasts gently. Then he kissed each nipple and buried his face between them. He took each nipple in turn and massaged it with his lips and grudgingly hooked her bra.

He stood still, watching her slip the silk dress over her lithe body so as to not break the spell and absorbed all the beauty and the softness, the desire dimmed for now, the fever that had consumed them abated. She buttoned his shirt and then held him tightly, looking up with tears in her eyes, "Goodbye. I truly love you."

"Good bye, Tiger. I love you, too. I always will."

With that she darted out the door and down the hall, her last trip down any halls of Space Corp. He stood and watched her go, the lonesome emptiness he had felt earlier now almost consuming him. He felt a great sinking feeling and actual physical pain as she went out of sight. Finally rationality overcame him and he thought to himself, *I've not lost her. I never really had her.* Art walked back to his chair and sat down slowly.

He put his feet up again, as he was before she came in, thankful for the dark now settling over the land. His mind was racing, thinking of the girl that just left, and the times he had spent just listening to her. He thought about the ecstasy of the past hour and decided that had to be it, no more, although he wondered how he would be able to resist again. He thought he should feel guilty but didn't. Then he wondered if there was something wrong with him. He *should* feel guilty.

At the appointed time on Monday Art and Chip arrived at the StressCo lab in anticipation of the Space Agency engineers' arrival. Promptly at nine o'clock Tina escorted them into the lab where Edgar was busy getting the clevis out of the large wooden box and standing it on end on the table with all the documents ready. Sam was standing

231

nearby, fidgeting a little as usual when he was nervous. "I sure hope this goes okay, Art," he finally said very quietly.

"Hey," Art leaned over and consoled, "these guys are professionals, the experts on this damned thing. I believe they'll find the problem."

Edgar glared at the clevis with some disdain. "Well, I sure hope so."

At 9:30 Tina entered the lab with three strangers following and said "Here are the gentlemen from the Space Agency, Mr. Kelly."

After introductions were completed, Sam asked, "Gentlemen, would you care for a cup of coffee?"

Bert Ellis, who appeared to be the lead engineer from the Space Agency, smiled at the thought. "Yeah, sounds good, but we'll have to pay you for it." The other two, Freddie Engle and Harry Andrews, who had been silent so far, followed suit as each withdrew a quarter from his pocket and handed it to Tina, who was watching in disbelief. Shortly she returned with a tray holding steaming cups with cream and sugar in pitchers she liked to use for important guests. Bert was standing by Art looking at the clevis and slowly asked, "That the item?"

Art confirmed that it was and then continued, "We're sure glad you guys got into the act."

Bert and Freddie bent over the clevis, examining it carefully. Freddie pulled out a large magnifying glass and then noticed a lighted magnifier work light on the end of the table. "Let's move it over here, Bert, under this lighted glass. We can see cracks better."

Art was surprised at that comment but decided not to interfere. Art and Sam watched intently as they turned the unit over and over and looked at the outer surfaces under the glass. Finally Harry moved into the forefront of the examination. "Let me see the strain gage installation drawing." Chip laid a copy of the specification and the installation drawing by the clevis and he began a detailed comparison of the installation methodology versus the specification requirements. Finally he looked up and commented to no specific person, "Looks like a damned good job to me. I don't see any problems."

Bert rolled the clevis so he could see in the barrel and spent the next few minutes doing a detailed visual inspection of the inside surfaces of the unit. He then turned to Art and asked, "Tell me again what you heard and what other data you have on this thing."

Art and Chip went through the entire sequence of events in detail, from the pop to showing Bert the plots of data from the previous stress runs. Art pointed to the spike in the data where the pop occurred and continued, "We're very concerned about it at this point, Bert."

Bert and Freddie smiled an all-knowing smile, giving Art some pause in his assessment of the effectiveness of their examination. "Well, you know the only loads this thing will see are in tension don't you?" Bert replied.

Art raised his eyebrow and peered at him as though he couldn't believe what he was hearing. "No, I wasn't aware of that. How do you mean?"

"Well, our stress people have calculated the launch profile of the vehicle and they're convinced that the only stresses this thing will ever see are in tension so we aren't concerned about compression."

Art felt a sinking feeling. He looked at Bert with a straight gaze that made Bert uncomfortable and somewhat hostile at having his position questioned. Art replied, "Well, I'm not so sure about that, Bert. We just don't know yet."

Bert ignored Art's comments and continued as if he weren't present. "Harry, open your briefcase and hand me that spray can. I want to see if there's a crack in this thing."

Harry complied and handed Freddie a can of dye penetrant that was designed to migrate down into small cracks when sprayed on. Engle took some wiping tissues and cleaned the outer surface of one side of the clevis and began to spray the dye onto the surface. He stood back and said, "Let's let that dry and then we'll spray on the developer and see if any cracks show up."

Art was standing by the table looking on in disbelief, struggling to hold his comments because he didn't know what their next move might be.

When the dye and developer dried Bert wiped the surface clean. He rotated the clevis to expose the other side and repeated the process. After satisfying himself that he had covered all the surfaces properly he placed the clevis under a black light lamp and performed a detailed inspection. In a few minutes he declared positively, "I'm satisfied there's no cracks. Freddie, you look to confirm that."

Freddie Engle leaned over and meticulously rolled the clevis from position to position and finally agreed, "I don't see anything. All the surfaces are clean and no lines showing anywhere."

Art and Chip had been observing this process carefully without comment. Bert turned to Art and asked, "Are you familiar with this process?"

Art confirmed that he was. "This is similar to the process that we use in finding cracks in aircraft engine cases and other metal parts. It works good for surface cracks."

"Yeah," Freddie replied. "We use it on some of our structural members."

Harry turned to Bert and asked, "Well, what's the next step?"

"I'm through. There's no problem here."

Art looked on in astonishment and Chip's mouth opened as if to say something and couldn't. Art stared at Bert with a deep frown and asked pointedly, "What do you mean, no crack?" His voice was shrill and agitated.

"Well, you see that there's no crack there," Bert argued, half defensively and half irritated at being questioned.

Art watched him with a fixed gaze that was typical when he was truly irritated. He asked sternly, "How about internally?"

Engle joined the discussion, "We don't think there's a crack internally. If there was a crack at all it would be external. Whoever heard of a piece of Inconel cracking internally?"

Art felt a wave of despair. He didn't want to accept this verdict without a proper exploration. "Well, we just don't know, Bert," he argued. "I don't think we can take a chance."

Bert was again visibly irritated and replied gruffly, "Well, it's our position that there's no crack. Our direction to you is to continue the test. I think that noise was in the press or somewhere else."

Art, out of the corner of his eye, saw Chip, red in the face, stalk out of the lab toward the back door of the building. Sam was sitting silently and motionless, afraid to say anything. Art was visibly disappointed at the lack of depth in the examination. "Will you give us formal direction to that effect?" he asked curtly.

Bert picked up his brief case, turned to leave and growled, "Well, since you saw fit to notify us in writing through contracts, I'm sure our lab director will answer your letter."

Art tried with one last-ditch effort. "Do you think the testing we did hasn't shown any reason to carry this investigation forward?"

"All I'll say now is that we don't think there's a problem. We're directing you verbally to continue. If you don't want to do that, take it up with your contracting officer."

Art watched as they stalked out the lab door toward the front of the building and then sat down in despair beside Sam. "Shit!" he growled. "Those people never even got close."

Sam had been motionless and silent through this exchange. He blinked nervously as he asked, "Well, now what?"

Art stood up and frowned, scowling at the clevis resting in its box. "They don't even begin to understand the problem. There's something wrong. I just feel it."

Chip returned to the lab with a defeated, subdued look and said quietly, "I've never seen such a damned ridiculous thing. Those people ain't got the foggiest idea what the hell they're doing. You can't find an internal crack by running a dye penetrant test on the surface. We told 'em up front it wasn't an external crack and they didn't listen." He was nervously pacing and asked gruffly, "What the hell do we do now?"

Art thought for a few moments. He looked at Sam and Chip when he continued, "Well, they said to test. I don't suppose we have any choice on that score. They seem hell bent on using these things, regardless of whether we know anything about 'em or not."

"How do you feel about continuing?" Chip asked slowly.

"Well, I suppose we have to. I'm satisfied with the press and I don't think there's any problem in the tooling." He turned and asked, "What do you think, Sam?"

Sam glanced at him, unsure of just what he did think. Finally he replied, with measured tones, "Well, if you guys agree that it's okay, I guess I'm ready."

Just then Tina appeared and asked cautiously, "What did you do to those people?"

Sam answered first. "What do you mean? To what people?"

"To the Space Agency people. They left mumbling about their decisions being questioned. The little short one said there wasn't no damned contractor going to question his decisions."

Art replied slowly, "They don't believe there's a problem and they're mad because I questioned their decision. At least, I suppose that's it."

"Well, is there a problem?" she asked bluntly.

Chip replied caustically, "Well, we don't know if there's one or not. We thought there was grounds but we don't know for sure."

Art continued, "We wanted them to investigate just to be sure there isn't. You know we have an obligation, at least morally, if not contractually, to point out problems if they show up."

Sam stood for the first time in a while and walked over to the clevis, glaring down at it like it was a serpent. "And you think this could be a serious problem. Right?" he asked.

Art, without expression, replied, "Right. I just want to make sure it isn't." He picked up his folder of data and motioned to Chip, "Come on, let's go see Tex. There might be something we can do yet, like talk to the people at Inter-Steel."

Tex shifted in his chair and leaned back with a concerned look. "I been wondering about you guys. How'd it go out there?"

They briefed him on the Space Agency's evaluation as they watched his expressions turn from surprise to concern and then to tortured rage. Then Art asked, "What next, Mr. Contracts? What are my options?"

Red was building in Tex' face, indicated by a very distinct change in the color of his lower ear lobes. Art knew him well enough to know this was a bad sign. Suddenly Tex took a paper weight, slammed it into the trash can sitting in the corner of his office, turning it over and scattering trash over the corner, leaving a large dent in the otherwise smooth trash can. "What the shit are they tryin' to do?" he yelled. "Don't they understand there may be one hell of a problem here? Don't those damned hysteresis curves mean anything?"

"I don't know," Art answered in a subdued tone, pondering the question.

"How the hell do they know this thing has stress only in tension?" Then, in a high pitched voice Tex yelled: "Shit. Shit!" as he stood up and stomped the floor.

Colleen, his secretary came rushing into the office asking, "Tex, what's the matter? Are you okay?"

He plopped down in his chair and looked at Colleen, "Yeah, I'm okay but I know some SOB's that aren't."

Colleen scowled at Art and Chip with a protective, steely-eyed look and Tex quickly replied, "It ain't them, honey, it ain't them. They're part of the solution, I hope."

Colleen gave them an acid smile, as though she didn't believe it. "Well, don't work your blood pressure up so. Settle down."

She turned and left the office as he regained his composure. "Well, as far as I'm concerned, we got a potential problem and I think we need to try to solve it somehow."

Art studied Tex inquiringly and then with great determination, declared, "Well, old buddy, if I can count on your support, we'll try to solve it, if we can."

"Fellah, you got it. We'll bend the damned rules as far as we can without goin' to jail."

As Art entered the building the next morning he saw a new receptionist sitting in Heidi's place. He stopped for a moment, staring, wondering where Heidi was. Then he remembered that she was no longer there. He thought again about their encounter on the floor of his office on her last day. He could almost feel her all over again, feel the warmth and the love pouring from her as he penetrated her and the long, lingering time he had enjoyed her. He said, "Good morning," as the new girl, cool and business-like, checked his badge for admission to the building and took the elevator to the third floor.

He entered his office, turned on the lights and went to Billy's alcove to check the coffee pot. Elmer laughed from his office door as he kidded, "I can always tell when you come in, buddy. You always check the pot first."

Art smiled at Elmer's humor. "Just like a bear to honey." He poured himself a cup and walked over to Elmer's office. "We need to talk about this damned clevis."

Elmer put his feet on the desk and leaned back. "How'd it go yesterday?"

Art gave him a briefing on the events and his conversation with Tex. Elmer, quietly listening, wrinkled his forehead and replied, "Well, it's like I told you. The bare clevis was supplied to us for instrumentation and conversion into a force sensor. I don't think they want you messin' with it beyond the instrumentation."

Art settled down further in the chair and glared out the window. "That's the way it seems, but if there's a problem we need to know."

"Yeah, I agree, but I think you've done all you can. You told 'em and they said there's no problem. I'm sure you're going to get a letter back through contracts that says that, too. As far as they're concerned they designed, qualified and built a part. Period."

He stared directly at Elmer as he asked, "But don't you think we have a moral obligation to tell 'em if there's a problem that they may have overlooked?"

Elmer squirmed a bit in his chair before replying. "Yeah, I think you have a moral obligation if you know there's a problem. But you don't know that yet, do you?"

"No. You're right, I don't know that yet. But I have indications that there may be and I want to find out for sure if I can. Can you imagine what would happen to a launch if we broke one of those damned struts before separation?"

Elmer was becoming more and more uncomfortable with the conversation, "Yeah. It doesn't take much imagination to see that 'N-Truss' back there would no longer be a truss and the vehicle would in all probability break up and destroy itself."

"Exactly."

"But they've made a determination that won't happen. I don't think you're going to get much further with it," Elmer said cautiously.

He felt Elmer melting under pressure and that surprised him. He had pictured Elmer as a fighter. "Well, Elmer," he asked, "what do you think I should do? Should I try to get an investigation going in spite of the Space Agency people or should I work it at a low level for a while and not rock the boat?"

Elmer folded his hands behind his head and leaned back thoughtfully. "Well, my gut feeling is that you should work it low level, test a whole group of those things and compile a good statistical data base and try to understand the hysteresis if you can."

"That's sort of what I think, too, right now. I'm gonna try to get Eddie to help me. He has a good feel for this kind of thing."

Elmer's tone became serious as he offered a warning. "Be careful, buddy, this could have lots of political ramifications and be very career limiting. I don't want to see you get burned. You got a good future with this corporation."

Art walked back to his office, pondering the conversation with Elmer and thought to himself, *Future, hell! If there's a problem in that structure, I have a moral obligation to find it if I can, and that's exactly what I'm gonna do.* He picked up his phone and called Chip, "How about coming over and let's call Dr. Arnette at Inter-Steel."

"I'll be right there. I'm anxious to talk to him."

As the phone started to ring on the other end Art pointed next door, "Ask Elmer if he wants to sit in."
Chip nodded and looked quickly into Elmer's office, only to find it empty. "Not there," he replied.
After a few seconds they heard, "Good morning, Phil Arnette here."
"Good morning, Art Cannon, program management and Chip Harrell, Quality Engineering with Space Corp in Hawkinsville here."
"Well, good morning, gentlemen. How can I help you?"
"I have you on the speaker phone here in my office. There's myself and Mr. Harrell from Quality Engineering. We think we may have a potential problem with some Inconel parts on the Space Shuttle booster aft struts."
"That sounds like something we need to talk about," Arnette replied.
Chip interjected, "Phil, as I understand it, you were the developer of this material. Is that correct?"
Phil laughed and answered politely, "Well, yes, I was. I've done the majority of the testing on it and without sounding like I'm bragging, I think I understand it better than almost anyone else."
"Great. Then you're the guy we need to talk to."
"Well, if it's about 718, I guess that's right. It's a very good material for the correct application but it, like any other exotic material, has got to be applied correctly. I've been working with it about seven years now."
They went into great detail to explain the problem and the symptoms. Phil listened intently, occasionally offering small comments and asking short questions. Then Art said, "I think that pretty well sums up what we've seen and know so far."
Phil responded, "Well, there may be a potential problem."
Art nodded and smiled at Chip, who was beaming. Phil continued, "The predominant failure mode of this material is compression. When it fails in compression it shatters like a shrapnel bomb. However, the tensile strength of it is enormous. It doesn't tend to fail in tension nearly as quickly as it does in compression."
Art commented, "And that's where we heard the loud shot noise."

"Yeah, that's characteristic of the material when it cracks internally in the micrographic mode."

Chip wrinkled his eyebrows and asked, "What do you mean by micrographic mode?"

"I assume neither of you are metallurgists?"

Art looked first at Chip and then at the phone with a grin as he answered, "No, afraid not. I'm an electrical engineer and a pretty good shade tree airplane mechanic and Chip's a quality engineer."

"No problem," Phil replied with a chuckle. "I'll just explain it to you without all the technical jargon."

"Please do," Chip responded.

"The material is, in my opinion, one of the better steel alloys when used correctly. However, it has a tendency to crack micrographically under excessively high compression overloads. What this means is that it will develop small cracks along the molecular bonds of the material. Try to imagine a crystalline structure, each crystal bonded molecularly to the other."

"Yeah," Art replied, "I studied crystalline structures in college chemistry."

"Same sort of thing. The tendency for these cracks to develop, at the molecular level, is much more predominant in the compression mode than in the tension mode. The cracks may be only along a small group of molecules but when it cracks this way, if the crack extends along enough molecular bonds, it may pop like a rifle, just like you heard in your test. These small cracks are cycle-sensitive also. That is, the more times the material is cycled, or compressed, in the regions where the material will crack, the larger and more numerous they become leading to a weakening of the overall strength of the material."

Art leaned back and contemplated what he had just heard. Then he glanced at Chip, who was intently listening. "You mean, Phil," he asked thoughtfully, "that we might not see these on X-ray, then?"

"That's right. About the only way to really see those small cracks is to section the material and use an electron-scanning microscope. I've done this on many occasions and have seen this phenomenon on lab samples that I purposely flawed. It will pop, in spite of what some people may try to tell you, when it fractures with a large enough crack."

240

Chip asked, "This crack we're talking about, will it propagate with additional cycles of use, say at least hypothetically now, on launch of the vehicle with a flawed clevis. Will those cracks grow inside and lead to a failure?"

"As I just said, they'll certainly grow and propagate under high compressive over-loads and will lead to a weakening of the part with use in time. But that's characteristic of many steels. But the answer to your question, without benefit of further analysis, is an unqualified yes. The cracks will tend to grow."

"So," Art asked, "we can expect the reliability of a unit to be in proportion to the loading and to the frequency of loads application?"

"That's true, predominantly in the compression mode. In the tension mode the tendency is not nearly so great but it could happen."

Chip leaned closer to the microphone and clarified, "Then as I understand the phenomenon, if we overload one of these things long enough or with a sufficient load, or some combination that is still unknown for this application, we could break one. Is that a true statement?"

"Yes. That's true. In the compression mode I would expect the unit to shatter at failure, sort of like a piece of glass. In the tension mode I would expect it to simply pull apart."

Art had been considering this and was concerned about the test program. "Phil," he asked, "how do you feel about our continuing the testing program?"

"I think you can do that okay. I think you've seen a case here that may just be a warning that you need to look closer at the material application. If one of those things shattered it could be very dangerous, especially at 400,000 pounds compression. Walls wouldn't make any difference in shielding people. Give me the dimensions of the part that you're working with."

Chip unfolded the drawings he had laid on Art's work table and read the diameter, depth and the wall thickness of the clevis. Phil replied, "Hold on, let me get my computer up." A few moments of silence elapsed in which Art looked at Chip and commented, "We may have really uncovered something here, old buddy."

Chip nodded as Phil came back on the phone. "It looks like, if you're testing at 400,000 pounds compression, you need to increase the wall thickness by at least one quarter of an inch, and maybe more, depending on the safety factor you want to use. I don't think a 1.4

safety margin in tension is enough to protect your margins in compression, given the characteristics."

Art replied, "Well, neither do I right now. I'll have to take this forward to the Space Agency and see what they want to do. We certainly appreciate your time and assistance."

"Hey, guys, call any time I can help."

Chip leaned back and sighed, blinked his eyes and complained, "Shit, I think we got a potential failure mode here. We need to do something about it."

Art was uncomfortable. "What do you think would happen if one of those damned things broke on launch?"

Chip sat up straight in his chair and without hesitation, replied, "Well, I think it's obvious. That N Truss back there would no longer be a truss, the vehicle wouldn't be restrained at the rear and would likely start to whip back and forth and tear out more struts and destroy itself."

"That's what I think, too." Art adjusted himself in his chair to a more comfortable position before he continued. "I think I need to talk to the Space Agency people about the qualification testing. I'm sure some of this must have shown up then."

"Good idea," Chip replied with a lighter tone than before. "I hope that settles the issue. I still can't get over those clowns and their dye penetrant test and their pronouncement that All is well".

After Chip left, Art sat back in his armchair and peered out the window at a flight of pigeons settling on the building next door and wondered about them and their structural problems. *Sure glad those little fellows don't have to depend on our engineering. Some of 'em might not make it.* He decided to fill Eddie in on the conversation and as he picked up the phone, Elmer walked in with a broad smile on his face. "Hi buddy," Art said, smiling as he replaced the phone.

Elmer sat down easily and burst out jubilantly, "Guess what's happening out there in *'cableland'*?"

Art looked puzzled before he answered. "I hope it's good."

"Good? Hell. It's better'n good. I just got my last manufacturing contract signed this afternoon. Now if the changes don't get to me, I'll meet the build schedules. I can't believe it," he croaked with glee.

"Great," Art congratulated. "How's it feel to be ahead?"

"I feel better now than I have in a long time. You know I've taken an awful lot of flack politically over these things."

"Yeah, I know, and I hope that'll all die down. You can't work trying to dodge every bullet they can fire at you."

After Elmer jubilantly left for Billy's office, Art was soon seated in Eddie's office. He went through a lengthy explanation, carefully presenting all the details he had just learned. Eddie sat with his brow furrowed and a worried look. Finally, he suggested, "Let's brief Ben on this. He needs to know."

Shortly a tall, stately, slightly balding man with deep blue eyes entered Eddie's office. "You must be Art Cannon?"

Art stood up and extended his hand, "Yes, I am. I've been wanting to meet you ever since you got here and after all the good things Eddie has had to say about you."

Art quickly perceived Ben was a bit shy as he watched a slight coloration come into his face and progress to areas where the blond hair grew thin. "Don't believe everything you hear. Sounds like you've made a new discovery in your clevis problem."

Eddie leaned back and continued, "Ben, Art has been talking with the originator of that material and I think he may have some significant data. I wanted you to hear it first hand."

Art reiterated the conversation and when he finished Ben slid back in his chair, wrinkled his brow and rubbed his chin in deep thought. He finally replied, "This is significant. We need to do some analytical exploration on that material to see if it's suited for this purpose."

Art started to interject, "But the Space Agency people are comfortable . . ."

Ben slapped the table in front of him. "I don't give a damn if they are comfortable. They just might be wrong. If they are, we need to tell 'em."

Art quickly replied, "That's exactly my position. If you and Eddie will help I'll try to bootleg some funds and set up a charge number."

"Beautiful. We can form a team and get some work under way. I've thought about those hysteresis curves that Eddie showed me and I can't see anything but trouble. I don't understand why someone else hasn't picked up on this."

"Well, there isn't much concern about 'em so far, Ben."

"In case it's of any interest to you, Art," Ben said quietly, "and it's definitely not for publication yet, you're gonna get a new boss up there in a week or so, so you might want to wait. I understand Billy's pretty hard to get things through sometimes."

Art sat straight up, wide-eyed and intensely interested. "Are you sure?"

"Loren announced it in the staff meeting this morning but he doesn't want it out yet," Ben continued. "But that may be a factor in your planning."

"It certainly is," he replied, still in disbelief. "What's going to happen to Billy?"

"Manufacturing. That's his strong suit anyhow."

Eddie had been quietly observing. "Plenty of surprises in this outfit. Who's coming in, or was it an inside promotion?"

"It's from outside. I'm not sure who," Ben replied. "All I know is that he was a high official in the Space Agency until his retirement"

"You mean we're getting some more retirees from the Space Agency over here?"

Ben smiled. "Looks like we're sort of a dumping ground, doesn't it? We're sure covered up with 'em. I think everybody and his cousin will eventually be here."

As Art stood up to leave, he said, "Ben it's sure been a pleasure. I'll create an interdepartmental work order so we can begin to look at some of this analytically."

"Well, let's hope it's a non-problem, but we'll need to know either way. I don't think we can afford to take any chances we don't have to."

CHAPTER FOURTEEN

Art returned to his office to plan a strategy for initiating a materials investigation in the aft strut clevises. He sat with his feet propped up peering out the window, watching the rain start to fall. After a while he took out a set of curves from one of the clevises and stared at the strange hysteresis, wondering what the real meaning was.

As he was about to lay it down, Elmer entered, looking as though he had seen a ghost. "What's wrong?" Art inquired, as Elmer dropped limply into the nearest chair.

"I just heard a terrible rumor, or at least I think it's terrible," he responded with a worried look. "I heard we're being reorganized and getting a new boss. I saw Harry Engle in the hall and he was non-committal as hell."

Art didn't wish to violate Ben's confidence so he refrained from any admission of prior knowledge as he asked, "How's that going to effect us?"

Elmer hung his head as he replied, "I don't know, but if we're gettin who I hear we're getting', we're all in trouble."

Art's interest was now rekindled. "Who is it?"

"A government retiree by the name of Garlin E. Hova."

Art sat a moment pondering this piece of information before answering, "I've heard of him. Where's he coming from?"

"From the Space Agency. He's one of those prima donnas that can't do any wrong. I've heard some of the old timers out there talk about him. He'll never change his mind or retract a statement or command regardless of what it is. He's just like running into a freight train head on. He won't move. There's only one opinion and that's his."

"Sounds bad," Art mused. "Surely he can't be that bad. I bet that's just rumor, Elmer."

Elmer squirmed uncomfortably in his chair and looked at Art with a questioning look. "You really think so? Another problem I got right now is the political mess I'm in over these cables. I thought when I got those contracts negotiated I'd be in good shape.

"Aren't you?"

"I just found out there's a bunch of changes that are gonna

impact my schedules. Like I told you, they're the last thing designed and the first thing changed."

"That's just the nature of that beast. People have got to accept that. It's not your fault."

"You know I'm bringing in somebody to help me on these things, don't you?"

He nodded, "Yeah, I heard that."

"Well, just between us, if we get G. E. Hova, I may be bringing in my replacement."

He tried to console Elmer. "Not a chance, buddy. Nobody else knows one tenth as much about that program as you do."

Elmer shrugged his shoulders as he left, somewhat settled down but still worried. He replied over his shoulder, "I sure hope so."

A large pigeon swooped by Art's window and startled him with the swish of its wings as he looked at the clock and thought he had better get started to outline a program that would help define the material characteristics. He asked for an analytical evaluation of the strut clevis design and a determination of the compressive and tensile modes with their yield and failure points combined with an analysis of the hysteresis characteristics of the material. Next he asked for an analysis of the impulse response of the clevis when it was suddenly hit with a shock load much as one would hit an object with a large hammer, simulating launch shocks.

He stared at the paper for a while, still considering the results he would like to see. He finally decided to ask for the natural resonant frequency of the clevis, which was the point that it would ring like a bell and for how long. As shadows started to cross the floor he looked out the window and said to himself, "Damn, I forgot to go home a couple of hours ago."

As he drove home he decided to discuss his strategy with Tex. He took a short cut through an apartment complex and saw a familiar figure he instantly recognized as his little friend Connie, accompanied by Al Creude going into an end apartment on the ground floor. *Well, looks like they moved in together,* he thought to himself, *I'm sure sorry to see a sweet kid like that go down so badly.* He soon turned onto Tex's street and found him in his garage tinkering with his favorite Model T Ford. "Hi," Tex responded warmly. "What you doin' out this way?"

"Well, I been worryin about that damned strut some more.

Guess I need some consolation."

Tex, with a serious look, asked, "Are you gonna get some analytical work going?"

Art related the events of the day, including his conversation with Phil at Inter-Steel. Tex wrinkled his brow in deep thought as he replied, "Hell, I think that's all you need."

"Well, I got some task statements worked out tonight for Eddie and Ben so they can go to work. Tomorrow I got to get it through the work order system so they can start to expend effort."

Tex frowned and leaned against the fender of the Ford. "Well, I don't know about that fellow Ghote up there. He may be slow to respond. He usually is."

Art smiled, pondering whether or not to tell Tex the rest of the story, but he finally decided it would be okay after Tex swore an oath of secrecy. Art proceeded to describe the impending replacement from the Space Agency, G. E. Hova. He noticed Tex grimace and squirm. "You know over fifty percent of that company is made up of those retirees now, don't you," Tex grumbled resentfully. "We're nothin' but a damned dumping ground."

"Tex, I know how you feel and I have to admit you got some justification. But there's some real talent out there. This fellow Garlin must be okay or he wouldn't have gotten to the level he was."

Tex scowled at Art as he replied gruffly, "Or else the sob stepped on a lot of dead bodies to get there."

Wanting to change the subject to one less controversial, Art commented, "By the way, I passed one of the apartments over on Mercer Street and saw Al and Connie going in. Guess they're living together now."

"Yeah. I've seen 'em. I've already seen her out with little Billy Sutherland over in the electrical shop, too. Al don't know it yet, but she's already shackin around on him. Gonna be interesting."

The next morning Art, Ben and Eddie reviewed the task outlines, after which he wrote an interdepartmental work order. After satisfying himself this was what needed to be done, he walked into Billy's office and saw him staring out the window into space, not the least bit aware of his presence. "Billy," he started.

As Billy jumped back to reality, he wheeled around growling, "What'cha want?"

Art laid the work order on Billy's desk. "Billy, I need some help in Ben Carr's area."

Billy scowled at the work order, dropped it on the table like it was hot and grunted, "You're playin' with fire, boy. You're playin' with fire. Leave it alone."

Art sat down in front of the desk so he could look Billy in the eye. Almost half begging, he pleaded, "Billy, we need to do this. There's a problem."

"No there ain't. The people out there say there ain't."

Billy held up a letter he had just received. "Here. They say officially there ain't a problem and you better continue testing. You better let it alone or you're gonna step on somebody's toes and then you'll be in deep shit."

Art was determined. "Billy, I think you agree there's a problem."

Billy scowled again, still ignoring the work order, "I never said no such thing. If they say there ain't no problem, there ain't no problem."

"I know all about that, but you have got to let me prove it. We got to know for sure."

"I ain't got to do nothin'," Billy stormed.

He glared at Billy as desperation was reaching a crescendo. He roared, "Damn you, Ghote, as one of the last decent things you'll ever do in your life, you're gonna sign that thing or I'm gonna throw your skinny ass out that damned window!"

Billy slid down in his chair in astonishment. He had never seen Art mad before. He started to grin as he replied quietly, "You're really serious about this, aren't you?"

"You're damned right I am, Billy," pointing to the signature line, as he demanded, "Now sign that damned thing."

Billy picked up his pen and signed his name to the bottom line and then gently counseled, "Old buddy, don't say I didn't warn you when the shit hits the fan. I got a gut feeling this'n has a lot of politics. It could be career-limiting and I think you got a damned good future with this outfit."

Art went quickly to Program Control with the authorization and opened a charge number against the project so he could expend funds internally. Then he almost ran over to Eddie's office and threw the task statement on Eddie's desk. "Get to work, boy. We got big things to do," he announced with a grin.

Eddie eyed the authorization in disbelief, picked it up and looked at the signature and just held it in amazement. "How in the hell did you do that so quick?"

"Persistence, man, persistence. I just knew how to get to Billy if I needed to. He's really a pussycat with a big bark."

Eddie dialed Ben excitedly. "Ben, you ain't gonna believe this but we got a go on Art's project." Then he paused a moment and continued, "Seriously, Ben. For real." Another pause. "Hell, I don't know unless he threatened to shoot him, or somethin'. I'll bring you a copy."

Eddie was elated as planning seemed to bubble out of him. "Maybe we can understand that thing now. First I want to collect all the data I can and then do some statistical research on the trends and at the same time begin to look at the characteristics of that material in other uses."

"Sounds like a good place to start," Art said jubilantly.

"Then I want to examine the design parameters and the specifications."

Art finally sat down as the excitement wore off.

"Buddy, you sure look like you're relaxing now. I been worried about you the past few weeks," Eddie commented.

"Yeah, Annie's been worrying about me, too. She said I been looking tired and stressed."

Eddie smiled and counseled, "Don't let it get to you. We'll work it out now."

"Yeah. I feel better, but I'm still worried about our change in management."

"But you got the funds approved so don't sweat it. By the way, how did you get Billy to sign this?"

"I threatened to throw him out the window," Art laughed.

Eddie looked in disbelief. "You're kiddin. You didn't really do that."

Still chuckling, he replied, "I damned sure did. I meant to get this thing committed before any new management comes in. That's an unknown and from what I hear, I might have a problem."

Eddie was leaning back in his chair laughing so hard he was about to fall out. "I never heard of such a thing. You actually threatened to throw your boss out the window."

"You know how Billy is. Sometimes you got to get down eyeball to eyeball with him."

He left Eddie and was soon briefing Tex on the in-house program and the letter from the Structures Laboratory at the Space Center that said, in effect, to continue testing because there was no problem. Then he asked, "How about if we go out to Sam's and get them started again. We need to cover his extra effort, too."

As Art and Tex entered the lobby at StressCo Tina greeted them with a big smile. "Well, well, if it isn't my two favorite contract managers. How're we doin?"

"Great, baby, just great. Tex and I need to see Sam."

Tex winked at Tina and slyly teased, "I came to see you. Art can see Sam."

She laughed and replied coyly, "Well, I can say one thing, you got good taste."

Art couldn't resist commenting. "Tina, he's just like a dog chasin a car."

Tina cackled loudly as she tried to reply, "Yeah, if he caught it he wouldn't know what to do with it."

Shortly the three of them were hard at work quantifying the additional expended effort. Finally Art asked, "How about getting Edgar and Chet in here?" When they were seated in front of Sam's old wooden desk, Art laid out the plans for their assistance in the research effort and said, "Guys, let's get our testing program in high gear and establish our best schedule. We're due to ship the first set to the Launch Facility pretty soon."

Chet looked inquiringly, doubt encasing each word as he asked, "You mean, there's no problem, like we thought?"

Tex smiled as he replied, "We still believe there's a problem but we've been directed to proceed on the production units. This is an independent analytical program and I'm directing you guys to support that totally." Tex turned his gaze to Sam. "Whatever Art asks you to do verbally, he'll clear with me first and then I'll cover you with a change order to your contract. I want you to keep accurate, and I mean damned accurate accounting records. Now, Sam, I mean accurate. Okay?"

Sam knew well what Tex was talking about and blushed as he answered, "I got your point, sir."

Art handed Sam a task outline. "Here's the initial task outline my in-house crew will be working on. I know you guys probably won't understand all the mathematics but here's a copy anyhow. I need you to cooperate with Eddie and Ben or anyone else that comes out looking for data so long as they're part of the team."

Edgar looked inquiringly at Art. "You mean there might be somebody who isn't a member of the team, like a spy or something?"

Art chuckled and replied, "I don't look for any of that, but just be aware of who is working the problem."

Edgar looked relieved. Sam, still concerned, suggested quietly, "You never know where an investigation like this will go. After all, some of 'em out behind the fence said there's no problem."

Art grinned as he answered, "You're absolutely right, and if we find there's no problem, that's great. But if there is one we sure want to tell somebody."

As Art and Tex arrived at Space Corp, they observed Harry Engle escorting a small, chunky stranger with a little paunchy pot belly, beady eyes over a small, thin mouth into the building through the front door. Tex asked, "Who's that with Harry?"

Art studied him as he approached the front door and replied, "Search me. Might be that fellow, Hova, or whatever his name is that Elmer's so afraid of."

Tex grinned and observed, "If that's him, we're in big trouble."

"How do you figure that? You met him?"

He leaned over in his characteristic all-knowing pose he used when he was trying to make a point that he was not really sure about either, "Notice how short he is. And that banty rooster walk and those little beady eyes? That guy has what's known as a 'Napoleonic Syndrome,' whoever he is."

"Buddy, you can see evil under most any rock. Even if it is him, let's give him a chance."

"Chance, hell," Tex replied quietly. "You give him the chance. I'll keep my damned eye on him. It's been too peaceful and I just got a chill, like somethin' bad's gonna' happen."

"Well I sure hope not. But things have gone pretty good around here for a while. Not great, but not too bad, either."

Elmer rushed into Art's office with a worried look before he could sit down and asked excitedly, "Did you get the word?"

He stared at Elmer quizzically. "What word?"

"Departmental meeting in fifteen minutes." Art looked beyond Elmer at the tall, neatly dressed stranger standing in the door and wondered who he was. He took note of the gold rimmed glasses and the shock of wheat colored hair with a youthful yet well seasoned face as Elmer suddenly realized he had not introduced him and quickly continued, "Oh, excuse me, Art, meet Ray White. He's the one I told you about coming in to help me."

Art stood up and extended his hand, "Welcome, Ray, I heard you were coming in."

Ray smiled warmly as he spoke, "Elmer's told me a lot about you, too. I'm sure lookin forward to working with you guys."

"Same here," Art replied. "Guess we better get over to the conference room."

As they entered the conference room Art observed that most of the ten people were present, all with program management responsibilities in various parts of the solid rocket boosters. He then noted that Billy was absent and turned to Elmer. "Where's Billy? He should be here."

Elmer looked quickly around the room and replied, "I thought he'd be here, too."

Just then Engle and the stranger entered the room and sat down at the end of the long conference table. Art noticed the placement of the people, the new stranger at the end seat of the conference table along the long side in the customary seat of authority and thought, Well, 'ol Tex called that one right.

Harry began, "Gentlemen, I've called you in to introduce you to your new department manager, Mr. Garlin E. Hova. He's replacing Billy Ghote, who is transferring to manufacturing because of his unique experience there. Garlin comes to us from the Space Agency after a long and distinguished career in responsible senior management. We hope he can lend us some of the experience, leadership, and knowledge that he's extended for these many years out there. As of today, Garlin has the position, the responsibility and the backing of management in his new endeavors." Harry turned and motioned to the front, "Garlin, the floor's yours."

Art was studying Garlin and thinking of what Tex had said in

252

the parking lot. He looked at his face with the small, tightly formed mouth and small beady eyes that might have the ability to look through a person if they chose to.

"Thank you Harry," Garlin said, with a drawl that Art had heard in the rural backwoods areas of the state. "Gentlemen, A'hm pleased to be here and to have the opportunity to take over this program. Ah'll get to know all of you as time goes on and we'll all reach an understanding of how we'll work together. Ah don't know what you know 'bout me but Ah'll tell you how Ah am. Ah'm a hard man but Ah'm fair, and I mean to tell you, Ah'm fair."

Elmer flinched, leaned over to Art and under his breath he mumbled, "Shit."

He replied, quietly, as Garlin droned on praising his own past accomplishments, "I always heard you better watch a damned guy that says he's fair. If he has to tell you he's fair, he's treacherous as hell."

Elmer squirmed like a worm in hot ashes and said quietly, "I know. That's something you demonstrate, not go around tryin' to convince people of."

Art picked up on the continuing remarks of Garlin: ". . . Ah expect to make some changes in the organization and in the assignments of you people. First assignment Ah want each of you to do is to prepare a briefin' of what you do and Ah'll assess 'em against your capabilities and Ah'll take it from there."

Art glanced at Elmer who was pale, and then back to Garlin, who continued, "One last thang, I'm gonna brang in a man I consider to be one of the top engineers in the industry as my deputy. He'll make any decision Ah'd make and when he speaks it's the same as me speakin. Last thang Ah want to say is that Ah run an open organization. Mah door is always open any time for any discussions about anything. Ah can hep' you in your work, or Ah can hep' you find another position either in or out of the company. Ah can council you on your personal life and Ah can hep' you in your religious life. However, there's a few organizations that Ah can't abide and if you're a member of one of them you better not let me know about it or you better get out now."

As Garlin sat down and Harry started to get up Ray turned to Elmer and Art and asked, "That was a strange thing to say. What'd he mean?"

Art shrugged his shoulders. "Beats me." Then he noticed a

small lapel pin on Ray's coat that had the form of a Scimitar outlined in diamonds and immediately recognized him as a probable member of the Shrine. He tried him according to the secret signs and symbols to be sure of who he was. When Ray responded correctly, he leaned over and said quietly, "Welcome, brother."

The next several weeks were uneventful and ominously quiet. Art and Tex spent a lot of time at StressCo where Art was pleased with the testing activities and the schedule they were maintaining. Eddie had been absorbing data like a voracious maelstrom sucking in paper, developing relationships, exploring concepts and possibilities and comparing these to design criteria often far into the night. One morning he burst into Art's office with an unusual gait and breathlessly exclaimed, "Look at this!"

Art jumped up from his chair, where he had settled down contemplating a hot cup of coffee and writing a report on his latest trip to San Francisco. "Hey, buddy," he exclaimed, "settle down and have a fresh cup of coffee. Then you can tell me why you're so excited."

Eddie came up short and burst into his good-natured laughter. "Yeah, guess I am a little excited. Does it show?" he asked, now more casually as he reached for a spare cup on the work table next to a set of file cabinets where Art kept all his programmatic data.

"No, not a bit. I know you go around that way all the time. Come on out to the pot and then we can talk all day," he answered with a slap on the back.

"Good deal," Eddie chuckled as he followed Art.

After pouring two cups, Eddie invited him to sit down at the work table. He stood at the black board and drew the hysteresis curve that had been such an enigma to him in his investigation. "See that curve?"

"Yeah, that's the typical one that we've seen all along, at least so far."

"Well, we've been missing something important that I just realized. We've got to know the natural vibration frequency of the vehicle. But look here now . . ." Eddie was pointing at the black board with a pointer he had found laying in the chalk tray.

"Wait a minute," Art interrupted, "you say you need the vehicle vibration frequency? Why?"

"Just a minute and I'll tell you," Eddie said hurriedly, as his excitement started to build again. "Look at the curve for the tension mode, just a single curve out and back, very repetitive."

"Yeah. I'll agree to that," Art answered quietly. "As we increase the load in the compression side we get that irregular error curve moving up the vertical axis and out the horizontal axis and then not tracking back to the origin, as one would expect when we release the load."

Exactly," Eddie triumphantly replied. "The thing goes way below the horizontal axis on it's way back to the origin, almost to and in some cases over nine percent error in each cycle."

Art stared at the curve for a moment and then jumped up excitedly from the chair. "Damn, man, it just struck me. Why in the hell didn't we see this before. This damned thing is frequency dependent and for each cycle of input load, depending on where the thing is on the curve, we're compounding the error with each cycle of input load into the strut."

"Exactly. We establish a whole new set of coordinates for each cycle, which compounds the error horrendously. See why I got excited?"

"Hell yes," Art exclaimed. "That's a huge revelation. Unless the data system on the vehicle measured frequency input into the strut, there's no way we could ever correlate data to the actual input because of compounding the damned error."

"There's no way of measuring the frequency of load input into the strut. I checked and there's no accelerometers in that area and without that information, the data acquisition system is useless."

Art peered at Eddie and then at the curve in deep thought. Finally he replied, "You're absolutely correct, I think. We got to know that."

Eddie was beginning to lecture now like a Pentecostal preacher as he continued, feeling more sure than ever since Art had agreed with him. "Also, if the strut and/or the clevis has a natural resonance frequency of the correct value we can get significant amplification of the load input at that frequency. What that really reduces to is, I believe, we could introduce another very large error in the measurement along with these cyclic errors."

Art studied this thought and quietly asked, "What is the frequency of load input estimated to be between the booster and the external tank attach ring?"

"Don't know for sure. I've talked to the vibration experts out behind the fence and they don't seem to know. One time I'm told it's three cycles per second, the next time I'm told it might be around thirty five cycles per second and the next time I'm told it might go as high as three hundred fifty cycles per second. I just don't know and I don't think anybody else knows yet either."

"Well, you know what that means, don't you?"

Eddie looked puzzled. "What are you getting' at?"

"What I think I'm saying is that we've got to do a much more thorough analysis of this thing than we first thought."

Eddie stared at the floor and then out the window before he answered. "Yeah, I agree."

Art continued, "The way this new fellow Garlin is starting out I'm not sure we can do that. He's very difficult to talk to, or at least to reason with. I haven't explained this to him yet but I know he's been over and smarted off to Ben about our questioning the design. Ben finally told him to leave."

Eddie was wide-eyed. "You can't be serious? Ben didn't say anything to me about that."

"Yeah, I know. He was afraid it might worry you so he's running interference."

"Well," Eddie replied with a sigh, "guess I better go over and explain this to Ben. How about coming with me?"

"Sorry, can't right now. I'm scheduled in thirty minutes to give Garlin a presentation on my work here. Then I got to go out to the Space Center and talk to the people out there on the qualification testing of the clevis units. They don't seem too anxious to talk, though."

"Well, let me know what you find out," Eddie said quietly as he exited.

Art sat contemplating the impending presentation and reflected on the rumors. He wondered about the decisions Garlin was making and wondered if he might be reassigned. There seemed to be little logic in some of the reassignments so far, such as major structures being run by two electrical engineers. It seemed to him that a strong structural engineer would be correct for that job. Art sighed. He had believe the guy knew what he was doing.

As he walked into the conference room he saw his friend, Hank Bonds, from structures, leaving the podium with Garlin lecturing him. "Ah want them schedules presented the correct way, do you hear. If you don't do it the way Ah want it done Ah'll help you find another position outside the company," he snapped. Art stopped, observing the scene and started to leave when Garlin said with a big smile that made him nervous, "Come in Cannon. Let's see if you can do any better."

Art looked straight at Garlin, believing the best way to face a bear in it's den is straight on. "I'll do the best job I can," he replied cautiously as he turned on the overhead projector at the front of the room.

Garlin interrupted Art as he started to present his material. "This here's Mr. Irvin M. Fishburne. He's reportin' in next week as my deputy and whatever he tells you to do, that's what you do. Understood?"

Art took a quick, casual look at the little man sitting beside Hova, trying to be as unobtrusive as possible but at the same time trying to size him up. He saw a small, curly headed man slightly smaller than Hova with a hard facial expression framed with a smirk as though he resented having to interface with the more common people in the department. His eyes weren't as beady as Hova's but had an insulting squint to them that Art resented immediately. He turned more directly, taking a closer look at the scowl and replied softly, "Pleased to meet you, Mr. Fishburne. I'll look forward to working with you."

A short, curt reply came back, "Name's Irvin. You'll be working *'for'*, Not *'with'!*. Get on with it. It's gettin close to mine and Garlin's lunch time."

Art carefully nodded and put up his first slide on the Integrated Electronic Assembly and went through a lengthy explanation of what the unit was and how he was managing the project. Next he showed the guidance gyros and then some of his instrumentation responsibilities. The presentation went without comment until he put up the slide on the aft strut clevis program and showed a sample of the data on the popping noise and the steps he had employed to diagnose the problem.

Garlin had changed his expression from blank to a scowl. "You mean to tell me you're questioning a design that was given to us.

You ain't got no contractual direction to do that."

Art looked straight at the pair without flinching. "We're not questioning the design yet. Right now we're just trying to find out if there's a problem. From the indications we see, there may very well be a serious problem."

"Ah don't want you doin that." Hova shouted.

"But if there is a problem we have an obligation to point it out to the Space Agency," Art replied sternly. He thought better of going into the revelations that he and Eddie had that morning, sensing this would be best at another time.

"Well," Irvin began with a sarcastic tone, "I know all the people that did that job and I tell you they're good at what they do. There ain't no problem and you better listen to your chief and let it alone if you know what's good for you."

Art stared at Irvin with strong emotions boiling up inside but little or nothing showing on the surface, a technique he had learned in his many appearances in court as an expert witness. "Irvin, there's sufficient grounds to believe we need to take a good look. We have a responsibility to do that. Do you realize what would happen if one of those struts broke on launch?"

"What do you think would happen, Mr. Cannon?" Fishburne growled.

"Well, in my professional opinion, as a professional engineer, I believe we would have a catastrophic failure of the vehicle system."

"Rubbish," Garlin interjected. "I'm ordering you to stop that activity now. We ain't got time for such as that."

Art decided to mount a counter-argument. "But, Garlin, I have an approved program with funds allocated and tasks outstanding. I can't just stop. Besides, I'm not spending that much of my time on it."

"Well, soon as those task requirements are used up, don't you spend any more money on it. Shut that time waster down. By the way, who's working it for you?"

Not knowing the degree of adversarial relationship that had developed between Garlin and Ben, he replied, "Eddie Rogers . . ."

Before he could say any more Garlin snapped, "You mean over there in Ben Carr's department?"

"Yes sir," Art replied as he saw Garlin's forehead begin to sweat and his beady eyes flash.

"That imbecile don't have brains to run a program of any kind. He and all his people are idiots. Ah don't want you working with 'em for any reason at any time."

Art was shocked because he knew the people in Ben's office and knew they were, for the most part, top notch people in computers and the finer engineering sciences. He stammered, "But Garlin, those people are sharp. I plan to use them to develop a hardware tracking system to go on our big mainframe computer over there so that we can account for all the hardware in the cycle."

"*NO!*" Garlin thundered. "There will be *NO* and I mean *NO* computers in the program management office. Those people are time wasters."

Fishburne sat up straight in his chair glaring. "Cannon, you heard the man. When you use up your allocations, shut this damned thing down and quit wasting money. And, there'll not ever be any computers in the Program Office. You're excused. We got to go to lunch."

Art was bewildered. He quietly turned off the projector, picked up his slides and walked out of the room without another word. In his office he sat down, turned around and peered out the window watching the pigeons flying gracefully from one perch to another, wondering again about their problems. After a long ponderous period he decided to brief Eddie and Ben. He also decided he was not about to yield to a flippant decree made without any kind of technical basis. There just might be a real problem in the vehicle and it just might cause a catastrophic failure.

Eddie was propped up with his feet on the table behind his desk eating a sandwich when he heard Art enter. "Hey, what the hell happened up there?" he asked expectantly.

Art sat down slowly and related the entire session while Eddie grimaced in mental pain. "Well," Eddie began when Art finished, "it's war again. Looks like it's time to start a strategy."

"What do you mean?" Eddie asked forcefully. "How the hell do we strategize against arrogant pomposity surrounded by absolute, abject ignorance?"

Before he could go any further Ben Carr entered, looked around and asked, "Who died? You guys look like a funeral."

Art related the preceding events while Ben's face turned red.

"That little sawed off sob. He don't know shit about anything . .,. got madder'n hell at me in the staff meeting when he tried to make a play to take over my department. He threatened then to not allow any computer assistance up there . . ."

"That's stupid," Art interrupted. "Why in hell shouldn't we use the tools we have? I'm afraid Tex was right again. We got a serious problem."

Eddie asked, "Well, Chief, what do you think we should do? How do we attack this animal?"

Ben smiled, kidding Eddie as he replied, "Well, you're the old war gamer and the operations researcher. What do you recommend?"

"Stealth, man, stealth," he quickly replied with a grin. "Let's proceed quietly and not say anything to anybody. I think we've got enough funds allocated so let's go on like nothin' was happening and collect all the data we can."

Ben asked, "What do you think of that, Art?"

Quietly contemplating the situation, he replied slowly, "Well, I think we'll be okay if they don't smarten up and go checking charge numbers and cancel the project on us."

"If they should," Ben continued, "we'll still be able to do a lot of bootleg work. Then when we get the data together we can present it first to our upper management and then to the Space Agency people, if there's any indication of a problem."

On the way back to his office Art passed Elmer's door, where he saw Elmer and Ray sitting with long faces. He asked, "What's up, guys? I thought Hank and I were the ones to catch hell today."

Elmer answered despondently, "Come in and shut the door."

Art immediately complied. Elmer grimaced as he said, "Well, my worst fears came through."

"What do you mean?"

"I mean that I'm being relieved of the cable program and kicked out of the Program Office."

Art stared in disbelief as Ray said dejectedly, "And I've been stuck with a new program I don't know anything about yet."

Art was visibly upset. He turned to Elmer and asked, "How could that happen, Elmer? Ray's a good man but hell, he needs time to phase into a thing like that. He can't just be dumped into a program that complex. Besides, nobody knows one tenth as much as you do about it. That's stupid."

"Well, I told you I was afraid. I'm sure politics got me. This fellow Hova's got a lot of connections and still appears to run part of the operations out behind the fence. He's an aggressive little fellow, just gobbles up everything in sight."

"Yeah," Art replied, "I know. After Ben's experience, he appears to want total control of the company."

"What's Hova's background?" Ray asked.

Elmer shrugged his shoulders. "I don't really know what his field is, unless it's killin' people."

Art half chuckled and answered, "Ben said he's not an engineer and doesn't appear to have a very good grasp of anything technical, but he's a good parrot because he's learned to remember facts and parrot 'em back to give people the impression he knows a lot."

"Worst kind of sob," Ray snapped. "That means he's insecure as hell."

"Where you going?"

"Don't know yet. Got any suggestions?" Elmer replied in disgust.

Art sat quietly for a moment and thought before he answered, "Definitely not to Engineering. You named that bunch 'F-Troop' for a good reason."

"Yeah, I know about that cesspool of incompetents."

Art finally suggested, "Go see Ben Carr. He's looking for some experienced people on big mainframe computers. You got a lot of that."

"Hey, that's a good idea, and Ben's a nice guy, too. I'll do that," Elmer replied as he pounded the desk with his fist to punctuate his determination.

Art looked at his watch, jumped up and exclaimed, "I damned near forgot. I got a meeting at the Space Center in thirty minutes. I'll see you guys tomorrow since I'll be out there late."

He arrived at Building AJ, hurried to the fourth floor and entered Room 447 where he found two people sitting at desks on opposite sides of the room. "Marshall Wilkie?" he asked.

One of the two responded, "I'm Marshall. You Cannon?"

Art extended his hand and Marshall shook it without enthusiasm. "I hear you guys been questioning the design of that clevis."

He answered quietly, "No, I'd rather say we're trying to understand it. I'm sure you know about the loud pop that we heard?"

Marshall leaned back in the chair and replied casually, "Yeah, I heard something about it. But the materials people said there wasn't a problem, so I forgot it."

Art felt uneasy, as though he were intruding into hallowed ground. He asked, "Did you ever hear anything like that during qualification testing?"

"Yeah. We heard it," Marshall answered. "I ran the test and we never could figure where it was coming from."

"Hmmmmmm . . .", Art parried, "that's interesting. You never did identify the source?"

"Nah, we finally decided it must be the test equipment. I listened to those things myself. We got up next to 'em and put our ear up close and when one would pop we'd stop and inspect. Never could find nothin'."

Art looked puzzled and asked, "How loud were the pops? The one we heard sounded like a rifle shot."

"Some were loud. Others weren't so loud," Marshall continued. "I finally put a battery of microphones around one of those damned things and tried to find the source. We never could."

Art was wondering why the subject was dropped without any further investigation. Then he asked, "Did you find popping in both the tension and the compression sides of the tests?"

Marshall looked confused now and slowly replied, "We didn't run any compression tests so I guess the answer to your question is no."

Art sat back in amazement and tried to frame his next question in a non-adversarial way. He sensed the conversation was beginning to turn hostile, which was not his intent. His quest was for technical information only, not a show-down over philosophy. After a few moments he asked, "Why didn't you run any compression tests?"

"Because the stress and vibration people told us there wasn't any compression load on those struts during the launch-boost phase. We just didn't see any need to do it, so we didn't. You know it costs money to run those tests."

Art felt his blood drain like sap from a tree in winter. He felt weak at the thought of not performing critical tests because he knew there was no way anyone could be sure what the loads would be. He could see no excuse for not performing a full set of tests to cover all contingencies. "What I'm hearing," Art began quietly, trying to hide his disappointment, "is that you did no compression tests at all. Is that correct?"

Marshall looked silently at Art. The other man in the office, still unidentified, glared from his desk and with hostility in his voice, snapped, "That's correct. That's what he said and that's the way it was. I was there, too."

Art did not want a confrontation. His mind quickly raced through the data he'd gotten while the other man in the office, who seemed to become much more hostile, continued, "You damned people better let those things alone. There's no problem in 'em and as far as I'm concerned, you're wasting time."

Art couldn't answer without becoming hostile himself, so he sat for a moment before he asked, "Could I get a copy of the qualification test report to study?"

A brief, quick retort came from both Marshall and the second man, "*NO!* You can't have a copy of the report. It was done by one of our vendors and we won't give it to another contractor." Art sensed the conversation was over and said, "Well, gentlemen, thanks for your time."

Marshall stared at Art with a steely-eyed look through slitted eyes and replied sternly, "Well, my recommendation to you is to let this damned thing alone. We've done the work and we don't like our design questioned."

Art turned as he started out the door and quietly responded, "I hope you don't feel like we're attacking your design because we're not. We don't know if there's anything wrong. We just want to be sure."

The next morning was Friday and Art went through his usual ritual of drinking a cup of coffee at his desk as he started mulling over the day's problems. He was almost through with his first cup when Ray entered and sat down with a glum look. "Mornin Art. I need to talk."

Art replied, knowing the full import of Ray's comment. "Brother, I'll do the best I can."

Ray began to pour out his concerns about lack of experience

in designing and building cables and a lack of experienced engineering personnel to support him in this effort. He finally concluded with, "I don't know many people yet, but it appears to me that there's a serious lack of management or something else going on here."

Art chuckled as he replied, "It's obvious, isn't it?"

Ray frowned and asked, "You agree then?"

"Yeah, but I don't know what to do about it. I think the problem is Frank. He's too trusting to manage a front line organization like this. I know of some cases where he's been seriously led astray, like Sonny Leech over in Logistics."

"Guess I don't know him yet," Ray mused, "but to take a new guy like me and dump him into a program like Elmer's just cold turkey and expect me to support the flight schedules was reckless. Then for Hova to just kick Elmer out like he did . . . I don't agree with that."

"Neither does Elmer, but since the company has grown to over a thousand people it's taking on the appearance of a monolith managing itself. I don't understand why they brought in Hova, but I suppose there's a good reason somewhere."

Ray shrugged his shoulders and commented quietly, "It should be obvious what sort he is. He's got no capability to manage people and I'm sure he'll kill some of us with stress."

Art felt the concern that Ray was obviously feeling. "Ray, just do your best and I'll help if I can."

He stood up with a serious look on his face. Then Art noticed a twinkle in his eye as the tension relieved itself. "Thanks. I feel better."

The phone rang as Ray turned to leave. Art heard, "Hello Chief, Eddie here. How you doin' this fine morning?"

He replied slowly, "Hello, Sunshine. What's up?"

Eddie paused a moment. "You don't sound too damned perky. Ben's coming down in a few minutes and I picked up some more data from StressCo yesterday we need to look at. I'm anxious to hear about your meeting at the Space Center."

He arrived in time to see Ben pouring the first three cups of coffee from Eddie's private pot. "I figured you'd want one, too, so I thought I'd just pour," Ben said as he handed him a cup.

"Gee, thanks. I can always use another, you know."

As the good natured jousting between the three friends came

to an end, Ben asked, "How about your meeting with the stress people?"

Art's grin became a frown as he related the conversation. Before he could get through Eddie was standing up and pacing the floor. When Art related the portion about omission of the compression testing, Eddie couldn't take it any more. He slammed a small booklet down on the table and said in a loud, excited voice, "What the hell. Don't anybody understand this damned thing? Don't they care?"

Ben tried to calm him down. "Eddie, we care and maybe that's all that's required right now. And there are others that care, too."

He sat down and stared at Art. "I can't believe that. And they even refused to give you a copy of the report, too?"

"Yep. They sure as hell did. I got a feeling they don't want us to look too close. Maybe they're eat up with pride in their product and don't want any outsiders involved."

"Well," Eddie continued, much calmer now, "I been working on the data and looking at the statistical significance of it. Every one of those things has the same type of characteristic, so that means the one that popped wasn't a fluke. It also tells me that the discontinuities in many of the compression curves are indicative of minor cracks as the loads are applied, although the cracks aren't large or loud enough to be audible to the ear."

Ben turned to Art and asked, "You agree with that?"

"I don't see a better explanation for that jagged line going up in compression right now. That's where the micro-fractures have to be occurring."

After they considered the possibility, Art spoke first, "I agree. It looks more and more like we're going to need some actual load impulse and frequency data. We're scheduled for the first Shuttle Flight in less than four months. Then we'll have access to the actual flight data, for whatever it's worth."

Eddie commented, his voice reflecting his skepticism, "I don't think we'll get any good flight data because the present instrumentation can't make the measurement."

Art contemplated that possibility. "Well, we've about proven to ourselves, at least, that we need the frequency and time correlation during launch to pull the data off the recorder tapes and get any intelligence from it. I think it's time I submitted an engineering change request to add accelerometers to the strut to make the frequency measurements. Also, I'll ask for a track of range time to be added to the data tape so we can correlate the load versus frequency and direction of travel against time."

"Okay," Ben agreed, "And I believe we need to begin to think about a test program, too."

Eddie raised his cup in a salute, "I'll drink to that."

CHAPTER FIFTEEN

Sitting in the quiet of his office, Art contemplated the meeting with Ben and Eddie to decide the direction their investigation should go. He considered the need for additional instrumentation on the Aft Struts to provide the vibration frequency and time information and the importance of knowing where on the hysteresis curve the strut forces actually were operating during flight. He decided to submit a request for an engineering change to the Change Control Board, which now had to go through the Logistics Office. This meant he had to deal with Sonny Leech, a move he had little pleasure in.

After an analyses of what he felt was needed, and concurrence by Eddie, he completed the request and carried it to the Configuration Control Board office, next to Sonny's office, for submission. Gayle Hart, the change board clerk, smiled as he approached and responded, "Hi there, I don't see you much since you moved to program management. How you been?"

Art sat down on the corner of her desk, glad to see an old and good friend again, "Well, it's this way. There just ain't enough hours in the day anymore, Gayle. Then, too, I'm sure Sonny would just as soon not have to deal with me if he can help it, since we're such good friends."

Gale giggled and replied, "Yeah, I know what you mean. Oh, by the way, did you hear about Lissie's promotion?"

Art sat up straight, surprised and asked quickly, "What promotion? I thought she was Sonny's star secretary among other things."

"Oh, she's still all the other things but she's now an Administrative Assistant. How about that?" Gayle said with an acid smile.

Art looked dismayed as he asked, "Hell, she could hardly do secretarial work. How is she going to be an administrative assistant?"

She laughed and then whispered, "In bed, baby. In bed."

He chuckled as he looked across the bay area at Sonny's new office in the corner and noticed a very young, slender girl with long bleached blonde hair, sitting outside the door where Lissie used to sit. "Where's Lissie sittin' now?"

Gayle pointed to another corner of the bay area where there was a line of private offices. "In the end office. She spends most of her time looking out the window when she's not in Sonny's office. They have coffee and a sausage biscuit in his office every morning and when the door's closed no one's allowed to enter or to call in."

Art looked at the office area and replied slowly, "Is that right?" Then he asked, "Who's that, his new secretary?"

"Yeah, that's Angela Morgan and believe me he's already trying to get in her pants. He gets his hands on her every chance and he's all but asked her to go to bed with him. She's so young and naive she doesn't understand what's going on."

"How long has she been here?"

"Oh, only about a week and a half. She started last Wednesday. She's cute, don't you think?"

"Yeah, she's a cute girl all right, but you better try to look out for her," Art replied as he stood up and handed Gayle the engineering change request . "I'd appreciate your taking care of this for me. It's important and we need to get it to the change board for approval as soon as possible."

Gayle took the small sheaf of papers and replied, "Don't worry one minute. You know I'll move it for you as quick as I can."

As Art rose to leave, he saw Angela get up from her desk and open the door to Sonny's office and start in. He hadn't looked directly at Angela until he felt Gayle flinch and heard under her breath, "Oh shit. Dear Lord. Oh! Shit!" Then he saw the door suddenly swing open and heard Angela emit a shriek as though she had been hit with a bullet. Sonny started screaming, "Get out! Get out!"

He saw Sonny and Lissie lying on the floor, both stripped completely naked and Sonny, big belly and all, still plugged into Lissie apparently in the midst of a huge orgasm. He was gritting his teeth and appeared to be trying to enjoy the climax while at the same time yelling at Angela. Lissie was squirming and yelling, "Get up, get up," as she tried vainly to reach the door and close it.

She finally succeeded in rolling Sonny, still in a huge climax, off her, made a dive for the door and slammed it as Angela staggered out screaming, "Oh my God! Oh my God! What have I done?"

She collapsed in her chair crying uncontrollably as the entire office suddenly became silent. Gayle rushed over, put her arm around her and said in her best motherly tones, "Easy baby, easy. Didn't he tell you not to open that door when she's in there?"

Angela, almost uncontrollably replied, "No! No! What kind of place is this? What kind of place is this?" Suddenly she bolted up from the chair and screamed, "I quit!" and ran out the front door across the parking lot toward the main building.

There was a long silence in the office as Sonny's door remained closed and then suddenly from somewhere across the junior walls Art heard a low, moaning, imitation of a cow mooing followed by laughter in the entire area as though all had been witness. Gayle returned to her desk where Art had been observing the scene in great disbelief and said painfully, "Poor kid. Poor kid. What a hell of a way to get introduced to the facts of life."

Art began to laugh uncontrollably while Gayle gave him a scornful look and snapped, "It ain't funny."

After a few seconds of reflection she looked at Art again with a big grin and asked, "If it weren't for Angela it'd be funny wouldn't it?"

Art had gained control of himself and replied amidst guffaws, "Yeah, baby, it's too bad, but that's one of the funniest things I ever saw. The angle was just right with Lissie's big bottom and that damned thing plugged into her and the shock on their faces."

Gayle began to laugh almost hysterically, "You're right," she gasped between huge heaves of laughter. "I wouldn't have missed that for anything in the world."

Angela ran into the Personnel Office, sobbing hysterically, and yelled, "I quit! I'm leaving now!"

Dean jumped up, ran into the outer office and asked excitedly, "What'd you say? You can't do that. You just started."

"Don't tell me I can't! I just did! I don't have to work in a place like this!" Angela yelled.

Just then Candy, Lissie's daughter, swaggered seductively into the office and interrupted the conversation, "Hi Deanie, ready for lunch?"

Dean motioned for her to go into his office and wait and as she complied, he asked sternly, almost yelling with excitement, "What the hell are you tryin to say, girl? What's wrong?"

Maggie, the Personnel Secretary, having heard the noise, came out of her office in a run. She looked at Angela and then at Dean and decided he was only making things worse. She yelled, "Dean! Shut up and sit down."

He turned red with rage and screamed back, "Don't tell me to shut up, woman. This damned crazy girl's all screwed up and threatening to quit."

Angela was becoming more and more agitated and screamed at Dean, "Threatening, hell! I just did. That son-of-a-bitch over there had Lissie down in the floor fuckin' her and I walked in on it. I didn't understand his game before, but that could've been me."

Dean was standing wide-eyed and mouth open, not knowing what to say. Candy, who had been peeping out the cracked door, heard the conversation and ran out of Dean's office yelling, "You're a damned liar!"

Maggie thundered, "Shut up Candy, shut your mouth and let me handle this." as she gently put her arm around Angela, who was sobbing uncontrollably with great heaves of her shoulders. "Easy baby. Come on into my office and let's get it all out." She lead Angela into her office as both Dean and Candy watched in disbelief.

Candy couldn't stand being told to shut up and screamed at Maggie, "Bitch! She's a liar. She's a damned liar. Sonny wouldn't want her skinny little ass for anything. I know."

Dean looked curiously at Candy and yelled, "How in the hell do you know?? He been fuckin' you too?"

Candy realized she was about to let the cat out of the bag. She laid her head back and stormed out of the office saying loudly, "I don't have to take that shit. I'm goin to lunch."

Dean cried afterher, "Wait, baby, I didn't mean it. I didn't mean it."

Just as Dean started to try to follow Candy and Maggie was trying to soothe Angela, Harry Engle walked quickly into the office and roared, "What the hell's goin on in here? I can hear you damned people clear down to my office." He took a look at Angela and asked Dean in a demanding voice, "What's wrong with her?"

Dean started stammering trying to explain. Angela, calmed down a bit, glared at Harry through red, tear-filled eyes, demanded, "Who are you?"

Harry thundered, "I'm the damned guy that's supposed to run this shittin squirrel cage. Who the hell are you?"

CORPORATE SPACE

Angela started to cry all over again and Maggie put her arm around her trying to comfort her. "There, there, it's okay. That's Mr. Engle."

Harry turned to Dean and demanded, "Mister, I want an explanation now, and it better be good."

Dean quaked and started to stammer almost unintelligibly. Maggie interrupted quietly and positively, "Mr. Engle, Angela walked in on something over in Sonny Leech's area that upset her and she thinks she wants to quit."

Harry, feeling that he was only getting part of the story, raised his voice again and demanded, "Well, what the hell did she walk in on? If she wants to quit, that's okay but I want to know what the hell's goin' on." He glared at them all equally with a steely look.

Angela turned on Harry with all her fury and in a high-pitched voice yelled, "I'm glad it's okay with you 'cause I just did. I walked in on that fat sob down in the floor fuckin Lissie. He's been after me, too, I know. And I'll tell you another thing, Mister Engle, he ain't gettin me. I have quit and I mean I have quit and there ain't nothin you can do about it."

Harry stood for a moment, transfixed, open mouthed, in utter shock. He finally managed to say to Maggie, "Get 'em both over here and tell 'em I want 'em now and I mean damned *Now!*" Then he turned to Angela and gently said, "Young lady, I'm sorry for this. I had no idea."

Angela glanced at him and between big snubs of crying replied, "Thank you, Mr. Engle. That's the first really decent thing anybody's said to me since I came here. But I'm gonna quit."

Harry turned, walked out the door and yelled back at Maggie, "Maggie, I mean *NOW.* "

"Yes sir," Maggie quickly replied as she picked up the phone and dialed Sonny's number. Gayle answered, "Maggie, he and Lissie put their clothes on and left the building."

"Where did they go? Mr. Engle's madder'n hell."

"Search me," Gayle replied. "Probably to Lissie's house or to a motel to finish up."

Maggie started to laugh and replied easily, "Well, tell 'em that Mr. Engle wants to see 'em soon as you can find 'em."

Gayle looked at Art, who was still sitting on her desk laughing and switched her phone over to the speaker mode so he could hear.

"What does Mr. Engle want with them? Does he know?"

Maggie chuckled as she replied, "Does he know? Hell yes he knows. Angela's here in my office and I'm gonna process her out unless I can talk her out of it and find her another place."

Gayle couldn't resist asking, "What happened over there?"

Maggie, trying to be as restrained as she could, replied, "Well, Dean and Candy got into a fight about it and Candy stormed out and finally Dean tried to run after her, but Mr. Engle came in. She almost let the cat out of the bag about her and Sonny, too. I don't think Lissie knows about that, does she?"

Gayle replied quietly, turning down the speaker volume and blushing a little, "No, I don't think she knows Sonny's fuckin' Candy, too. I'm certain Dean doesn't know. Of course he's getting' all he can, too."

They heard Angela start to sob again as she yelled in the background, "You mean he's doin both of them? I got to get out of here. I'm leavin."

Maggie quickly replied, "I'll call you back later," and hung up.

She turned to Art and said, "I hope Maggie and I didn't embarrass you."

He patted her on the shoulder, still laughing. "Lady, I wouldn't have missed this show for anything in the world. I just hope Angela comes out okay. I think she's making the best decision though. Sonny'd hound her to death. He's that vindictive."

Gayle laughed and jokingly replied: "Come back for the next verse. I'm sure it's gonna get hot over here again."

Eddie was in the process of examining a new set of data he had just discovered from his research when Art walked in. "Look what I got," pointing to the data spread out on the table.

"What is it?"

"Failure data on other similar structures and the results of the analyses that were done afterwards. Also, I got a copy of the Specification that those clevises, and I assume the entire strut, was designed to. In fact, I think the entire vehicle may have been basically designed around that general specification. If it was, we may have an even bigger problem than we thought."

Art's interest was immediately riveted. "Explain what you're saying. I think I just heard something I don't want to hear."

Eddie grinned and continued, "Well, data here in this stack" pointing to one of the stacks on his work table, "is data on aircraft wings and on oil rigs in the North Sea that failed. This stack here," pointing to another stack, "is other structural failures. Now, what happened, particularly in aircraft and oil rig designs is they used this specification originally . . ." pointing to a copy of Mil-Handbook-5.

Art interrupted Eddie's explanation, "Well, what's wrong with that? It's used everywhere you look."

"True," Eddie replied firmly. "but it's for structures that don't move much, like a bridge truss, or a table leg, or something that doesn't have a dynamic environment. What we need is a stochastic, or in other words, a dynamic design approach that takes into account all the variables introduced in a moving structure like this one."

Art watched Eddie thoughtfully for a few seconds and then asked, "Explain what you mean by *'stochastic'*".

Eddie smiled as he continued, "A stochastic analysis in this case is one where we introduce variables to simulate the true environment we expect the part to see."

"I see," Art responded studiously, stroking his chin. "What you're saying is we want to design the strut assembly, including the clevis, using dynamic environments that we expect the unit to see during launch."

"That's right. There's both high and low frequencies and loads. Each one has it's own effect on the performance of the part and on safety. That's why the selection of materials and their response to the dynamic environment is so critical."

Art sat down in a chair with a serious expression. When he had considered the information for a few moments, he asked, "Do you mean to tell me the design doesn't take into account any dynamic loads at all?"

"Right now I believe that's what I'm telling you. It took into account such things as your test program where you apply one cycle of tension load, from zero to 400,000 pounds over a period of minutes, not where the unit was being pounded at thirty five or three hundred, or whatever times per second in several directions, like we think it may be."

"What about the selection of Inconel 718 for this?"

"Well, that's a damned good material but I think it's incorrectly used. Properties of materials change over different usage

273

regimes and what we have here, I think, is a classic case of improper design. First the specification was inadequate and secondly, if the design was correct I don't think we'd see that hysteresis like we do."

"Eddie, that's a significant statement."

"Yeah, I know," he replied with a deep sigh. "But this design wasn't understood very well. You can look at the data acquisition system and see that it's got about as much chance as a snow ball in hell of getting any usable data out of those strain gages you're installing."

Art frowned as he considered this while Eddie turned to a table and continued, "Look here at this data." He unfolded a sheaf of papers containing calculations, graphs and diagrams of aircraft wings and continued, "This was a wing attach problem on one of our fighter bombers. The attach points were stressed and designed, using the static design case, for a life of five thousand flight hours without failure. It was intended to inspect these every five hundred hours and replace them at four thousand hours to stay inside the safe operating region. But look here, failures started to occur at one hundred hours, catastrophic failures, where the wing actually separated from the aircraft. Analysis showed under-design but a redesign using stochastic techniques, which in truth are not well known to most stress analysts, solved the problem. No more failures."

Art was deep in thought when Ben walked into the office and quipped, "You two look like you made a major discovery."

Art answered, "Your boy here," motioning toward Eddie, "may have stumbled onto something bigger than I really want to get into."

"Actually I'm a little scared where this thing might lead to, Ben," Eddie added.

Ben sat down and asked quietly, "Let's look at it. If there's a problem you know we can't walk away from it."

"I know," Art agreed. "I'd be the last to advocate that but I don't know about questioning the design philosophy of the entire vehicle structure."

Ben peered at Art and then at Eddie with a very serious look. "I agree. That's a hell of a statement."

Eddie began to explain his data and the relationship of various parts of the Space Shuttle system to the specifications that govern the design. Ben sat patiently, absorbing all the data, it seemed to Art, at once. He marveled at the intellect and the easy exchange between these two. Finally, after he was through, Ben leaned back in the chair and replied ponderously, "Well, guys, it's just like a cat eating a grind stone. You do it one bite at a time. I think this data is significant and what it tells me is that we've got one hell of a job ahead of us."

"That's my opinion too," Art responded.

"I'm not sure anybody here is capable of doing the entire analysis. I think we need to do as much as we can and present it to the Space Agency for further resolution."

Art shifted in his chair, very uncomfortable with challenging the vehicle design. He studied the curves with Ben and Eddie watching quietly. Finally he said, "Well, guys, there's going to be real live people flying that damned thing."

Ben replied, "People just like us."

The next two weeks were hectic, as usual, with the work load that Art, and his colleagues who were responsible for other booster systems, had to contend with. He observed Irvin Fishburne, the new Deputy SRB Program Manager, attempting to consolidate his hold over the group. He also observed the retired people from the Space Agency brushing him off as though they thought he had nothing to say. It soon became obvious that Garlin Hova depended on him and never questioned any decision he made. Art decided the only way to get along with Fishburne was to be as obnoxious to him as he was to everyone else. After a particularly difficult day, Ray entered Art's office, plopped down in a chair and breathed a large sigh as he asked, "What's with this little sob? He ain't got the brains the Lord gave a Christmas turkey."

He grinned as he looked up at his friend. "I agree, but I don't know what to do about it. Looks like he's got Hova's full attention."

Ray looked frustrated and replied quietly, "About all I know to do is quit. Those two are obviously here for the duration." Then Ray looked at the chart that Art was preparing and asked, "What's that?"

"This is a hardware status accounting system. Since Hova decreed we can't use computers, I need some way to track all my hardware through the flights. Right now I think I have a problem in guidance gyros."

He nodded his head. "What kind of problem?"

"I only have thirty nine units in the system. That gives me six flight sets and three spares. I have to send each set back to the factory for refurbishment and retest after each flight and it takes four damned months before they're ready to go back to flight status. I won't be able to support the current launch schedule when we're launching two or three times a month with assets I have now."

Ray nodded again and replied studiously, "Yeah, I never thought of it that way, though, because so far all of my cables are throw-away. But I'm gonna build a bunch of reusable ones soon."

"Then you're going to have to know what assets you have and where they are in the schedule to support the systems."

Ray jumped at the realization, "Hell, I got to do something about that, don't I?"

Art smiled as he replied, "You better or you'll end up in a crack. Bad. When it comes time to build up the forward and aft skirt sections for flight you might not have enough hardware."

Ray stood up with his brow deeply furrowed. "I better forget Fishburne and get busy on doing something like that myself," he replied as he left the office.

The quiet of Art's office was broken by the entry of Delmer Carter and Bill Wilkins from the Space Agency. "Hi, guys," he said cheerfully as they walked in. "Pull up a chair."

Delmer looked at the charts spread over the desk and asked, "What's that?"

Art smiled and replied graciously, "Well, have a seat and I'll tell you."

Seated comfortably around the work-table, Delmer began, "I'm interested in this. Let's talk IEA's later."

Art beamed at the interest and went into an indepth explanation of the chart, how it would track, and how he could use it to allocate flight hardware for each flight, and how it was to be updated.

Delmer stood up, stretched, and commented, "That's beautiful, that'll really work, but I got a question. Why in the hell don't you build a computer model and put this thing on the computer. That's the only logical way to do it."

"Can't, Delmer."

"Why not? Hell, I'm not a programmer but I could almost do that. I know you can," Delmer replied in disbelief.

Art smiled sarcastically at Delmer. "Well, I don't want to

undercut Garland, but we're not allowed to use computers in the Program Office."

Bill leaned back in his chair and stared quizzically at Art before demanding, "Why in the hell not. You're supposed to use any tools you can to further this program."

Art replied quietly, "Well, I got to try to support my management the best I can but I'll tell you that Garlin had decreed that we shall not use any computers up here."

Delmer frowned and demanded in a caustic tone, "Why?"

"Because Garlin hates Ben Carr."

"What the hell has that got to do with it?" he demanded.

"Garlin tried to take control of Ben's department but Ben won out at the Staff Meeting. He recognized him for what he is, I think," Art replied. "But listen, you guys didn't hear this from me."

Bill snickered and quipped, "I'm not surprised. That's the way he was before he retired; strutted around in his coat like a little banty rooster and tried to take over everything in sight. Don't worry, we know the problem."

"Yeah," Delmer interjected. "We're glad the little SOB's gone. Some of 'em used to call him *'Little Hitler'*." He sighed and looked wistfully at Art's chart. "Total stupidity," he mumbled as he turned and peered out the window at the white, puffy clouds drifting by.

Bill picked up a large sheet and asked, "Can I have a copy?"

"Sure. This one's for the gyros but I'm going to do one for all my hardware. I'll give you a copy of each one and each update."

"Beautiful. I'm going to see about getting' this on a computer out at the Agency if you don't mind."

"Not at all. I can't work the problem here, so maybe we can solve it that way."

The next few days were consumed by Art and his counterparts preparing and presenting to the Space Agency the regular monthly review of events and hardware status to support the first launch of the Space shuttle. The review, as always, was very indepth with significant questioning and discussions of problems. Garlin rarely supported any of the people he had working for him in these meetings, but instead turned on them frequently with a vengeance. Then Irvin always followed with his caustic comments, to the embarrassment of everyone including the Space Agency people. These two earned the disrespect of, and in some cases had instilled fear in people beyond reason.

At the midpoint of the meeting Tim Large, a former Stanford foot ball player and a hard working engineer in charge of parachutes used for recovering the boosters after launch separation, was trying to solve a major schedule problem. The discussion bantered back and forth among the attendees about how to solve the dilemma due to a lack of parts.

"Tim, how come the subcontractor can't pull his schedule in a month on that hardware to support your contractor?" Hap Jordan, manager of the Space shuttle Program Office at the Space Agency asked.

Tim, harried and frustrated, answered, "Well, sir, he's working two shifts a day now. The problem is these last minute design changes we put on him to incorporate into the rigging. Those weren't his fault. His suppliers are trying their best to supply him the new rigging now."

Garlin, getting redder and redder in the face because Tim insisted on telling the truth instead of saying "We'll pull it in" when he didn't believe he could, finally turned on him with all the hostility he could muster and snapped like a pit bull, "*Tim! Ah want that sachedule compressed a month or else.* Do You Hear Me? Ah Said A Month! *Now You DO IT!*" he yelled.

Hap looked disdainfully at Garlin and counseled, "Easy Garlin. You're on the other side of the fence now. You don't work for us any more," and then kidding, added, "besides, you're liable to have a heart attack."

Garlin turned red again and yelled in a shrill voice, "Don't you talk to me that way, boy! Ah don't have heart attacks! Ah give 'em, and Ah'm gonna give him one if he don't pull that schedule in."

The room was deathly silent as Garlin looked around the room at his other presenters. He said loudly in his best intimidation style, "That goes for the rest of you, too!"

Fishburne, who had been sitting with his usual smug smirk, followed Garlin's lead, "Anybody else here that can't do his job, I'll be happy to fire him right now."

Garlin nodded his approval and said in a normal tone, "Okay Tim, continue."

Tim had been standing at the podium quietly watching.

Without a word, he grinned, walked around the table and stood between Garlin and Irvin seated at the long conference table. All conversation stopped as Garlin and Irvin peered up at this massive six foot four, 270-pound giant leering down at them. Tim glared at Garlin and then at Fishburne for a moment. He handed Irvin his presentation slides and continued to glare at Garlin for a few seconds.: The room was so quiet one could have heard a pin drop. When he finally spoke in a firm, quiet voice, much as one would do when he met his maker, he growled in his most threatening tone, "No! *YOU* continue. I don't have to take that kind of abuse from any body. I've taken your smart mouth for the last time. I quit."

Garlin started to say something. Tim stared at him with a steely-eyed look and boomed, "Shut your damned mother-fuckin' mouth before I cram my fist down it! Don't you say a fuckin' word or it might be your last!" Tim turned and walked out of a stunned conference room of fifty people.

The Space Agency people sat staring in disbelief. "Well, well, well," Irvin stammered, "I was gonna fire him this week anyhow. He's not doin' his job."

A tall, lanky, red-headed 60-year-old ex-Space Agency employee named Gus Strothers, now working for Space Corp, glared contemptuously at Irvin from the back row along the wall and replied with a cynical laugh, "Now, Fishface, you know that's a damned lie. Let's just get on with the meetin'."

Garlin coughed a couple of times as tension relieved itself at his discovering he were still alive and barked, "Next presenter."

Word traveled fast through the company that someone finally put down the unholy duo and left Irvin speechless for once. Ray came into Art's office the following week and sat down. "Sure has been quiet around here since that meeting with the Space Agency Program Office."

Art leaned back in his chair, "Too bad you weren't in there to see that. Old Gus finally put the cap on it."

Ray started to laugh and finally replied, "Yeah, I heard. That guy is a master at putting him down. And Gus is such a nice guy, too."

"He sure as hell don't like Fishburne."

"Yeah, and I'll bet somewhere he earned everything he got,

too."

"Have you noticed that when one of those two clams up the other one clams up?"

Ray sat quietly for a moment and pondered this. Finally, he said, "I wonder what kind of a relationship they have. It can't be healthy, at least from Fishburne's point of view. I really wonder about 'em, but they're both married with families."

"Yeah, and the contrast with Garlin, supposedly the leader of the flock over in that little fundamentalist church out there in the back woods and Fishburne, coarse, crude, belligerent, cursing sort of person with no seeming consideration or respect for anything but Garlin. Very interesting alliance."

Ray had been gone from the office for an hour as Art was finishing up his hardware scheduling model. He looked up to see Irvin swaggering into his office. "Hi Irvin, what's up?" he asked as politely as he could, still feeling all the hostility that was evoked now just by the presence of this little enigma.

"What the hell's all them papers? It's not like you to work, you know," Irvin said in a half hostile, half joking tone of voice.

He picked up one of the sheets and replied, "Oh, you mean this?"

"Yeah, that," he snapped, "What the hell is that? Don't look like nothin' we ever used before in a Program Office."

"Just how many Program Offices have you ever worked in?"

Iwvin swelled up and almost choked as he yelled furiously, "That's none of your damned business." He picked up one of the sheets and started to examine the numbers and the columns.

Art explained, "That's the published flight schedule for the first ten missions and utilization of gyros. You can see we need to buy seven more flight sets by mission twenty-five or we're going to run out of assets."

Irvin pitched the sheet on the table. "Who authorized you to spend time workin on this trash? Who did?" He was almost screaming in his high-pitched voice.

Art leaned back in his chair and stared at him. Without blinking he replied, "I am authorized to support my hardware in this program in any manner that I need to, within bounds of policy of the company. I didn't feel I needed specific authorization to do any specific task."

"You mean you did this on your own? That borders on a computer model. Did you know that?"

"How would you know, Fishburne?" Art responded sarcastically, trying to get the upper hand in the conversation he knew was going to deteriorate anyway. "For your very elementary information, that's a flow chart that will keep track of the hardware assets as we fly and refurbish and build. I need that to do my job."

"Like hell," Irvin yelled, red faced and obviously agitated. He grabbed the copies and started toward the door yelling, "Give me this shit. If I ever see you wasting company time on such trash again I'll fire you. In fact, I ought to do that right now!"

Art was mad, but remembered the days of combat with Sonny. Then he stormed at Fishburne in like fashion, "I need fourty-two more units ordered by the end of next month to meet schedule."

"How dare you question the quantities of hardware in this program? You got enough through Flight 51. If I find you wasting time on this shit again I'll have Mr. Hova fire you on the spot."

Art, starting to laugh inside, stood up, stretched up his full six foot one frame and then stretched it as far as he could so he could look down on Fishburne and started around the corner of the desk in a long stride. Irvin let out a shriek, "Get away. Don't you touch me," as he beat a hasty retreat down the hall still carrying the charts.

Art yelled down the hall, "And don't come back up here, either. "

Ray ran out of his office next door as Fishburne disappeared: "What the hell's goin' on in here?"

Art sat down and answered between chuckles, "That little pipsqueak buddy of yours has heard about the hardware model and he wanted a copy of it. He ordered me to stop work on it and 'not waste company time.' Then he grabbed some copies of it and ran, like the damned coward he is."

"Why would he do that?" Ray asked with a puzzled look.

"Only if he'd heard from some of the people at the Space Agency who have a copy. They liked it and want to use it."

Well, they should."

"I suspect somebody made an issue of tracking flight hardware and he probably wants to get credit for developing the system. I'll bet we'll get a tracking system and he'll take credit for it."

Ray looked as though he couldn't believe what he was hearing, "You think he'd really do that?"

"Yep. I'm sure that he would. But the important thing is we get a system on a computer. Maybe that'll happen now."

"Don't bet on it," Ray replied, "the way Garlin hates Ben Carr, he'll never allow that to happen."

Neither Art nor Ray saw much of Fishburne or Hova for the next two weeks, except a casual passing in the hall. Fishburne seemed to have forgotten the chart incident but Art and Ray made a pact to watch him closely. Finally, one Friday afternoon at four o'clock, the department's shared secretary, Nancy, appeared with an announcement, "Staff meeting in fifteen minutes in the conference room."

"You gotta be kidding. That's only fifteen minutes before quitting time and I promised to fly co-pilot with Ed to New Orleans on a charter tonight."

"Sorry, Art, I'm just following orders. You're not the only one that's mad."

By this time Ray had overheard the ordered meeting and demanded to know, "Whose brain storm was this?"

"Fishburne's," Nancy smiled cynically as she left. "Good luck. You'll need it."

At 4:15 the subsystem managers for the Solid Rocket Booster program were assembled in the conference room. At 4:20, five minutes late, Irvin and Garlin swaggered to the front of the room. Garlin opened the meeting with, "Gentlemen, Ah know y'all want to go home but we got somethin we need to do. We got to have a way to track hardware we fly on this program. Irvin here has worked the last couple of weeks devisin' a method to do that." He turned to Irvin, "Irvin, explain the system and then give 'em each a set of sheets for their hardware. We gotta have these filled in by Monday at 9 a.m. to submit to the Space Agency. You'll have to do 'em and give 'em to Irvin so he can have the data keypunched and printed. That way they'll look like they was done on a computer."

Irvin stood, turned on the view graph machine and began a lengthy explanation of the exact same system he had fled Art's office with. Charlie Welch, who was sitting beside Art, slipped Art a note that had been passed down the rows. He opened it and read, "Looks like you called it right--Ray." Art chuckled and observed Ray suppressing a laugh. At five o'clock Irvin finished and handed each person a set of sheets with the admonition, "Remember, 0900 Monday. Don't be late."

As the meeting broke up Art looked at his watch. He had just enough time to make the flight with Ed. He walked quickly to his office and called Ed at the airport, "Hey, buddy, I got stuck in a meeting. I'm on the way."

Ed replied patiently, "Don't rush. The passengers are gonna be late and Old Bessie is gassed. I've got a weather briefing and the flight plan's filed with ATC. All we got to do is call the tower and get our clearance and go."

"Great, I'll see you shortly."

As he turned to leave the office Irvin came in the door. "Better take those home with you, sonny boy," he quipped.

"Yeah, guess I better," Art replied caustically, not wanting to be delayed. "Let's see how 'your' system works out."

Irvin smiled his acid little smile. "It'll work. I understand you got to catch an airplane? Is that right?"

Art glared at him as he replied, "Yeah, something like that."

"What'ya mean somethin like that?'" Fishburne asked, his voice coming up in pitch. "Where you goin?"

"New Orleans, Lakefront."

"That's a private field. You must be flyin' it?"

Art looked at him cooly as he answered, "No, Irvin, I'm not the pilot in command tonight." He flinched a little and continued probing. "Sounds like pilot talk to me."

"Yeah, I fly a little sometimes."

Irvin flashed something between a smirk and a smile as he continued, "I used to have a student pilot's license and soloed a 150 Cessna. What you flyin' tonight?"

Art glared at him as he picked up his Jep charts and approach plates and replied, "Aero Commander 560."

Irvin's eyes got wide, "Oh, a big one, yet. What kind of license you got to fly something like that?"

Art, brushing beside Irvin on his way to the door replied, "Excuse me, Irvin, I got to go."

As Art started out the door Irvin, not giving up yet, continued, "Then you are flyin?"

"I told you I'm co-pilot tonight and for your information, I'm flying co-pilot for probably one of the finest pilots in the business. See you later."

As he disappeared down the hall Irvin called out, "Great. Maybe one day we can go out and I can teach you a few things."

Art called back as he rounded the corner to the elevator, "Sounds great, Irvin. I'd like that."

CHAPTER SIXTEEN

After convening a meeting with the integrated electroncis assembly engineering support group from the Engineering Department, now called *F-Troop* because of general ineptitude, Art was concerned about an electrical interface problem. He knew the criticality of this unit since it formed the electronic brains of the booster, taking data for, and responding to, commands from the Orbiter computers. Dirk Watson, lead technician with a senior engineer's rating, was typical of the level of people that Art had supporting the various engineering programs. Although Dirk was a good person and was diligent in his efforts, he had neither the academic credentials nor the technical background.

Dirk asked, as he stroked his Abe Lincoln-type beard, "Art, I don't understand the software interface between this unit and the ground test equipment. How can we find out about that?"

Art sat back in his chair and replied quietly, "I suppose you can go ask Gus Strothers. That's his area."

Dirk looked unsure about that approach. "Well," he answered, "I think you better interface with him at your level. Besides I got to go see *Brother* Garlin about a problem he had in church."

Art was taken aback. "What'd you say? 'Brother Garlin?'"

He laughed and asked, "You don't understand do you?"

"No, I suppose I don't."

"Well," he began, "I'm an ordained minister, as you know."

"Yeah. I think that's fine."

"Brother Garlin is the senior elder out at Tall Pines, one of the churches that I hold revivals in sometimes and he had a problem with one of the teen-age girls out there. I need to council him on how to deal with it."

Art's curiosity, as well as his caution, was aroused as he studied Dirk. "How come the parents don't handle it?"

"We give the parents guidance and Brother Garlin, as the senior elder and spiritual leader of the flock out there, in the absence of the pastor, councils the girl in the way that he sees fit. She's seventeen now and was seen out in a dance hall and then she went to a picture show."

"Oh," Art replied, realizing that Dirk had inadvertently told him about a relationship that could have significance. He was sure that if the IEA program came down to a challenge of wills between himself and Dirk he would lose. He made a mental note to play that one carefully and stay out of a political fight if he could.

Art reflected a moment while Dirk talked about the church philosophy of evils on dancing and picture shows. He thought about his friend, Coleman Anson, who was raised in Garlin's church and was brought up in the fundamentalist dogmas that they relentlessly espoused. Coleman committed an unpardonable sin, he joined the Masonic Lodge and found himself shunned and outcast not only by the church he had been raised in but also by his family. Coleman had related to Art, "This has gone on for twenty years, Art. Be careful of that group. They're vicious to anybody outside their own clavern."

Art had taken this piece of advice seriously and wondered if Garlin knew or would find out he and Ray were Thirty-second Degree Masons. He looked quietly at Dirk and wondered if there was going to be any problems. Well, if there are, he'd just have to figure his way through. Sensing that Art was deep in thought, Dirk interrupted, "Hey, you're a thousand miles away. Anything wrong?"

He grinned and replied cautiously, "Yeah, I guess I was just about a thousand miles away." He covered his concerns by continuing, "I was thinking about the parity problem. Guess I best go see Gus. I'll let you know."

"Great," Dirk replied with relief at not having to perform the duty himself.

As Art entered the third floor from the elevator, he saw Garlin coming down the hall and started to raise his hand politely to wave when he suddenly heard Garlin bark, "Cannon, Ah been lookin' for you!"

"Oh," Art tried to reply pleasantly. "Do you need something?"

"No!" Garlin barked, mustering the most unpleasant voice he could find. "You're gonna need something like a job if you submit any more engineering change proposals like that'n you put in over yonder. You should know better'n that."

Art looked puzzled and thought for a moment before asking, "Which one you talkin about, Garlin?"

Garlin appeared to become enraged and was intent on making

a scene. "You better know which one, mister. That'n you put in to make changes in that instrumentation system back there on them struts."

Art stared his boss straight in the eye and replied, "But there's a serious problem there. Have you read the proposed change?"

"Don't need to!" he barked. "Ah already told you, there's no problem there. Ah canceled that thing and don't you put another'n in! You hear?"

He felt his blood pressure start up and his boiling point approach rapidly. Then he replied quietly, "On what basis did you make that decision?"

Garlin turned red at having his decision questioned and stormed, "On the basis that Ah say so and that's all you need to know. Now you better listen to me!" Garlin was becoming animated, waving his finger at Art as his temper got the best of him.

Art contemplated his next statement carefully for a moment and then continued, "Well, you're delegated the authority and the responsibility to run this shootin' match. If you decree there's no problem back there, we'll just have to wait and see."

Garlin thundered, obviously not satisfied with the outcome, "Are you questioning my authority?"

He smiled and replied, "Never, Garlin. I'm one of your strongest supporters. Don't you know that?"

This took him aback for a moment and much of the hostility seemed to leave before he grunted curtly, "Well, you better listen to me. That's all Ah got to say."

Art smiled as he turned to stalk off and replied quietly, "Yes sir." He observed the small figure moving off in an obvious attempt to convey who was really boss.

At Gus Strothers' office Art found Gus propped up in his chair, leaning back with his feet on the desk smoking one of his favorite cigars and reading a thick document on prelaunch test requirements. Gus looked over the top of the document and grinned at the sight of his friend and said, "Howdy partner. Where you been so long."

Art smiled as he seated himself at the table beside the desk. "Been busier'n a one-armed paper hanger workin in a whirl wind. How about you?"

"Hell, man," Gus began. "Don't let it get to you. It'll all work out okay."

"Yeah, I guess you're right, but some things do worry one at times."

"I know what you mean. I got a ton of 'em down at the launch site. What can I do for you?"

"Well," he replied, "my guys over at *'F-Troop'* need an answer and they're afraid to ask you directly."

Gus dropped his feet off the desk and looked surprised. "What? Afraid to ask me directly? Hell, that's what I'm here for unless they're some of them damned screw-ups that don't know enough to ask an intelligent question."

"I think they believe you're some sort of image way up here in the tower they can't approach, is all there is to it."

"Well, I'll fix that," Gus replied with a laugh. "I'll go over there and buy them suckers a cup of coffee and sit down with 'em and visit for a while and then they'll see I'm a team member. How about that?"

Art grinned as he replied, "Great. That should solve the problem. Now tell me, was parity even or odd on the data buss coming off the Orbiter command data link into the IEA."

"It's even. I had it set up that way because I thought it would make a better check to validate the data coming off the system. Got any problem with that?"

"No, they just needed to know."

Gus picked up a thick document, put his feet back on the desk and turned the pages for a moment. Shortly he pointed to a paragraph about half way through the manual, "See, right here. It's spelled out. All they would'a had to do was look in the book."

Art kidding, replied, "Now Gus, you know that's too easy."

He put his feet down off the desk and had started to continue when Irvin Fishburne stormed in with a scowl. He ignored Art's presence and roared, "Strothers, I don't understand you. You got the nastiest, low-downest, meanest mouth I ever heard!" he yelled. "You get me out here in front of people and put me down and try to embarrass me every way you can! You try to make me look bad and try to show people I don't know nothin! You're just a constant asshole to me." Fishburne was becoming highly animated, swinging his arms and pointing his finger at Gus, but maintaining his position well in front of the desk for protection.

Irvin was venting his full fury and Art was speechless at the hostility. Then he almost screamed, "Strothers, why in hell do you do that to me? WHY??"

Gus leaned back in his chair, slowly replaced his feet on the desk and took a long draw on his cigar before answering, which obviously irritated Irvin even more. He screamed again, "Mister, I asked you a question!! Why do you do that to me??"

Gus leaned further back until Art was sure he was about to turn over and then, squinting through the cigar smoke with a big smile, perfectly timed for maximum effect, replied, "Yeah, Fish, that's right. I do those things, don't I?"

Fishburn, feeling victory at hand, yelled, "You admit it! You admit it!"

Gus, still grinning and squinting through a perfectly round smoke ring he blew from his cigar, replied calmly, "Yeah, Fish, but there's somethin' you don't know."

"Whatt'a 'ya mean, something I don't know? What don't I know?" he yelled.

Gus looked straight at him and chomped down on his cigar for a moment as though he were smashing a fly under foot and quietly replied, "Fish, I'm the best friend you got around here." Then he leaned back a little further and watched Irvin start to hyperventilate as he realized how badly he had been taken again.

After a quick reflection on his position, Irvin stomped the floor and screamed, "Damn you Strothers! Damn you! You did it again!" He turned, ran out the door and down the hall.

Art and Gus started to laugh uncontrollably. After a few moments Art wiped the tears from his eyes and said between heaves of his sides, "That's the funniest thing I ever saw."

Gus finally got control of himself. "The little 'som-bitch walked into that'n, didn't he?"

Still laughing, Art left and decided to go see how Eddie's analysis was coming. As he entered his office he saw Ben and Eddie intently studying a large printout. "I think we're getting' somewhere," Eddie greeted warmly. "You know we got a staff of programmers working on data reduction now, don't you?"

Art looked surprised. "Well, I knew you had some but I guess I never asked how many."

"Six part time when we can spare 'em. We're debugging the programs now and I think we're about ready to make a run," Eddie replied confidently.

Ben interjected, "But I sure as hell don't like what I see. I want to double check everything."

"I agree," Eddie continued. "But we better start thinking of some hardware tests we need to run to try to get some empirical data to double check with."

"Yeah", Ben said thoughtfully. "Looks like we need a lot of testing, maybe even more than I first thought."

Art sat down and studied the data and curves. Finally he said, "Looks like the zero point drifted pretty erratically."

"Yeah, it sure did," Eddie replied, "and right now I don't see any good reason."

Art continued, "If we could null out the error and establish a firm zero point to start from, we might be able to get a fix on stress values that the clevis sees as it makes the excursions."

"Well, maybe yes and maybe no," Eddie explained. "The error was cumulative either in a positive or in a negative direction and the probability of doing a correlation of error is low because we don't know what the frequency of the load input is."

Art pondered this for a moment and then Ben commented quietly, "If we had the accelerometers installed back there and an IRIG time correlation on the recorder we might be able to construct an algorythm that would give us that."

Art glanced apologetically at Ben, who was looking wistfully at the pile of paper from the computer test run and replied quietly, "Well, forget that. That ain't gonna happen."

Eddie stared at Art questioningly. "But you submitted a proposed engineering change to do that. I saw it."

"Yeah, I did and Garlin canceled it. And he threatened to fire me."

Ben pounded the table and almost yelled, "Damn! Damn! How in hell could he do that? He had no justification! He had no right! We need that data!"

"I agree a hundred percent, but I don't think we're gonna get it. We'll just have to try to figure out something else if we can," Art replied dejectedly.

Eddie now appeared limp and disgusted. "Well, we have to have it.

There's no other way to make the loads correlation with these hysteresis characteristics and the random errors it generates in the data."

"I know," Art replied wistfully.

Eddie continued, almost hysterically, "According to the analysis we've done the original design of those clevises was marginal at best."

Ben walked to the window and peered at the grass blowing in the wind for a moment and then turned with a vengeance, "How the hell are we going to get any amount of testing done on this thing with the attitudes up there?"

Eddie grunted, "Yeah, I been wondering that myself."

Art slid down in his chair a bit further and sat quietly for a moment. "Let's decide what we want to do and I'll find a way to do it if there's any way possible. You know we got the first launch next week. I hope we'll get some data back that we can use.

Eddie turned sullen with a deep frown as he grunted, "I'll tell you what we'll get—nothin'! Nothin' that has any intelligence because the design of that damned data system is wrong."

"He's exactly right. I just finished an analysis of that thing, not that I didn't trust yours, but my data correlated with your analysis. That data system is not usable for anything except to tell you that there was loads data back there," Ben said.

"Okay," Art replied. "Let's concentrate on the design of the clevis and try to develop some good feel for the integrity of the design if we can, and then if we get any intelligence we can use from flight data, so much the better."

Eddie frowned and replied, "I don't believe we'll get much."

"Well", Art continued, "If we do, maybe we can use it for correlation. It'll tell us whether or not the data was all tension, as claimed, or whether or not we have compression data as well."

Ben wrinkled his brow and replied thoughtfully, " Welllll, maybe not because of the large hysteresis. It just depends on the cumulative error. I don't have much faith at this point."

"Ben's right, Art. Let's outline some tests and try to figure out how we can do 'em."

For the next hour and a half the three of them sat around the table devising both static and dynamic tests. Finally, Ben sighed and commented quietly, "Well, I think this battery of tests is what we need to run, but they're gonna be expensive."

Eddie thumbed through a stack of work statements for impulse test loads. "I don't know where in the hell we'll do this one. I don't have any idea where we can get equipment that can apply a load of 400,000 pounds thirty times per second."

"I don't know either," Art replied, "but I think it's important to check our calculations with real data. If there's a way, we have got to find it."

The next morning Art was still pondering the test program and how to implement it. Finally he decided to see if Tex had any ideas. He poured himself a cup of coffee at the pot and started down the hall when he heard his phone ring as he passed his office door. He darted into the office spilling hot coffee on his hand. While silently swearing at the coffee, he answered, "Cannon here."

"Hello there, guy," came the female voice on the other end, "This is Heidi."

"Well, well," he answered with a big grin. "I didn't expect such pleasure this morning. It's been too long."

"Well, I've been thinking about you and us and the program and all and I thought I'd call. I know you've got a first launch coming up in just six more days. I'll bet you're busy."

"Yeah, it's been pretty hectic lately."

They proceeded with small talk for a few minutes. Art was glad to hear from her and thought about the night on the floor of his office. He had worried about her and still felt badly about giving in the way he had. He knew all too well it could be addictive with someone like Heidi.

"I've missed you so much. I hope you aren't mad at me."

"How could I ever be mad at you, silly girl," he replied, trying to be as casual as he could.

"Well, I felt bad, sort of like I led you on that night I quit."

"Baby, that was a beautiful night and besides, it took both of us, you know."

"I know, but I don't want to hurt you or cause you any trouble. I just wished it could go on forever that way."

"Yeah, but baby, you know how it is."

"Yeah, and I'll never change, but that's not what I called you about."

"Well, you know you don't need an excuse to call."

Finally, she asked, "I've met someone I like a lot and I just wanted to see what you thought about him. I've only been out with him a couple of times so far."

He laughed and replied, "Now Heidi, you're the only one who can make that decision."

She was silent for a moment before continuing, "Well, I suppose that's right, but I value your opinion."

He felt a slight tremor of both relief and concern. "Heidi," he asked quietly, "how do you feel about him?"

"Well, I'm not sure. I was excited the first time I went out with him but now we've had two dates and I'm just not sure."

"Well, baby," Art advised, "about all I can say is, don't rush into anything. If there's anything there today it'll be there tomorrow and after that. If it goes away, it's probably your instinct telling you to stay away."

"Yeah," she replied wistfully. "That's sort of what I thought, too. I think he'd like me to go to bed with him and I was kind of tempted last time but something just kept eating at me and I didn't give it any chance to develop."

"Baby, my advice is not to do that. If all he wants is your body then he'll grow tired and be gone and all you'll have is a well-used bottom."

"I know," Heidi replied. "And that's not going to happen again, ever, unless that one special person comes back."

He laughed at her comment, wishing again that it would be possible to continue a relationship. He knew that he had strayed one time too far and didn't intend to repeat it again because he loved Annie too much. He knew that he would eventually forgive himself for one mistake but if it became a regular thing, it would create far more problems than it would happiness. He continued thoughtfully, "Heidi, I just don't know what I'm ever gonna do with you."

"Well, since you've adopted me, or I've adopted you, or someone had adopted someone, I don't know either. It's too bad we couldn't have made it," she laughed.

He knew she must be lonely. He thought about his and Annie's relationship and how good it was to have someone to really care about. He carefully replied, "Baby, don't get in a rush. That guy is out there and all I can say today is someone is sure missing a hell of a deal."

"Thanks," Heidi replied, "I'll just not rush and see where it goes and above all, I'll keep my pants on. Tight."

"Good girl, that's the way to play it and if this one doesn't work, there'll be one that will. I know because you're too much woman for it not to."

"Thanks. A girl needs her ego pumped up along. I know you're busy but I'll call you one day for lunch. Okay?"

"Great. I'll look forward to it. See you baby."

After Heidi hung up Art left the office and found Tex hard at work on one of his other contracts. He smiled as he asked, "Where you been? I ain't seen you in several days."

Art sat down in the side chair beside the cluttered desk and said quietly, "We need to plan a strategy."

"Oh shit. I see another conspiracy comin'. What the hell you in a crack about now?"

He laughed at Tex, whose eyes were twinkling with mischief and continued, "Well, you see where I come when I need a good conspiracy."

"Hell, you know a good strategist when you see one."

He outlined the test program that he needed to run as Tex listened intently. When he finished, Tex asked, "What do you think it'll cost?"

"Well, I don't have any bids or anything, but my rough, gut feel is about $65,000," he replied, wrinkling his brow.

Tex leaned back, stared at the ceiling and was quiet for a moment Then, without a word, he pulled out the StressCo contract file. "Let's see something a minute here." He started punching numbers into his calculator like a machine gun and shortly frowned. "Well, all we can legitimately bury in the contract is about $10,000. We could go out on a limb and hope the auditors don't catch us and stretch it to maybe $15,000. That sure as hell leaves you short."

"Yeah," Art replied despondently. "And I know better than to go ask Hova to let me spend any corporate risk money. He's opposed as hell to this program."

Tex leaned back and stared at the ceiling again. "Yeah, you can say that again. The little son-of-a-bitch decreed that nothin' was wrong and he ain't never gonna change that. What you gotta do is force him to accept it without getting' killed. Now how do you do that?"

"I know you're waiting for me to say 'modification to the basic contract'".

"Yep," Tex responded. "That's the only way I see to do it and he better never know the mod came from you. I don't know how you'd do that since any change has to originate through the Program Office at the Space Center, be approved by their contracts and funded as a directed add-on to this contract. Then he's got to honor it."

Art frowned and almost whispered, "I feel a method comin on, Tex. I feel a plan!"

"I knew we could count on that," Tex replied with a laugh.

Before the hour was over Art entered Joe Harper's instrumentation lab at the Space Center. He outlined the problems with data on the clevis ends and went into detail about the hysteresis curve and it's potential effects on the data as well as the vehicle data system. Then he said, "Joe, I need to rewrite a large part of the specification to put in changes that require the analyses we need to understand this thing."

Joe looked pensive for a moment as he pondered the problems. "Well, I agree that's a strange phenomenon and I think we need to understand it, but can't you use the changes clause in your overall basic contract to do those tests? You know you and I did that on the Saturn program years ago."

Art felt panic and decided to tell him the real problem.

"So," Joe began after Art finished, "you need a specification revision put on your contract through our contracts office to get around Hova. Is that right?"

"That's right, Joe," Art confided.

"Well, when that little SOB was out here we had a hell of a time with him. Sometimes we had to work around to get the job done in spite of him. He's a typical boil on the ass of progress. Write whatever you need and I'll put it on your contract."

Art felt a large load lift. "Thanks, buddy. I knew I could count on you."

"Hey, any time. We got a job to do. I know you're trying and you know you can count on me."

Minutes later he entered Tex's office. "You're back early. Did he throw your ass out?" Tex asked, anticipating the worst.

"Hell no, man. Carte blanche. How about that?"

"You mean you can structure any test program you like?" Tex asked in amazement.

"Well, anything within reason. I found a guy who understands our problem. I'm going to Eddie's to start writing a specification now."

"Beautiful. If I can help, let me know."

As Art started across the parking lot he saw Irvin Fishburne coming out the door of the adjacent building. Fishburne glared at him across the driveway and growled, "I been lookin' for you, mister."

Art smiled as he answered quietly, designed to infuriate Fishburne even more, "Well, you found me."

"I want to know how come you turned in those schedules early."

He peered at Irvin with a puzzled look. "You said Monday. I didn't give them to you until Tuesday. I was late."

Fishburne glared at Art with a razor edge look and slowly replied, "But them other sons-of-bitches didn't turn 'em in 'til Friday. And I know you went off flyin' to New Orleans. Now how'd you do that?"

"What do you mean, how'd I do that?" Art replied with disgust, stretching to his full height so he could look down on Irvin. "I filled out the damned forms was how I did that."

Fishburne looked strangely at him, somewhere between total doubt and a sneer. "We know that's too much work to get done on a week end, don't we?"

"You're right, Fish, it took me until Tuesday."

Irvin had become frustrated and stormed, "But you couldn't 'a done it that fast. I planned for you to work all week on that little task."

"Why, Irvin?"

"To keep your ass out of mischief, that's why," he snapped, his voice getting higher and higher. "I don't trust you and Mr. Hova don't trust you. You ask too many questions."

Art was exasperated and resolved to needle him some more to see how far he could push him. "But I thought we were supposed to ask questions. I'm just trying to do a good job for you."

"Good job, hell! You're supposed to take directions from me and not do anything that I don't approve of. Do you hear?"

Art was becoming amused at the high state of agitation he was witnessing and replied quietly, "Yes sir. I'll try to do better. I'm always on time for my program reviews. My schedules are always updated and correct. I don't have any delinquent hardware. What would you like me to do differently?"

Irvin's face was red with anger at still not being able to get the upper hand. He got as close to Art as he dared, "You did those damned charts on a computer, didn't you? I know you! You're one of them damned computer weenies."

He stared down at Irvin with a knowing smile as he replied with quiet sarcasm intended to agitate him even more, "Well, old buddy, I didn't give you a printout did I? I believe it was all *writ by hand*, just like you said."

Irvin was turning redder in the face, "Damn you! I know computer work when I see it!"

"Irvin, you're gonna have a stroke." Art passively advised.

Irvin was starting to breathe hard and yelled, "Confess, damn you, confess! You know what Mr. Hova said about computers. *Now confess!*"

With his voice almost a whisper, Art glared down, "Never, Fish. Never."

He started to walk off as Fishburne yelled, "I'll get you for this!"

Art entered Eddie's office and Ben asked, "Well, have we got a plan yet?"

Eddie sat up attentively with no trace of a smile and looked as though he was expecting the worst. Art began, "Better than that. We got a ticket to do whatever we need to do."

Eddie flopped back in his chair, as if he had been shocked. "What the hell did you do? How'd you get around Hova?"

Art laughed at Eddie's enthusiasm. He related the session with Tex and the plan they came up with and then the meeting with Joe Harper. Eddie was curious and asked, "Does Joe understand the full ramifications of this thing?"

"No, but he knows there's enough problems to justify the work we need to do and he'll support that."

Ben frowned and asked, "Don't you think Joe has the right to know the full story?"

"Yeah, but if Hova got wind that we were looking at data for anything other than the specification change, he'd undermine us through his underground network and cut off the funds."

"You think he could do that?" Ben asked cautiously.

"Hell yes. Even though he's gone from out there a lot of those people are still afraid of him."

Eddie replied quietly, "Yeah, Ben, he'd cause Joe a lot of trouble and we don't want that."

CHAPTER SEVENTEEN

Two days before the first launch Art and his colleagues in the Program Office who held responsibility for specific systems such as propulsion, structures, range safety pyrotechnics, electronics, and many others that made up the boosters gathered at the Launch Facility to form an analytical support team. This was in case there were problems in the vehicle, the as-yet unflown and unproven monolith sitting on the launch pad like a huge white eagle ready to take its place in the heavens. The team was headquartered in the Vehicle Assembly Building, a formidable structure billed as the largest building in the world in volume. To enter this building one felt as though he were entering a huge man-made cavern from which he may never return. The openness around huge structural beams and high-bay areas stretched almost as far as one could imagine, almost four hundred feet straight up. The doors seemed large enough to move an average sized office building through with ease.

Launch Control was located in a wing extending south parallel to the launch pads located two miles to the east. There were huge glassed windows overlooking the entire launch area, providing the engineers and technicians a panoramic view of the entire field of activities.

Each time Art visited this facility he was awed by its massiveness. On this historic trip for the maiden voyage of the first Space shuttle, dubbed STS-1, he stood in front of the building with his friend, Egor P. "Boomer" Johnson, pyrotechnics manager, whom he had worked with for many years on other programs dating back to the now "old" Saturn/Apollo program. Boomer's pyro would separate the boosters from the external tank and initiate the recovery sequence, parachuting the boosters back into the sea so they could be recovered, refurbished and reflown. A separate safety system under Boomer's responsibility was installed to blow up the boosters in case of emergency. The Range Safety Officer would initiate any emergency destruct action by remote control from the launch room, if necessary, by pressing a button on his control console. The two of them stood quietly for a few moments, just staring into the cavernous building through the open three hundred foot hangar doors. Finally

Boomer asked, "How'd you like to work down here, Art?"

He thought for a moment before replying, "Every time I see this thing I feel like I'm in a cave. There's no windows except in Launch Control."

"Yeah, I don't think I could manage it either."

Shortly they entered Launch Control where an organizational meeting was due to begin to coordinate technical elements of the team and familiarize everyone with the launch sequence. As they rounded the corner Boomer stopped short, staring across the open space at the launch pad and the tall gantry that held the magnificent machine, Columbia, mounted on its gleaming white external tank and flanked by the two long, cigar-shaped solid rocket boosters. The two of them stared at it for a full minute. Finally Art commented, "Impressive, huh?"

Boomer, with tears in his eyes, replied quietly, "But what the hell if my system had to destroy it? I don't think I could deal with that."

Art, feeling deep compassion for his friend and knowing full well how he felt and why, remembered the old Saturn V days when he and Boomer had stood near this same spot and admired the magnificent rocket before it made its maiden voyage. He turned to Boomer and gently replied, "Boomer, we ain't never blown up one yet and we're not gonna start now. But if it ever has to be done, well . . ."

Boomer grinned as he regained his composure. "Yeah, I understand but I still worry. I always wonder about the Range Safety Officer with his finger on the destruct button, and whether or not I could actually punch it."

Art started to move toward a seat by a console. "Yeah, well, he's a very special person, very special."

After the meeting and assignment of duty stations for the prelaunch and launch activities, Art decided to visit the hangar floor and check on assembly of the next flight set of boosters. Traveling to the launch facility had been difficult because of Hova's restrictions on travel. He considered a trip to the Launch Facility to be a plum and didn't like to give out plums to anyone except a select few of his cronies if he could help it.

These restrictions had caused dissention, considerable problems and cost the program significant sums of money because of a lack of coordination and hands-on experience. Art thought on his way down the elevator to the main deck: *You can say whatever you like about old Billy but you could always get him to come around. But this Hova is a different breed of cat, non-engineer, shallow technically and totally unyielding.*

As he stepped off the elevator and turned down the passage toward the hangar deck he saw a familiar profile that he recognized as Frank Starnes, Chief of the Astronaut Corps at Houston. Art called out, "Frank!"

Frank turned, with his face lighting up at the recognition of his old friend, and replied jovially, "Well, I'll be damned. Are you working this one?"

Art extended his hand when he got within distance. "Sure am, fellow. How's everything in Texas?"

"Well, we're like that proverbial dog eatin' peach seeds. We're nervous as hell. You know this is the first test launch we ever had with a pilot on it."

"Yeah, but you got some good ones. So far as I know right now we got a good vehicle."

Frank smiled and replied confidently, "Man, I got the best there is. I got my real ace, Charles P. "Smoky" Stover and one of the super fighter pilots of all times, Hank Bogish as co-pilot."

"Yeah, you're top quality all the way," Art replied. "I know about Smoky from the Lunar exploration days but I don't know much about Hank."

Frank smiled as he answered, "Watch that boy go. He's got a real future in front of him. He flies that Gulfstream simulator like nobody I've ever seen except Smoky. That's why I chose him. But you know 'ol Smoky, Mr. Cool all the way." They approached a coffee machine in the alcove near the entrance to the hangar deck and Frank asked, "How about a cup of coffee? Tell me what you're doing."

"Well," Art replied as he accepted a cup of steaming machine coffee, "I'm program manager for the booster electronics systems, most of the instrumentation and the guidance gyros, among other things."

Frank sat down in a chair next to a small refreshment center and studied him a moment. He finally asked, "Art, I know you and I know you'll be straight with no bureaucratic bullshit. Are there any problems that you know of?"

He looked solemnly and quietly at Frank, fully recognizing the concern and the seriousness of the question. "I can't speak for everybody, but so far as I know, there are no problems."

Frank grinned, relaxed, and replied, "Beautiful. I remember when you told us about problems on Skylab and nobody would listen and then boom, just like you said. I also remember problems on the Saturn you flagged."

"Well," Art continued quietly, "if I did, you know I'd tell you, don't you?"

"Yeah, I know. I remember once when you got fired for refusing to lie to us."

Art chuckled as he replied, "I didn't know you knew about that. Hell, I hope that story ain't circulating around."

"No," Frank laughed. "Dr. Hans Mueheller told me a long time ago. He was upset. You know that cost that company its contract ultimately."

"Well it should have. If we can't be honest I don't think we should be involved."

Frank thought a moment. "I got to get up to launch control in a minute. We're starting the twenty-four-hour countdown in thirty minutes, but tell me, do you suspect any problems in the vehicle anywhere. Is there anything lurking that we don't know about, something that may have slipped by somewhere?"

Art drew a deep breath before continuing. "I'm chasing one right now. We've done a lot of analytical work on the aft struts and there's a possibility of a problem, but we're not sure. We've got a lot more work before we're ready to ring any bells."

"Serious problems?"

"Not sure yet. It could be, but then we may be chasing a ghost, too."

"Hell, we never chase ghosts. If there's any indication, we got to know."

"Well, it's my plan to complete the analytical work, present it to the company management and then give all the data to the Space Agency."

Frank grew quiet for a moment and stared off into the vastness of the building. "I sure hope there's no problem. Do you know what would happen if we broke one of those damned struts?"

"Well, we don't have any hard data, and I hope we never have to find out but I think it probably would lead to a catastrophic failure and loss of mission."

"Yeah," Frank snorted. "And loss of crew. Well, keep after it." He extended his hand and said, "It's good to see you again, buddy. I'm glad you're back on the team. I got to git."

As Art walked into the assembly area to begin his inspection of the hardware in buildup for flights two and three, he heard the loudspeaker announce, "Countdown for launch is beginning. T minus twenty-four hours and counting." He felt shivers go up his spine and remembered the launches of the mighty Saturn V and the shock waves that beat the building relentlessly until the vehicle was clear of the area. He still heard the shock waves coming from the five big Rocketdyne F-1 engines thundering beneath that big beautiful pencil arcing ever so gracefully into the sky and beyond.

He was awe-struck that day as he sat in launch control and saw that beautiful sight and watched the Werner von Braun with his dedicated and talented group of people he brought with him from Germany at the end of World War II, and marveled at their magnificent achievements.

He remembered watching him, like a kid with a new toy, sitting in his chair focused on the vehicle moving ever so slowly at first, gripping the chair arms and straining until his knuckles were white, saying over and over, *"Go! Go! Go!"* Shortly the launch controller at Houston, in his calm, deep staccato voice, announced over the communications link between Houston and the launch facility, "Staging complete, second stage ignition." He remembered the look of relief and the yell of success from the launch crew as they monitored the many consoles and watched the mission as it progressed smoothly and according to plan. In his mind he heard Mission Control come on the link again and say "Two hundred miles down range, altitude one hundred miles velocity twelve thousand five hundred miles per hour. One minute thirty seconds to staging."

He walked across the hanger deck and up the stairs to the forward skirt assembly fixture where the next forward sections of the boosters were being assembled for flight two. He watched the people below on the floor and could feel the electricity of the moment building, the suspense he knew would culminate in the launch of that very sophisticated and magnificent bird poised out on the launch pad.

He imagined the hold-down arms swinging back and first ignition of the main engines as they come up to speed as if to say, *"Go, Go, Go, Fly!"* Then he imagined the ignition of the big solid rocket boosters strapped to the side of the external tank. He saw the belch of flame and the rapid acceleration of the entire vehicle to the 254,000 foot altitude where the boosters would separate and parachute back into the ocean for recovery. Then in the theater of his mind he watched the Orbiter perched on top of the big external tank like a locust on a limb, gulping fuel for near-orbital insertion as the three main engines on the rear accelerated the craft at breakneck speeds.

He directed his attention from the floor below and stepped into the forward skirt through the access door from the work platform surrounding the structure some fifteen feet in the air where he found his friend and chief manufacturing engineer, Leonard McCroy. "Hi, buddy," Leonard greeted.

Art smiled and extended his hand, "I was wondering if you were around anywhere. How you doing?"

"Great," Leonard replied. "How you like your new mounts?"

He directed his attention back to the Forward IEA and shook the mounting bracket nearest him. "Looks good, Leonard. What do your guys think of it?"

"They love it. That old one was sheer hell to install and we didn't think it would hold a hundred pound box down in case we had a rough launch. But this one will do the job."

Art grinned as they emerged from the forward skirt. "Leonard, you look nervous," he said.

Leonard looked sheepish and confided, "You know I'm always nervous at these damned things. I keep running over the thousands and thousands of things that could go wrong and worrying about what we might have left loose or what we might have left off. You know how it is."

"Yeah," he replied quietly, fully appreciating how Leonard felt. "I sure as hell do. But you've always been an old mother hen."

As they started down the stairs Leonard replied sternly, "The first son-of-a-bitch that I catch up here that doesn't care better get the hell out of my way fast. We can't tolerate that."

"I agree. By the way, where you going to watch the launch from?"

Leonard relaxed and smiled as he replied, "Guess I'll be at

launch control with you guys on stand-by. I've got a couple of consoles up there."

"Great, I'll see you up there at T minus three hours".

The next morning Art was up and out of the motel at daylight. As he drove into the parking lot at the Vehicle Assembly Building he stopped and gazed transfixed at the beautiful vehicle standing on the launch pad. He saw road barriers up and guards at their stations to assure no unauthorized people were admitted to the area. He thought out loud to himself, Okay, baby, we've given you wings, let's see you fly. His mind again flashed back to the awesome first flight of the Saturn V.

He remembered hearing Launch Control calmly say, "T minus thirty seconds . . . T minus twenty seconds, Automatic Sequencer On. . . . T minus ten seconds. . . nine. Ignition. . . seven. . . six. . . five. . . four. . . three. . . two. . . one. . . We have lift-off. We have lift-off." The swing arms had moved back, releasing the vehicle from their grasp, clearing the path for the huge monolith as it began to rise and initiate its roll program to move it out away from the stand and then to accelerate upwards under power from the five big Rocketdyne F-1 Engines that would gulp three hundred and eighty six thousand gallons of propellants in just one hundred and sixty eight seconds of life to place the mighty vehicle at an altitude and velocity where the second stage could take over and boost it higher and faster before it, too, was spent. The emotion was almost more than he could stand. He still got tears in his eyes as he again listened to the thunder that emanated from the big engines and remembered the stream of flame belching from the flame pit arcing upwards through the deflectors turned outward toward the sea and the clouds of steam from the cooling water flooding the flame pit to prevent the erosion of concrete. Art sat for a moment and silently shook his head with a sense of pride beyond all other feelings that he could muster at the moment, at being a member of this exclusive team.

He arrived in the Engineering Room where the team was beginning to assemble while the count down progressed. He noticed the count clock in front of the building. T minus six hours and counting. He checked his watch and saw it was now barely seven a.m., which meant the launch will be on time at 1 p.m. He saw Frank

Starnes approaching and greeted, "Mornin' Frank."

He smiled his big, hearty smile as he replied, "Mornin yourself. You ready?"

Art grinned from ear to ear as he replied confidently, "Yeah, man. I'm really ready for this one. I can't wait to get back into space."

Frank looked serious for a moment and asked quietly, "Art, are you guys worried about the struts on this vehicle?"

He sobered and replied, "Well, they're all from the same lot manufacture. If there's a problem, and I want to emphasize '*if*', it's in these, too."

"Okay. I just wanted to know. I spent a lot of time worrying last night about everything I could think of to worry about and that was part of it."

He put his hand on Frank's shoulder and continued calmly, "Yeah, I know, I didn't sleep much either. We're chronic worriers, but it's gonna be okay."

Frank grinned, "Well, I believe it is, too. I gotta go get the boys out to the vehicle by T minus two so they can run the final checks."

At T minus one hour Art joined Leonard McCroy at an instrumentation console and listened to the Launch Control conversations between the controller and the space craft on the pad.

"We don't have lock on the data link," he heard Smoky Stover, the chief pilot say.

"OK, Columbia, understand no lock," Launch Control replied in their methodical manner. "Hold one."

"Roger," came the reply from Smokey.

Art looked inquiringly at Leonard and asked, "Problem?"

"Yeah. Seems those damned computers don't want to talk to each other for some reason. I think they could launch okay but you know Frank as well as I do. He'll never let 'em go unless it's right."

"Yeah," Art replied, as he punched up the computer codes for the data link display, "I agree with him, too. Especially on this one."

Instantly he had a mass of numbers, symbols and words that would befuddle the uninitiated's mind. He intently studied the lines of code, deciphering each one, scrolling back and forth on the screen for a few moments and finally said, "Looks like some sort of formatting problem."

He listened to the conversations between Launch Control, the cockpit and the team of software experts in the adjacent room. Leonard, intently listening, asked quietly, "Do you think they should delay the launch?"

"Let's see what they come up with. Those guys are the experts."

Leonard grimaced as he concluded, "Well, if there's any doubt, I vote for delay."

"Yeah, me too." He quickly scanned all the other key parameters for the craft and saw that all other systems were *"Go"*. "Looks like this is the only anomaly so far."

Leonard shook his head, "But it may be enough to scrub."

The Count Clock was at T minus twenty minutes and the software people were feverishly trying to link the computers. At T minus ten minutes the Launch Controller was asked, "Gentlemen, what's your decision. We are approaching a critical point at T minus nine and we must make a decision."

The calm voice of the chief launch engineer echoed over the console speaker, "Gentlemen, we have a problem we don't understand right now. We recommend scrub until tomorrow."

They heard the launch controller in his usual calm, staccato voice reply, "Houston, you copy that?"

"Roger, we understand scrub and concur. We'll recycle until tomorrow, launch at 1330 hours."

"Roger," the launch controller replied. "We're recycling now."

Late that night Art and Frank Starnes, sitting alone in the launch support room chatting about old times, looked up to see Smokey Stover entering. "Hi Smoke," Frank greeted. "I thought you'd be over in the crew quarters asleep."

"Nope. Couldn't sleep," Smokey replied, "I'm concerned about that damned computer. This has got to be a good flight."

Frank turned to Art. "Smokey, meet a good and old friend of mine, Art Cannon. He's been a member of the team for a lot of years. He's one of the guys that helped put your ass on the moon. He was a friend of the Doctor's as well."

Smokey's poker face suddenly lit up. "I'm sure pleased to meet you, Art."

Art extended his hand to a genuinely warm handshake. "The

pleasure's all mine, Smokey. I been a fan of yours for a long time. I've been envious of every damned flight you ever made."

Frank laughed as he continued, "He's another one of them fly boys, Smokey. I know he'd rather be up there in the cockpit with you as here on the ground."

Suddenly Frank raised his hand. "Quiet a minute. They're discussing the software on the net."

They heard Houston say, "Format looks good. I believe that dropped bit was the problem."

The launch controller answered, "Engineering, do the computers talk like they're supposed to now?"

Next came a voice from the adjoining room, "Yes sir, they're working fine now that we corrected that bit error that was holding off the *'hand shake'* between the computers."

Launch Control asked, "Have you isolated the source of that bit error, engineering?"

"Yes sir. We fault isolated down to the component part and have replaced the printed circuit board. Everything checks out. All values are nominal, all data rates between the computers are nominal."

Quickly Launch Control asked, "Houston, do you copy?"

Houston replied, "Houston copies. Hold one. We're in a conference looking at the computer schematics." Shortly Houston came back on the net and continued, "Houston concurs. We want to run a few cycles to satisfy ourselves. Can we recycle back to T minus twelve Hours?"

"Uh, Roger, Houston, we can recycle the countdown on the computer back to T minus twelve and you can continue running tests on the system until T minus six without interference in the count."

"Roger Launch," Houston replied. "We'll start testing in one-five minutes and continue until T minus six hours. Will the crew be ready for tests at T minus six hours."

Smoky picked up a mike on the console and barked, "Roger, Houston. This is Stover. The crew will be ready."

Suddenly the communications net was very quiet. Finally Launch Control asked, "Stover, where are you?"

Smokey picked up the mike again, laughed and answered, "I'm in the standby room listening to you guys work.

"Oh. We didn't know."

"Well, sounds like you did a good job. I'm headed to bed

right now for a good night's sleep. See you on the pad."

Frank turned to Art. "Well, I got to get this one in the sack, see you tomorrow."

After Frank and Smokey left, the Support Room was empty except for Art, who was still bubbling with excitement. Testing activities could still be heard in muted tones from speakers on the various consoles in the room and the many lights on the consoles would change status periodically. The Houston engineers, Cape engineers and various contractor engineers from around the country were working long and hard to assure a successful first flight for Columbia. He leaned back, drew a deep breath of satisfaction and pride as he stared across the open fields to the launch pad. He marveled at Columbia standing erect, like a magnificent fledgling ready for first flight. She was bathed in a shroud of white light that made her stand out like a beautiful snow-capped mountain.

He noticed the clock on the wall saying 1:30 a.m. Eastern time. It had been a hell of a long day, but meeting Smokey made it all worthwhile. He again leaned back in the chair and resumed his gaze out toward the launch pad and imagined himself for a few moments sitting in the cockpit with Smokey. He went through the start and liftoff sequence and remembered the films he had watched so many times of the Apollo launches with the earth dropping away, slowly at first, and as the vehicle increased velocity, the amazing speed at which the earth began to get smaller and smaller. Finally the horizon appeared as a semicircle and continents began to come into view.

He sat for a few moments wishing, no, almost demanding that he be allowed to see this beautiful and awesome sight. He felt awkward, cumbersome and earthbound. He wanted in the worst way to experience, to see, and to feel the thunderous thrust and awesome acceleration as the vehicle moved so rapidly away from the Earth. He imagined the thrill of flying this new breed of craft, this super-ship, compared to the old Apollo craft, which were of themselves majestic and beautiful. This is the ultimate flying experience. A flight like this would be almost worth dying for. If you could make this voyage just once perhaps it wouldn't matter if you returned or not. He wondered what the noise level would be in the cockpit, if it would be loud, how the vibration levels would be, what the visibility would be.

Then his thoughts reverted to Earth flying as he relived the take-off roll in the magnificent P-51 Mustang that he loved so much. He thought of the acceleration and the high noise level as he eased the throttle up to take-off power and the big Rolls-Merlin engine began to scream with it's deep, throaty, symphonic voice of authority, a characteristic thunder like no other, as it eagerly delivered all sixteen hundred horsepower and started to accelerate slowly and then faster and faster until she broke free of the earth bonds and joined the eagles as she pointed her long, sleek nose skyward and climbed like a homesick angel into the heavens. He opened his eyes and looked out at the beautiful Shuttle standing on the launch pad with the moon coming up over the horizon, adding its light to the search lights bathing all parts of Columbia, the launch pad, and service structure, holding the magnificent machine to Earth for just a few more hours.

Next morning he was up and out of the motel by 8:00, thinking of the hot cup of coffee he would get at the restaurant and drink as he drove back to the Space Center. When he rounded the corner of the adjoining building that contained the restaurant, he almost ran over Garlin Hova coming out of a room near the corner of the row of buildings on the ground floor.

Almost simultaneously he saw Art and barked coarsely in his best intimidation voice, "What you doin' down here, boy?"

Art replied pleasantly, "Good mornin' Garlin. Are you staying here, too?"

Garlin was trying to unobtrusively pull his door up a little tighter as he continued spewing venom at Art for being at the launch site. Art noticed some activity through the almost-closed blinds and partially-opened door and thought this was curious, but was distracted back to Garlin, barking with his usual coarse bull-dog snap when he felt either uncomfortable or threatened, "I asked you a question, mister. What you doin' down here?"

Art chuckled inside for a moment and replied jovially, "Well Hap, out at the Center put out a list of people required to support the launch. My name was on it and you approved it. I'm on the way back out to Launch Control now."

"How'd you get in there?" Garlin roared. "You don't know nothin' 'bout launchin' a space shuttle. Who else is up there with you?"

Art smiled, amused at the attempts to intimidate him. "Well, there's about thirty of us in the Booster section. Anybody specific?"

Now flustered, Garlin started to stammer, "No, no, I don't care who's up there. I just care about you and them others that work for me."

"Well, I suggest you check your list if you want to know who's down here officially. And, yeah, it's true, I don't know anything about launching a Shuttle because we ain't launched one yet."

Just then Garlin's door opened wide and Fannie, Garlin's personal secretary, started to walk out of the room with, "Baby, I'm ready. . ." As she saw Art her surprise turned to shock; her face turned ashen as she quickly stepped back and tried to close the door. Garlin, whose back had been to the door, looked quickly around and nervously jerked the door shut with a bang. "Well, well, maybe I'll see you out there." He turned without another word and started to walk nervously toward the ice machine.

Having completely forgotten about the coffee, Art thought as he started the engine on his rental car, *Hell, I think I walked in on one of the scandals of the year. Now I know why Fannie frequently disappears when Garlin makes trips. I wonder what the congregation out at his little fundamentalist church would think of that.*

He turned onto the highway and joined the stream of traffic to the Launch Center. *But I suppose it's none of my business anyway. All that knowledge can do is make life more miserable, which it probably will now that he knows I've caught him.*

Art arrived at the Launch Center, checked through security, and entered the control room already buzzing with activity. He saw Boomer sitting at the same data console that he, Frank and Smokey were watching earlier in the morning and said, "Howdy, partner, how's the count comin?"

Boomer looked up quickly, "Beautiful." Shortly the door to the Launch Support Room opened and Boomer saw Hova and Fishburne enter. Irvin looked around the room for a moment and spotted Art and Boomer, and as he started towards their console, Boomer looked up and growled, "Aw, shit, man, what did we do to deserve this?"

Art peered at him curiously, having not seen them. Boomer nodded toward the pair, "Look comin here. Tweedle Dee and Tweedle Dum."

He turned to see Irvin approaching with a big smile on his face. Art quietly turned to Boomer and counseled, "Hang in there, buddy. It's okay. He's not armed."

Irvin, followed by Garlin, came over to the console and slapped Art on the back and asked, "Well, well, guys, how's it goin?"

Art glanced cautiously at him as he replied, "Hello Irvin. Good so far. Looks like we got a clean *'Go'* from our side. The computers are shaking hands now and communicating great."

Garlin turned to Art and, with a stern glare designed in part to offset the previous incident at the motel, growled, "Are you tryin to be smart? Whoever heard of a computer shaking hands?"

Art choked back laughter and Boomer had to turn his head to fake a sneeze to hide his obvious snickers. Finally, Art was able to say, "Well, Garlin, that's a common usage term when two computers link up and start to exchange data on command from each other."

"Common, huh?" Hova snorted. "How they do that?"

"Well," he replied quietly, "there's several ways. One way is through software in the computer so that the computers can synchronize and either read into each other's memory or read from each other's memory."

Irvin was beginning to frown which meant he didn't understand either. He started one of his cutting remarks just as a very large, strong-looking, security guard approached, towering over the both of them, and asked, "Let me see your badge, sir."

Irvin stammered for a moment and finally reached into his pocket. "Here!" as he curtly shoved a badge toward the big guard.

The guard studied the badge a moment and replied courteously, "Sir, I'm sorry but you're not authorized in here. You'll have to leave."

Hova stepped up and entered the conversation in his best intimidation voice, "Ah'm Garlin Hova and Ah'm the SRB Program Manager for Space Corp and Ah authorized him to be here."

The big guard asked again, courteously, "Let me see your badge, too, sir."

Garlin sputtered a moment, and finally handed him his badge. The guard, who was six foot seven and weighed some 270 pounds, looked at the badge, frowned and jutted out an already square jaw supporting an extremely short crew cut. He said courteously, "I'm sorry, sir, you'll have to leave, too."

Garlin fired off his best broadside with a snap like a pit bull and yelled, "Listen you, I'm G. E. Hova and I'm an official on this program and if I say we're authorized, we're authorized."

The big guard had obviously heard all he wanted. He swelled his big frame up at least two more inches, towering over the two of them and replied, "Sir, if you're an official then you have a place in the VIP viewing room. I don't care if you're Jesus Christ, you have exactly thirty seconds to be gone from this room or I'm physically gonna throw both of you out. I could arrest you for being in an unauthorized area."

Irvin looked painfully at Garlin as though he thought the best thing to do was retreat. As the two of them hurriedly left Boomer turned red with laughter along with a number of people on other consoles. Art was dismayed and asked, "Why do you suppose they tried that?"

Finally Boomer got his laughter under control. "I sure as hell don't know unless they still think they can bully everybody when they want to, but when they hit 'ol Felix here, that was it."

The Launch Controller barked over the speaker system, "T minus three hours and counting." Tension began to build as anticipation of the impending launch overcame all emotions. Art saw the van going out to the launch pad with Smokey and Hank Bogish and knew the ship would be in good hands. He went back over the meeting he had with Smokey last night and this morning and was thrilled all over again at seeing one of his heroes, whom he placed on a level with Duane Cole, Art Scholl and Bob Hoover, three of the world's greatest pilots.

He and Boomer, along with Scott Vann from Powder Kegg Corporation, sat watching the count down progress to one hour and then down to thirty minutes. In what seemed to be no time at all, the launch controller announced "T minus twenty minutes and counting." Art suggested, "Let's bring up the communications circuit from the cockpit and listen in." Shortly they heard Smokey's voice going over the checklist for the final time.

Smokey started checking the throttle settings for launch on the three main engines as Boomer commented quietly, "Listen to that guy. That's got to be the coolest and calmest man I ever heard." Smokey went through each item with the same solid, staccato voice he had heard on recordings, the first of which was his trip to the moon. The excitement in all the voices was obvious except for Smokey. He seemed like he was just cranking up another airplane for a pleasure flight.

Scott marveled as he asked, "Do you think anything could ruffle him?"

Art chuckled as he answered, "Haven't you heard? That's Mr. Cool. That's why Frank chose him."

Boomer leaned over and commented, "There ain't many men alive that could tackle this one. This is a real first, a totally unflown vehicle with nothing but theory behind it."

Hank and Smokey were in deep concentration on the computer link-up. Art heard the launch count progressing to T minus thirty seconds. Finally Smokey said, "Looks good, Hank. She looks good. Check tank pressurization."

Quickly Hank replied, "Tank pressurization in the green. All systems on this side are *'Go'*".

As the count reached T minus twenty seconds Art quickly programmed in a window on the console that showed the heart rate for each of the pilots. He pointed to the corner and Boomer looked in disbelief. Smokey's heart rate was all of seventy-four beats per minute while Hank's heart rate was running at one hundred and fourty three beats per minute.

Suddenly, as the count approached T minus ten seconds he heard Smokey say to Hank, "Son, give your heart to God because the Space Agency has sure got your ass."

At T-minus-nine seconds the Launch Controller barked over the speaker system, preempting all other conversation with the realization that the moment of truth had arrived, "Main engine ignition." Then he droned on, as if it were an every day occurrence, "7, 6, 5, 4, 3, 2, 1, booster ignition. We have lift off. We have lift off."

Art, Boomer and all the others stared intently as the automatic functions of Columbia took over. In a deafining roar that seemed to be concealed inside a huge cloud of steam, the ship emerged and crept upward ever so slowly at first. It cleared the gigantic clouds of steam belching from the pits as the flame from the booster nozzles and the three main engines were deflected into the torrents of cooling water. Quickly it began to gain speed as it cleared the tower, accelerating at an amazing rate on its course into the heavens. At the appropriate time the computers initiated the roll program, causing it to roll ninety degrees to the right to establish the down-range trajectory out over the ocean.

Art was thunderstruck at the immense power being displayed by the two boosters, eight and one-half million pounds of brute thrust as Columbia thundered into the sky with a vengeance. Shortly he heard Smokey, "All systems are still *'Go'*".

He heard Houston reply, "Roger, Columbia, all systems are go. Approaching Max-Q." In a few seconds Houston came back on the net, "Columbia, Max-Q."

"Roger, Houston." "By Max-Q. You are Go for throttle up."

Smokey promptly replied, "Roger, Houston, throttle up." Smokey advanced the engine throttles to full power and felt the vehicle accelerate even more as it left the region of maximum aerodynamic pressure and vibration and transitioned to supersonic flight.

Art stood, peering out the window at the long smoke trail, as Columbia surged into the heavens at breathless speed. He waited for the Boosters to separate at 254,000 feet. Soon, he heard launch control say, "200,000 feet. Coming up on booster sep."

Smokey, sounding gleefully happy, replied, "Roger, Houston." In what seemed a fleeting second, Smokey came back on the net, "SRB separation, engines nominal."

"Roger Smokey," Houston replied. "We confirm separation. Looks good and clean." Art and Boomer peered into the sky and saw two small pencils moving out away from the now tiny glow of fire from the three orbiter main engines burning at one hundred and ten percent power, as the boosters fell away. Houston continued, "two hundred and ninety thousand feet up, ninety miles down range."

Boomer had picked up a pair of field glasses and loudly exclaimed, "They're away from the Orbiter. They're chuffin' now, about to burn out." He continued to watch the boosters on the remote video monitors as they fell back toward Earth. As they approached 30,000 feet altitude he observed the parachutes opening to lower the boosters into the sea where they would be picked up by two small ships.

In a few minutes, which seemed forever to the launch crew, they heard Smoky say, "ET separation clean. OMS engines burning for orbital insertion."

Art slapped Scott Vann on the back and yelled, "Shit, man, we did it! We did it! Look at that bird go. Just look at it." He was beside himself with glee, as he joined every one else in the room in laughter and shouts of success. Shortly they heard from the console again, "Roger, Houston, we confirm orbit."

Then, as if to answer the many questions about whether Smokey's blood was real or made entirely of ice water, there was a slow statement coming in over the communication link. "Houston," Smokey started, sounding meek and awed, like he was almost praying, "You can't imagine how beautiful this is. God. It's beautiful up here. This machine is magnificent. I had no idea. I had no idea, even through all the preparation. You can't fully appreciate the magnificence of this thing until you actually experience it."

There was complete silence until the mission controller in Houston replied very slowly, and reverently, "Yeah, Smokey, we can only guess right now. Some more of us are ready to follow your lead. Bon voyage."

CHAPTER EIGHTEEN

After returning to Hawkinsville from the first launch of Columbia, activity returned to normal for Art and his colleagues, focusing on launch number two. Mission control had asked for a survey of lost tiles, which were a part of the heat shield designed to protect the vehicle from frictional heating in the atmosphere during re-entry, and Smokey had confirmed that they could see a few missing on the top surfaces after opening the cargo bay doors. Art was amused to hear Mission Control report publicly that the bottom tiles were in good shape except for a few small places. This was an obvious slip because the crew had not gone *EV,*" or in other words, performed any outside extra vehicular activities requiring a space suit.

Tex entered Art's office, where he had a small TV set on watching and waiting for any news of the mission in progress and slouched down in a chair, obviously very deep in thought. "How's it goin?" he asked slowly with his Missouri drawl.

"Fine, so far. I don't think there's any serious problems."

Tex squirmed a bit and looked out the window at the pigeons flying to and from the window sill and then finally asked, "Tell me somethin', buddy."

"Sure. What you want to know?" he answered as he continued writing on his report.

"You been in this business a long time."

He stopped writing and looked up quizzically at him. "Yeah. I guess so."

"How in the hell did they know about the bottom of that damned thing? They don't have no TV camera up there they can look with, do they?"

He laughed as he answered Tex, who was obviously bothered by this point, "Ever hear of spy satellites?"

Tex looked up quickly.

"Spy satellites? Hell, I never thought of that but how the hell do they look at the bottom?"

Art laughed heartily at him as he squirmed in his chair, "Well, old pilot friend, you know this damned thing flies up side down and backwards as a rule? I know you never flew your Mustang that way during the war unless it was some accident during combat, but that's it."

"Hell," Tex exclaimed with a blush, "I knew that. Why didn't I think of that before."

As Tex turned to leave Art's phone rang. "Excuse me, Tex."

Tex waved his arm and quipped gleefully, "You answered my question. See you later."

Art picked up the phone and heard Eddie: "How about comin' over here and look at this flight data off the struts with us?"

"You got it already?"

"Well, we got the quick look data from telemetry. I'm trying to get the raw data from the computer lab now. I think it's a bunch of crap, and so does Ben, but we might be missing something."

"Be right there."

Art was amazed at the plots he saw on the paper Eddie spread out in front of him. "Look here," he commented as he pointed to the curves. "The axis is perfectly straight across the page. That means the data is always referenced to zero and we know that's not true; no consideration of the hysteresis error in those units and there's no frequency data to begin to see how the system responds. Is that how you guys read it?"

"Exactly," Ben replied thoughtfully, "but even further, I think these plots indicate compressive loading."

Eddie was sitting with a dejected look and slowly began to turn red in the face. "Hell, man," he finally said. "If I recall correctly, there was no qualification testing done on these units in compression. That's what you said, wasn't it?"

Ben was standing and replied gruffly, "Yep. That's what he said."

Art studied the two of them. "That's right, and what I see now is at least requalification of those units."

Eddie slammed the table with his fist so hard he sloshed coffee out of Ben's cup, "Hell, you know as well as I do that's not gonna happen."

Ben slid back in his chair while Eddie mopped up the spilled coffee with a paper towel and continued thoughtfully, "Well, this is where we did a good thing in getting this testing program set up.

Maybe we can get some good data to tell us it's okay when we get through with it."

"I sure hope so," Art replied quietly as he saw his good metallurgist friend, Alf Bennett enter. Alf was always jolly, affable and full of good jokes.

Alf looked around and perceived all was not well. His usual big smile faded as he peered at one and then the other. Finally, he asked, "What's wrong? You guys holdin' a wake or something?"

"Yeah, something like that. Come in," Art replied.

Ben motioned towards a chair. "Alf, we got a problem. If we wanted to know about the stresses in a piece of material and didn't have all the facilities to run stress-strain diffraction patterns, how would we do it?"

"Well, first I'd run some tests using a stress crack compound and then look at the patterns that occurred under those tests. That'll give you a good first approximation and tell you whether or not you need to go further. Besides, it's cheap."

Eddie hopped up from his chair and quickly agreed, "Alf, that's a good idea. Why didn't I think of that?"

Alf flashed a big grin and patted Eddie on the arm gently, almost fatherly. "Because, son, you're not a metallurgist."

Eddie asked eagerly, "If we do that, will you interpret the data?"

He turned to Art and, without answering Eddie's question, and asked, "Is this on that strut problem we were talking about?"

Art nodded and replied, "I think we need your help."

He slid down in the chair while he contemplated the request, considering his answer carefully, "I'll help on one condition."

"What's that?"

"That nobody knows I'm involved. You guys are playing with fire."

"In what way?" Ben asked.

"Well I probably shouldn't tell you, but I was in a meeting this morning with Hova and Fishburne and some of the stress people from engineering. They were trying to pump me about the materials in that thing and I told them I had no data and wasn't involved with it. I said I hadn't looked at it and had no reason to."

Ben leaned over the table and asked cautiously, "Who were they?"

Alf wrinkled his brow a bit, trying to recall as he answered, "Well, there was Lem Grayson and Arnold Sanders. Then, Fishburne called in George Tyrone."

Eddie jumped up from his chair and exclaimed, "I know all those damned guys. They don't know nothin' about stress loading and structural engineering. Besides, they're all from the Space Agency and retired out there twenty years ago."

Ben stared at Eddie sternly. "Now, Eddie, don't make any general statements because there's some really good people in that agency."

Eddie sat down and replied, "Ben, I know that and I love working with the good ones, but you know as well as I do that some of those people retired the day they went to work. Some of them are just parrots who got nothing to contribute but noise. These guys are that sort."

Art came to his defense with, "I agree, Ben. I know those people and they couldn't engineer their way out of a paper poke."

Ben smiled and, as the gentleman he was, replied, "I'll accept that and what Eddie's saying is that this is part of the dead wood."

"Exactly! Those damned guys were a part of the clique that Fishburne ran and that's why they're here now."

Alf had been watching the exchange with interest. He commented quietly and, as always, cautiously, "I'll deny I ever said it because Hova does have a position of authority up there and can be a lot of trouble if he gets a clear shot, but those aren't the only ones they've brought in like that."

"Yeah, Alf. I'm sure that's true," Ben answered. He stood up, looked solemnly out the window and turned, facing the group. "To hell with Hova and all that damned click. We got a responsibility to try to solve this thing. We'd be less than honest if we didn't try."

Art replied with a grin, "It's more than that. We have an obligation. There's enough doubt now to try to find out what the true story is."

Alf smiled and picked up the conversation again, "Well, if you guys will listen to your good Jewish friend here, you'll get started on the stress cracking right away. But just keep my name out of it. My boss is afraid of him so I have to be, too."

Art put his hand on his shoulder. "Alf, if he ever gets after you, there's a secret to dealing with him."

He jerked around and looked straight at Art. "Secret? What the hell are you talking about? Let me in on it."

Art grinned as he continued, "I've learned that when he jumps on you if you'll jump back just as hard as he jumps on you, he'll turn tail and run."

Eddie shook his head. "Yeah, but that'll make him hate you even more, won't it?"

Art looked at them and continued, "No. You're already at the bottom of the barrel. You are, in his eyes, a sinner and damned for hell and the only thing left for you is to exterminate the impure from the Earth."

Eddie was wide-eyed, and quickly asked, "Why do you say that? That's not rational. Nobody can stand in that kind of judgment."

"I agree, but here's the deal."

Art spent the next few minutes relating the research he'd done on the small fundamentalist group that Hova headed and then related the story about his Masonic Brother who was kicked out by the church and shunned by his own family because he had joined the Masonic Lodge.

Alf stood up and growled with determination, "Well, I'm Jewish and I suppose that makes me something of an outcast around here, but I sure as hell ain't gonna let that impact my thinkin'. Besides, I'm a practicing Mason and proud of that, too."

Art stood and put his arm around Alf's shoulders. "Alf, you got more friends in a minute than those two can buy all day."

Alf grinned as he replied, "Yeah, I know, but I get pissed when I find out things like that."

Ben was slouched down in his chair, looking past them out the window in deep thought. Finally, he said, "Well, I'm of the opinion that the reason he's trying to find out what we're doing is to try to cover up for somebody somewhere if there's a problem."

"You really think so?" Eddie asked.

"Sure. Then he's got another debtor out there that he can control one way or another, either gratitude or blackmail. Going behind our backs says that he doesn't want us to know he's interested nor does he want to get too close, so it won't look like he sanctioned our investigation."

"Exactly," Art replied with a frown.

"Probably the only reason he keeps Fishburne around is to do his dirty work so he can maintain the aloof, pious image while he's cutting throats as fast as he can."

Ben grinned as he thought about Hova. "Well, guys, my position is that we press on. When we get results we can tell the world. If not, we'll go away and be quiet."

Alf stood in preparation to leave and said, "Well, get that stress cracking material and call me when you have something to look at."

"Sure will," Art replied, "and thanks for the help." He turned to Eddie. "Continue to try to get the real, raw data from the flight and I'll get started on the stress cracking process with Tex."

Alf asked as he started out the door, "Does Hova know about those tests?"

"No, I don't think so," Art replied. "The contract change to implement our new specification revision came through contracts to me. He gets a synopsis and the change number, but he seldom reads 'em. Fishburne may pick up on it but then again he may not."

"Let's hope not," Alf replied. "It'll make things a lot simpler if you don't have to involve them."

Eddie replied firmly, "I don't think that'll be a problem. They'll want as much distance from it as they can get. The secret was getting it through before they knew it was coming."

"Absolutely," Ben replied, "but if they do pick up on it they'll be pissed and try to shut us down again."

Art left the building, crossed the parking lot to Tex's office and noticed the clouds building for a squall. "Buddy, it's gonna rain cats and dogs out there in a while," he announced when he entered Tex' office.

"Right now I wouldn't much give a damn. What's up?"

"Well, we got to see Sam about doing some stress crack testing."

"Some what?"

"Hell, I never heard of it either, but Alf said we needed to do it. Sounds good to me. I was hoping you'd know something about it."

Shortly Tex, Art and Sam were huddled around StressCo's

conference table deeply involved in telephone discussions with Tom Bennett, an applications engineer from Sam's strain gage supplier. Art asked, "Tom, do you think this process will give us stress data on these things?"

Tom replied cautiously, "Stress cracking is a good way to obtain a first approximation to define the patterns you would want to scan if you ran diffraction tests using a low-powered laser, or some other technique. It's not going to tell you, for example, what the forces are but it will tell you the relative magnitude and direction of the forces by the spacing of the cracking lines as the part either stretches or compresses. The stresses will be normal, or ninety degrees to the lines, sort of like throwing a rock into a pond."

"Thanks, Tom," Sam replied. "We'll be gettin back with you soon."

"Okay," Tex said, turning to Sam, "I'm giving you verbal go-ahead to order the materials and I'll cut you a change order when I get back to the office. You'll have it by tomorrow at the latest."

Sam grinned as he replied, "Yes sir, I'll proceed right now." Then he turned to Chet, "Get your order made out for the materials and let's call it in today and get the stuff over here. Then develop the test procedures that you need and let's move out. Call Chip from Quality and coordinate the test procedures with him."

Art, pleased with Sam's initiative, said, "Hell, Sam, you've got this damned thing down to a science now. We didn't have to tell you anything to do except to get movin."

"I think I finally got you damned guys figured out."

Tex laughed and kidded, "We'll see, buddy, we'll see. I want to see your pricing before I let you off the hook."

Art turned to Chet as he rose and started to Sam's coffee pot, which had finally stopped dripping, "Are you ready with the fixtures to check the drift of the zero point on these units?"

Chet looked a little embarrassed. "No. I planned to have the fixtures designed and built by now, but I just finished the design. I just now got in part of the materials."

Tex smiled and comforted Chet. "Hey, you're ahead of me. I still haven't issued you a change order but I expect to get it out of typing maybe tomorrow."

Sam glowed to think that he was ahead of the project and quipped, "Well, what did I tell you about how we'd work with you guys. You just give me a verbal and I'll move . . ."

Chet overrode the friendly exchange. "We're running five units on this test program. Correct?"

Art replied, "Yeah, that's right. We'll run 'em for thirty days, five units. We'll take the data and see how the readings drift over a long period of time under a constant load. I want to know if the calibration of those things changes over a period of time with them sitting there with the rest of the Space Shuttle attached stationary like they will be on the launch pad before launch."

Sam looked bewildered and asked meekly, "I know you want this but what the hell is it going to do for you?"

"Well Sam," Tex began, before Art could explain all the technical reasons, "you know that thing sits out there on the pad before launch and the loads are supported by the upper ball joint on the forward end of the boosters where the external tank attaches and the tank and orbiter combination hangs down on them. Then, the side loads of the entire structure are supported by the aft struts."

Sam nodded. "Yeah, I understand that." Then he realized the value of the measurements. "I see," Sam replied proudly, "you want to know if any of the measurements move with time after this thing is stacked?"

"Exactly," Art replied. "That's part of this test program. The balance of it will tell us how your sensors respond to the dynamic excitation. That's the part that Wilkie Labs claim they can do, but I'm still worried about their quote."

"What are they going to do?" Chet asked. "I know we're shipping some units out there."

Art continued, "We need to apply a four hundred thousand pound impulse in ten one-hundredths of a second and I'm skeptical about their equipment."

"Sounds pretty tough," Chet commented as he picked up his materials from the table.

"Well, if we can get a complete strut we need to determine the natural resonant frequency. If not, we'll have to try to model it on the computer from this data and figure it out that way. What we really need to do is fully instrument these damned things in flight and then we wouldn't have to be guessing."

Tex grinned as he commented, "Well, you tried that and almost got your ass fired."

"Yeah," Art agreed, "but they got a long way to go to get me."

The next day just before quitting time, Art appeared in Tex's office and gleefully announced, "Hey, Columbia's in the last orbit. Let's go out to the Center and watch her land. I know where there's a monitor in a ground station."

Tex jumped up, almost tripping over his trash can looking like a kid in a candy store. "Shit man, let's go."

Shortly they checked in through security and entered the telemetry ground station, where Art greeted old friends as he and Tex took a seat in front of the big monitor screen where Columbia would appear momentarily. There were smaller monitors around the room at consoles for the Hawkinsville mission support team. Tex slid down in his chair a bit and asked, "How the hell did you know about this place?"

Art smiled and replied, "Most of these people are old Apollo people I've worked with for years. We go way back."

Tex was pleased to get to watch the first landing of Columbia from such a vantage point. Suddenly he heard the conversation between Smokey and Mission Control. "Your turn looked good. Chase planes will intercept at thirty thousand feet and escort you down."

"Roger Houston," Smokey replied, "everything feels good so far. I can see a chase plane below now."

"Uh, roger, Columbia, your trajectory is right on course. Speed looks good, attitude looks good."

Shortly Columbia broke through the thin cloud layer and Smokey said calmly, "We have the runway in sight."

"Roger Columbia, she's all yours."

Suddenly Smokey called, "Uh, Houston, the auto-land system No-Op light just came on. The system is off the air. It won't reset." There was a quick feeling of panic. The automatic landing system that had been planned for the first few landings had failed.

"Columbia, this is Mission Control. You'll have to hand-fly her down," the ground controller announced, still retaining the stoic calm that had been so characteristic throughout.

"Roger. We'll land her like we should have in the first place."

They listened to the controllers give Smokey position and speed data, "Come right two degrees. You have a ten knot wind from three zero degrees. Altitude is twenty thousand feet, speed is three five zero knots. Glide slope looks good."

"Roger, looks good from here."

The conversation soon became more rapid from the ground. "Altitude five thousand feet, speed three hundred knots. Glide slope good," as the data continued in a chant to Smoky.

Smokey had all but neglected to reply. Art knew he was extremely busy in the cockpit with his glider that had the glide ratio of a brick. Smokey occasionally grunted, "Roger" just to let them know he was aware of their tracking, but the real activity was in the left seat of Columbia as it sped on its way back to earth from which it had departed in such a hurry a few days before. The controller was concentrating on calling out altitudes and speeds. "Five hundred feet, speed two seventy five knots; four hundred feet, speed two fifty knots; three hundred feet, acknowledge gear down, speed two hundred twenty five knots."

Smokey replied, "Gear down and locked."

The controller continued, "Fifty feet, two hundred twenty five knots, twenty five feet, fifteen feet, five feet, touchdown."

Tex jumped up and yelled, "Son of a bitch, did you see that, right on the fuckin' numbers! Right on the numbers!" Tex was beside himself while Art just stared at the screen in disbelief.

The controller calmly continued, "Welcome home, Columbia."

Everyone was ecstatic, especially those who flew and really understood this feat. Tex was still gyrating and almost yelled at Art, "From two hundred and twenty miles out in orbit and he literally hit the damned numbers on the runway! Shit man, that's impossible! Tell me he didn't do that!"

Art replied proudly, "Hey, old buddy, I told you, that's a real pro. One of a kind."

As they started to leave the laboratory, Bud Cox, the lab director, approached Art and extended his hand, "Hi, buddy, how you been. I heard you were on the program but you ain't been out to see me."

Art smiled and replied, "Thanks old friend, it's been too long. By the way, this is my buddy, Tex James, an old Mustang P-51 jock from W-W-2."

Bud extended his hand and greeted Tex warmly, "Pleased to meet you. We go back a long way. You're welcome here any time there's room for you to watch any launch or landing."

Tex, elated at the invitation, smiled and replied, "Gee, thanks, Bud. I'll sure take you up on it."

Art extended his hand as they left, "Thanks, Bud. I'll see you soon. We'll work over some old times."

The next day Art went to his office early, put on the coffee pot and sat down to contemplate the day while he waited on the coffee. As he sat in his chair watching the birds fly over in flocks, as they do in the fall, he heard Ray come in. "Sure smells good," Ray remarked as he sat down in one of the side chairs.

"Sure does. I need a cup this morning. Fishburn and Hova have been too quiet since I got back from the Cape. I got a feeling it's gonna be a bad day."

Ray sat ponderously for a moment. "Yeah, I'm sure, but how is anybody's guess. Let's have a cup of coffee and to hell with him. I need to talk about cable designs."

"Sure. I'd rather drink coffee any time than worry about Fishburne. But he's the one to watch. Hova'll have him do the dirty work."

They returned to Art's office, each with a steaming cup of fresh coffee and delved into the design of a forty-foot cable that had so many connectors coming off of branches that it almost looked like an octopus. Just as they were starting to verify the interconnects between the connectors where the wires came out to connect to other cables, Fishburne strutted in and announced, "Well, Mister Smart Guy, you had your day when you got me and the chief thrown out of the Firing Room at the launch. I just been lookin' for the right opportunity and now I got your ass. I'll have my day today."

Art looked up and replied quietly, "Irvin, you know that's not true. You were somewhere where you weren't supposed to be and you can't take that out on me."

Fishburne smiled like he was about to commit mayhem, which Art thought sometimes he would really like to do. "Well, you keep showing up in places you got no damned business so we thought we'd just clip your wings for a while. Your travel is terminated. You can't go anywhere and I mean anywhere for any reason."

Art was thunderstruck. He looked up in disbelief. "But you know I've got to go to the west coast next week for the Rate Gyro meeting."

Irvin smiled a toothy smile as he gloated. "Not any more you don't. You're grounded big boy, 'til you learn some humility."

"Irvin," he boomed, "you know I'm one of the speakers."

"Well, guess they'll have to get themselves another speaker, won't they? The one they had has been a bad boy. You got to learn you don't get away with that shit."

Art was red in the face and trying to control an emotional explosion coming on. He glared at Fishburne and said sternly, "You went into that room by yourself unauthorized. I didn't have nothin' to do with that."

Fishburne was laughing with glee at having hit a nerve. He continued sarcastically, "You got to learn to support your bosses. You don't put the old chief down and get away with it."

Art was furious. "You mean to say that you're willing to sacrifice important business for a personal vendetta? Is that what you're saying?" He was shouting and started from behind the desk toward Fishburne, who retreated quickly out in the hall yelling, "Don't you touch me, mister! Don't you touch me!"

Ray was sitting, wide-eyed, in his chair as though he had seen a killing. "I don't believe that! I just don't believe it!"

Art sat down in his chair and sarcastically replied, "Someday that little SOB is gonna go too far and somebody's gonna kill him if he doesn't kill somebody else first."

"Boy, you got that right," Ray croaked, still in disbelief.

He peered at Ray with a worried look. "Guess I better call George out on the coast and tell him I can't make the meeting."

"What will it mean to the program?"

"Well, it's gonna mean that the reuse and refurbishment plan for the launches is going to be delayed because this is the sort of thing that has got to be worked between several different companies and centers."

"Well," Ray continued, "you did win the fight for the new gyro test station at the Launch Center. That'll help, won't it?"

"Yeah," he mused, "that's gonna give us a good pre-installation test, but they need desperately to have a full-up factory test with the results coordinated with everybody. That way, we're less likely to let any guidance problems get through."

Ray had a grave look as he said, "I've heard that those two will let anything happen to prove a point. I guess it's true."

Art leaned back in his chair and drank a long swallow of his now almost-cold coffee, and grunted, "Yeah, and they'll never change a decision once it's made, no matter what. To listen to some of the stories from the old timers out at the Center, it'd make your blood run cold."

"Yeah, and I bet they never let any of it get to upper management where it could hurt 'em. They always had a patsy or an excuse."

Over the next three weeks Art and Eddie, assisted by Ben and others, worked at every opportunity on the collection and reduction of data from the first flight. Finally, Eddie called them together in his office. "Well," he began when they were seated at his work-table, "I finally got raw launch data and it's worth what I thought it was. Nothing."

They studied the charts and followed Eddie's explanation. "See here, again the axis is linear and we know that's not right. There's no IRIG time channel for correlation of frequency. We don't know what the hysteresis has done to the results and we don't know what the error magnitudes are."

Ben sat with a frown. Finally he added his assessment. "Well, the one thing it does prove, I think, is that there is both tension and compression loads on these struts and nothing more."

Eddie was ponderously staring at the pages of data, two graphic traces from each of the six struts. After a few moments of contemplation, he broke the silence, "Well, one thing we can be sure of, I think, is that it certainly says there is a problem."

"Right now, I'm of the opinion that we're going to invalidate the design," Ben replied coarsely. "From where your analysis is going, it looks like there isn't sufficient material to assure the strut's integrity."

Art was moving around in his chair as though he were uncomfortable with the entire issue. He wrinkled his brow and rubbed his chin ponderously as he said, "But then again, if there's no problem, that's a good answer, too."

"Yeah, I agree and I hope it works out that way, but Eddie's stochastic model may show results we don't want to see. I was actually hoping this flight data would show us we were wrong but it doesn't show us anything about this problem."

Eddie slowly walked to the window in deep thought. Finally he said, "Well, I think I'll factor this data into the model and see what that tells me and then I'll insert the Mil-Handbook-5 calculations and see how that data compares. Maybe then we'll have a good feel for where whoever designed these things started from. Maybe we can learn their thought processes."

Art leaned back in his chair and agreed. "Well, I think that might be good to do. Of course, we roll out tomorrow for the second launch and maybe that one will give us some better data."

Ben snorted as he stood up. "Not with this damned data system. There's no changes in the design is there?"

"No," Art confessed. "I guess that was just wishful thinking."

Eddie chuckled and asked sarcastically, "Remember the fateful engineering change proposal you submitted to redesign this system way back when it could have been done?"

He nodded as Ben reminded them, "Almost got your ass fired, didn't it?"

"Yeah, and now we're stuck with garbage," Eddie retorted.

Art returned to his office feeling dejected and worried. He poured himself a fresh cup of coffee and sat staring out the window watching the pigeons go and come from the sills. Then he saw a flight of geese headed South for the winter. *Lucky guys. No worries, just able to fly all the time. Hell, maybe I should chuck this mess and take one of those corporate pilot jobs. But, then, I'd be gone all the time and I wouldn't get to see Annie and neither of us would like that. Besides, they don't pay very much.* As he started to leave the office for the day, his phone rang and startled him so that he jumped. He picked up the phone and answered, "Cannon here."

The voice uttered a sigh of relief. "Damn, I'm glad you're still there."

He immediately recognized his friend Arnold Truax from the launch center. "Hello Arnold," Art answered cheerfully, "how's it goin' down there?"

"You know we roll out tomorrow for the second launch, don't you?"

"Yeah. Is there a problem?"

"Yeah, I'm afraid there is. You know those damned little wires coming off those strain gages in the aft engine nozzle actuators?"

"Yeah. I have those installed here by StressCo."

"That's the one. Well, we broke one installing the actuator and we've worked all day trying to repair it. We can't get it to re-solder and we're gettin desperate. We don't want to roll out with open work if we can help it."

Art frowned and replied, "Arnold, I told you guys not to mess with those damned things if you had a problem. They're tough and I know you don't have anybody that can do it."

"Well, we were hoping you could tell us how."

He chuckled and replied, "I only know one person who can do that and she does 'em all. I think I better get her on the plane tonight. You'll just have to bite the bullet and roll out with some open work."

"Hey, I'd rather not do that if I can help it."

"Arnold, believe me. This is the best way. Just write it up on the squawk sheet as 'Pad Repair' and I'll get Sara on the plane. I'll work it and call you back in a few minutes."

"Then you don't think we can fix it?"

"Arnold, I'm sure you can't. I'll call you back in a few minutes." He rushed into Tex's office in almost a run. "We got a problem at the Launch Center! We need Sam to get Sara down there quick. They roll out tomorrow and she's got to repair one of those damned nozzle actuators."

Tex looked at him incredulously. "You mean they broke one of those sensors?"

"Yep, they broke a wire and they been screwing with it all day and can't fix it."

"Shit man," he growled disgustedly, "I bet they ruined the whole thing. Ain't nobody but Sara can fix that."

"I know. Let's get Sam and get her down there. You'll have to send one of the Quality Inspectors, too."

"I agree," Tex replied hurriedly as he dialed Sam at StressCo. "Sam, we got a problem at the Launch Site. They're rolling out SL-2 tomorrow and I need to get Sara down there quick to repair one of those damned engine nozzle actuator wires."

Tex switched the phone over to the speaker as Sam answered. "You're not serious, man. It's quittin' time. Hang on a minute and let me try to catch her." They heard Sam yelling out his office door, "Carol. Carol! Get Sara for me, quick. We got a problem."

There was silence for a moment and then Sam said excitedly, "There goes Carol running across the damned parking lot. She's about to drive out in that old '49 Chevy pick-up truck she drives. Hurry, girl! Hurry!"

Tex couldn't restrain himself any longer and burst out laughing. Sam retorted quickly, "What's so funny?"

Tex, still laughing, replied, "I can just see that now, Carol running across the parking lot trying to catch that old truck."

Sam was suspicious of a joke and replied cautiously, "You are serious aren't you?"

Art entered the melee, "Hell yes he's serious!"

Sam chuckled as he replied, "I ain't never seen such a pretty thing as Carol running with her dress tail flying in the wind. First time I ever seen her legs. Man, what a sight."

Shortly Carol, out of breath, entered Sam's office with Sara in tow. He looked at her and began patiently, "Sara, how quick can you go to the Launch Site? They need you down there."

Sara turned pale, shifted her fresh tobacco chew and asked, "You gotta be kiddin' Mr. Sam. Why duh they need me down there?"

Sam, trying to settle the excitement in his voice so as to not upset Sara, replied slowly, "Well, they broke a wire on one of those nozzle actuators that you built and they need you to fix it."

Sara clearly had a problem, obvious by her shifting from foot to foot and looking like her face was about to pop. Her jaws were beginning to swell and she began to look like a caged animal. Sam recognized the symptoms from experience and motioned her toward the bath room. She gratefully went in and spit out her chew. When she came out she grinned and continued, "That's there's a plug you owe me, Mr. Kelly."

He laughed and replied, "Okay, Sara, I owe you one. Now what about the Cape?"

"I ain't never been there, Mr. Kelly. I'm not sure I can find my way around. In fact, I ain't never been out'n this state and ain't never been no further south than Bug Tussle. I ain't never been on no air plane, neither."

Tex, in his best fatherly voice, came on the speaker phone gently, "Sara, we know all that, but there's a problem that we don't think anybody but you can fix. We need you real bad. Don't worry about going alone, we'll send your Quality Man, too."

Sara's tone shifted a bit. "Well, can I take my husband? He ain't never been much further'n the county line, I know. He's plannin to lay by part of his corn t'morrow, if'n hit don't rain t'night."

Tex frowned and was thinking fast. "Well, Sara, he'll have to stay in the motel. He can't go out to the launch site because he's not an employee of Sam's."

Tex heard a very dejected Sara: "Oh, well, well . . ." as she was trying to make up her mind about going.

Art understood what a big thing this was for her. He knew she had little or no understanding of such worlds as this and felt great empathy. He had watched her walk across the parking lot to her old pick up truck more than once and marveled at the old blue jeans and denim or plaid shirts and the walk that she had as though she were still hopping rows out in the corn field. He also marveled at the wonderful, and very unique touch she had in soldering these impossible little wires in impossible places, wires almost invisible to the naked eye. Suddenly he proposed, "Sam, put Sara's husband on the payroll as of today and classify him as a tool carrier. Then you can send him, too."

Sam saw Sara's face light up as she exclaimed, "You really mean it, Mr. Cannon?"

Sam answered quietly and evenly, "Yeah, Sara, he means it and I mean it. As of this morning he's on the payroll as a tool carrier and he can carry your tools for you."

She leaned back and laughed a hearty laugh typical of country folk, as she exclaimed, "Man, mister Kelly, he'll never be thu same after this. He ain't gonna believe it. Yeah, I'll go but not before mawnin'. We got to milk and feed tuh'night and git somebody tuh do it fer us whilst we're gone. Hot doggies, we're gonna' finally ride one of them damned air planes."

Sam smiled at Sara. "Thanks, Sara, I'll send somebody out to the farm after while and let you know when to leave, and don't worry, we'll see you don't get lost. You're too valuable."

Tex breathed a sigh of relief. After he heard Sara leave the office, he continued, "Well, guess if that's what it takes, that's what we'll do. You got another employee but I never heard of a tool carrier."

Sam kidded him, feeling for once he had a definite advantage. "Yeah, but you have now. I'll get reservations made and let you know in a little while."

"Fine, we'll get 'em cleared in through security and arrange for escorts to pick 'em up at the airport."

The next morning Sam called to assure them Sara, her husband, and the Quality Inspector were on the airplane and headed for the Launch Site. Art breathed a sigh of relief while Tex leaned back in his chair and chuckled, "I'd sure like to see those three when they get in that Vehicle Assembly Building and out on the pad up in that vehicle."

Art started to laugh and replied, "Yeah, that's probably the biggest thing that ever happened to them. It's odd how some people have grown up in the middle of this and have been so disaffected by it all. Here they are in the middle of one of the greatest technological centers in the country and they seem to be totally oblivious."

Art was in his office early the next day to be sure that the escorts for Sara and her entourage were in place and there were no problems in getting them from the motel into the Vehicle Assembly Building. He called Arnold at home before he could get out the door. "Arnold, have you got Sara and company all situated for the day?"

Arnold laughed as he replied, "Yeah, mother hen, I took care of it. Last night we took 'em out to a sea food restaurant down on the beach and they couldn't believe their eyes. Are you sure she can do this work? She didn't seem like she knew much about anything."

"Hey man, she's the best. She's never been out of the state until now and if it weren't for Sam Kelley, she'd still be milking cows and feedin' chickens."

Arnold became serious as he asked, "Well, can she really solder these things?"

"Arnold, she's the only one that can. She's an artist. You looked at the workmanship that went into those things, didn't you?"

"Yeah. It was outstanding."

"Well, she did that, and I mean all of it."

"Okay, if you say so, but it's hard to believe she can do work like that."

"Rest assured friend. Take good care of her, she's valuable."

Late that afternoon he called Arnold back at the Launch Site. "How'd the repair job go?" he asked quickly.

He replied apologetically, "Well, to be honest, it ain't yet."

Art sat straight up in his seat and looked in disbelief at the phone, "What do you mean, it ain't? You damned guys didn't turn the transporter over on the way out to the pad did you?"

Arnold, still quiet and reserved, replied, "No. They won't let her go out to the pad."

"Why the hell not? Don't you want that thing fixed?"

"Hey," came the quick reply from the other end, "there was a telecon early this morning about her between your guy Hova and our management and he said not to let her go out there because she was so country. They were about to send her home but I argued that maybe she could teach us to do it."

Art was furious. He stood up and paced back and forth across the office dragging the phone across his desk, almost yelling at the mouthpiece, "That's the most asinine thing I ever heard! If you want that repair made, send her out there. Send the entire US Army out there with her if you want to but let her do her thing!"

Arnold was sheepish in his reply. "Well, she's been trying to teach some of our people all day and she hasn't been able to get 'em to make any acceptable connections yet. Her quality man isn't much help. He knows the processes but he can't do it either."

Art boomed at the phone, "The damned quality man isn't supposed to be able to do it. He's supposed to only know if it's done right. Besides, she's not a damned instructor. She's a do'er and a hell of a good one!"

Arnold sensed his furor and replied quietly, "Settle down, Art, I know it's frustrating, but give me some time. Maybe she can teach these people. Hova and Fishburne are the ones that submarined us. Let me try to work it out."

"Okay. I'll call you tomorrow and see how it's goin'," he said as he hung up the phone in disgust.

He sat in his chair for a few minutes and stared out the window, watching people from the company going home. *Shit, I might as well go home, too, for all the good I've done.* He looked at his coffee cup. *Maybe just one more cup before I go.* He picked up his cup and started to get up from his chair and said to himself, from somewhere deep down in his subconscious, *No, I been drinking too much of that stuff lately. I'm gettin too nervous.* He resolved to just go home.

When he arrived at his office the next morning he saw the light on in Ray's office and peered in. Ray turned with a start and replied cheerfully, "Good morning. What are you doin' here so early?"

Art grimaced as he replied, "I just couldn't sleep. I got an idiot situation at the Launch Center and it's buggin' me."

Ray smiled knowingly as he replied, "Yeah, I was talkin to Arthur Wong down there yesterday afternoon and he told me. He thought the gal could do the work but I guess they shot you down, huh?"

"Yeah, another typical case of not knowing their ass from first base about the technical aspects of this damned program. If those people try to fix that thing with no more experience than they have, they'll ruin it and have to pull it off and send it back up here for a full re-instrumentation. It costs over thirteen thousand dollars each for that."

Ray frowned and asked, "What you gonna do?"

"I don't know. I've called down to check on progress. Fishburne and Hova hate me enough now and I'm afraid if I cross 'em they'll just make my life more miserable than they already have. Guess I'll just wait and see what happens."

Ray got up and came to the door where Art was standing and replied sternly, "Fuck 'em and do what's right. I think the coffee's done. I came in early to work on these damned cable designs. I got a hell of a schedule and I ain't gettin much support out of F-Troop."

Art smiled and replied thoughtfully, "Yeah, I got the same problem."

As the day progressed with one problem after another, Art hadn't had much time to worry about the actuator repair. He had resolved technical issues and worked a dozen other critical problems in schedules, designs, contract requirements, document and specification generation, and the many other duties typical of a manager of a major system. At shortly before five o'clock, a full half hour after the bulk of the people had gone home, he sat down in his chair and reflected on Annie's arrival home tomorrow and how he would be glad to see her. He really missed her lately, perhaps because of the constant strain and pressure. Suddenly his phone rang and he almost jumped out of his chair. He snatched up the hideous little monster that had become an adversary, and answered gruffly, "Cannon here."

"Hello there," he heard a jolly voice say, "this is Arnold."

He glared at the receiver and wondered why he was so jolly. "What's happening?" he asked bruskly.

"I can't believe what I've seen."

Expecting the worst, he asked, "What did they do?"

Arnold sounded overjoyed but stammering a little, he replied, "Well, you know Hova submarined us on the repair."

"Yeah, yeah, I know about that," he responded impatiently.

"Well, he did it to himself again. We brought in the best technicians we had and Sara worked with 'em 'til late last night and back on it early this morning, and up until noon. Those guys never got to solderin' that stuff any good."

"Well, I told you she wasn't no damned instructor!"

"Wait! You ain't heard the good part. Joe Hendricks in repair operations gave up and called Buck Miller, who is director of manufacturing. Buck got pissed, I mean he really got pissed when he came down here to the lab. He said it couldn't be done the way Sara was trying to show 'em."

"Go on, go on." Art was intensely interested now.

"He picked up a piece of cold stainless steel here in the lab they'd been using as a practice piece and ordered Sara to put a pad on it and then solder two wires to prove that she could."

"Well, did she?"

"Did she? Man! Did She! She made those damned people look like monkeys. That thing was perfect. Buck blew up and yelled, 'You mean you damned people have kept this woman here three days trying to teach you something as simple as that?' Poor old Lem. When he told Buck that Hova ordered him not to let her go out there, Buck blew up and yelled, 'Lem, you work for me! I don't give a damn what Hova said! You jerks get this lady out to that damned launch pad and let her do what she came here to do!'"

Art burst out laughing as the tension drained. Arnold, enjoying telling the news, continued, "Well, they got her cleared to the pad and up on the work platforms and man, in less than an hour she climbed down out of the vehicle and walked out of there like nothin' you ever saw. That red plaid shirt reminded me of a big cardinal struttin' his stuff.

"Damn, I wish I could have seen that!"

"Well, it was good as new. Her QC man inspected it and then our QC man inspected it. Then the government man came away shaking his head and saying, 'How the hell did she do that? I just don't understand but I saw her do it..' Then the government QC man turned to Buck out there and said, 'Buck, hire this lady. I don't care what she costs.'"

Art cackled with glee and asked between guffaws, "What did Buck say?"

"Buck said 'I sure as hell wish I could. She'd replace at least a half dozen and maybe more.'"

"Beautiful," Art croaked. "Just beautiful. We saved a chunk of schedule and a big chunk of money."

"Yeah, and Buck ordered me to take 'em all out to dinner tonight and then to get 'em back on the plane to Hawkinsville tomorrow. He's tickled to death. They were a sure hit, especially the tool carrier. He was all eyes. Sara treated it sort of matter-of-factly, you know, like she did it every day, but I can tell she's had the time of her life."

Art was still chuckling. "Thanks Arnold, go give 'em a fittin' party tonight. They're good people and deserve the best."

"You bet I will, and thanks."

Art sat down and laughed like he'd not been able to for a long time. Suddenly Tex came into his office, saw him sitting holding his sides from laughing and asked curiously, "What's wrong with you, boy? You okay?"

Art finally got himself under enough control to relate the conversation amid guffaws of laughter and soon Tex was laughing so hard he couldn't sit still. Finally he was able to say, "Well, maybe them turkey asses'll listen next time we talk. You think?"

CHAPTER NINETEEN

Art, Tex, Eddie, and Ben, assisted by the analytical team Ben had assembled gleaned, all the data they could on the aft strut and similar design problems in other programs to establish a firm technical basis for their investigation. Eddie was busy compiling data and completing his stochastic computer model that would give him the correct answers in the dynamic regime, where the system actually worked. He needed actual data from the Wilkie Labs contract to validate his model and many pages of calculations. Late in the fall, Tex entered Art's office and said, "I almost forgot, I gave your test contract out at Wilkie Labs a go-ahead but I got some reservations for some reason."

He nodded and replied, almost prophetically, "Yeah, me too, but their engineers say they can do it to our specifications. Let's try it. Okay?"

"Okay," Tex replied, raising his eyebrows . "Sam's gonna ship two instrumented units out there tomorrow and they sure as hell better not damage that instrumentation."

"You got that right."

"I got a clause in the contract that makes 'em liable for any damage." Tex chuckled and continued, "I know they're hard up for work and they're willing to commit to anything."

"Yeah," Art replied thoughtfully, as he slid back and propped his feet up on the desk, "I only hope they can do it."

Three weeks went by so fast it seemed they never were. They had gone through the usual monthly program review with the customer and Art had come through unscathed. Others were not so lucky because of various problems and the lack of support coupled with their usual adversarial relationship with Hova and Fishburne. No mention of the aft strut force sensor testing program was made because of Fishburne and Hova's hostility.

On Tuesday of the fourth week since Wilkie Labs had been turned on contractually to perform the test program, Art called Tex. "What the hell's goin' on out there? They need to be sending us some data. Is there a problem?"

Tex snorted his usual comment when he was irritated, "I was just thinkin about them damned people. How about I call 'em and if there's a problem we'll sure as hell go out there?"

As they arrived at Wilkie Labs the snow was coming down in earnest. They were escorted into the conference room where the test engineers sat quietly around the long conference table with their contracts manager. The atmosphere was tense, a feeling of doom seemed to be coursing through each individual, or at least through Art and Tex. When the meeting convened, Tex looked at the Wilkie contracts man, fearing the worst, and asked bluntly, "Well, what'd you fuck up this time? I got a bad feelin."

The contracts man, taken aback, started to stammer. Finally he said forcefully, "Well, we had some problems. Your specifications were too hard. They were difficult."

Art had a sinking feeling and quickly replied, "Well, we all knew what the ground rules were."

The Wilkie people became more and more uncomfortable. The lead test engineer replied quietly, "We got a lot of data but we were never able to get the impulse rate you needed out of our machine because it just won't respond that fast."

Tex turned red and demanded, "Didn't you know what the machine would do before you started? If you didn't you sure as shit should have!"

Art was agitated. He looked at all the people at once and asked, "Well, what the hell *did* you do?"

The lead engineer handed Art a sheaf of data and charts and replied, "Here's what we have."

Art spread the sheets out on the table and studied the impulse data. "Well, at least you got a start. There's a hell of a discontinuity in a critical area. Did you try to re-run this part?"

The Test Conductor sitting at the end of the table who had said nothing until this point answered, "No. I ran the tests and we can't re-run it. We wrecked the machine."

Art looked at him incrediously. "You did what?"

The Test Conductor repeated quietly, "We wrecked the machine, broke it bad. We can't get any repair parts for at least six months."

Tex stood up and glared, "Shit! In other words you defaulted

340

the contract!"

The contracts man jumped to his feet to be on an even par and almost yelled, "Hell no! We got you a lot of data and we got you the other data you wanted, including the natural frequency of those things."

Tex roared, "But this was the most critical part of the data." He glared at Art and demanded, "Can you use it?"

He shook his head back and forth unknowingly, unsure, and feeling sick inside. "I don't know. I'll just have to discuss it with Eddie," he finally said.

Clearly disgusted, Tex picked up the balance of the data, handed it to Art and growled, "I'll get back with you on our contractual position. I think you got a problem."

Neither one said much on the way back to the plant as they slipped and spun along in the snow, now really getting deep and slick. Finally Tex broke the silence, "I'm afraid we'll have to pay 'em most of the money for this damned thing, anyhow. I can withhold their profit but the direct costs . . . "

Art was looking ahead intently trying to define the road as he answered quietly, "I was afraid you'd say that, but we'll just do what we have to do. If Eddie can't use the data, maybe I can talk Hova into letting us expend a little overrun and go up to the Earthquake Center. That's where we should have gone before."

Tex stared at him dejectedly and grunted, "Yeah, and on that day they'll start serving ice cold beer with meals in hell, too."

Eddie's assessment of the data wasn't good. "Damn, I was afraid of that," he complained. "I guess we got had but I might be able to extrapolate some and get something we can use. But look, there's that big void right in the middle of the curves. I need that to verify the calculations but maybe we can verify the bounds of them."

Art stood up and announced, "I'm gonna see Hova about going to the Earthquake Center with this damned thing."

Eddie stared at him with a bewildered look. "Man, you're not serious?" he asked.

"Well, don't you agree that we should go there?"

"Yeah, absolutely. But that's like sticking your head in a hungry lion's mouth."

"Well," he replied, "I got to try. Maybe I can. Maybe I can't. The worst he can do is fire me and I'm not sure that'd be all bad."

He left Eddie's office through the snow to the headquarters building and took the elevator to his office. He pulled off his coat, sat down in his chair and stared out the window for a while contemplating the wisdom of approaching Hova. "But," he said to himself finally, "If I don't ask, I sure as hell ain't gonna go. If I do ask about the worst thing that'll happen will be an ass chewin' and I'm used to that." With this resolve he took a deep breath and walked to Hova's office on the second floor adjacent to a large secretarial area with all the trappings of power. He felt the deep blue carpet under his feet and looked at the artistically done wooden, felt-filled wall panels alternated with, at least, copies of fine art. As he approached Fannie's secretarial desk, he thought to himself, It's not too late to listen to Eddie. "Hi Fannie," he greeted casually.

Fannie smiled with her best business smile, still wondering how much he really knew, and asked, "Yes, can I help you?" He could sense that she was not nearly so friendly as she had been prior to the launch of SL-1.

"Is Garlin in?"

"Yes sir, he is. Just a moment." He watched Fannie nervously fumble with the intercom before she was able to say, "Mr. Cannon is here to see you."

A deep growl emitted from the speaker, "What's he want?"

"He didn't say, sir. Just a moment." She asked in her best business voice, "What is it you want, sir?"

Art was dismayed at the problem he encountered seeing the man he was supposed to work for. "Tell him it's a test problem I need to discuss with him."

She relayed the message and after a moment that seemed like an eternity, like the lamb to slaughter, he heard the gruff response, as though he was getting his *'mean'* tuned up, "Send him in."

Art didn't like the way this was shaping up, but entered the office and saw Hova, Fishburne and two other of the old buddies from the Space Agency that he knew were close during those days. He resolved to present his case anyway.

Garlin glared at him and in his best intimidation voice demanded, "What you want down here?"

342

He started to sit down at the table where the others were seated in front of Garlin, who was sitting in his immense executive chair with the large padded arm rests and high back that extended far above his small stature. Garlin snapped, "I didn't invite you to sit down, mister. I want to know what you want first! You may not stay long!"

Art glanced clandestinely at Fishburne and noted a big grin on his face, as though he were enjoying what he saw, perhaps even hoping to see some of his blood spilled. He decided to play it low key and not infuriate Hova if he could help it. He remained standing and continued in a low, almost humble voice, "Garlin, the test data that Wilkie Labs was able to supply us was not adequate for analysis. I want your permission to take the testing up to the Earthquake Center so we can get some good data."

Garlin issued a smile that seemed to say, *Now I got you, you son-of-a-bitch,* leaned back in his chair, glared and demanded, "Is this for that damned boon doggle you been workin' on?"

Art blinked and replied, "Well, it's for the aft strut force sensor project. You know we have a new set of requirements and a new specification to comply with."

Garlin looked at Fishburne. "You know about this?"

Fishburne stammered a moment and admitted, "Yeah Chief, I just forgot to tell you. We got a change order to do some additional testing but I still think it's a waste of time and money. What he's trying to do is to show up the structures people out there and say they don't know how to design this damned booster."

Art turned to Fishburne and countered sternly, "Irvin, you know that's not true. We're trying to determine if there's a problem or not. If there's no problem, that could be the best answer we could find."

Garlin frowned and snapped, as he liked to do with an audience, "Well, mister, Ah'll tell you one thang. You're wastin' time and money. Ah told you to shut that thang down a long time ago and Ah mean for you to shut it down. Now Ah mean to tell you," his face was getting red, "you shut that damned waste project down. Ah know you and your kind. All you want to do is rock the boat. If you don't shut that thang down Ah'm gonna faare you! Understand? I'm gonna faare you!!" Garlin was standing up, shaking his finger up and down like Sonny had done so often and shouting, "Ah'm not gonna let you attack my friends like that. Ah know that thang's all right without your having to mess around in it!"

Art was desperately looking around the room for a little encouragement, but all he can see was a smirk on Fishburne's face and a big smile on the other two people's faces. He quickly reaffirmed that what Garlin liked best was an audience of cronies to perform in front of. He assessed his position and decided it wasn't good. Garlin could actually fire him if he decided to and then he knew the project would be really dead. He decided to try a little diplomacy. "Well, Garlin, I guess I work for you and if you say shut down, guess I will."

Garlin squinted at him as though he didn't believe what he heard. He growled, "Whut 'choo say?"

Art smiled and repeated, "Well, I work for you and if you say shut it down, I guess I'll shut it down."

"That's what Ah thought you said, mister, that's what Ah thought," Garlin snorted. "It's about time you listened to me!"

Fishburne joined in. "Yeah, it's about time you listened to somebody here. I'd 'a fired you before now if it hadn't been for the chief here. You better be thankful he's here to protect your ass."

Art smiled and replied quietly and evenly even though inside he was seething like a maelstrom, "Well, if you say we shouldn't go to the Earthquake Center, we won't go. I'll close down the project as quickly as possible and submit a final report to the contracts people and we'll be done with it."

Garlin jumped up again and roared, shaking his finger, "You submit any final report to me before you give anythang to anybody! You hear!"

"Yes sir. I had planned to do that, anyway," Art answered.

Garlin was still standing and thought he smelled the sweet smell of victory. "Well, Ah want to know everything you plan to give to anybody outside this company. Nothin' and Ah mean nothin' goes out of here that Ah or Mr. Fishburne don't approve. Do you hear?"

"Yes sir. Loud and clear."

He sat down, glaring at Art, as he continued, "Okay Cannon, you understand. Now you can go."

Art shut the door behind him as he heard Fishburne begin to laugh. "That'll teach that bastard a little humility, chief. I couldn't 'a done it any better."

As he left, he resolved to strategize the closeout of the

program with Ben and Eddie. He stopped by Tex's office and briefed him on the results of his session and the two of them sloshed through the ankle deep snow to Eddie's office.

They sat down around the work-table and Eddie immediately perceived doom and gloom. Art began, "We got to have a strategy session. Better get Ben if he's here."

Shortly Ben joined the group and Art outlined the discussion he had endured. Ben was outraged. He got up, stomped around the room and stopped before the window, cursing. "Those damned idiots," he stormed. "If they had a fuckin brain among 'em all they'd be dangerous. Don't they care that the investment cost of one of those damned craft and launch systems is over two billion dollars. And they're willing to play politics with lives and that kind of money just to protect their damned buddies." Ben stomped his foot and blared, "Shit, man, that's totally unacceptable."

He came back to the table where the others were seated, his face red and his thin blond hair encrusted in a band of perspiration. "We got to have a way to deal with this. That damned Hova has taken control of the company. That little son-of-a-bitch actually dictates the moves that Engle and all the others make. He's done it through intimidation, threats, blackmail, and every other underhanded, undermining scheme he can find but he sure as shit ain't gonna do it to me!"

Art replied sympathetically, "Yeah, I know. But let's see where we are and see if there's an option."

Eddie said, "Well, I'm ready to make the final model run in a few days. I've validated the thing with all the test data I can find and I think it's correct. All I need to do is put in the calculated data and the data our crew is developing from other analyses and then I think we can get a feel for the real problems in it."

Ben asked, "How long will it take you to finish extrapolating and reducing what data you got from the Wilkie tests?"

Eddie looked at the floor for a moment in deep thought. "About a week, I'd say, and then we can put some of that into the model for correlation. I should have some firm, justifiable answers from the analyses in two weeks or less, Ben.".

Art had taken the calendar from Eddie's desk and studied it intently. "Well, maybe we can start putting together a presentation about the last of November or the first of December and give it to

Hova just before Christmas."

Ben snorted and replied, "Hova, hell! I'm gonna invite all the upper management of this damned company. I'm gonna have every one of them swingin' dicks in that meeting and they're gonna take a damned position, one way or another."

Tex leaned back in his chair, from where he had been relatively quiet up until now and interjected, "Let me make a suggestion." He wrinkled his brow as he stroked his chin in deep thought, "Let's play this thing politically correct. These people ain't gonna be thinkin' of much besides getting out of here for Christmas from about the middle of December on. After they come back from Christmas and New Year's leave, they'll be rested and ready to start thinking serious about problems then. How about if you hold off on presenting this thing until the first or second week of January?"

The room was silent as Eddie spoke, "Well from an old tactician's point of view, I agree."

Ben and Art nodded agreement as Ben replied, "Yeah, I think so."

Art tapped the table lightly with his knuckles and said, "Okay, after the first of January, as soon as you can schedule it, Ben."

At the end of the two-week period when Eddie had the data complete, Art and Ben watched him enter the execute command in the big Univac computer. The monstrous beast was silent for a few moments before a stream of data started coming off one of the printers. Eddie frowned at the numbers in the neat, tabulated columns, and mumbled, "Damn, damn!"

Ben looked at the big plotter and pointed, "Let's graph that stuff so we can tell more about it."

He nodded and entered a plot command. They watched intently as the big plotter drew the curves and finally Eddie grunted, "Damn, we got more of a problem than I thought we had."

They carefully studied the plots as Eddie pointed at two bell-shaped curves and explained, "This one is the strength curve and this one is the load curve." He stood a moment and scratched his head thoughtfully before continuing. "But look at the large area of overlap. It's in this overlap area where the load exceeds the strength on this compression curve and that's where a failure could occur." Then he looked at another curve that had just finished plotting and commented, "It's probably gonna be okay in tension, but even then I think I'd be afraid of it. I don't give a damn if they did pull one to failure through the ears in their qualification test."

Art and Ben were silent as they studied the curves from the simulation. Finally Art asked quietly, "Did you compute a probability of error on this thing?"

Eddie, looking quiet and solemn, replied, "Yeah. There's a three percent probability of error, or in other words, there's a ninety seven percent probability that we're correct on all counts."

"How about probability of failure?" Ben asked.

Eddie picked up another set of data that was coming off the printer and replied, "There's a ninety-five percent probability that we're going to break one strut in the first twenty-seven flights and a near one hundred percent probability of vehicle and crew loss if that happens."

Ben was staring at the numbers with a puzzled look. He commanded, "Run the model using the Mil-Handbook-5 data numbers."

Eddie thumbed through his notebook and busily started re-entering data. Soon the computer was humming again and printing out data. He entered the plot command and soon exclaimed, "There's about a one point four safety factor using the Mil-Handbook-5 static data, about what we been working toward in the entire design. Looks like there's no problem if you believe this data."

Ben snorted, "Well, as far as I'm concerned, that validates the model."

"Yeah, that's right", Eddie replied. "We've got to stay in the Stochastic Design realm to accurately predict what this damned thing is gonna do in flight."

"Yeah," Art said. "It's sure not static. Looks like we're running on some thin margins so far."

"We got to go do it, guys. We got to make the presentation and tell 'em what we found. We owe it to our management to present it to them first and then we got to set up some meetings out at the Space Center and tell them so they can do something about it," Ben said.

Ben turned to Eddie and continued, "We need to absolutely validate the model and data and then we need to offer some recommendations. I think Art's concept of installing another strut across the 'N' to make an 'X' truss with two sides is the near term answer. That way if one broke, the vehicle would be failure tolerant and would likely survive. The way it is now, with just that damned 'N' down there, it hasn't got a chance in hell if it breaks just one strut."

Art, still stroking his chin in deep thought, replied, "I got to be absolutely sure of what we're saying in there because we're going to get some rough criticism if anybody can prove us wrong,"

Tex leaned back and said with a smirk, "There's some people out there that don't want to hear this story."

Eddie chuckled and croaked, "Yeah, I can name two right now."

The next few weeks were spent validating the model, data, concepts, and calculations. Finally the presentation was put together and was ready to be presented in as simple terms as possible, with the knowledge that some of the people like Hova were not technically knowledgeable, and would not relate to a stream of mathematics. However, as Eddie pointed out on numerous occasions, it must justify itself and present enough technical data to satisfy scrutiny. Just before the Christmas break Ben was finally satisfied with the presentation. "Well, guys, it's not long until our 'D-Day', but this thing holds together. Now let's decide who all we're going to invite to the meeting."

Eddie had prepared a list of possible attendees. "Well, we need the Director of Engineering, Chief Engineer, Fishburne, Hova, Quality Manager, Engineering Stress Manager, Materials, Structural Engineering, and I think we need to invite Chip Harrell and Arney Edwards who have worked the quality portions of the program for us."

Ben leaned back almost to the point of turning over and frowned as he asked, "Who else can you think of? That's a pretty complete list. You've got all the decision makers on it."

Art interjected, "Well, there's some of those guys from engineering who were involved in the original design specification. I don't know what their involvement was specifically in the actual hardware design but I do know they were involved in the system design."

"Okay, I'll put 'em on. Anybody else?"

Each of them sat for a few minutes contemplating the meeting before Ben broke the silence. "Well, I think that about covers it." We've got enough of the decision makers that if there's any possibility of making a decision, we can make it. The company is properly represented."

On the third of January at the end of the Christmas and New Year's break they met to discuss the presentation date. Ben said "Well, Monday is a bad day and Friday they're all wanting to get ready to leave for the weekend. Let's pick Tuesday or Wednesday of next week, late in the afternoon. There's no staff meetings then, and everybody should be available. I checked with travel and they're all in town."

Art suggested, "Let's go for Wednesday. Okay?"

Eddie smiled and replied, "I think I agree. People are usually settled in better on that day with their mind on their work, over the Monday blues and far enough from the weekend not to be a problem."

"Okay," Ben grinned. "I like your logic. I'll send each of 'em a memo today inviting 'em for a meeting at 2 p.m., January 12th, 1983."

Eddie stood with a victorious smile, feeling good about the work. "Done. I'll sure be glad to get this thing out to the Space Center."

That afternoon Ben had his departmental secretary, Alice, deliver a memo to each of the participants. When she delivered Fishburne's invitation, he let out a shriek as she retreated to the hallway. "What the hell have you done?" he shouted at her.

Alice didn't understand what he was talking about and finally regained her composure. "Sir, you better discuss that with Mr. Carr."

"Carr hell," he shouted. "Get Cannon in here!"

Alice looked at him coldly, "Sir, I'm not your departmental secretary. I would recommend that you get your secretary to do that." With that she turned abruptly and disappeared down the hall.

Fishburne glared after her, dumbfounded at her attitude and his lack of intimidation. He tried to call Art's number. The phone rang and rang and he finally slammed it down, not knowing that Art and Tex were at StressCo checking the instrumentation schedule for the next set of aft strut clevises to be shipped to the Cape. Fishburne was beside himself as he ran across the area to Hova's office and burst in yelling in an excited voice, "Look what that damned Cannon's done now. He's called a meetin' to tell the world about this damned thing."

Garlin cracked a small, slitted, all-knowing smile. "No, Fishburne. He's put one over on you. Look who signed this thing," holding up his own copy. "We forbid him from doing this and he got Carr to do it. Them damned people over there in that computer area don't know what the hell they're doin' anyway."

Fishburne sat down and exhaled a big sigh. "Well what the shit can we do to stop it? I'm afraid they'll upset the apple cart out there. If we go out criticizing those people we'll lose our hold over 'em."

He smiled wryly as he replied sternly, "Well, Irvin, Ah obviously can't be a part of that meetin'. Ah'll take the day off and go do somethin' else, so Ah won't even be here. You go in there and raise hell with everything they say. Ah mean totally disrupt that meetin. Then we can order 'em to cease and desist and shut it down."

"You really think that'll work?" Fishburne asked, becoming thoughtful and meek.

Hova glared and growled with a cold, beady-eyed stare designed for maximum effect, "Mr. Fishburne, it better work and I *mean* it better work."

Fishburne blinked, fearing the worst if he should fail, and answered quickly, "Yes sir. You can count on me."

As he started to leave Garlin said quietly, "On your way out, tell Fanny to come in here."

Momentarily Fanny appeared. "Come in and close the door, Fanny." When she was seated in a big over-stuffed wing-back chair in front of his desk she looked quizzically at him. "Mah enemies are trying to strike at the sources of good and righteousness again. They're trying some tactics that might loosen my hold over people Ah need to control. But if Ah can overcome 'em, my hold will be stronger. Do you understand?"

Fannie nodded, not at her boss this time, but at her elder and mentor. "Yes, yes I do. What can I do to help?"

Garlin grinned, "Well, Wednesday of next week you'll take the day off and meet me over at the lake cabin. Ah feel the need to continue your purification. The need's gettin mighty strong now. Understand?"

Fanny blushed a little and replied, "I'll be there. I want to get all that divorce behind me and learn the right ways. I like what you're teachin' me, I mean the techniques and all."

He grinned as he said, "Yeah, so do I Fanny. We'll continue your education 'til you're completely cleansed and ready to face the world again."

She looked quizzically at him and asked, "When do you think that's going to be?"

"You got a long way to go. I'll let you know when it's time."

Fanny stood up, displaying a shapely leg as her dress fell apart at the open seam down the front. "Do you like this dress?" she asked shyly.

"Yeah, Fanny, Ah been lookin at it all mornin and the more I look at it the better I like it. Now you be there instead of comin' in to work. Ah won't say no more about it."

She turned around shyly and replied, "Don't worry, I'll be there."

At the appointed time in the main conference room all the invitees gathered around the large conference table. Those who could not find room at the long main table found seats along the wall in side chairs. Art was seated along the wall with Eddie while Ben seated himself at the table next to Chief Engineer Ingram, who was sitting next to the two end seats for Hova and Fishburne at the end of the table. At the appointed time Art stood up and announced, "Gentlemen, Mr. Hova and Mr. Fishburne haven't arrived yet. Let's give them just a few more minutes."

He sat back down as Eddie whispered, "I'll bet they don't show."

After a tense ten minutes of waiting Art got up to offer the introductory remarks and explain the purpose of the meeting. As he approached the podium Fishburne burst into the room and went directly to the second seat at the end of the table and announced loudly and antagonistically, "Okay, Cannon, let's get this damned thing over. Mr. Hova decided not to come. He doesn't have time for trash like this."

Without responding to Fishburne, Art walked around the room and handed each person a copy of all the slides in the presentation. He felt apprehensive about Fishburne and about Hova's snub of the meeting. He purposely handed Fishburne the last handout, anticipating the worst, and then walked to the front of the room where he put up his first slide.

"Gentlemen, this is a presentation of the analytical work that we have done on the aft strut clevis end. This project has gone on at a low level for the last four years, due primarily to a lack of funding and support. We believe we have uncovered a problem and want to present our data and our work to you prior to advising the engineering people at the Space Center."

Fishburne was flipping through the presentation rapidly, creating as much noise with the paper as possible, and yelled, "This is a bunch of shit. How in hell can you call people together to listen to this?"

Art replied quietly and evenly, with all eyes focused on Fishburne trying desperately to set the tone for the meeting, "Mr. Fishburne, if you'll just follow the presentation and listen to the explanations I think you'll understand as we go."

"Understand hell! I understand already! This is a bunch of shit!"

Ben reached around Wayne Ingram and laid his hand on Fishburne's shoulder, "Hang on, Irvin. Just be patient a few minutes."

Fishburne flashed a vitriolic glared at Ben. Hova's hatred was clearly reflected in Fishburne's eyes and Ben sensed that this meeting was going to be interesting to say the least. Art flipped to the next view graph and started to outline the design of the Solid Rocket Booster structure, the attach points and the instrumentation that went into making up the force sensor system. "As I'm sure you all know, the SRB is attached to the external tank in the rear through an N-truss formed by the three struts attached between the external tank attach ring and the SRB aft attach ring. The geometry of that truss forms a fixed, or rigid, mounting there for the aft end of the SRB to the ET . . ."

Fishburne interrupted loudly, "Don't waste my time with that shit. We know all that. Get on with it."

Art looked at him and replied, "Well, Irvin, we weren't sure just how much everybody knew about this particular system so we wanted everybody to be aware of what we were discussing."

Ben was looking perturbed now but didn't say anything. Eddie was watching Ben's face turn red and his brow begin to sweat from anger and wondered just how long it was going to be before he came down on Fishburne.

Art moved to the third slide in the presentation and started to explain the way that the strain gage force sensors were installed and how they were tested. Fishburne had thumbed beyond where Art was and saw a line that said the probability of losing one vehicle in the first twenty-seven flights was ninety-five percent. Fishburne, again interrupted Art, "Are you trying to tell me we're going to start crashin these damned things?"

Art glared at him, seething inside, and replied sternly, "Irvin, you're ahead of me. Let me address that when I get to it."

Irvin felt he was penetrating Art's concentration and continued, "Look here, you even put this shit on paper with the company logo on it. You can't do that!"

Ben turned to Fishburne and ordered sharply, "Fishburne, shut up. He did do it! Now be quiet!"

Fishburne stood up and glared at Ben, sat down and sarcastically yelled, "Don't you tell me to shut up! I'll have your ass fired."

Ben had realized Fishburne's game was uproar. He looked at him and answered, "Fishburne, just listen. That's all we ask. You'll get a chance to comment later."

Fishburne glared at Ben as he growled, "Well, don't you tell me to shut up, mister. I'll talk all I want to whenever I want to. I'm the deputy SRB Program Manager and don't you forget that! You hear?"

Ben, realizing there was no further point in any more discussion, sat back down and looked around the room at the shocked faces. "Continue," he said.

The next two slides Art put up over the constant din of interruptions and sarcasm pouring from Irvin Fishburne, still with the company logo on them, defined and introduced the problems that they had found with the aft strut clevis and its role as a force sensor in the instrumentation system. These included: (a) design deficiencies in the aft strut clevis structure; (b) the lack of any qualification testing in the compressive mode; (c) the probability of failure and loss of one vehicle in the first twenty-seven flights; (d) the inability of the data system to accurately take and record data; (e) the problems introduced in the calibrations, response times, and accuracy of any data collected due to the strange and abnormal hysteresis curve displayed by the clevis units in the compressive mode; and (f) other problems as they related to the static and dynamic characteristics of the vehicle.

Trying to drown out Fishburn's noise with his own volume, he pointed out the fallacy of design using the static Mil-Handbook-5 specification. He contrasted this data with using a Stochastic, or Dynamic rationale which set Fishburne off even more vehemently than before. Art offered a set of recommendations which included addition of a fourth strut to make the structure failure-tolerant and recommended an indepth investigation of the design by a qualified, PhD level team supplemented by personnel from Space Corp and the Space Agency.

Fishburne couldn't stand any more and jumped up again. "That's the most ridiculous thing I ever heard!" he screamed. "How can you, as a supposed professional engineer and hopefully somewhat intelligent person put out this garbage?" .

Art bent down, looked straight at him and snapped, "Fishburne, if you'll listen, we'll tell you how we could do it and we'll give you supporting data to show you how."

Ben, looking around Wayne Ingram, who was frowning at Art, yelled, "Fishburne, *be quiet!*"

Ingram glared at Art now and asked curtly, "Do you mean to say there's a possibility of losing a vehicle?"

Art, now ignoring the noise from Fishburne, replied loudly to get over the uproar, "Yes, that's what I'm saying, but it's not all bleak. We haven't lost one yet and there's a way out."

Ingram looked sternly at Art and demanded, far from the good natured attitude he had always shown previously, "There had better be, mister. You better have some good data to support yourself."

Art turned back to his slide with Fishburne still raving about the presentation being on the company logo paper and continued, "I'm going to let Eddie Rogers present the technical part of the material." He handed his pointer to Eddie and sat down at the corner of the table so he could change slides as he needed them.

Eddie cast a jaundiced eye at the crowd all arguing among themselves, Ingram scowling at Art and now at him, and Fishburne trying his best to create any and every diversion he could. He wondered if he really wanted to expose his body to that kind of abuse. However, being the fighter he was, he approached the podium and nodded to Art for the first slide.

Eddie, pointing at the screen, began by discussing how he developed the model and showed a myriad of stress/strain curves and, amid the constant confusion created by Fishburne, fielded questions by the stress engineers present. Finally, the manager of Stress Analysis confessed, "We've never seen this type of methodology before in design."

Eddie smiled as he replied, "Well, I'll be glad to work with you and teach you what I know, but it's all embedded in higher mathematics."

Fishburne was increasing his diversion now, fearing that Eddie was going to make some progress in defining the problem. He knew Garlin would be very unhappy if that happened and Eddie got a consensus to present the data to the Space Agency, as Art had said he intended to do. After over an hour of lecturing by Eddie, and ducking hostile outburst after outburst by Fishburne and cutting remarks by Ingram, who had not sided with Fishburne but just simply didn't seem to understand the problem, Eddie started to show how he developed equations from his research for some of the curves that he had presented on previous slides. He had talked almost completely in a din of distractions, yelling and arguments the entire time and was wondering if he would survive.

Fishburne, in desperation and with a total lack of understanding, yelled, "That's bullshit! There's no validity to any of that!"

Ben had all he could take and jumped up on the other side of Ingram, who was ducking as low to the table as he could get to avoid being hit if fists should start to fly. Ben yelled across Ingram's head, "Fishburne, shut your damned mouth or leave the room."

Fishburne was both desperate and furious. He yelled back at Ben, still over the top of Wayne Ingram, who was still crouching low in his chair, "Don't you tell me to shut up, you son-of-a-bitch. I'll have you know I'm responsible for this in Mr. Hova's absence and I say it's a sack of shit! There's nothing to it! I'm terminatin' this meetin' now! If there's anybody that disagrees, I'll fire your ass and if you think Mr. Hova won't back me up, just try. You know as well as I do who runs this damned company!"

Ben swung over Ingram's head at Fishburne, who retreated quickly to the front of the room behind Eddie, yelling, "Don't you touch me! Don't you dare touch me! This damned circus is over *now!* All of you get out'a here *now!*"

Wayne Ingram, taking his cue from Fishburne, stood up, glared at Eddie and boomed, "I'm a good mind to fire you both right now for even daring to question the design of this vehicle. How in the hell do you expect me to go out there and tell them there's a problem?"

Art was mad. He yelled over the uproar in the room, "Wayne, if there's a problem, I damned well expect you to go out there and tell 'em."

Fishburne, thinking he had support from Wayne Ingram now, approached Art in a loud, abusive manner. "You've sat here for two fuckin' hours going through a bunch of gibberish that don't make any sense at all and you expect me to go out there and tell those people there's a problem in that vehicle."

Wayne joined Fishburne in chastising them. "How dare you even question Mil-Handbook-5. Did you know that most of that vehicle was designed using that requirement? You can't question that!"

Fishburne was going around the room picking up all the handouts and yelling at the participants, who were cowed, "Give me that damned shit. I don't want even one copy out of this room."

Sam Hardiman, who was Director of Engineering, rose quickly from his chair with a disgusted look on his face and stalked out of the room. He looked at Ben, who was standing nearby with a scowl that could melt an alligator, and growled, "What a bunch of shit. Don't make any sense at all."

Fishburne charged the corner of the table where Art was picking up the slides and the surplus handouts and yelled, "Give me that shit. I'm gonna fire you right now for this."

Art looked him straight in the eye and said coldly, "Damn you, Fishburne. Go ahead if you think you can get away with it."

Fishburne retreated after grabbing the materials and yelled in his high-pitched voice, "I'm sure Mr. Hova'll talk to you when he gets back tomorrow. He'll fire you, I know."

Eddie was thunderstruck and sitting on one corner of the table as Fishburne made his rounds demanding all the material from each participant. Art was standing at the front of the room watching the people leave after Fishburne had so successfully wrecked the meeting. Then Fishburne came over to Art and demanded, "I want the originals of this shit from you, too. You ain't gonna keep nothin'. I don't want none of this bull crap around here for any reason. I'm gonna fire you, too, Rogers, if you don't give me all the rest of this shit."

Eddie was mad and shaken with disbelief. He mustered up all the calm he had and replied, "You got all I have here."

Fishburne said, "Cannon, I'm gonna' clean out your files."

"Like hell you will!" Art started to walk menacingly toward Fishburne, who beat a hasty retreat yelling, "I'll get security up here, then. I'll call 'em now."

Eddie approached Art and said calmly, "Give it to him. It's not worth getting yourself in jail over."

Fishburne screamed with glee at hearing Eddie's advice. "That's the best thing you can do, Cannon. Give it to me, or I'll put your ass in jail and then I'll fire you."

Art settled down, knowing that Eddie wouldn't cave in this way if there weren't a good reason. He walked down to his office while listening to the banter from Fishburne at how stupid they were to try to cross Mr. Hova, how no one does that and gets away with it and how Mr. Hova gave heart attacks to people that he didn't like. Art largely ignored the noise and handed Fishburne his originals and the copies that he had on his desk. Fishburne demanded, "Is this all?"

"Yeah, Fishburne. That's all. Now get your little ass out'a here."

"Well, it better be. If I find any more of it around here, I'll sure as hell fire you. Now this damned project is shut down now," he screamed. "Do you understand me Cannon, *SHUT DOWN NOW!!!*"

Art replied sternly, "I heard you!"

"But are you gonna comply?" he yelled.

Art stared at him and replied quietly, to his surprise. "Fishburne, you made your move. You better pray that nothing ever happens to one of those vehicles. If it does, I'll assure you that I'll tell this damned story. I'll tell the world about it, and most especially, I'll tell the investigating committee that I know will be appointed."

Fishburne shrank back and, in a shrill voice yelled, "Are you threatening me, Cannon? Are you threatening me?"

Art glared at him as he started to the door. "No, Fishburne, that's a damned promise. If anything ever happens to one of those ships, you better bet your ass you and Hova will be held accountable!"

CHAPTER TWENTY

As the sun started to set on the cold, short, January afternoon after the meeting where the team had tried to present the results of almost five years of research and investigation, they gathered in Ben's office to lick their wounds and discuss the outcome. They were sick at heart and disappointed at the way the meeting had gone and the lack of progress at identifying the problem to the Space Agency, a problem they considered critical and potentially life-threatening, not only to the program but to the astronauts flying the vehicles.

They were very concerned about the implications for their career with the company, a career each of them had hoped would be a terminal career for them until retirement. They knew full well as long as Hova had a position of authority, each lived in great jeopardy. Eddie, seated at the side of his work table with Art at one end and Ben standing gazing out the window watching the early evening shadows begin to fall, said, "I ain't never been through such a damned brawl. I didn't know such things still happened to civilized people."

Art laughed sarcastically and replied slowly, "Well, old buddy, you know it now. You've seen upper management at its worst."

Ben interjected, "Well, it's obvious that Fishburne's mission was to disrupt the meeting, for whatever reason they had planned."

Eddie frowned, propped his feet up on the table and began to think like the tactician he was. He said, "Well, it's a hell of a way to start a new year out but from a tactical point of view, if I had something to hide or was trying to protect somebody somewhere, I think that would be my approach. He obviously doesn't want anything to feed back to the Space Agency."

Art was gazing at Eddie with a puzzled look. "But, Eddie, why wouldn't he want to tell anybody out there if there's even the slightest indication of a problem?"

Ben had been quietly contemplating the scene. Suddenly he leaned forward and spoke with determination. "Well, we've got a hell of a lot more than an indication, we've got a good analytical base to believe there is a problem."

"I'll tell you one reason," Eddie volunteered.

"What's that?" Ben asked.

"Because Hova decreed there's nothing wrong and you know if he decrees something there's no power on Earth gonna make him change it, no matter what. He'll let the entire program go down the tube before he'll admit he's wrong about anything."

Ben grunted disapprovingly, "I can't imagine a person that hard-headed. There's got to be another reason. He's protecting somebody."

Art approached Ben's coffee pot in the corner. "Anybody join me?" Both Eddie and Ben declined and Art poured himself a cup of thick, stale black coffee, but at this juncture he didn't pay much attention to that. He sat down at the table and took a long sip and began, "Well, Eddie, I bet you never had so many threats of being fired in one day and you're still here."

"You guys don't have to worry about that. They'll never fire you now," Ben replied cautiously.

"Why do you say that?" Eddie grunted in disbelief.

"Simple," Ben replied sarcastically, "We hit a hell of a nerve somehow and I think they're afraid of you. I think they'd be afraid of what you might do with that data. You've got too much knowledge."

Art grumbled, "Yeah, but Fishburne took everything we had. We don't have that data any more."

Eddie chuckled sadistically as he replied, "Don't you believe it, buddy, don't you believe it. Fishburne didn't get it all. He just thought he did."

"Then where is it?"

Ben pointed toward the computer center, "Well, I got a hell of a lot of it in the memory of that thing out there and if I know Eddie, he's got copies of everything stashed somewhere."

"How'd you know that, chief?" Eddie asked.

Ben laughed heartily. "Because I know you and I know you're a pack rat."

Art was quiet, thinking over the events and weighing their futures with Space Corp. "Well, I still think we've destroyed our future with this company, so long as Hova is here and I don't see him moving anywhere."

"Hell, maybe somebody'll offer him a job somewhere," Eddie grunted.

"Not likely," Art retorted. "Politically, the company thinks it needs him because of the way he's able to deal with old friends and enemies either through the buddy system or fear."

Eddie was pondering this train of thought. Before he could make any comment Ben answered, "Well, strategically we put the company on notice. We've done all we can except to do without being whistle blowers."

Art looked at Eddie and Ben and asked, "Should we do that? What do you guys think?"

Ben shrugged his shoulders. "You know as well as I do that whistle blowers always die and seldom get much accomplished. I think the prudent thing now is to just be quiet for a while and hope one don't break."

Art shifted as he replied, "Or the calculated probabilities don't come true."

"I agree we've compromised our futures but what's important is we had to get the message out to the responsible people. We did that and now they have assumed that responsibility. I don't know what we should do next," Ben said.

Eddie answered slowly, "Well, we could go to the Space Agency ourselves, but I don't think that would be smart. Whistle blowers always end up getting sacrificed in the fall-out and very little else comes out of it."

Art smiled wryly. "Yeah, I agree, Eddie. The system has to work and if we can find a way, we have to see that it does."

"If there's any weakness in our argument so far it's because there hasn't been a strut broken yet. That's their only strong point," Eddie added.

Ben came to life and said, while pointing his finger at Eddie to emphasize the point, "Yep, that's true, but the conditions haven't been right yet for that to happen. If the loads should exceed the capability of one of those things in compression, I'm satisfied it's gonna shatter and then, boom!"

"Hova and Fishburne would make the most out of it if we blew the whistle," Art interjected.

"Yeah, I don't think we'd get much of an audience now. And we don't have a vehicle failure yet to say we told you so," Ben answered slowly.

Suddenly the door opened to Ben's office and Alf Bennett slowly entered the room. "I thought I might find you guys holed up somewhere. How you feeling?"

"Come in, Alf. We're just going over the meeting," Art replied, glad to see his friend.

Alf smiled as he took a chair at the side of the table next to Ben and volunteered, "I never seen such a damned thing as that. That was a cat fight to top all cat fights. Fishburne was determined to wreck it and Wayne Ingram was looking for an excuse, too."

With a puzzled look, Ben replied, "Do you really think so, Alf? He was hostile but I thought it was only because he didn't understand . . ."

Art interrupted, "Maybe he was embarrassed because he didn't see the problem or didn't have enough understanding of structural design to see it. I can't imagine why, though."

Alf grinned as he replied, "Well, there's a lot of pieces of the puzzle. I can give you one that you obviously didn't have before the meeting that I accidentally got a while back."

All eyes were riveted on Alf. Ben said quietly, "Go on Alf."

Alf smiled, squirmed down in the chair a little further, blinked and began, "Well, when you attacked the design of the clevises you unwittingly attacked Sam Hardiman."

Art leaned forward with a shocked stare. "Alf, that's not true. Sam hasn't been a very effective Director of Engineering, but we didn't attack him. He had nothing to do with that design, as far as I know."

Alf grinned and continued quietly, "Therein lies the fallacy. You've got to know the beginning of this project to understand. Do you know Sam's origins?"

"No. All I know is he came here just a couple of months before I did from Rutherford Engineering where he was some sort of group supervisor, but outside of that I don't know much."

Alf continued, "At Rutherford he was a group leader of a small design group of three or four engineers, a young man on his way up. One of their tasks was to design this aft strut clevis."

Ben looked at him incrediously. "You got to be kidding, Alf. You can't be serious."

There was a long moment's silence before Alf replied, "Well, Sam and Wayne are very close at work and socially. They're almost a symbiotic pair. If you attack one you attack the other. That explains Ingram's hostility. He thought you were attacking Sam."

Eddie, sitting straight up and staring with disbelief at Alf, couldn't restrain any longer and interrupted, "But that's not true! We didn't attack him even if Wayne thought we did. I'm sure that he and his group did the design to the specification. It's the specification that's wrong, not the design."

Art propped up further on the table to be sure he didn't miss a syllable. He stared out the window as he commented, "I agree with Eddie. However, Wayne perceived you were attacking Sam and that's why he came on strong. That only reinforced Fishburne."

Alf continued, "Well, I think that explains Wayne's actions in the meeting, but do you think he'd really allow a problem in the vehicle without telling anybody about it?"

Ben shook his head, "I just don't know. It might happen but my impression of him is no. But I just don't know."

Eddie shifted position as he interjected, "I think in spite of Fishburne we've relayed the message loud and clear to all our decision makers. Let's see what he does."

Art nodded in agreement. Eddie suddenly took on a very concerned look and asked, "Won't Hova have to at least give the Space Agency a copy of the data whether or not they agree with it?"

Alf scowled at Eddie. "You don't know, I'm sure, of the hold that they've got on this company. He isn't called Little Hitler for nothing, and then there's the Court Jester, Fishburne. Damn! What a pair. . ."

Ben nodded agreement, "Alf's right. He'll suppress it and I'm of the opinion we can't go out there unofficially and survive. The Space Agency people would have to come back here if we did and I think Hova has enough of a hold on those people that he could still suppress it."

Eddie looked dejected and advised, "Art, I'd recommend you take all your old laboratory notebooks out and lock 'em up in a vault somewhere. That's all the records you have of what you did, other than your contract files."

Art answered in surprise, "You don't think Fishburne would try to take those, do you?"

Ben interrupted, "I wouldn't be surprised at anything those two did. When Hova gets back here tomorrow there's no telling what they'll try to do. I think Eddie's right."

"Okay, I'll put 'em in protective custody. It's after six and I'm gonna' go home and forget about it. We did the best we could."

"Yeah," Eddie replied. "At least this company's officially on notice. What they choose to do about it from now I suppose is their business."

The next morning as Art walked to his old Buick to drive to work he wondered if Hova would try to fire him or whether he would just ignore him for a while and try to get at him in some other way. When he arrived at his office and poured himself his usual first cup of coffee, Ray suddenly appeared and sat down. He looked at Art for a moment without speaking and then asked, "You okay, Brother?"

Art chuckled at the concern. "Yeah, I'm okay. We got battered a little yesterday, but I'll survive."

"Battered, hell," Ray exclaimed. "I heard part of that damned abortion and saw Fishburne out at the shredder after the meeting. What's gonna happen next?"

"Well," Art started slowly, "we did our work and we presented our case the best we could. We notified the proper company officials of the problem and possible consequences. I suppose those who make corporate decisions have got the ball. They were all there except for Hova and Harry Engle."

"What if they should really try to fire you?"

"Ben thinks they're too afraid of us to try that without some other really hard issues. I believe as long as we do our work they can't bother us."

Ray pondered this for a moment. "Yeah, I agree. It'd be better to keep you where they can watch you for a while instead of having you out like a loose cannon ball."

That afternoon as Art was walking slowly down the hall, still pondering the events of the previous day, Hova rounded the corner and stopped short. He went into his automatic scowl and glared for a moment with his little beady eyes flashing. Art looked at him and said, "Good afternoon, Garlin." He was expecting the worst.

Garlin snarled at him, "Don't you good afternoon me, Cannon! Ah heard about your fiasco yesterday. If you ever do anything like that again Ah'll faare you on the spot. Instantly, and Ah mean instantly!"

Art looked straight into the beady eyes and replied sternly, "Well, in the first place, it wasn't a fiasco. We presented valid technical data to this company about a problem that's really there. I think you better know that."

Hova turned red at what he considered Art's defiance of his authority, and shouted, "Are you being insubordinate to me? Are you?"

"No sir, I'm not. I'm just telling you what we did yesterday," Art countered quietly, shifting his position and looking straight at Hova.

Hova shouted, "Ah know what you did yesterday. If it hadn't been for Mr. Fishburne you'd have this company in real trouble. He saved the day for us all. Do you hear?" Hova was beginning to talk excitedly and to wave his arms.

Art felt he had him on the defensive and if he were going to be fired he would have already done so. He thought that Ben must have been right, and decided to press the point further. "Well, Garlin," he continued, "the data we presented was correct. I wish you'd just listen. I'd like to go through the whole thing with you."

Hova was beginning to breathe harder as his anger mounted. He shouted, "Ah don't need to go through it. Ah know there's no problem in that thang and Mr. Fishburne heard you and your bunch of incompetents yesterday. That project is shut down and Ah mean right now. Don't you spend another dime on it and Ah mean not another dime. If you do you'll be guilty of d'rectly disobeyin' a d'rect order. Do you hear me? Ah mean *none!*"

Art looked at him with a quiet, unintimidated look that infuriated him even more. "Yes sir. I hear you. I'll have a final report written for you and we'll shut the project down."

Hova turned to stalk off down the hall and snorted, "Well, that final report better not have any negatives in it, mister. It better be totally non-controversial. Ah'll tell you that right now."

Art turned down the hall, entered his office and dialed Eddie before he sat down. "Eddie, Art. I just met Hova in the hall and we had a hell of a session."

Art heard Eddie gulp and go silent for a moment and then ask cautiously, "What'd he have to say?"

Art related the conversation and heard Eddie laughing before he finally replied, "Shit man, Ben and Alf were right, they can't afford to have you out running around loose. They'll have a harder time getting to me but buddy, you're in the lion's den."

"I'm giving you official direction to write me a final closeout report. I've been ordered by Hova to make it totally non-controversial, so I'm passing my orders on to you to make it non-controversial. Okay?"

Eddie chuckled on the phone and jousted, "Well, we're not gonna rock the boat, are we?"

Art laughed as he replied, "Be serious. I think we better not press our luck for a while. Let's play the game and sit tight and pray that nothing happens to one of those flights."

"I agree," Eddie replied seriously, "I'll get you a report out. What do you want it to say?"

Art pondered this point for a moment. "Well, do you think if you wrote the report around the Mil-Handbook-5 data you could write a non-controversial report?"

"Yeah, I could do that and they're not smart enough to know the difference. He'd accept that and we wouldn't have to compromise our stochastic work."

"That's what I was thinkin', too," Art concluded, half thinking and half listening to Eddie's last comments replay themselves. Finally he continued, "Yeah, I think that's the way to go. Let's do it. Be sure we don't compromise any of our original work, though."

"You got it, chief. When do you want it?"

"Well, I'm in no hurry. Just when it's convenient."

As the months went by, Art concentrated on his other duties as best he could in providing instrumentation and electronics for the Shuttle flights, which were usually launching on or close to schedule. He and his counterparts were having trouble keeping an adequate supply of hardware at the Launch Site to support the build-up of the boosters because of tight Congressional budgets. There never seemed to be enough funding to do the job right the first time.

After months of highpressure work, fighting seemingly impossible odds to sustain the flight schedules with inadequate hardware quantities, and continual haranguing by Hova and Fishburne to keep up, the pressure was adversely affecting people. They were driving the entire program management staff harder and harder. Art was having to provide a significant part of his own engineering work because of the lack of competent engineers in *F-Troop* and it was beginning to take it's toll. He and Tex had travelled the bounds of the country, coast to coast now since Hova had released his travel ban and he was pushing his subcontractors to the limit.

Finally, Art was desperate for enough rate gyros and Integrated Electronic Assemblies to support the flight schedule. They were still required to run the Mission Models, as they were now called, to make the hardware allocations to the various missions by hand because of Hova's even deeper hatred for Ben and his refusal to allow any computers whatsoever into the Program Office. Art had set up and was running a mission model on his own computer at home and thereby relieved himself of the long, laborious hours of doing it by hand.

Each time there was a mission model exercise, Fishburne came to Art's office and sneered, "Well, when are you gonna give me the new allocation schedules?" He was suspicious, and correctly so, that Art was running the model on a computer somewhere but he didn't know where.

Art always glared at him with contempt and asked, "When are you gonna let us use the computer center for this damned thing?"

Fishburne would turn and leave without saying anything further beyond some occasional snide remark but was still trying to figure out how Art performed the task. His schedules were always up to date and hand written in pencil. Fishburne so far had not seen him making the transfer from the computer run that he generated the night before onto the forms that were required for the "Fishburne model".

Annie had finished her course work and had elected to come home to write her dissertation because she was beginning to worry about Art. She saw the stress beginning to show and didn't like it. Frequently, she said, "Baby, slow down. It's getting to you. You don't need this pressure."

His standard reply was, "Don't worry about me, hon, I'm okay." This kept up until one day she was visiting with one of the other System Managers' wives and they began trading notes. Lorrie said, "I'm not sure about what to do with Ed. His blood pressure is going up and he's getting to where he won't sleep. Did you know that he shares the same secretary as Art does and she's got *five* of those guys to work for?"

Annie shook her head and replied, "Well, I can't get Art to go to the doctor to check his. I don't know what I'm going to do."

The day following this conversation, as Art was walking down the hall to the secretarial pool he heard loud voices coming from Manuel Garcia's office. Manuel, a small, trim man in his mid fifties, well-grayed hair and distinguished looking from his Latin heritage, was in charge of the insulation and thermal curtains that went around the base of the booster that protected it from heat from the nozzle flame. He heard Hova saying loudly, in his best intimidation style, "Ah don't want no excuses! Ah want that hardware at the VAB tomorrow or Ah'm gonna faaare you. Ah don't believe you can't get them people to work tonight and get it out."

He heard Manuel reply desperately, "But Garlin, it's not a matter of them workin' tonight. It's a matter of parts they don't have."

Hova yelled at him in his usual intimidation style, "Ah don't accept that. If they don't have parts, Ah expect you to get 'em and get 'em now. You hear what Ah said? *Now!*"

Art stopped to listen to this exchange, which had become frequent for himself and the other managers. Everyone received a generous share but there were a few individuals who seemed to be under constant attack, who appeared to have been singled out to be the whipping boys. Then, there was the little court jester, Fishburne, who always came in to do the mopping up after Hova had chewed the poor individual out unmercifully about some problem, either real or imaginary. He watched the small frame of Hova, the perfect embodiment of the Napoleonic complex, walk out of Manuel's office, neatly dressed, wearing the dress coat that was part of the constant uniform he always wore.

Art walked into Manuel's office and saw him sitting at his desk dejected, and worried. "Hey buddy, don't let it get to you."

He smiled weakly. "I try not to, but he's totally unreasonable. I tried to get funding six months ago to get these parts so we could supply the flights without this sort of thing and you know what he told me?"

Art sat down and asked, "What'd he say?"

"He said I had all the parts I needed. He said that Mr. Fishburne had planned the flight hardware and I had all I needed through Flight 51. I tried to tell him this was gonna happen and it did. He won't listen and he's threatening to fire me over it." He was turning pale and beginning to sweat.

"Hey friend, you feel okay?" Art asked quickly.

"No, I don't. I sure don't. I think I'm about to be sick."

Art touched his forehead and he felt cold and sweaty. He knew that something bad was wrong. He directed, "Just sit quiet a minute." He quickly stepped around the corner to an adjacent office and called the nurse's station, "Jane, Art. You better get up here quick, you may have a coronary on the way."

Shortly the nurse ran into the office and saw Art holding an unconscious Manuel's head. She quickly injected a syringe of stimulant into his veins and yelled at the nearest secretary, who was among the small crowd gathered outside the door, to meet the ambulance and show them the way in.

"Let's lay him down and get his shirt open." No sooner had they done that, he began breathing hard. The nurse worked feverishly over him. Suddenly he stopped breathing and she immediately installed the emergency breathing equipment she had brought and started to pump his heart. Shortly he started to breathe again and a little color returned to his face. "Damn," she said under her breath. "Hang in there Manuel, hang in there."

Soon the ambulance crew ran into the office, bundled him up on a stretcher and whisked him out for a quick trip to the hospital emergency room. Then Art walked slowly to his office, reflecting on all the things Annie had been saying and resolved to listen better. After all, he thought, that could have been me.

In a few minutes Ray came in and sat down. He looked solemnly at Art and announced quietly, "I just found out they didn't make it. He died enroute."

Art turned and looked out the window, silent for a time. Ray sat starting off into space. Finally, Art said brokenly, full of emotion, fighting back tears, "That little guy was my friend, Ray. He was a good friend. He came out of the jungles of Central America and got himself an engineering education and did a hell of a good job. He made some real contributions to this program. Now he'll be forgotten and never receive any credit for what he did."

Ray was equally solemn as he answered, "No. We'll always remember him. Those that knew him, any way, and those that appreciated him for what he was and for what he did. We'll remember him on each launch."

He turned and looked through tears at Ray, "Well, maybe that's all we can expect anyhow."

Ray was thinking about the last few months of stress and strain and about the last few minutes of Manuel's life and stood up. As he started out the door he said quietly, "Well, all I can say is Hova and Fishburne got another one but I'll but be damned if they're gonna get me. I'm gonna find me a decent job somewhere."

Art looked at his friend and replied, "Well, we can't say that directly, I suppose, but I think you're right. Remember when he sat in that meeting up there and stormed at us that he didn't have heart attacks, he gave 'em?"

"Yeah. That's what I was thinking about. Maybe we just saw one."

"Maybe."

Two months after Manuel's funeral and his replacement by a retired Space Agency buddy of Hova's, Eddie rushed into Art's office breathless and blurted, "Art, Ben just quit. I had no idea."

He looked up with a jerk. "What'd you say?"

"I said Ben just quit. He just told me he's accepted a job in Washington state."

Art was staring at him with disbelief. He leaned back and asked quickly, "Why'd he quit?"

Eddie was visibly shaken and nervous. "He told me he had learned that our names were truly on the shit list in the company, that Hova had filed bad performance reports with the corporate office on him and probably on us, and that our chances of any further advancement with this company are none to zero."

"Well, we thought something like that might happen, didn't we?" Art grunted.

"Yeah, but now that we know it's happened, I'm pissed."

"All we know for sure is about Ben. How'd he find out?"

"He's got a friend at corporate headquarters somewhere and she told him she'd seen his record and wanted to know what was wrong. He told her and scared her to death. Looks to me like people in the corporate office are afraid of him, too. They all seem to think this contract hinges on him."

"That's not true! In fact, I think he's a detriment not only to the contract, but to the entire program."

"I know," Eddie replied. "But the people there don't know that."

"Yeah, I hear you. This's just another example of how the little bastard will get you one way or the other. If he can't do it head on in public, he'll get you in the back."

Eddie was beginning to settle down a bit. "You're exactly right. He's a vindictive little shit and he'll get his revenge any way he can."

Art propped his feet up on the desk before he continued. "Well, I don't blame Ben. He's the guy that really should be running this program, you know?"

"I agree. By the way, you got any hot coffee up here?"

"Yeah, come on."

When they returned to the privacy of Art's office, Eddie smiled for the first time since he had come in. "Maybe we should do the same thing."

"Well, I don't know. You got to make your own decision. We've been here for a long time and I'd like to see this program through."

Eddie nodded slowly. "I know how you feel. I feel that, too."

He continued, "This vehicle is so damned important to the well being of our country. There's so much riding on the success of this program. I keep thinking back about the old days with von Braun and the group he brought from Peenemunde. Somehow I just feel I'll be letting him and the rest of those people down if I don't stick it out."

"Well, I sure wish we had him here now. I know this thing would be a hell of a lot further and a hell of a lot better."

The breeze blew in the window that Art had opened and flapped the curtains back and forth. They both sat watching the curtains and listening to the pigeons come and go from the lofty perches on the window sill. Finally Eddie asked, "Suppose they have any problems?" pointing to the pigeons.

Art pointed at one large one and replied, "That's an old one that keeps coming around here. I bet it's seen some hard winters. I think they have their problems just like we have ours."

Eddie replied, "I hope they don't have any structural problems like we do." He studied the old pigeon and finally it flew off. "Well, they have an escape. They can fly off. What was it you used to say,

'Fly with the eagles or scratch with the chickens?' Well, I'm beginning to feel more like a damned chicken every day."

Art gazed at him. "Yeah, I understand, but there's no escape for us, buddy. We got to live with ourselves."

Suddenly Art's phone rang. He recognized the voice as that of his program manager on the IEA contract from Connecticut. "Art, we have fault isolated the unit that failed checkout on the vehicle day before yesterday, after we got it back up here. We have a problem in the voltage regulator circuit of the MDM power supply. It's lost regulation and over-voltaged the mux board and burned out a bunch of integrated circuits. We'll have to change the MDM out."

Art wrinkled his brow and thought a moment, "Well, I think that's what we better do. Do you have a spare?"

"No, you wouldn't authorize purchase of any spare units when we told you we needed 'em and now we're stuck, just like we told you we'd be."

Art replied, "Well, Mark, you know that I tried to get funding for that over a year ago. Hova wouldn't allow it then and has disallowed it every time since. Fishburne told him we didn't need those spares and he's not about to let us buy 'em."

"I know that but that doesn't solve the problem for us, does it?"

"No, it doesn't and we'll just have to try to work around it. I'll call Bob and see if I can get you one shipped out today from Oregon."

"Okay, Chief, we'll be waiting to hear. Meanwhile, we'll go as far as we can on the repair."

"Okay, buddy. I'll call you back in a little while and give you the status."

Art hung up the phone and growled, "Shit! Snake bit again. Some more of this damned mismanagement. I'm about to impact a check-out schedule because I can't keep enough spare parts on hand."

Eddie shifted uncomfortably. "Watch it. That's what got Manuel."

"Well, buddy, it ain't gonna get me."

In the coming months as fall faded into winter, Tex entered Art's office and announced, "Well, Sam is ready to ship another set of your clevises down south for assembly. I hope we can get some

372

follow-on for him. It's a shame to let that team break up out there. They did a hell of a job for us."

"I agree, Tex, which reminds me, I haven't gotten that final report from Eddie yet."

Tex looked blank. "Which final report?"

"The one on the clevis breakage problem we did. You remember that program, or do you want to forget it?"

"Hell, how could I forget that? Why hasn't he given it to you?"

Art looked puzzled. "Hell, I don't know. Guess I better ask him. It seems like I never get a chance to get out of this damned office anymore. This shit just keeps piling up."

"Tell me about it. I'm gettin too old for this kind of rat race. I'm gonna have to have some help down there." Tex quipped in true fashion as he left.

Art replied, "Keep your head down, your back to the wall and your eyes forward, buddy."

He laughed as he went out the door and retorted playfully, "You're the one that better do that. I see the deals you pull up here to keep your shit moving. If Hova ever knew some of the strings you pull, he'd kill you."

"Yeah, but don't forget who helps me with those strings."

He stared intently from the open door. "If he ever found out just how much we work around him to get some of this work done, he'd kill us both."

"But if we didn't we'd never accomplish much, would we?"

"You got that right."

Art leaned back in his chair and wondered, I wonder why Eddie hadn't gotten him that final closeout report. Ben's quit and it had been almost ten months. He decided that the best thing might be to go over and ask him. Eddie had been keeping close to his office and not coming around the Program Office. Soon Eddie greeted him with a smile, "Howdy. I was thinkin' I needed to call you."

"Oh? Business or monkey business?"

He became serious as he answered, "Business. I just accepted a hell of a job offer this morning."

Art looked at him in disbelief and finally asked, "You what?"

"This is a dead end for us, Art. You need to get out, too.

Hova and Fishburne made it clear that we're doomed here."

Art sympathized with Eddie. Hova had taken charge of the new Computer Center manager, who had replaced Ben, through his usual intimidation and threat of firing. He was dictating all activities in the computer center now, although he still wouldn't allow use of computers in the Program Office simply because he had issued a public decree that it would never happen.

"Well, buddy, I understand. I'll miss you. We've done some good work together."

"Yeah, but I'm not leavin' town. I'll still be here and I still care about this program."

Art felt the loss deeply but realized it was inevitable. "Well, I might follow you one day. I know Ray's negotiating for a new position, too. If he gets it, it'll be a hell of a step up for him. I'm gonna stick it out a while, though and see if it changes any."

Eddie grinned and replied, "But this one seems to always change for the worse. Hova's killin' it. By the way, I'll give you your final report on the day I leave and I'd strongly advise you to keep it until the day you leave, if you're smart."

Art looked at him quizzically. "Why? It's non-controversial, isn't it?"

"Yeah, it is, just like we were ordered to do, but you know as well as I do that they'll never understand it and it'll cause another firestorm. It's written around Mil-Handbook-5 and it's simple as hell, but they'll never figure that out. It leaves all our other work intact."

As budgets got tighter and tighter on the program because of a lack of congressional budget support for the Space Agency, Art was not able to get authorizations for new hardware when he needed it, which further compounded his schedule problems, as well as those of his colleagues in the program management office. The Shuttle flights were going well, or seemingly well to the casual observer, but the realities of the situation caused tremendous stress on people trying to swap hardware around to keep the program on schedule and viable.

Hova and Fishburne had become more dictatorial because of their own incompetence and ineptitude which led to gross errors in management. There had been two more casualties from the ranks of the Program Office, fortunately not deaths, but heart attacks which drove the individuals from the program for their own survival. Art

374

had come to believe that Hova knew what he was talking about when he said, "Ah don't have heart attacks! Ah give 'em!"

Sam Kelley at StressCo was ready to complete the last set of strut clevises on his contract but due to the hectic and frequent flight schedules, Art wasn't able to keep enough hardware flowing in the system between launch, recovery and return to Sam for re-instrumentation to keep him on schedule. Then, too, the units were beginning to look tired and ill-used after just a few flights, in spite of their certification for use on twenty flights before throw away. The general condition these units were falling into was causing great consternation for Art and his chief inspector, Chip, because of their fears of the material and potential for breakage and disaster. Each time he approached the subject of procuring new, fresh hardware, Hova rejected the request, sternly reprimanding him with, "Mr. Fishburne has told you what you need through Flight Fifty-One. If you manage your stuff right, you'll have plenty."

After an inspection of the last units that Sam was going to instrument, Tex and Art drove back to the plant, neither feeling like conversation. Tex especially had become very depressed about the poor physical condition of the units and primarily about one that could not be screwed into the test tooling. "Those things look like shit. That one is so out of round that it ought to be scrapped now", he said.

"I agree buddy," Art replied. "But they're supposed to be good for twenty missions. Hova's not gonna let me replace them until they actually fly twenty missions, no matter what."

Tex frowned, pondering just what that really meant. He finally said, "Well, I wouldn't want to use some of those damned things again after one mission with all those dings and gouges all over 'em. Especially that last one. It looks like warmed over hell."

"That's the reason for dimensional checks on that set. I want to know, too. I suggested that to Chip, and our government inspector thought it was a hell of an idea and imposed the requirement."

Tex leaned back in the big soft seat in Art's old Buick. "Well, I'll have to say one thing."

"What's that?"

"We're lucky to have the government QC man we've got. I just don't think there's one much better. He has a hell of a grasp of this program. It's too bad we couldn't have involved him in the analysis and that damned presentation you and Eddie gave."

"Yeah, but we had to keep that in-house until our management decided to give it to 'em out at the Space Center," Art replied.

Tex rolled down the window to spit out a piece of chewing gum he had been chewing on since before he went to StressCo. "Damn, that stuff gets hard after a while. Do you think he ever knew what you were doing?"

Art shook his head. "No, I don't think so. There weren't any problems on the basic contract, which was the limit of his responsibility."

Four weeks before the clevises were scheduled to ship, Chip called Art, "Hey, we got a problem. Better come out here."

Art felt a sinking feeling. "What is it?"

"We got one with an elongated hole in the ear where the pin goes through. If we try to fly it that damned pin will be loose and cause all kinds of slack in the joint."

"Are there any more like that?"

"We'll know by the time you get here. I called Oscar from the government office, too. He's on the way out."

Soon Art, Chip, Tex, and Oscar Markham, the government quality inspector, were gathered around the long bench where Chip had the units laid out for inspection. Chip took his standard fit pin and inserted it in the hole to check the dimensions.

To everyone's shock, the pin rattled around when he shook it, displaying a significant misfit between pin and hole. Oscar quickly commanded, "Gimmie that micrometer." He checked the dimension of the pin and then checked the inside dimension of the hole. Next he looked at the drawing and checked the dimensional requirements and the tolerances before he replied, "That ain't even close. Reject it."

Chip smiled and without a word, handed Oscar a reject tag he'd already written up and pointed to the disposition block. Oscar beamed, "Well, you beat me to scrappin' that one, didn't you."

Chip grinned as he replied, "Nothing else to do. That thing isn't flight worthy at all. The rest of 'em are marginal as hell, too, but they do meet the spec, barely."

Oscar picked up the micrometer and started checking the inside dimensions of the holes. Finally he commented, "Yeah, these meet the drawing but I sure as hell don't like what I see. You can see how they've stretched and deformed."

Oscar turned to Chip and asked, "Have you done the dimensional checks?"

"Yeah, all but the threads on that one that's out of round. We've got to get a thread die to try to clean up the threads and see if it will go into the tooling."

"How do they look visually?"

"Well, nothin' to write home about but this one here was the only real reject so far. We may have some more thread problems though, because a couple of 'em look like there's galling where they've been stressed."

"Okay. We better check that, too."

Chip continued, "The thread die and gage we got on order won't get it for at least a month or maybe five weeks. They have to make these big ones up special and that's gonna kill the shipping schedule."

Art frowned and turned to Tex. "I don't know anything to do but gamble on these remaining units because Hova won't accept any excuse if these things are late. We'll have to go ahead and instrument and hope these threads check out when the thread gage gets here."

Chet, Sam's engineer, who had been standing quietly, stepped forward, "Well, we screwed these units into the test fixtures that we use to test in the big press back there, but that's a looser fit than the thread gage."

"Yeah, and the threads in those mounting blocks probably crept a little too," Tex added. "Just remember, you been using the same test tooling a long time."

"Okay," Art continued, "I guess we better gamble. If we have a thread problem, maybe we can dress it down to meet the drawing."

Sam worked his crew through December and through the Christmas holidays every day except Christmas day. Art was pleased with the willingness as he watched Sara do her intricate soldering and was always amazed at the delicate touch she had on the tiny wires.

Three weeks after returning from the brief holidays, Art was collecting data to run on his home computer mission model rather than go through the laborious hand analysis required by Hova and

Fishburne. Suddenly Jan, one of the departmental secretaries ran into Art's office breathlessly. "Mr. Hova wants you immediately," she said.

Art looked up and asked with justifiable concern, "What's he want?"

Jan replied excitedly, "You know better than to ask that. I don't know. He's in a meeting in the conference room."

"Okay. Okay. I'll go see what he wants," Art answered grudgingly.

He walked into the conference room and saw six of the structures people seated around the long conference table, with two structures people from the Space Agency. Hova glared at Art as he walked in and before he could say anything or take a seat, he growled, "When you gonna ship them clevises?"

"Well, we have some mechanical problems right now. They're scheduled to ship the middle of the month. I think we'll make that okay."

"Boy, your ship date just changed," Hova growled. "You ship those things Wednesday."

Art looked at him in disbelief. "But we can't. We have problems on one. We're having to polish out the threads and we just got a thread gage yesterday."

Hova was plainly irritated and snorted, "Mister, Ah don't care about any of your flimsy excuses. Ah told you to ship them things Wednesday and Ah mean you'll ship 'em Wednesday or else."

Art felt anger welling up and said with a loud, course growl, "I told you I couldn't do that. I got mechanical problems with 'em and I'll ship when they're ready and not one damned day sooner. You can't run around changing my schedules without letting me know."

Hova felt he was about to lose control of the situation and pounded the table to a very silent room, yelling, "Ah said Wednesday and Ah mean Wednesday. Now you do it! You do it!"

Art looked at him and replied in an equally loud voice, "I told you and I won't tell you again, not one damned day before they're ready." With that he turned and walked out of the room and back to his office.

Hova and Fishburne avoided Art for the next few days. He had asked Tex to have Sam's crew on extra overtime to try to meet the date if he could. Finally Wednesday morning arrived and he had gotten a buy-off from Chip and Oscar. Everyone felt they were as good as could be.

He took the special air shipping documents to Hova's office for his authorization because of the additional cost of shipping this way, and asked Fanny, "Is Garlin in?"

"Yes sir," she replied in her best business tone, still looking sheepish and wondering just how much he really knew. "Go on in."

He pushed the door open and saw Hova sitting on one of his large soft couches with two of his old Space Agency buddies laughing about some trivia that had occurred years before. He saw Art, assumed his best scowl, and growled, "Whatta' you want??"

Art felt rage build up to the point that he knew he couldn't go on this way. He threw the shipping documents down on Hova's lap and said quietly, "If you want those things shipped you better sign this now."

Hova started another tirade about the schedule and how his attitude had better change or he's gonna fire him while signing his name to the shipping document. Art grabbed the papers off his knee when he was through signing and without another word walked out of the office with Hova's mouth going like a circle saw in a saw mill. He entered the large work area where Fannie and the other secretaries looked curiously, having heard the noise through the open door. Without a word, Art turned and walked back to his office and said to himself, "Well, that's it. I've got to do something."

Art closed the door and sat staring out the window for at least a half hour, watching the pigeons. He considered his position and the problems he was having, and when he thought about leaving the program he got cold chills. He felt caught in a trap with no good way out. His friends at the Cape and in Houston were all valuable and he hated to seemingly abandon them. After a while he resolved to try to make life a little easier by staying away from Fishburne and Hova at every opportunity and hoped they didn't try to find him for any reason.

There had been quite a large number of Space Shuttle flights since the fateful day in which he and Eddie tried to warn the company about the problems in design. He pondered this for a while, finally concluding, "Well, it's held together so far. Maybe we were just chasing a ghost. But dammit! The numbers were there to support our position. Maybe we're just gonna be lucky."

Suddenly Art was brought back to reality by a quiet knock on the door. He put his feet down from the desk and said quietly, "Come in."

Ray entered the office with a look of concern mixed with a smile, as though he had accomplished something big. "Hey, buddy. You never shut your door. You okay?"

Art smiled as best he could after his latest encounter with Hova and answered slowly, "Well, I'm still alive, I guess. How about you? You look like you captured something."

"I did. I got me a hell of a position and there's one for you if you'll go. How about it? This place is killin' both of us."

He peered out the window for a moment before answering, "I been sittin here thinking about that very thing. I just had another battle with Hova. Seems like they're gettin more frequent and more ugly now. Or maybe I just hate the little son-of-a-bitch more since Manuel died. I don't know . . . but I got to do something, I guess."

"Well, it's time you started looking after yourself a little, you know."

"I know. I don't feel good a lot of the time anymore and I know it's stress brought on by him and his shit."

"Well, it's obvious he doesn't respect anything or anybody. He ain't got the decency of a pole cat in the middle of a beauty contest. How 'bout comin' over to Acro Engineering with me? Those guys all know you and they'd love to have you."

"That's a good place, Ray. A damned good bunch of professionals," Art replied with a smile.

"Frank Symon, the president over there told me when he made me the offer that he'd like to get you over there."

He sat for a moment considering the offer. He and Ray had become much closer friends since Eddie and Ben had left the company, feeling as though they were on a lonely outpost together. Finally he replied, "I feel like I have an obligation to the program and to the rest of the guys here and at the Cape. You know, we got some really dedicated people in the program."

"Yeah, but look at the hell that Hova puts us all through. I know it's because you tried to warn them about that strut problem. Since there ain't been one broke, he thinks he's got the upper hand. And you're the last one, too. All the rest are gone."

"Well," Art said with great introspection, "we predicted one out of the first twenty-seven. Adventurer next week will be twenty-five. Hell, maybe he's right. Maybe there's no problem back there like we thought."

"Hey! You guys did what you should have. You found a potential problem and worked it as far as you could. It could have been, and who knows, it just might be yet."

"I sure as hell hope we don't ever have to find out."

"Yeah, me too, but back to gettin' you out of here. How about it? Eddie, Ben, and all that crew you had working knew they were washed up."

"All because we challenged Hova."

"Don't make no damned difference why. It's a dead end. Shit, man, you got too much to offer to be pigeon-holed here."

He knew Ray was right and finally agreed, "Okay, buddy. You go over and see what it's like. If you like it, then maybe I'll come over and talk. Okay?"

"Well, I guess that's better than nothing. You're the hardest headed sucker I ever saw when it comes to takin' care of yourself. You know that?"

"Hell, Ray, it's time to go home. You gonna' turn your resignation in next week?"

CHAPTER TWENTY-ONE

Art leaned back and quietly studied a series of equations he had just finished solving on the large blackboard in his office. He sipped a warm cup of coffee and contemplated lunch before the monthly hardware schedule status briefing he was to present, as he mentally solved and resolved one portion of the first equation to be sure it was correct. Suddenly the telephone rang.

The voice was excited and strained. He recognized it as one of his old flight instructors, Johnny "Ace" Barnes. He said in a quavering voice, "Adventurer just blew up!"

Art was fully aware of his propensity to kid at times and answered jovially, "Yeah, and I bet you flew your 195 today, before you put on the wings, of course."

"I ain't shittin! I just saw it on TV! I saw it!"

"Yeah, John. Got any more jokes?" As he realized the seriousness he felt panic, his whole body became weak and near collapse. "You're serious aren't you?"

"Hell yes!" was the urgent reply.

It was unusual for Art to miss watching or listening to a launch but he had to prepare for the briefing and hadn't paid much attention since the beginning of the count-down on the previous Friday, when all seemed to be going well with his systems. "What, what happened? Where'd it blow?"

Almost incoherently came the reply, "About seventy-four seconds into the launch before SRB separation. Nobody knows what happened yet."

Art turned from his desk and quickly switched on his little TV. His secretary, Jan, passing the door heard the commotion and stuck her head in the door. "What's the excitement?"

He looked at her incredulously, still only half-believing. "John just said Adventurer blew up. That couldn't have happened, could it?"

"How could it? How could it?" she said over and over as she rushed to see the TV. Immediately they saw news commentators busily interviewing everybody and everything. Then they showed the launch and explosion pictures over and over and over.

Ray had heard the commotion from his office and appeared at the door prepared for the worst. "What the hell's going on?" he asked. Then he slumped down in a chair. "Damn. Damn! Damn!" he yelled.

Jan, standing by the TV on Art's credenza, began to sob.

All pretense of work stopped as they watched the newscasters. They studied all the stop frame shots and saw the right booster move out away from the structure and then slam back into the side of the external tank.

They watched the flame progress toward the forward end of the booster and the horrendous explosion that followed. Then they saw the solid rockets free from the structure starting to go into wild, uncontrolled trajectories. Moments later they saw the boosters explode as the Range Safety Officer ignited Boomer's pyrotechnics imbedded into the sides of the long pencil-like rockets before they could change course and return to the coast. They split open and fell harmlessly into the sea in a pile of scrap.

Struggling for words, Ray finally asked, "What--what happened? What the hell could have happened?"

"Must have been structural. Must have been. I sure as hell hope one of those damned aft struts didn't let go."

Jan looked through her tears at Art and asked, "What are you talking about? You were working on those things!"

"Yeah, we sure were, for five years. Then we presented the results to the company management and nearly got ourselves killed by Hova and Fishburne."

You told them it would happen?" she asked, wiping the tears and looking curiously at Art.

"Remember that horrible meeting about a year ago?"

"When Fishburne made such a fool of himself?"

"That's the one. Eddie and I told management there was a ninety-five percent probability this could happen to one of the first twenty-seven vehicles. This is twenty-five."

Ray commented slowly, "Looks like you might have been right."

Jan was looking incredulously. Didn't you tell anybody else?"

"Only our management. The Space Agency people never knew about our years of work . . . "

Suddenly Art's phone rang again. The strained voice on the

other end replied, "Art, Bill Allison at Mission Control in Houston."

Recognizing an old friend from the days of the Saturn V launches, he replied, "We're watching here, Bill. I can't believe it. I just can't believe it. Were you working the launch?"

"Yeah. But this is an unofficial call. It's our opinion that we broke one of those aft struts. A couple of us here knew you spent several years analyzing a potential problem in that area. What do you think?"

Art leaned back in his chair. "Bill, we had good technical reasons to believe there was a design flaw there. You know what happens when you break one member of an 'N' shaped truss."

"Yeah, I always agreed with your premise. It doesn't take much imagination to see what could happen if you broke one."

"We were sure she'd go unstable and start to whip the end of the booster just like a rope tied to a tree when you snap it."

"Yeah, I knew you were afraid of a catastrophic failure if that happened. What do you think?" Bill asked, now returning to his methodical, analytical patterns.

After a few moments of contemplation Art answered, "Well, I've been watching all the playbacks and it looks like that may be what happened. However, don't jump to conclusions yet."

"Don't worry. I was thinking about our brief discussion several years ago when you were down here. I just wanted your opinion but there'll be an investigation and an official opinion will be issued."

"I'm sure there'll be a hell of an investigation."

"Think about it a while. I'll call you back in a couple of hours."

"Okay, Bill. That should be long enough to begin to develop some sort of feel for it."

Jan looked quizzically at Art: "Is this part of that instrumentation job you were doing at StressCo? That's right, isn't it? It was StressCo?"

"Yep. We found what appeared to be a structural design problem."

"Then you knew one would fail?" Jan asked.

"No, not for sure. We worked all those years trying to understand it."

Suddenly the intercom speaker in the building came on with.

"I'm sorry to announce that we just lost Adventurer. We don't know what went wrong. All we know so far is that there doesn't appear to be any survivors. The explosion occurred seventy-four seconds into the launch."

After the announcement, the offices were a mad-house of confusion. The people couldn't believe the tragedy. Art heard some of the secretarial people crying in the halls and others trying to ask "Why" in stunned tones of disbelief. Jan, still sobbing said, "Well, I knew you were doing something but I didn't know what. "Is that why Hova hates you so much?"

"Yeah, partly. That and other reasons bound up in his ego and religion."

Ray, turning sideways in the chair so he could see Art better asked, "I'd think any son-of-a-bitch in his right mind would want to know about that! Period!"

"Well, Hova and Fishburne thought I was questioning the strut design. Some of their buddies out at the Space Agency wrote the specifications for it," Art replied vehemently.

"Well, what did he do about it?"

"He solved that problem like he solves most of his problems. He issued a decree that said there was nothing wrong."

Art called Eddie Rogers at his new office, "You heard?"

"Yeah, about five minutes ago. I was just about to call you. I got the TV on and what I'm seeing scares me to death."

"Yeah, me too. You think our prediction came true?"

Eddie was serious. "Well, all of our analysis and computer models said one of the first twenty-seven didn't it? And this is twenty-five. It's scary as hell. Looks like it failed just like we told 'em it would."

Art asked Eddie to switch to the same TV channel he was on so they could compare notes. As the films of the accident were run and re-run and details of the launch narrated by the media, Eddie yelled excitedly at the phone, "Look there, looks like something coming out the bottom. Black smoke!"

"I see it, probably from incomplete combustion or something like that. Looks like a rough booster."

Eddie's keen eye watched the progress of the Shuttle up by the Launch Support Tower and then on through the roll program. He suddenly exclaimed, "There's more black smoke. That damned booster looks like it's moving back and forth to me."

"I see it! I see it!"

"Art, the only thing that can mean is we broke a strut on lift off. You know we've had other rough boosters, too."

Eddie was sweating and feeling as though his stomach were tying itself in a knot as he replied excitedly, "Come over here. We got to talk about this."

Jan, who had been watching the pictures and listening to the conversation, began to cry again softly. Amid sobs she said haltingly, "Why did it have to happen? Why? Think of those poor people!"

With a cynical look, sliding further down in his chair, Art replied slowly, "Eddie and Ben quit Space Corp over this. I guess if I was smart I'd 'a quit too. Looks like we were right."

Jan wiped her eyes and said, "I still don't understand why they wouldn't listen."

Art turned his face into a smirk. "Well, the one we had to tell and the one that needed to know is so damned smart that you can't talk to him. He knows everything; solves everything by decree. End of discussion."

Jan looked shocked. "Well, if that's the case, and you told them about it, somebody should sure pay for it."

"I agree. I promised Fishburne that the story'd be told and one day he'd be held accountable." Art answered as he got up to go to Eddie's office.

Soon he was seated around Eddie's worktable with his office-mate, Stan Hicks. He turned to Eddie as they continued to watch the media reports, "I'm convinced we broke one of those damned things. I believe that right booster was rough enough to set up enough shock levels to exceed the allowable compression loads in the clevis and the damned thing shattered."

Eddie, in deep thought after a moment of contemplative silence, responded, "We know if you break one strut the entire structure is not failure tolerant and becomes unstable. The second strut likely broke due to overloads caused by whipping of the booster created by the guidance system trying to get back on course. Of course, that whipping of the booster would force the seals to open. We know that happened because we saw flame blowing out from the side, probably through a joint that was forced to open. Then when the third strut broke, the aft end of the booster swung out so far that the nose cone impacted the external tank, ruptured it and slammed back into the side of the ET. With the propellants pouring down the side, they exploded and she went up."

"Yeah, That's my sense of it, too," Art replied.

Stan interrupted, "Well, what would cause a rough booster?"

Eddie peered thoughtfully at Stan over his glasses and replied, "Well, several things. I would suspect either a crack or a void in the propellant grain, improper acoustical tuning of the internal geometry of the rocket motor, chipped or broken places on the points of the star configuration inside the grain, and lots of other things that I haven't even begun to think about. I'm not really a solid propellants expert but I did research it."

"Did you ever find any evidence of another rough booster like this before?" Stan asked.

"Yeah," Eddie replied. "We found some interesting characteristics in this particular motor design."

Stan, who was a civil engineer with little rocket experience but excellent experience in structural design, sat up straight as he asked, "Like what?"

Eddie replied, "Well, you know the boosters are what we call *segmented* motors because each one is made up of a number of segments." Stan nodded his understanding.

"When the fuel is still liquid, each segment is poured full in a mold inside the motor case where it sets up hard. During assembly at Cape Canaveral, the segments are stacked one on the other and sealed at the joints."

Stan nodded. "That's the bands you see around the motor?"

"Yep," came the reply. "The O-ring seals are inside the cover, or bands . . ."

Impatiently, Stan interrupted, "What's this got to do with the failure?"

Art picked up the explanation. "Inside at each interface between the segments is a thing called a restrictor. This is a flat plate-looking affair and protrudes into the flow of gases to aid proper combustion in a normal burn of the grain. As the propellant burns it causes a highly-sheared flow. In other words, there are small shock waves set up which lead to the formation of vortices, or high velocity eddy currents, in the inside of the motor."

"You mean, sort of like little whirl pools?" Stan asked.

"Yeah. These vortices cause smoke rings and move down toward the nozzle end of the motor. The upshot of that is if there's is a crack, a void, or a mismatch on the mating surfaces these vortices can become unstable and cause extremely high vibrations. This can cause a larger fracture or opening in the grain, which would in turn quickly cause a larger vibration. These shocks can, under the right conditions, become regenerative, or in other words, they can cause other larger ones to form. Then they become dangerous."

Stan exclaimed, "Then the thing will self-destruct!"

"Exactly," Eddie replied. "I know that on SL-11, for example, we found this situation and it was a real eye opener."

"Then what happened?"

"It was found in those tests, and especially on SL-11 that pressure variations can be very significant, especially on large rockets like this one. This is the largest solid rocket motor that's ever been flown."

Stan, sitting up straight and paying close attention to every word, acknowledged that he had read this but never thought about the significance.

"SL-11 was the first booster instrumented to make this particular measurement and it, quite by coincidence, turned out to be an extremely rough firing, much rougher than expected. The shocks were far worse than anybody thought it could be, almost to the point of losing it like we lost Adventurer.

"Then you think something set off a series of these big oscillations?" Stan asked.

"Well," Art replied, "we don't know yet, but you can be sure the booster was running rough right from the start. It's hard right now to say what caused that. I think that probably the black smoke and the debris coming from the rear was from partially burned grain and chunks of unburned fuel being excreted from the rear of the nozzle."

Stan leaned back in deep thought before commenting: "So, you suspect a rough booster with vibrations causing shock in the structure big enough to shatter one of those aft struts."

"Exactly," Eddie replied emphatically. "But I want to know if there were hard-over, or sudden, guidance commands to the nozzle. If there were, you can be sure that a strut broke at that point and I'll bet my last cent that occurred at lift-off."

Art leaned forward. "I agree and if that occurred the structure became unstable, allowing the booster to whip while the guidance system tried to get back on trajectory. It probably set up a ripple similar to tying a rope to a tree and then whipping one end. That could force one or more of those seals to open and cause a burn-through."

Eddie interjected, "Yeah, and when the last strut broke it allowed the booster to swing out, rupture the ET, spill fuel as you saw in the film, and then slam back into the side of the structure. Then, BOOM!"

As the three sat silently contemplating, Art suddenly remembered he owed Bill Allison a call.

He dialed the number and Bill answered. "Mission Control. Bill Allison."

"Bill, I'm over at Eddie's. We've been studying all the data we have and we're almost certain that Adventurer broke one of the aft struts and the structure became unstable . . ."

After explanation of the theory that Art and Eddie had just put together Bill replied, "Well, that sure makes sense, doesn't it?"

"Yeah, to us it does. I don't see anything else that could do it that way. When they recover the right booster maybe we'll learn some more about that."

"Yeah, but you know the Range Safety Officer blew it up. I don't know if we'll ever get anything back or not."

Art almost prayed, "Let's hope, Bill. Let's hope."

There was a moment of silence.

Finally Bill asked, "Does Starnes over at the Astronaut Office know about your investigation?"

"No, Frank didn't know. I told him at the launch of SL-1 that we were chasing a possible problem. But, no, he didn't know. Nobody at the Space Agency ever officially knew."

Bill was quiet for a moment and then asked, "Can I tell him about your work on the struts?"

He considered this a moment before answering, "Well, it's got to go to the commission that I know will be appointed and I guess this is as good a starting point as any. Yeah, go ahead and tell him."

The next day Art was in his office early. There was a noticeable, almost ominous absence of the presence of either

Fishburne or Hova, as though they were trying to avoid seeing him. Suddenly his phone rang.

"Hello Mr. Cannon," came the jovial voice over the phone, which Art instantly recognized as Oscar Markham from the Government Inspection Agency.

"Hello Oscar," Art replied, smiling at hearing his friend again.

"Looks to me like one of those damned struts failed yesterday."

"How'd you figure that?"

Oscar, extremely adept when it came to ferreting out problems, chuckled. "I looked at the damned TV same as you did."

"I didn't say anything, Oscar."

Oscar coyly responded, "I know that and officially, I know you're not going to. But for your information, I impounded all the data at StressCo where you did most of your testing and instrumentation work."

Art smiled and felt good that Oscar was on the job as he always was. "That's a good idea, Oscar. I expect the commission may want that before this is over."

"Yeah, and I expect they'll want to talk to some gentlemen still here at Space Corp too."

"How did you know about that?"

Oscar chuckled as he replied, "Don't worry, buddy, I got my ways. I know what goes on. Any good Quality Inspector never lets anybody buffalo him about anything."

Art laughed. "You sly fox. But you couldn't say anything officially."

"That's right. But I sure was interested. One of these days I want you to sit down and fill me in on the whole program, unofficially of course."

"Sure, I'll be glad to give you the whole story on the thing. Unofficially, of course."

"I didn't have any agency delegation on that damned investigation. I'm just another government inspector trying to do a good job."

"Yeah, Oscar. I've wished for a long time there were more like you."

Oscar laughed, obviously liking the feeling of being appreciated. He asked, "By the way, will you talk to a friend of mine about it?"

Art sat up quickly and with an apprehensive tone, asked, "Who's the friend?"

"Well, he's a reporter . . ." Oscar trailed off slowly.

Art stopped to consider this a moment before replying, "I don't want to disappoint you or your friend, but no, I refuse to go to the media with anything. I don't think that's the way to go right now. I'd be blowing the whistle and you know that whistle blowers always die one way or the other."

Oscar, disappointed, pushed his request insistently. "Yeah, I know very well about that but I told him you would. I think he can help you get this out to the commission. He knows a lot of people at Headquarters."

"I'm sorry, Oscar, but I won't call him," Art said emphatically.

"Well, what if he calls you?"

Art understood Oscar's predicament. He made a commitment and couldn't deliver. He finally weakened, "Well, I got no control over who calls me, but I don't want to discuss this thing with the media yet."

Oscar breathed a sigh of relief into the phone. "I got your point. I'll just tell him he can call you and you can tell him to go to hell if you want to."

Later that afternoon Art received a call from Mark Huffinger from *Aero News*. Mark opened the conversation with "How are you today, Mr. Cannon?"

Not believing that he was really interested in his welfare, Art replied, "Well as can be expected, under the circumstances."

"I understand. I've been conducting an investigation into this accident and a mutual friend of ours said I could call you. Is it okay if I ask you some questions?" The voice sounded both desperate and insistent.

Art laid down his pencil and leaned back in his chair before saying quietly and forcefully, "Mark, I don't think it's appropriate that I make any statements now. I guess I decline to comment on anything until we have more data."

Fearful of losing the contact, Mark became more insistent. "I understand, but I've been talking to some of your old team members and know about your aft strut investigation."

"Oh? I'm not aware of anybody that you've talked to."

"Let me assure you I have but I won't reveal any names at this time. Can you just confirm some things if you won't give me a statement?"

Art wanted to terminate the conversation but because of Oscar's friendship he was reluctant to do so. He finally conceded, "Well, I suppose I could say yes or no to anything you asked."

"Great. Did you perform a series of tests and analyses that would indicate there was a high probability of strut failure?"

Art blinked and wondered just how much this guy really knew. "Yes, we did that."

"Did the results indicate a potential failure?"

Art again, without wanting any discussion, replied, "Yes."

"Did you predict a failure on each two and seven tenths launches?"

Art now knew that he had access to data presented in the meeting he and Eddie held almost two years before where they presented their findings to Space Corp management. Just before the presentation Eddie found an error in one of the charts that mistakenly said there could be a failure each two and seven tenths flights instead of the correct number, twenty-seven. Art replied, "No, there was a typo error in a chart and we corrected that in the presentation you obviously know about."

Mark laughed a little uneasily and asked, "Was is corrected to say that there could be one failure expected each twenty seven flights?"

"Yes, it was. There was no further discussion on that point."

"I understand. Now, you officially presented this data to the company management. Did you ever at any time present this data to the Space Agency?"

Art flinched. "No, we did not."

"Why not?"

"The company made a decision not to do that."

"Just one more question. Did you ever recant or change your conclusions?"

Art replied quietly, "No. Most emphatically, we never did. We stand by the work we did."

"Thanks, Art. You've been a very reluctant interviewee but you've also been a big help."

As Art hung up the phone, Fishburne suddenly appeared in the door. "Mr. Hova wants you in his office now, mister!" he said in the harshest tones he could muster.

Art glared at him with total contempt. "What the hell does he want, Fishburne?"

"Get your ass down there and see!"

As Art entered Hova's plush office with all the finery, he observed Hova sitting at his desk, almost invisible in his huge over-stuffed executive chair. Art began to feel almost sorry for him as he thought what he must be going through. Hova started out, "Art, we've had our differences. Ah know that and Ah think we need to bury the hatchet and make amends. Ah'm gonna appoint you to a position of second deputy down here and give you a large raise. How does that sound to you?"

He glared at him without saying a word and noted that the snap and bite was gone, along with the sarcasm and the apparent hatred he so lavishly displayed. Art had never expected to hear such a statement from Hova. Suddenly he felt his blood pressure surge from an urge to drive his fist through the small mouth making the sounds from behind the massive desk. Finally, all he could manage to say was, "I can't believe that. I just can't believe you'd do that."

"Well, son, there's a lot of things we can't believe in this world. But we all got to continue to work for the best and for the glory of the Lord. Ah've always tried to do that, you know."

Art's stomach started to churn as bile seemed to boil up into his throat, hunting for an escape onto the blue carpet. He started to sweat as he glared at Hova, studied the countenance carefully for a moment and replied, "Shit!" He turned quickly and started to the door.

Hova yelled at him as he realized he wasn't for sale, "Ah'll get you for this!"

"Yeah! I'm sure you will!"

Fishburne was listening outside the door and appeared to be near panic when Art stormed out. "You better listen to the 'ole Chief, fellah, if you know what's good for you."

He glared at Fishburne as though he were Satan himself. "What the hell's wrong with you? You scared, or something? You better stay out'a my way, bastard! I made you a damned promise once. I ain't forgot!" Art stomped out of the building, got in his car and just drove for an hour, considering what his next move would be. He decided just to play it low-key for a while and see what the recovered booster parts would reveal and then plot a course from there with Eddie.

Both Art and Eddie watched the news media intently during the next few weeks and were dismayed to see all the attention given to O-Ring failure. Eddie called him several times and vehemently grumbled, "Can't they see what the real cause of the accident was. It was that damned strut. The O-Ring was only a consequence, a secondary failure."

He had quieted Eddie down each time by saying, "Easy buddy. When they get the booster parts back and see the failure mode in that O-Ring joint and see the others that had failed or were on the verge of failing further up-stream, you'll see a change in attitude." Art was worried about having not recovered the booster parts and began to think that the salvage crews were not going to find anything. Finally there was a miraculous find, the segment that actually burned through. However, as fate would have it, this would be the only part ever admittedly found. There would be no opportunity to examine other joints.

The following week late in the afternoon, just before Art left his office, he got a call from his old friend, Frank Starnes at Houston. "I'm glad to hear from you, Frank. I was hoping you'd call."

"Well, you could have called me."

"No I couldn't. But I knew you'd eventually do it. I'm sittin' on a powder keg up here."

"What do you mean?" Frank roared. "Were you working on the cause of this accident?"

"We believe we were. We tried to get it out to the Space Agency a year ago and were stopped cold by Garlin Hova and Irvin Fishburne.

Frank was beside himself and Art could imagine the ex-Marine Colonel's rage. "I know that little son-of-a-bitch. He'd fuck up a wet dream. He don't know his ass from first base. He's nothin' but a fuckin' parrot; alligator mouth with a jay-bird ass," Frank yelled.

"Easy Frank. Easy." Art counseled the old combat Colonel.

"Now I understand a hell of a lot more. I didn't know he was involved, him and his little 'yes-man' who's sucked his ass for most of his damned miserable life!"

"Yeah, Frank. It's a long story. I'll tell you one of these days. It's not pretty."

"Yeah, yeah. I want you to." Frank was regaining control of himself and Art could feel the rage beginning to diminish. He knew Frank wasn't one to cross lightly. He thought back to the story he had heard about him single-handedly shooting his way out of an ambush in Korea. When the enemy count was made it was found that he had killed eighteen of the enemy soldiers. However, he also knew that he was a man capable of being as kind and gentle as any human in the world but was terribly intolerant of incompetence.

Finally, Frank growled emphatically, "I'm sending a couple of astronauts up there to see you tomorrow. Will you talk to 'em?"

"Damned sure will. Give them my phone number and I'll pick them up at the airport. They shouldn't come over here, though."

"They'll be coming up in a T-38. How about 10:30 out at the military field. Their names are Donald Davis and Sid Cameron."

The next morning Art was at the military airfield a little before 10:30 and watched a sleek T-38 enter the traffic pattern for a smooth landing. Shortly the little craft pulled up to the hangar and shut down the engines. Two pilots climbed down from the cockpit. "Art Cannon?" one asked. He smiled, extended his hand and replied, "That's me!"

"I'm Don and this is Sid. Where can we talk?--Privately?"

"We'll use a friend's real estate office, if that's okay."

Don grinned and answered, "Great. Frank said there might be a problem."

The three quickly became good friends, having found a number of mutual acquaintances both inside the agency and on the airshow circuits. On arrival at the office, Heidi stared at the two in their flying suits. Art introduced them to Heidi, who was thoroughly impressed at having met two bonafide astronauts and one who had actually flown the Shuttle. Sid kiddingly said to her, "You should meet the guy we work for, John P. "Smokey" Stover, chief astronaut, an old Apollo Astronaut who actually walked on the moon." She looked as though she couldn't believe what she heard.

Heidi asked, "Art, is he serious?"

"Serious. Did you find Eddie?"

"Not yet. His office says he's still out of town."

As they took seats in a small conference room adjoining Heidi's office, Sid grinned, "By the way, I almost forgot, Smokey says hi."

Art rummaged around in his brief case and pulled out copies of the presentation that he and Eddie gave and copies of his notebooks.

For the next two hours he and the two astronauts engrossed themselves in a deep discussion of the sequence of events, tests and findings that they had made during the test program. Finally Don walked over to the window in deep contemplation and said, "Well, this may be what we're lookin' for. It sure as hell holds together as far as I can see."

Sid responded, "Yeah, I agree." Then he turned to Art and asked, "Will you write all this up as a sequence of events and send to us? We need a copy of this presentation, too. I want to be sure it gets to the Commission just as you laid it out."

"Sure. I have all of my old lab notebooks and I'll just extract the events from that and send it to you."

"Great. Let's get something to eat and we'll head back south."

Three weeks after Art's meeting with the astronauts the presidential commission started to probe the accident and concentrated, to Art and Eddie's dismay, on the O-Ring failure as the principal cause. It seemed that the Space Agency was pushing the investigation in this direction. Art had submitted his data to the astronauts and was waiting for something to occur, such as a chance to discuss it with the commission. After a month had gone by with no response, Art had begun to voice extreme concern to Eddie.

During of one of these sessions in Eddie's office every few days Oscar phoned from the front lobby. He had learned they were holed up periodically discussing strategy on getting information to the commission about the struts. He was obviously disturbed and walked quickly by Eddie's secretary without a word. She had learned to expect this when Oscar was bothered and had joked on occasion, "When that guy gets locked in on something, he's got a one-track mind and I don't know what to do to help him."

"Oscar, you look like you just saw a ghost." Eddie commented as he entered and closed the door.

"Might as well have. I just found out something."

"What's that?"

"Well, you know your astronaut meeting you had here a while back?"

"Yeah, but I never heard anything from it."

"You didn't need to. They turned all your material over to the investigation commission."

Art looked puzzled and asked, "Well, that's what I would expect. Wouldn't you?"

"Yeah," Oscar continued bitterly. "And the commission sent all the data here like you would expect them to do, too. Right?"

"Right, since this is where much of that design was done."

Oscar leaned his large body back and his blonde hair fell over his face. He nervously brushed it away. "Do you know who's on the investigation board here in Hawkinsville?"

"Well, I would assume there's a group of Space Agency people."

"Correct," Oscar said. "But they have a contractor board of advisors and guess who's chairman."

Eddie turned pale. "Not Garlin Hova?"

"Correct again," Oscar said excitedly. "Both Hova and Fishburne are on it and guess who got your material when it came in and guess who is still covering his ass by destroying your data?"

Art pounded the table and jumped up with a loud exclamation, "Shit, Shit!"

Eddie looked shocked and defeated. Oscar, staring at them with desperation, replied, "You'll have to find another way, guys. You'll just have to find another way. Hova's shut off this channel."

Art stood up and uncharacteristically paced the floor. "What if we went directly to the commission, Oscar? What if we went in there and said, 'We need to talk to you?'"

Oscar frowned and replied, "On what basis or authority would you do that? I'm sure Hova has thought of that and has covered his ass that way too. I don't think you'd get anywhere."

Eddie looked at Art with frustration and rage showing on his face. "I'm afraid I agree with Oscar . . . I don't think we'd get far with a direct approach. Besides, that's going to put us in the category of whistle blowers and all we'll do is suffer and accomplish nothing to boot."

"Yeah," Art replied after a few moments' thought. "We got to have somebody to run interference for us out there, somebody that we can depend on to keep that from happening if we can. We still have got to get the story out and try to get that damned thing fixed."

Eddie looked at Oscar and asked, "Have you seen the hearings on TV?"

"Yeah, they're trying to tear a hole in some of these Hawkinsville folks. They're gonna blame *them* for the problem, it looks like."

Eddie slumped further down in his chair as if trying to hide from his frustration. "And the sad part of it is that those damned guys aren't to blame. Not one of them. Maybe they made some bad decisions, but their decision to launch wasn't the cause of the accident. It wasn't the fault of Powder Keg, but they're gonna' get blamed for it. I smell a damned cover-up."

"Yeah, I do too, but it's that little beady-eyed five-foot-four egomaniac's cover-up I see. Damn him anyway." Art growled.

Oscar tried to put Art at ease. "Well, you guys tried before it happened. You warned 'em."

Art stood by the window overlooking the office complex courtyard watching the birds, like he watched the pigeons from his office at Space Corp while he contemplated options for their next move. He finally commented, "Well, I just don't know what to do from here except wait and watch for an opportunity and hope it arrives."

Friday afternoon Art looked up to see his good friend and ace aircraft mechanic, Mack, driving into his driveway in his old yellow Ford truck. Mack jovially entered the garage where Art was working on Annie's Triumph and sat on a stool. After a few moments of good-natured chit-chat, he asked, "I need your help."

"You know anything I got is yours. What you need?"

Mack smiled warmly. "I got a damned Bonanza up at Thomas Field I been trying to solve an intermittent alternator problem on for a week. I've changed alternators and regulators and just about run out of ideas. Can you help me tomorrow?"

"Sure. What time will you be there?"

Mack grinned his usual big, happy grin. "Well, I'll be there at eight o'clock."

Art shifted his position against the fender as he considered the early hour on a weekend. "Well, how about if I get there by nine or so?"

Mack laughed and replied, "Yeah, sure, sack hound. Any time you get there'll be okay. I got the rest of the annual inspection to do."

Assisted by the "The Big O", as the other A&P mechanic was affectionately known, and an hour of troubleshooting and repair, Art looked up and saw his friend, Gary Stafford, enter the hangar. "Hello buddy. How's the new 210 Cessna doing?"

"Great," Gary beamed as he watched Art finish tying up a wire bundle on the Beech.

"We just fixed an alternator problem, broken wire. Real snake of a problem because you couldn't see it."

Gary was interested in the Shuttle program and knew of Art's role in the solid rocket boosters. He was particularly saddened when the Adventurer blew, both for the crew and for the beautiful machine that was so quickly reduced to rubble. He looked at Art thoughtfully. "I haven't seen you since Adventurer. What's happening with that seal problem that caused the explosion?"

"Well, first off, the seals were *not* the primary cause of the explosion. It looks like the commission is going to conclude that but they haven't gotten the full story. Their conclusion is wrong".

Gary's surprise registered quickly and with dismay he blurted, "What the hell did cause it, then?"

He invited Gary to the front of the hangar where there was an old park bench in the sun by the front ramp situated to watch airplanes taking off and landing. Art leaned back and in his usual manner crossed his legs and stared across the field at the windsock outlined against a distant silo. looking for a good place to start. "Well, old buddy, I'll tell you the story, if you have a few minutes. I don't talk this much because most people don't understand but I know you will."

He spent the next thirty minutes giving Gary an overview of the problems and the obstacles he ran into over the years and described the real culprits in the accident. Gary was shocked and enraged. "I got a good friend who is a U.S. Senator. I'm going to have him call you."

Art looked at Gary and shook his head. "No, Gary, I don't want to get into the political arena with this. Those people will feed you to the press and then you're dead."

Gary looked perplexed and continued, "No. That's not the case with Frank. He'll protect your name and your identity. I guarantee he won't compromise you, and he'll get things working. How about it?"

"Do you think he'll really do something instead of just talk a lot and do nothing?"

"I guaran-damn-tee you he will. I know this guy. He's a go'er. We grew up together."

Art stared at him with a searching look for a moment as if to try to decipher the real motivations, and then decided he was serious. "Well, I trust you. He can call me at home if he wants to but I won't call him. So far I've not called the first person, and I won't start with him. That way nobody can accuse me of being a whistle-blower."

"He'll call you next week, I guarantee."

Monday Art explained Gary's offer to Eddie, who stared at the ceiling for a few moments before slowly replying. "Sounds okay. Yep. Sounds good," as he turned around in his chair and crossed his legs, which seemed to give him more assurance in his decision. "We need somebody like that if he's serious. Maybe this'll work."

Art sipped a cup of coffee, frowned and slid down further in his chair. "Well, I sure hope so. At least, I'll see what he says."

That night after Art and Annie had finished dinner and were in the process of washing dishes, the phone rang. She answered and excitedly said, "Washington's on the line!"

"Who is it?"

"Senator Carson, he said."

Art looked at Annie with a big smile. "Well, well."

He heard a friendly voice on the phone. "Art, this is Frank Carson. I was talking to a good friend of mine last night, Gary Stafford, and he suggested that I give you a call on the Adventurer accident. He seems to think you have data that the Commission hasn't seen and you're having trouble getting anybody to listen. Is that correct?"

"Yeah, Frank, that's right. We have a lot of data that the Space Agency never saw. We think it's important that it be considered before they make a wrong decision."

Carson was silent for a moment but finally replied, "Well, I'm not an engineer so I'd like to have my assistant who takes care of all the science things contact you. Can we do that?"

"Sure," Art replied, and then proceeded to discuss his concerns about not being branded a whistle-blower and being barred from ever doing business with the Space Agency or other governmental agencies again.

"If you cooperate with us, I'll guarantee that won't happen. Of course, you may have to testify before the Commission. Can you do that?"

"Sure, I'd be glad to, but you know as well as I do that one individual like me can't take on a corporation the size of Space Corp, and when you combine that with hostile government agencies, I wouldn't have a chance in the world at defending myself."

"I understand, but those are problems I can work."

"Okay. I'll talk to your guy."

Wednesday evening Art received the next call. "Hello Art, this is Leonard Bowles. I work for Frank Carson."

He was feeling greatly encouraged. The deep voice on the other end sounded business-like and sincere. "Well, I'm pleased you called. Frank said you would."

"Yeah. Sorry I couldn't get to it sooner but I got covered up in other problems. Frank tells me you have some information that the Adventurer Commission hasn't had the benefit of. Is that correct?"

"That's right. My colleagues and I did a very indepth analysis over a five-year period of the ends of the struts and we believe that was the initial failure on Adventurer."

Art sensed a sudden attention to detail on the other end. "How about describing the program and the conclusions and then tell me why you think that."

Art spent the next hour in detailed discussions. Finally, Leonard concluded, "Well, I just wish people had listened two years ago. I can tell you now that the National Association of Sciences has done an indepth analysis of the vehicle and the accident and what you have told me correlates very closely to their findings. You need to be talking with them. Will you do that?"

Art smiled at this revelation. This was the first independent data he'd had that supported their findings, and what better support could one ask for than this respected group? "We'll be glad to work with anybody who can get this thing out in the open and get it fixed. Our objective is to fix the vehicle so this doesn't happen again. We can't stand another loss."

"Exactly. I plan to be in Hawkinsville sometime in the next two weeks. I'll call you and we'll get together. Okay?"

"Great. I'll get Eddie and we'll have a good round table discussion." As Art laid down the phone he felt tingly waves of satisfaction ripple up his spine. *Maybe. Now just maybe we'll get this thing fixed.*

His next move was to inform Eddie, who again expressed some of the same reservations that Art had voiced to Gary about getting involved with politicians. "We sure as hell ain't gettin' anybody to talk to us any other way, so let's go for it," he finally concluded.

The next day Art decided to visit the Space Center Propulsion Engineering Lab to see an old friend, Ching Woo, who could help him get data on guidance commands issued to the boosters from the Adventurer computers and transmitted back to the ground by the onboard telemetry system. He barely entered the lab when Ching spotted him. "Hey, old buddy!" came a warm welcome from a corner filled with file cabinets and three desks.

Art peered around the cabinets and saw the small, wiry, well-dressed engineer whose large glasses almost covered the broad smile that seemed to consume most of his face. He put out his hand. "Hello old friend. It's been a long time."

Ching looked studiously at him for a moment before he resumed the big grin. "I'll be damned, you're starting to get gray-headed. Remember when we used to bet on who'd do that first? You owe me a cup of coffee."

They shared a good laugh as they had shared many good laughs and projects over the past years. Art put his arm around Ching, genuinely glad to see him. "You're right, and I'll pay off right now. Come on."

They each poured a cup of coffee after Art deposited twenty cents in the coffee kitty. Ching suddenly looked straight at him as he was accustomed to doing to people when he was serious. "It's good to see you Art, but I know you didn't come out here this time of day just to buy coffee. How can I help you?"

He returned the serious look. "Ching, you always were a wizard at reading me."

Ching laughed easily as he replied, "Well, it's easy if you get to know a person and how he operates inside, I guess."

Art looked wistfully at him and asked, "Do you have or can you get me a copy of the telemetry data on the nozzle inputs to the right and left boosters on Adventurer?"

He pondered the request. "If I don't, I can get it. Let's check my files." He checked measurement numbers to identify which measurements Art was interested in, selected one of the file cabinets and rummaged through the enormous amount of data. He finally said, "Here it is, I thought I had that." He unrolled the data from the Orbiter showing engine nozzle control commands from launch until the explosion.

Art looked quickly at the bottom of the set of curve traces and found "Time Zero", the starting time for the launch. It was evident, as Art had suspected; the right booster was being fed quick, erratic guidance commands to try to stabilize the vehicle on it's planned trajectory. Ching looked at the curves and scratched his head. "That's odd. Look at those commands going to the thrust vector control. I never saw anything like that."

He studied the curves intently for a few minutes. "Can we say with any authority that these commands became erratic about seven-hundred milliseconds after lift-off?"

Ching traced along the chart with his finger on the time scale. "Yes, that's when the erratic commands started, at seven tenths of a second. What would cause that?" he asked curiously.

"Broken strut."

Ching pondered this a few moments as he stroked his chin: "But the problem has been blamed on a leaking seal. How are they related?"

Art put his hand on Ching's shoulder. "It's my theory that the seal burn-through was a result of the strut breaking and this confirms that. I had to know about these commands before I had absolute evidence that this was the case."

"Well, I'll be damned."

As Art described the data, Eddie became ecstatic. "Well, I think that about clinches it. I'm sure that's what happened. It's so obvious, I don't see how they could miss it."

"Well, the only way they would miss it is if it were withheld. That panel is supposed to be a Blue Ribbon set of people appointed by the President, but that doesn't mean they can't be led astray or be wrong."

Two weeks went by with no call from Leonard Bowles. Art and Eddie began to wonder if something was wrong. The third week went by and still no call. Art was getting discouraged again and Eddie had convinced himself that Leonard Bowles was not sincere to begin with. In the middle of the fourth week, Eddie's office partner, Stan Hicks, barged in with the afternoon newspaper and vehemently threw it face up on Eddie's desk. One of the lead stories on page one was captioned "Frank Carson Throws Hat In Ring For President." Eddie read the story caption in disbelief. Then he scowled at Stan. "Well, that's the end of him, I guess. We'll never hear another word because he won't want to get near any controversy."

Stan sat down with a dejected look. "I'm afraid you're right. I thought you guys had something going there."

He dialed Art and asked with apprehension, "Have you seen the afternoon paper?"

"Yeah. I just got it out front."

"Well I predict that's the end of Carson. You just watch."

"Well, buddy, maybe he wasn't the right one anyway."

Eddie was plainly irritated. "Shit. Doesn't anybody out there give a damn?"

Art glared at the phone as he shared the disappointment. "We got to believe they do, buddy, we got to believe they do. Don't get discouraged yet."

As the weeks dragged on Art and Eddie became more and more discouraged about getting the real cause of the accident investigated. Hova and Fishburne had avoided Art, which suited him fine because the less contact he had with those two the better he liked it.

The Space Agency was starting to make an effort to regroup, restructure and make design changes in the Boosters, most of which were things they would like to change because of previous unadmitted design deficiencies of one kind or another. There was a monumental effort to redesign a historically troublesome seal that had been a continual source of problems during assembly. It seemed the wheels of many efforts were spinning along as though they were running in quick sand. The usual mode of problem solving was taking over, that of throwing millions after millions of dollars at a problem, either real or perceived, before attacking the real problem. Of course, the contractors were eager to "fix" everything in sight because of the added work and the added profits. They saw millions of dollars worth of effort going into such things as picture books to justify the seal theory and satisfy the unknowledgable congressmen who were running hither and yon like fleas on a dog suddenly dumped into flea' powder. "To an old war gamer like me, I don't see any way to turn 'em away from this damned seal theory. The news media has got too much momentum on it now," Eddie commented.

The next afternoon Art received a call from Tex James, his old contracts man. Tex typically popped off a couple of jokes before asking, "How about coming out to see me? I got a new job."

"Where the hell are you? I went down to your office yesterday and they were noncommittal as hell about where you were."

"You'd never guess in a million years. I went to work for Sam out at StressCo. I was impressed with his little company, and besides, they needed help."

"Well, I'll be . . ."

"Then, too, I got thoroughly pissed and fed up with the way Space Corp was being run by Hova and his little yes man that I just quit and went to work out here day before yesterday."

Art was marveling at this revelation when Tex changed his tone. He sounded urgent. "I think you really need to come out here."

"Well, I could come this afternoon or tomorrow."

"How about in the morning. Sam'll have on a pot of coffee, I promise."

Art arrived at the front of StressCo at nine a.m. to a warm greeting by Tina Little, who had moved from receptionist to executive secretary. She asked, "Did you know Heidi had a little girl last night?"

Art looked astonished: "Hell, I didn't even know she was due yet. I thought she had another couple of weeks. The last time Annie or I talked to her she did."

Tina's eyes twinkled: "She was early. They're both doing fine. Tim is tickled to death, too."

"Well, that's great. We'll have to get 'em a baby gift."

Sam interrupted the conversation as he entered the lobby. "Hello, there my friend," he greeted Art as he noticed the gray in his hair seemed a little more pronounced, more silvery now, and the slump in the shoulders just a bit more. After all, it had been almost two years since he had worked with Sam and they had developed a deep friendship and respect for each other.

When Tex entered the room, Art's eyes lit up at seeing his old friend. "Well, old buddy, you sneaked out on me but you made your escape to a good place."

Tex laughed sheepishly as he replied, "Just ran out of gall. I couldn't take it any more. The damned place is totally dominated by Hova and the little court jester. I had all I could handle. Sorry I didn't tell you before I left."

Sam looked serious as he said, "Art, we know about all the work we all did on those struts."

Art nodded his concurrence. "Yeah. We worked hard."

"Tex wasn't at that meeting, if you can call it that, where you guys presented your findings. But he knows what went on."

Art nodded as he looked at Tex. "Yeah, I told him about all I could think of."

"Well," Tex started, "I know you well enough to know that you're trying to get the design changed, like it should have been back then."

"Well, we haven't gotten very far."

"I got two things for you."

"What's that?"

"You know that years ago I worked for Powder Keg."

"Yeah. I remember you telling me that."

"Well, there's a group of people there that don't want the company blamed."

"Oh?"

"Yeah. They don't think the seal was the problem either. I've talked to 'em and they want to talk to you. How about it?"

"Hell yes," Art replied. "Those people could do some good, and since they're about to get blamed, I'd think they'd want to defend themselves."

Tex, being the realist he was, flashed a typical wide, knowing grin. "Only if they're not paid to take the blame. You know that there's always a patsy in something like this and the company may be willing to take the blame, but right now they're not."

"Okay, who do I talk to?"

"Fritz Lugar. Fritz is an old friend and he's moved up as director of safety. He'll call you Friday night at home at eight our time. He's going to be out of the plant until then."

Art beamed at the thought of again pursuing the elusive solution to repairing the Shuttle. "Sounds good. Maybe we're not dead in the water yet." He turned to Sam and continued, "Oscar told me he had impounded all the data and records you had out here."

"Yep. But I already had it protected."

"Good, we may need it yet. By the way, I got to go back to Isle City, Washington Saturday morning. Guess I'll be gone most of next week. We got to do a design review on some hardware changes up there."

Sam chuckled as his eyes danced. "I'm surprised Hova and Fishburne would let you out of their sight. How'd you manage that?"

"Well, you'd never believe how easy it was," Art replied with a knowing grin. "I think they were afraid to say no. Besides, it's official business in the great redesign of everything on the vehicle."

"You mean it's 'get well' time," Tex replied cynically.

At the time appointed for a call from Powder Keg Corporation, Art's phone rang. He heard a very pleasant young lady's voice, "Mr. Cannon?"

"Yes."

"Just a moment for Mr. Lugar, please."

Art felt a spurt of energy flow through his body. Shortly a friendly voice on the other end said, "Art, this is Fritz Lugar out at Powder Keg. I believe we have a mutual friend, Tex James."

Art smiled at finally talking directly to one person he believed had a good reason to help. "We sure do, Fritz. Tex is a hell of a fellah. I have the highest regard for him."

"So do we. Wish we could get him back. How about telling me about the Adventurer accident and the data you have. You probably know that we're about to be blamed and I don't want to take any lumps if we aren't due."

"Well Fritz, I want to preface anything I might say with one requirement I feel strong about."

"What's that?"

"I don't know you people out there very well, but I want your assurances that there'll be no media involvement in anything I'm about to say. What I'm really saying is that I don't want any publicity. I want to work the problems within the system."

He heard a sigh of relief from the other end. "You got a deal. We feel the same way."

With this reassurance, Art spent the next hour briefing him on the findings and conclusions of the strut clevis program, and the scenario of the accident that he was convinced was correct. Fritz interjected small questions periodically and clarifications of technical data but for the most part, listened to he explanation.

"This is all very interesting," he replied finally "Did you know that High Flier Aircraft, the people who built the Orbiters, have done an independent study on the accident?"

"No. This is the first time I've heard that."

"Well, you'll be interested to know that they told us almost exactly the same thing. Of course, they don't have all the background data you have, but their summation is very close to what you just described."

Art grinned as he felt a shiver run over his back at another independent verification of their work.

"Well, that's good. That's a second major correlation of our work. I also found out recently that the National Science Association has a study that supports us, too."

"Well, I'm sure you know of the study that the Eddie's Aircraft Company did on that same subject, don't you?"

Art frowned. "No, I know a lot of people out there but I didn't know they were even looking at it."

"Well, during their studies of the design of certain elements of the booster systems, they did an indepth analysis of the aft struts and their interactivity with the vehicle system. They concluded, and very strongly concluded, I might add, that was the failure mechanism and their scenario is almost the same as High Flier's and yours. So that's four totally independent analyses that support the same conclusions, except yours was two years before the accident."

"Well, it certainly gives us credibility. Maybe somebody'll listen."

After a brief discussion of the three other corroborating studies Fritz asked, "Can you and Eddie get away for a visit out here to discuss this with our management and senior technical people?"

"We sure can. I'll see when Eddie can come."

"Don't plan it yet. Let me go back and work it with management and then I'll extend an invitation with several options. I'll need to get a lot of people together."

"Sounds good. I'll brief Eddie and we'll wait to hear from you."

Art couldn't wait to tell Eddie the good news. Soon he had him on the phone enjoying his ecstasy about the possibility of finally getting something done. Eddie asked, "How come, do you suppose, that these reports haven't circulated from High Flier and the Academy? I've never seen anything on them and the Commission doesn't appear to be paying any attention to 'em. I can't imagine Hova would have that much influence."

Art sobered a moment and now was plainly puzzled. "Well, buddy, that's a hell of a good question. If they're there, and I have no reason to believe they're not, it seems to me that the Commission would be zeroing in on that pretty hard unless there's a cover up of some kind going on. But I don't see why."

On Monday after Art's arrival in Isle City, overlooking the beautiful Pudget Sound, he and Bart Haggardy, chief engineer, were hard at work on design changes required by the Space Agency. Suddenly the meeting was interrupted by Electro's receptionist who had gotten a first edition newspaper from the stand out front of the small plant. "Just thought you guys might want to see this," she said quietly as she sauntered into the laboratory where they had documents, wiring schematics and hardware spread out.

Art read the headline, "Document Destruction Charged." He felt a chill go through his body to think that anybody would do such a thing. Bart squinted at the lead. "Hell, man! That can't be right. I don't believe that. It's just another one of them damned media sensations."

Art, quickly perusing the lead text in the story replied

cynically, "I sure as hell hope so, Bart." The news media capitalized to the fullest on this latest revelation. Art had rationalized to himself this was a mistake; no one would be so low as to deliberately destroy evidence.

Bart laughed cynically as he reconsidered his first remark. "Don't let yourself get naive, old buddy. You should know better 'n most folks that there's a real den of wolves out there. Didn't Fishburne teach you anything?"

Art sat up with a start and stared at Bart.

"What's the matter?"

"You just said the magic word, *Fishburne*". He quickly dialed Oscar's number. Finally, after what seemed an eternity, Oscar answered. Art was almost in a panic with fear about his records in the files. "Oscar, all of my program records on those struts are in my files in my office and I'm out here. I'm worried."

Oscar started to breathe hard. "Oh shit. I never thought of that and now all these accusations about records being destroyed."

"You got access to everything there," Art stated in almost a panic. "How about asking one of your inspectors to go up to my office and check?"

"I think we better do that. I'll call you back."

Later that afternoon Oscar called. "Art there's a problem." Art was silent, expecting the worst. Oscar continued, "I sent Darcus Stroud up there to check on the files. She's a good friend and I can depend on her. She went through all your old files."

"What did she find,"

"Nothing! There were copies of the old contracts but there was no analytical data, curves, or anything else. It's all gone, man! Gone!"

Art felt his body grow weak as he silently berated himself for having not thought of this possibility and done something to protect his files earlier. "Did she look in any other places?"

"Yeah, she went through all five of the cabinets and found nothing. Then Fishburne came in and demanded to know what she was doing and she told him she was looking for the old strut clevis files."

Art nervously asked, "What did Fishburne say?"

"Fishburne told her that they were all there in the drawer . . . No one had bothered any of your files."

Art looked at the phone in disgust and yelled, "That's a damned lie, Oscar! You saw those files up there!"

Pain was obvious in Oscar's voice. "Yeah, I sure did. I know that one drawer was overflowing. Remember I was kidding you about needing another file cabinet?"

"Yeah, I remember. I wonder who did it, I mean who actually performed the act?"

Oscar laughed cynically. "I'm sure Hova directed it and Fishburne did it after you left but there's no way to prove that."

Anger was overtaking Art rapidly as he yelled at the phone, "Well, I'll tell you one thing, those damned files were government property. They belonged to that contract and nobody and I mean nobody had the right to go in and destroy 'em."

Oscar replied quietly and sympathetically, "Well, Art, who's to say what's to be kept on any contract. Only the people involved with it can make that decision."

Despair was obvious in Art's voice and manner. "Yeah. You're right. I'm just disappointed, that's all. All those years of work just trashed to try to cover up something."

Art sat dejectedly for a long time thinking about all the work that had gone into developing the data in the file drawer. Bart watched his friend sympathetically but said nothing, aware of the despair he felt and how he'd feel in the same situation. Finally, Art said slowly, "All the derivations that Eddie did and all the meeting notes of all the sessions we had over the years. Just gone to shit!" The bitterness was obvious. He felt helpless and most of all he felt betrayed again.

Finally, Bart laid his hand on Art's arm and said gently, "Hey, you did the best you could. You got to remember that."

"Yeah, but I wish I'd thought of this." He finally, almost apologetically, dialed Eddie's number. After four rings, Eddie's answered. Art related the revelation that he had just had. Eddie was silent for a few moments before answering cynically, "Well, I just didn't think they'd go that far."

"I know, but we believe they destroyed our report for the Commission. Why didn't we think about this?" Both were quiet for a moment. Finally Eddie continued sullenly, "We should have known they would. They let seven people die in Adventurer and then there was your buddy that died from stress up there in the Program Office.

Then, too, don't forget those two that had to leave because of induced heart problems."

"Yeah."

"I don't believe they'd stop at anything. There's probably others we don't know about. Seems to me that's a pretty heavy load to have to defend on Judgment Day."

Art, now somewhat philosophically, continued, "Well, guess the media was right for a change. There were records being destroyed. I'm sure they don't know which records, but guess we gotta give 'em one this time, don't we?"

"Oh," Eddie replied with a start, "I was so caught up in all this mess that I almost forgot to tell you something that's gonna blow you even more."

Art looked quickly at the phone and thought, *Now what?*

"I just found out since you left that Hova's been promoted to senior vice president and Fishburne has been promoted to SRB Program Manager at Space Corp."

Art stared at the phone in disbelief and finally growled bitterly, "Well I guess I'm not surprised. They'll deserve anything they get from that move."

"I always heard that crime didn't pay, but maybe it really does," Eddie said.

A week went by with no word from Powder Keg, then two weeks. Art was beginning to get impatient. Eddie called him almost every day asking if he'd had any word, and he always answered with the same "No, but don't give up yet."

Almost a month later Eddie met Art for lunch at their favorite home cooking restaurant, a small hole in the wall place where the waitresses kidded then about being "charter members". Eddie was already seated at a back table in a corner when Art entered. "Look here!" Eddie snorted as he threw out a newspaper face up in front of Art before he sat down. *"Space Agency Awards $100 Million Booster Contract To Powder Keg,"* read the page 1 headline.

Then under the lead, a sub-head stated, "No Second Sources To Be Considered." Art felt limp and sank down in a chair while Eddie squirmed in a rage. "Those damned people. No wonder we ain't heard. They're gonna step up and take the heat and keep the Space Agency's skirts clean. I see it comin! They've made an economic decision!"

Art replied with a frown, "I believe you're right, but the sad thing is the Space Agency wasn't to blame to begin with."

Eddie leaned back dangerously far and out of nervous energy, jumped up and started to pace the floor. Other patrons in the restaurant looked curiously at him as he walked back and forth by the table they were occupying in the corner. "Shit man! Shit's all I can say. The damned momentum behind those seals is gonna be insurmountable and they're not doin' anything about the real problem. What we gonna do, Art? What the hell can we do?"

Art sat dejectedly with his head down weighing their options. "Well, buddy, I'm out of airspeed, altitude and ideas, all at the same time. I don't know. But we have to do something."

Finally Eddie settled down in the chair and appeared to be mulling over an idea. He looked at the floor and then straight at Art. "You know Stover, don't you?"

"Yeah. Met him once. What you got in mind?"

"How about if we send him copies of some of the data we saved and explain the failure scenario to him? Do you think he'd run with it?"

Art pondered the question a moment. "Well, he's not known to be bashful and he'll sure as hell fight for what he believes."

"Well?"

"Okay!! He might be able to do something. Maybe he can't but then, who the hell knows. It's worth a try."

As the days passed, they grew more impatient. Finally Art phoned, "Eddie, I've waited long enough. I'm gonna send what data we got left to Smokey. It can't hurt."

After two weeks went by with no response from Houston, they were again feeling discouraged. Finally, in near desperation Art called his friend Bill Allison at Mission Control. "I was just thinkin' about you. I was talkin to some of the guys over in the Astronaut Office and one of 'em mentioned you had sent down some data to Smokey," Bill began.

"Yeah, we did. I was wondering what happened to it?"

Bill hesitated a moment before he replied, "Well, all I know for sure is that he sent it to the Commission in Washington. He's been under a lot of heat himself lately.

"Yeah, I can imagine. But I know he's in there pitchin' hard."

"He is. I almost feel sorry for the guy. He lost some close friends."

Art asked, "What do you think will come of the data he sent up there, of mine, I mean?"

"I wouldn't count on much. There's so damned much focus on the seal that I don't think anybody at Headquarters is in the mood to consider anything else now that they've got somebody to stand up and take the blame."

Art's frustration was showing. "But Bill, that isn't fixing the problem. It just won't do."

"I agree but I think they're willing to gamble . . ."

"Well, that's a hell of a gamble."

"I agree. If I hear anything I'll let you know. By the way," Bill continued, "you ought to know that Hova's down here now. One of the guys said he had his girlfriend with him, too. Looks like he feels pretty confident since he got that promotion."

"I knew he'd gone somewhere, he and Fishburne both. It's been pretty quiet here for the past couple of weeks."

"Well, don't count on it. From what I've been able to learn you and Rogers have been the subject of some discussion. Looks like he found out about Smokey sending that data to the Commission."

"I hope Smokey's okay. Are they after him, too?"

"Afraid so. Just wanted you to know."

Art left for Eddie's office and found him sitting dejectedly in his chair. "Well, did Smokey strike out with the bureaucracy?" Eddie asked cynically.

"Yeah. I'm afraid he did." Art briefed Eddie on his conversation with Bill.

Eddie frowned, slid down in his chair, crossed his legs and started to swing his foot rapidly. "The stakes are high, Art, the stakes are high."

"Yep. I've got to do something." He stood, slowly walked over to the window of Eddie's office and peered at the birds flying in and out of the trees. He saw a mother robin trying to teach her young ones to fly. Art stood a few moments and watched a little one struggle.

Eddie, in almost total frustration, stood up and pounded the desk with his fist. "How in the hell did we get into this mess? How could such a beautiful program go so wrong? How?"

Art dreaded going to work Monday because of the adversarial relationship that was becoming more and more dominant now since Fishburne and Hova were feeling untouchable after being appointed to their new executive positions. Their strutting and attitudes had become truly Napoleonic, as though they had been granted royal status. He was afraid they would be back in the office and he didn't want to see either of them if he could help it. Annie felt Art should leave Space Corp and frequently said so. His reply was always, "Baby, I can't quit until we get this thing right."

Art started the day off with a cup of coffee from the communal pot. There wasn't much joy in this now since all his old friends had left and Hova had filled their positions with cronies. He sat and thought about Elmer, Billy, Ray, Ben, Tex, Chip, and especially about Heidi. He smiled when he thought about Heidi's new little girl. Then he thought about the time they had in the floor of his office and wondered what it would really be like to be married to a woman like that. Suddenly his phone rang. "Cannon here," he answered.

The voice was strange to Art, authoritative and gruff. "Mr. Cannon. This is Dr. Foley." Art immediately recognized him as having been one of the Commission members. "A friend of yours called me over the weekend and said I should talk to you about Adventurer."

"Oh. Who?"

"Fellow named Stover. Know him?"

"Hell yes. I thought he had been neutralized."

"When can you come up here? I know the report's been submitted but I sure as hell don't agree with it. There's too many loose ends. I, for one, don't believe most of the stuff that they put in it, but then, I'm just a physicist. Them damned lawyers and generals don't know much about technical details."

Art felt his heart leap with joy. Maybe this was the key. "When can you see me?" he asked quickly.

"Well, I'm pretty booked until Wednesday or Thursday. How about then? I want to leave Washington and go home no later than Friday."

415

"I'll be in your office Thursday morning at nine o'clock."

"I'll look forward to it. See you then."

Art was ecstatic. He quickly dialed Eddie and briefed him with renewed expectation and hope. Eddie, being the realist that he was, looked back at the others that had shown an interest and for one reason or another, mostly due to politics or self-interest, had backed off. "Well, don't expect too much out of it and then you won't get disappointed. That's all I can say."

After Art hung up, he once again let the eternal optimist side of his personality come through, the side that Annie always said made him interesting. He leaned back in his chair and took a long drink from his coffee cup and actually enjoyed the taste of the hot liquid running down his insides. As he sat enjoying the morning sun and his coffee, his phone rang. "Cannon here," he said.

"Mr. Cannon, Mr. Fishburne wants you in his office in five minutes." He recognized the voice of Fishburne's secretary who now sat out in the large secretarial bull pen where Hova's secretary, Fanny, sat.

"What's he want?"

"Don't know, sir. He just said to have you down here."

As Art entered Fishburne's richly-appointed office, the one that Hova had occupied until his promotion to an even bigger and better office, he saw Hova, Dean Aikins from personnel and Wimp Hammonds, the chief of security, sitting on opposite couches. "Cannon!" Fishburne barked, "You got a problem!"

Art stared at the audience, wondering why this collection of people.

"Oh? What you mean?"

Fishburne threw Art's personnel file on his desk. "I been reviewing your file and it's a damned mess. You got more black marks than the law allows. You don't know the first thing about following orders. Besides, you and this Stover fellow are guilty of conspiracy. He's gonna get his, too! You can bet on that."

Art stared at Fishburne coldly. "Fishburne, you don't know what the hell you're talking about. That's the most ridiculous thing I ever heard."

"While we were at Houston we found you had sent a bunch of your shit down to Stover. That's clear and absolute insubordination."

Hova was watching with obvious enjoyment. Art was sure he was

416

proud of the years he had been grooming Fishburn and now to see him perform this way must have been a great joy.

Dean was nervous and for once had nothing to say. Wimp was all business, obviously following orders.

Art glared steely-eyed as he could at Fishburne. "I hope you're not going to try to make trouble for Smokey. He didn't ask for that data."

Hova couldn't remain quiet any longer. "Well, mister smart guy, I tried to reason with you and get you on our team. You either play the game our way or you don't play at all."

"You mean I sell my soul to you and close my eyes to dishonesty and incompetence? That's what you wanted me to do!"

"No, Cannon." Fishburne was looking as though he were savoring the moment, a moment he had wanted for a long time. "You're fired. Mr. Hammonds will escort you back to your office to get your coat and then to the door. He'll take your badge as you leave. Here's your final check."

Hova stood and said, "Let's all pray."

As Art walked back to his office under the watchful eye of the security man, he felt a relief mixed with sadness. He wondered what the meeting in Washington with Dr. Foley on Thursday would lead to. Once more he thought, *Does anybody out there really care?*